Praise for Mardi Oakley Medawar's award-winning debut novel, *People of the Whistling Water*:

"Mardi Oakley Medawar has a feel for the Crow and the incoming whites as few other writers could. Her characters, white or Indian, are *people* . . . This is our history."
—Don Coldsmith, award-winning author of *Runestone*

"Rather than emphasize two cultures' diversities, Mardi Oakley Medawar celebrates their similarities with poignancy, wry humor, and precise characterization."
—Suzann Ledbetter, award winning author of *Nellie Cashman, Prospector,* and *Trail-Blazer*

"Ms. Medawar has an astonishing talent for turning mere words on a page into characters so vivid and real, so deliciously human, you'll swear they can't possibly be fiction."
—Penelope Williamson, author of *Heart of the West*

Don't miss the next Tay-bodal mystery:
The Witch of Palo Duro (St. Martin's Press)

Also by Mardi Oakley Medawar . . .
People of the Whistling Waters (Bantam)
Remembering the Osage Kid (Bantam)

And coming soon . . .
Rainwater on the White Road (Signet)
Brothers of Thunder (Bantam)
Murder at Medicine Lodge (St. Martin's Press)

MORE MYSTERIES FROM THE
BERKLEY PUBLISHING GROUP...

THE HERON CARVIC MISS SEETON MYSTERIES: Retired art teacher Miss Seeton steps in where Scotland Yard stumbles. "A most beguiling protagonist!" —*New York Times*

by Heron Carvic
MISS SEETON SINGS
MISS SEETON DRAWS THE LINE
WITCH MISS SEETON
PICTURE MISS SEETON
ODDS ON MISS SEETON

by Hampton Charles
ADVANTAGE MISS SEETON
MISS SEETON AT THE HELM
MISS SEETON, BY APPOINTMENT

by Hamilton Crane
HANDS UP, MISS SEETON
MISS SEETON CRACKS THE CASE
MISS SEETON PAINTS THE TOWN
MISS SEETON BY MOONLIGHT
MISS SEETON ROCKS THE CRADLE
MISS SEETON GOES TO BAT
MISS SEETON PLANTS SUSPICION
STARRING MISS SEETON
MISS SEETON UNDERCOVER
MISS SEETON RULES
SOLD TO MISS SEETON
SWEET MISS SEETON

KATE SHUGAK MYSTERIES: A former D.A. solves crimes in the far Alaska north...

by Dana Stabenow
A COLD DAY FOR MURDER
DEAD IN THE WATER
A FATAL THAW

A COLD-BLOODED BUSINESS
PLAY WITH FIRE
BLOOD WILL TELL

INSPECTOR BANKS MYSTERIES: Award-winning British detective fiction at its finest... "Robinson's novels are habit-forming!"
—*West Coast Review of Books*

by Peter Robinson
THE HANGING VALLEY
WEDNESDAY'S CHILD
INNOCENT GRAVES

PAST REASON HATED
FINAL ACCOUNT
GALLOWS VIEW

CASS JAMESON MYSTERIES: Lawyer Cass Jameson seeks justice in the criminal courts of New York City in this highly acclaimed series... "A witty, gritty heroine." —*New York Post*

by Carolyn Wheat
FRESH KILLS
MEAN STREAK

DEAD MAN'S THOUGHTS   TROUBLED WATERS
WHERE NOBODY DIES

SCOTLAND YARD MYSTERIES: Featuring Detective Superintendent Duncan Kincaid and his partner, Sergeant Gemma James...
"Charming!" —*New York Times Book Review*

by Deborah Crombie
A SHARE IN DEATH
LEAVE THE GRAVE GREEN

ALL SHALL BE WELL
MOURN NOT YOUR DEAD

JACK McMORROW MYSTERIES: The highly acclaimed series set in a Maine mill town and starring a newspaperman with a knack for crime solving... "Gerry Boyle is the genuine article." —*Robert B. Parker*

by Gerry Boyle
DEADLINE   BLOODLINE   LIFELINE

DEATH
AT RAINY
MOUNTAIN

Mardi Oakley Medawar

BERKLEY PRIME CRIME, NEW YORK

DEATH AT RAINY MOUNTAIN

A Berkley Prime Crime Book / published by arrangement with
St. Martin's Press, Inc.

PRINTING HISTORY
St. Martin's Press hardcover edition / 1996
Berkley Prime Crime mass-market edition / January 1998

The Putnam Berkley World Wide Web site address is
http://www.berkley.com

ISBN: 0-425-16141-2

Berkley Prime Crime Books are published
by The Berkley Publishing Group, a member of Penguin Putnam Inc.,
200 Madison Avenue, New York, New York 10016.
The name BERKLEY PRIME CRIME and the
BERKLEY PRIME CRIME design are trademarks
belonging to Berkley Publishing Corporation.

PRINTED IN THE UNITED STATES OF AMERICA

10 9 8 7 6 5 4 3 2 1

FOR
DEBBIE OAKLEY-RAY AND HELEN OAKLEY-WILSON
MY SISTERS
AND FOR MY ADOPTED NAVAHO SISTER
TOYA ANDERSON
WITH MY THANKS FOR THE YEARS OF
ENCOURAGEMENT AND FAITH

AUTHOR'S NOTE

Although this is a work of fiction, the names of a majority of the characters are real, and this work is based on the actual lives of these very men. I have done this intentionally. On too many occasions their names have been misused, their extraordinary lives distorted. I am only a storyteller. As such it is not my responsibility to right a plethora of wrongs. But during the course of telling a story, I can give my people back their heroes. I can restore to these heroes their names.

Mardi Oakley Medawar

ONE

They say that we came from the Crow. Before that, from the Mandan. Maybe we did. Personally, I don't believe it. I do believe in the stories that tell about a time before the Lakota came from the north country and when we, the Kiowa, like the Southern Cheyenne, lived near the Black Hills. But since the time of my grandfather's grandfather, we have lived in this place, a verdant land just above the Red River, a river that separates our country from Texas. For all of my grandfather's time this has been our homeland. And our most sacred place within this homeland, the Rainy Mountain.

In the summer season of 1866, I was somewhere in my early thirties. Thirty-two, thirty-three maybe, no more than that. What is clear in my mind is what a terrible summer that season was. It all began to go wrong when our principal chief, Little Bluff, died. For thirty-three years Little Bluff had been responsible for keeping an independent, furiously stubborn people, lacking even the basic understanding of the term *compromise*, united as a single race. Then, to our great dismay, he died. Not on the battlefield, further adding to his legend with a richly deserved hero's death, but in his sleep like a tired, used-up old man. Only to honor him would the six bands and the multitude of sub-bands converge at the humidity-drenched base of the Rainy Mountain during the full and punishing heat of summer, fighting mosquitoes and, as it almost happened, one another.

We Kiowa have never lived as the white man has portrayed us, in big groups, in a gigantic village sprawling across the prairie. It's a very romantic notion, but stupid. Consider the practicalities. Each band and sub-band had its own chiefs and minor chiefs. A band generally comprised sixty to eighty lodges, a sub-band, twenty to thirty. When the entire Nation came together it made for an impressive sight of thousands of lodges stretching along a river. But we could not live that way. With so many people using the same water source, the water supply was quickly polluted. The great herds of horses ran out of grazing land. Then there was the threat that a single village could be easily destroyed by warring enemies or disease. The seldom-mentioned reason for camping apart is that with so many chiefs in one area, the chiefs fought among themselves. These men, accustomed to absolute authority, were disinclined to share.

For these reasons, based solely on self-preservation, the bands typically lived apart. The Nation as a unit only came together once a year, for the annual Sun Dance. It was during these two weeks of religious ceremony, held in the early spring, that marriages were announced and summer raid parties amassed. The Nation then split up, each band going its own way. For the Nation to converge again as a whole after the Sun Dance, there had to be an extraordinary reason. Now there was. The Sun Dance of 1866 has been inscribed on the Kiowa calender as the Silver Sun Dance. It had already been held, the Nation had scattered, raiding parties were sent out, and the summer buffalo hunt was in progress. Then Little Bluff was found dead in his bed.

Runners were dispatched to call back the bands. The various chiefs were told to bring their bands and meet at Rainy Mountain, along Rainy Mountain Creek. This creek feeds into the Washita River, a river that cuts through the very heart of our country. It was further down the Washita and backing into the Washita Mountains that the Blue Jackets were busy establishing a new fort they called Fort Sill. Until two years ago the Kiowa were at a relative peace with the Blue Jackets. They gave us presents all the time because they were deep inside our country and because we, like they, had made war against the Gray Jackets. Our smaller war with the Confederacy was because of the Caddo. The Kiowa and the Caddoes have never gotten along. Our animosity was exacerbated when the Gray Jackets began supplying the Caddoes with guns and ammunition, which they used against us. Our chiefs called a war council and it was unanimously voted to cut the Caddoes off at their source. Our warriors went after the Gray Jackets' supply wagons and took the shipments intended for the Caddoes. Because of us, the Gray Jackets were fighting two wars. One to the north and a second harrying campaign in the backyard of their home countries of Louisiana and Texas. The Blue Jackets liked that. What they didn't like was that the Kiowa warriors also raided them, stealing their horses and mules. The Blue Jackets made a big fuss about losing their animals, especially when the Kiowa warriors had the effrontery to sell back their own badly needed stock at exorbitant prices. The Blue Jackets started talking loud, made threats, and stopped giving presents.

This was a great mistake.

The warriors retaliated, attacking Blue Jacket supply wagons, taking the presents they felt were due. All the chiefs agreed, refused to call their warriors back when the Blue Jackets formally protested. Little Bluff pointed out to these irate officers that his warriors were only taking payment due them for the use of our land on which the Blue Jackets were building their forts. The Blue Jackets have been shooting at Kiowas ever since, but there weren't enough of them in the Territory to worry about. The Kiowa warriors thought this little war was funny. Besides, the Blue Jackets and the Gray Jackets were more intent on fighting each other so, for the most part, the Nation left them alone to get on with it. What white men did to each other was none of our concern. We had troubles enough of our own, for that terrible season there was at work much more than heart-wrenching grief for the loss of Little Bluff, the voracious insects, and the ruthless weather. The monsters of greed, lust, ambition, and murder had been released from a human heart for very human reasons.

Somehow, I, Tay-bodal, had lived all my thirty-odd years without ever once combating these evils, and I was unprepared for what I was about to meet. That season changed my life just as surely as it almost redirected the future course of our nation. Something chose me to stop it. Some guiding spirit maybe. Who knows. But there is little doubt in my mind that whatever it was, it was powerful, for at that juncture in my life, I was the unlikeliest candidate for the task. For you to fully appreciate this, you have to know just what this guiding spirit was given to work with.

Not to make a meal of it, I was a loner. Generally considered a man of no consequence. Even my name, Tay-bodal, is less than awe-inspiring. Literally translated my name means, Meat Carrier, (the hind-end portion of the buffalo, no less).

Smallpox left me bereft of family when in my early twenties. Once I had gone through all the stages of grieving, I realized that I had become fully independent. There was now no one to hold me back, make me a responsible person. I could go my own way, forge my own destiny. I was young and delusional, and actually came to believe that my being alone was my own choice. I had to see all of that as a good thing. If I didn't, I would have gone mad. A second bitter truth about me during those days was that I was considered odd. Too odd to be asked to join a permanent band and much too odd to be invited into any of the warrior societies.

Oh, as a youngster I had belonged to the children's societies, the first being the Rabbits. Which meant that a mob of little pot-bellied boys ran around dangerously armed with bows and arrows, allowed to shoot at anything that breathed. We were encouraged to go after rabbits but generally we went after slower-moving targets, such as unsuspecting older sisters as they gossiped and preened themselves, and dozing camp dogs. During religious functions when the men danced in their societies, we Rabbits disruptively hopped around making a general nuisance of ourselves. Next came the Herders society. This induction happened around age ten and was supposed to be a high honor. What it was, was enforced labor, for the responsibility of tending and guarding the horse herds fell to the Herders. Boys remained in this society until they reached the age of nineteen or twenty. From the Herders promising candidates were invited to join proper warrior societies. The fact that any offer was couched in the terms of an invitation was irrelevant. If asked, the inductee was obliged to join. No representative from any of the societies ever broached me, I never went beyond being a Herder.

Being passed over did not mean that I wasn't proficient with weaponry or was thought to be a coward. No one has ever said that about me. What they did say was that I was eccentric. Which was true. Plants and their varied uses had always fascinated me. So, too, did the anatomy of animals and people. I regarded every life form as something miraculous and I burned with a deep hunger to understand just what made these forms so different yet so uniquely the same. Which was why I dissected the first rabbit I ever killed instead of skinning it out and presenting it to my mother as a good son ought to do. While the other mothers of Rabbits were proudly roasting whole rabbits, my mother was forced to make a stew of mine, which she served up along with the usual fare of seasonal fruits and seared chunks of buffalo, while enduring my rather lengthy monologue on the size of a rabbit's heart, lungs, and liver.

As a Herder I attended every birth of a foal with badly concealed glee. But it was when I was seventeen and autopsied a still-born foal that my specialness became the subject of concern and behind-the-hands speculation. But what damned me, prevented my natural progression from boy to warrior, happened a year after the incident of the stillborn foal.

Travelers of the Jesus Road all know the story of how the young Jesus met with learned elders and astonished them all with his wisdom and knowledge. Even though I had never head of Jesus at that time, I did relatively the same thing. I plunked myself down in the counciling circle of Buffalo Doctors and Owl Doctors, astonishing the living snot out of both groups of elders with my temerity and my self-taught theories. Needless to say, my elders weren't especially filled with wonder for my wisdom and were less than impressed with my knowledge. Even less so when I accused them of being out of touch and backward in their methods of healing. My father humbly offered the offended men presents to make amends for the bad manners of his unique son, but despite this I was branded an incorrigible and my natural ascension from boy to warrior came to an abrupt end.

I've always felt badly about that, but only for my father's sake. He was a proud man. He deserved a better son. But living the life of a man of no consequence proved to be the most freeing experience of my young life. Branded as unfit, I was no longer subjugated by older warriors who had formerly been quick to tell me what to do and to criticize my pale efforts. At nineteen I was suddenly liberated, able to go my own way, study plants and animals to my heart's content. Nineteen is such a thoughtless age. I was so happy with my new freedom that I never gave a thought to what my father was feeling. Until the day we were alone together in the eagle pit.

My father was a quiet man. He only spoke when necessary and his long spells of silence used to bring my naturally wordy mother to the brink of frustrated tears. Sometime around my eighth year she got used to it I guess, for she would talk and my father would nod as he ate. That is my clearest memory of childhood: mother talking, father nodding as the three of us shared the evening meal. It was only when he cleared his throat, indicating that he was on the verge of speaking, that she shut up, snapping her mouth closed as hard and as tight as a snapping turtle's. And then she sent me a warning look, driving me into deeper silence.

Father is going to speak.

My mother and I braced ourselves for this rare occasion and held that pose for however long it took him to say whatever was on his mind. It wasn't until I was nineteen and in the pit with him that I realized why he was this way. His profession was the cause of his long silences. You see, my father used to catch eagles. Brown eagles, not the eagles with the white heads. White-headed eagles were no good to him. Only the tail feathers of the brown eagles were of worth to us, the Kiowa. White-headed eagles didn't have the speed, the courage, or the cunning of the brown ones and being admirers of the brown eagle, we never wore the feathers of the white-headed eagles for any reason. Eagle catcher was a profession requiring long hours of patience and complete silence. When the dismal truth occurred to him that none of the societies were tempted to invite me into their ranks, he decided that he'd better train me as his apprentice. Having a useful occupation would give me something to do other than collecting plants and spending unseemly amounts of time studying dead animals.

Being an eagle catcher is hard work. An eagle can never be shot dead by arrow or bullet, for the spilling of its blood would kill its magic power, making the tainted feathers worth even less than the feathers of the white-headed eagle. A brown eagle must be taken alive and then killed without bloodshed. This requires digging a deep pit in very solid

ground because eagles are smart; they stay to the high country where the ground is rocky and unforgiving. So there I
was, in the autumn of my nineteenth year, toiling away with
all the arrogance of a nineteen-year-old eager to show off
my superior young strength to the middle-aged quiet man
that was my father.

After he paced out the width of the pit, wide enough so
that the two of us could sit in it together without rubbing
shoulders, we stood in the center back to back, both of us
armed with wooden shovels. I attacked the hardened ground
with unbridled zeal. I shoveled like an escaping badger, dirt
flying everywhere. My father was content to take his time,
raising neither a sweat or a dust storm. After about an hour
I was so exhausted I was delirious. My father didn't say a
word as I raved and wasted water by pouring our only
supply over my sweat-and-dirt-coated body. He just kept
on shoveling. Alone. After he had hauled away his son's
unconscious body from the dig site. He had to stop digging
long enough to do that because the sprawled body of his
son had been in his way. Had I fallen into a faint outside
the measured area, he simply would have left me there un-
disturbed. But I had inconveniently puddled at his feet.

After digging that pit single-handed, he cut and gathered
long poles to lay across it. By then I was able to help him
cut armloads of long grass to lay over the poles. Then I
went with him as he hunted and killed a coyote. Coyotes
make the best bait because their rather pungent aroma carries for miles. My father laid the carcass on top of the grass
concealing the pit. Then he told me something that really
upset me.

"You first."

Which meant he expected *me* to climb down into that pit
and sit underneath that reeking, dead coyote.

The stench was unimaginable. Descriptive words fail.
The hours we sat together in that pit, utterly silent,
breathing in that noxious aroma, seemed like a lifetime. To
make the experience even more horrible, not one eagle took

the bait. At dusk we finally scrambled out. I hurried with all the speed my cramped-up legs were able to produce running down the side of that hill. At the bottom there was a knee-deep creek. I frantically bathed, washing coyote smell and innumerable fleas off my body. I was slightly appalled that my father hadn't chosen to follow. I had always known him to be a rather fastidious person. His choosing not to bathe struck me as being most curious. When I returned he would not allow me to make a drying fire. During our only conversation of the day, he explained, in his hesitant low-voiced way, that a fire, even the faint odor of a dead fire, would alert eagles to our trap. They would stay away. So I shivered myself dry, ate a hunk of dried meat, and slept sporadically through the most uncomfortable night of my life. And the next morning I realized to my horror that he expected me to go back into that pit.

Three days. For three days we sat together under that rotting, maggot-infested coyote. After the second day, I didn't bother bathing. What was the point? Being clean only made the essence of decaying coyote worse. On the third day, an eagle struck when I was crazed from the confinement, my sense of smell burned out. The shock of the attack almost made me cry out. Only my father's quickness stopped me. He grabbed my head, pulling me against him.

"First pass," he whispered.

There were more passes, the eagle striking the carcass glancing blows, raining us with dust, dry grass, and other things I did not want to think about in that dark hole as the eagle tested just how dead that coyote was. Finally the thing landed, sinking its talons deep, tearing at the putrid meat, and all the while turning its head, ever on the alert for danger. Because we carried the same scent as its meal, it never suspected that danger would not come from the sky but from below ground. When the eagle relaxed, my father raised his arms through the poles and grabbed it hard by the legs, pulling it down into the pit with us.

I have no idea which of us screamed the loudest, me or

that fighting eagle. Had there been room enough in that pit, I know I would have run around inside it like a madman, for the eagle was fighting, beating my father with its wings, ripping his arm open with its talons, at the same time the poles were caving in, and what was left of the decomposing coyote falling on top of me. My father, unfazed by all of it, snapped that eagle's neck. The pit was ruined, the blind no longer in place. Sunlight was at last able to shine down on us. My father looked from his prize to me, his only son, as I huddled and whimpered against the wall of the pit, covered from head to toe with coyote gore.

That was the only time I ever heard him actually laugh.

He bathed with me after that. We spent at least an hour scrubbing ourselves clean. And that night we built a fire and I treated his wound, sewing it up, dressing it with tallow and a poultice to prevent blood fever.

"You're very good at this," he said as I tended him.

I basked humbly in his praise, was extra careful as I attended him.

He watched me quietly, then said, "I think you should do this kind of work. You're not very good at catching eagles."

Our eyes met and he smiled. I was speechless, recounting all the disappointments I realized he suffered because of me, yet realizing too that despite my legion of faults, he loved me unconditionally. That is the memory of my father I will hold in my heart forever. Two years later, he was taken from me by the pox.

I was days behind the Nation as it gathered at the Rainy Mountain. I had been studying new theories put forward by practitioners belonging to other tribes. I greatly respected those men of other nations, and their wisdom was beneficial to my own people. So involved was I in this study council that word concerning Little Bluff reached me almost too late. Next I faced the arduous task of travel. Because of my craft and my love of homely comforts, I owned more possessions than a single man with an ounce of sense ought to have. With no wives to do the packing or sons to drive my small herd, whenever the bands moved I was always the late arrival. The one shining relief in my singular existence was that because of my craft and because I had no wife tying my loyalty to her relatives, I was free to stop and make camp with the first convenient band or clan. As I stopped at the campsite of a small band constructed on the periphery of the central camp, I had no way of knowing that this would prove the last season this small luxury would be accorded me. My life as an orphan and bachelor, which I had convinced myself was thoroughly enjoyable, was dwindling away, and the days remaining could be counted on the fingers of one hand. Had I known, I believe I would have fled.

The first time I ever saw the man who would become one of my best friends, I was suffering the fires of the noon sun. Because of the appalling heat, I wore only a breech-cloth and an old pair of moccasins. The ground was so hot I couldn't sit down because the hardpan earth burned my skin. Instead I squatted on my haunches, hands cupped around squinting eyes. Only my long hair, which felt like a cumbersome weight, protected my back from the sun's determined assault. In the shaded distance, safe from the burning rays, the important men of the council were already in their places, seated in semicircular rows according to their importance.

The first row was filled by the principal chiefs of the six clans. Behind them were the subchiefs and the chiefs of small family bands. The third row contained the recognized members of the two healing societies, the Buffalo Doctors and the Owl Doctors. From the fourth row into infinity were the Nation's warriors of varying ranks. Because I had been as prompt for the council as I had been for the gathering of the Nation, the only place left for me was in the full glare of the sweltering sun *behind* the row of boys, members of the Herders society. The boys sat just outside the tantalizing shade canopying the men attending the council. Now and then the delicious trim of shade skittered over them as a frail breeze awakened the frothy canopy of the oaks, elms, and birches. As the fickle shade soothed them and they sighed loudly, I hated every one of those boys.

The burial of Little Bluff had taken place at sunrise. I loved Little Bluff very much. He had been a gallant man, and my boyhood memories were always of him astride a fast-running horse as he led the charge to ward off an enemy war party that threatened our village. He made my blood pound with pride that I had been born a male. Even more when I realized, at such a young age, that our mutual masculinity was a shared bond, that in essence this hero was my older brother. Now he was gone, and deep in my sorrow, I stayed to myself until it was time for the burial. Because I'd isolated myself, I had no idea of the second tragedy that had occurred during the short hours before the funeral. It was not until an hour later that one woman told me about the afternoon council that women and children were not allowed to attend. She didn't say why, and in our culture, questions are considered rude. I can only assume that she believed I already knew why and she had no more time to spare talking to me. Confused, I walked away, leaving her to her chores. As I hurried to join the council, the one thing I knew was that it had not been convened to elect our new principal chief. That election could not be done without the votes of the women. This council, then, was for something else entirely, and whatever it was, it was very serious.

Cursing, shifting my weight, and settling again, I vaguely heard The Cheyenne Robber's name called. During the course of our separately lived lives, I had heard his name many times. He was the kind of warrior they sang songs about. Because I had never seen him, I hadn't paid much attention or given much credence to the extravagant stories told about him, and frankly, some of the stories had beggared my imagination. Four men, two walking before him and two following, all four of them heavily armed, were The Cheyenne Robber's escorts. As I watched them bring The Cheyenne Robber forward, a pole twice the length of his considerable shoulders positioned behind his head, wrists lashed to either end, my mouth fell open.

To say he was magnificent is to demean him. He was beyond magnificent. He was the most beautiful human being I have ever seen. Seeing him for the first time I was so overawed that I rose to my feet and just stared. In age he was a good fifteen years my junior. I'd always thought myself an impressive size at almost six feet. He was at least half a dozen inches over that. My arms, my legs, were thin sticks against the mass and muscular curve of his. But it was his face I found most astonishing. His features were absolutely perfect, skin smooth, flawless. He was so beautiful, he didn't seem real.

Unconsciously, my fingertips traced the side of my face, felt the deep creases around my mouth, the scattering of holes left by the smallpox fever I had survived. As too many of my people had the same scars, I did not feel ugly because of them but I was made aware that compared to his my face was a bit lupine, cheekbones too prominent, eyes small and wide set. His nose, wonderfully Romanesque, was perfectly proportioned to his face. My nose had a bony ridge and, being stubby, ended almost an inch above my upper lip. His generous mouth was pursed in anger. Mine naturally looked like that, so drawn up that my lips appeared to be continually hovering on the brink of a pucker. My self-evaluation ended when The Cheyenne Robber turned his head, coal black eyes making contact with mine for a fleeting second as the charge against him was shouted. Then I sat down. I should say I fell down, for my knees buckled and I landed with a rather undignified thump on my back-end.

Murder.

This incredible human was accused by the relatives of the murdered man, Coyote Walking, of the crime. I sat there with my head bowed, the sun piteously hammering my poor brains. Looking back again toward the drama, The Cheyenne Robber's maternal uncle, the war chief named White Bear, known to the whites as Satanta, because pronouncing his name correctly, *Set-Tainte*, seemed beyond them, was going head-to-head with the trial's chief prosecutor, Kicking Bird. A primary leader in his own right, Kicking Bird was not only the prosecutor, he was also the maternal uncle of the victim. To make a bad situation even more dangerous, White Bear, Kicking Bird, and Lone Wolf, all of them long time antagonists, were the three candidates presently seeking election as our national principal chief, to replace Little Bluff.

When the enormity of this information crystallized inside my overheated brain and the ramifications became all too clear, I became even more dazed. Rising, I pushed my way through seated bodies, walking into the shade. There I plunked myself down beside my peers, the healers, on the third row. I was—I am even now—a doctor. In those days neither healing society publicly acknowledged me. But neither did they denounce me. I had been practicing my craft for too many years and had proven time and again that I had the *gift*. Being a thoroughly arrogant little swine I had let it be known that, if asked, I would join neither society. It needn't be said that I was never asked.

The reason I chose not to disciple myself to the Owl Doctors was because I felt that they put too much emphasis on prayers and visions. The Buffalo Doctors, the physickers, were closest to my calling but I disagreed with their belief that all illnesses and wounds were ailments of the blood. As I had done at a tender age and continued to do as a man, I protested the practice of dangerously bleeding patients. I was baffled and frustrated that the Buffalo Doctors pointedly refused to accept the fact that it was possible to bleed a person to death. What I have always done is sew up wounds, set broken bones, treat the symptoms of presenting illness with medicinal herbs.

It badly ruffled doctorly feathers when I appeared and sat myself down in their number. Because of our rift they had always counted on my good manners not to force myself on them uninvited. Normally I acceded, kept myself separate, but on that day I was too desperate for the shade they enjoyed. I ignored their side glances and barely audible grumbling. This was not difficult. The shade was delicious, and now that I was so much closer to the proceedings, I could both see and hear everything properly. I forgot about my ill-at-ease colleagues and leaned forward, hanging onto every word White Bear spoke.

In that season White Bear was in his middle age. He was an enormous granite block of a man. Having virtually no neck, his head erupted between massive shoulders like a joke. Down through the years I've heard some very unkind remarks made concerning White Bear. The most unkind was the comment that for all his legendary nobility, White Bear was actually as vacant as a cow. The person making this statement never knew the living White Bear. He'd formed this unjust criticism based on a photograph taken in 1870. This person, supposedly a historian, somehow failed to take into account the photographic process of the day, which required the subject to sit completely still. This was almost an impossible task for a man like White Bear. I was among those present when the photograph was taken. I know why his effigy was captured with a certain, shall we say, bovine aura? Thoroughly unused to sitting still, and the photographer managing to be especially fiddly with the camera, White Bear dozed off. He snapped awake the same instant the flash powder exploded. In that same startled second he lifted one corner of his mouth in an inauspicious and rather dull-witted half smile. That second has been frozen in time, that photograph displayed in museums and history books and reprinted for sale to collectors. What that photograph can never show is that second following the flashing explosion, we were all laughing uproariously at White Bear's good-natured expense. Had any of us realized that this hilarious accident would result in an official portrait, we would have put guns to that photographer's head demanding he try again. But we didn't know, and it did become the official portrait. Since then I have often heard people say, "The camera doesn't lie." *Yes it does.* It's a pathological liar.

As a survivor of those years, I will tell you the truth. In life, White Bear moved so quickly he was a blur. His mind was faster than a Gatling gun and he was so eloquent that even at the height of the fifteen years' war between the Kiowa Nation and the United States, White Bear was hailed in Washington, D.C., as "The Orator of the Plains." He loved playing practical jokes on his neighbors so much that he was considered a menace, and his own relatives fought a running battle as to whose turn it was to live next door to him. He could out-eat ten men, and he needed sex the way normal men need air to breathe. He had a laugh so genuine and so booming that standing too close when he was given to gales could cause one's ears to bleed. To be blunt, he was a man too big for this planet.

And I miss him.

Owl Man, an Owl Doctor, was seated next to me. My head was throbbing because I had been too long on the back row, my brains were baked hot from the sun. A wave of nausea was making itself felt when, miraculously, there was a faint whisper of refreshing air. Glancing left I saw the eagle feather fan that had been resting against Owl Man's folded arm moving ever so slightly and for my benefit. There was no time to mutter my thanks. Events before us were rather rapidly plummeting to a new low.

White Bear and his much smaller nemesis had actually resorted to shoving one another. Relatives of both men leaped to their feet, shook their fists, raucously cawing. Lone Wolf, the third candidate in the run for Little Bluff's post, made a great show of springing between White Bear and Kicking Bird, holding both men apart with long, outstretched arms. Then he gave a speech! When Lone Wolf finished, White Bear began. Kicking Bird fumed and rolled his eyes the whole time he waited for White Bear's final word. Seconds after it was said, Kicking Bird immediately launched his own diatribe.

I sat there mouth agape. I couldn't believe it. One man was dead, another on trial for his very life, and the three men supposedly up to the task of replacing the wisest chief ever to draw breath, were politicking. I looked around, taking a quick read of faces, desperate to know if this impressed anyone else as being bizarre. Apparently not, for each face was intent, nearing enthralled.

The moment Kicking Bird finished speaking, the relatives of White Bear and Kicking Bird formed two lines. In these lines they faced each other, eyes narrowed, mouths snarling, tossing insults back and forth. Meanwhile, two young men ran the separate lines distributing arrow shafts. Each man in the challenging lines was given two shafts. A hush fell over the assembly as the men in the opposing lines growled grizzly growls and beat one shaft against the other. The effort created a clacking noise that became increasingly louder than the war drums they mimicked, and carried to the distant minor camp where the women and children of this, the main camp, had been sequestered. The women heard the steady tattoo, and understood this sound meant that Kiowa was declaring war on Kiowa. Their answer was a single-voiced shrill staccato. The grief, so heavy in that strident cry, turned my blood cold. Tiny rat feet raced up and down my spine. Lone Wolf, who moments before had offered himself as a clear-headed mediator, went pale in the face.

Fearsome Warrior is a hackneyed phrase, woefully inadequate, glibly used by those who have never known the bowel-loosening terror of being surrounded by . . . Fearsome Warriors. Lone Wolf knew, for he was. The men surrounding him had only that morning smiled, called him brother. Now, they were dangerous strangers. It's to his credit that he was afraid. The rest of us were afraid for him.

Owl Man was the undisputed leader of the Owl Doctors, the religious seers and healers of the spirit. He was prehistoric, owning a face deeply scored with lines, and a wizened body. Thanks to the abysmal heat, his body, except for a modest covering over the groin, was fully exposed and it was not a pleasant sight. Still, in those moments when he rose, straining against desiccated tendons, straightening just a minutia the natural curl age had visited on his spine, he was a comforting presence.

Gradually, as each man in the challenging lines became aware of Owl Man, the clacking ceased. The distant sopranic voices of the women wafted a few more moments, became soft, then faded completely. Silence hung on the humid air, ominous, heavy; still Owl Man waited with effect. The men who had seconds before filled everyone with consternation now looked glum, shuffled their feet, sent the opposing side blaming looks. That old man, armed with only a withering stare, had reduced those battle-hardened men to a bunch of fearfully contrite little boys.

"This is shameful," Owl Man said in a croaky voice. "I am astonished that I have lived to see such a day. Brother turning against brother." He shook a sad gray-white grizzled head. "Shameful."

Kiowa people were taught from the womb to respect age. It was typical of our breed that all of the men present became penitent. With one exception.

White Bear.

"My nephew stands lashed to a pole!" he roared.

Kicking Bird rallied, then countered, "For a reason."

White Bear whirled on the smaller man. He raised a fist, bringing it dangerously close to Kicking Bird's nose. Admirably, Kicking Bird did not flinch.

Lowering his fist, White Bear spat between Kicking Bird's feet. "He is accused only by you."

Kicking Bird's face mottled with fury. "He is accused by my entire clan."

White Bear spat again. Kicking Bird lunged, the two men

bumped chests. Lone Wolf did not move to intervene for a second time.

"I will speak!"

Again heads turned in Owl Man's direction. He had yelled in a volume no one would have credited to him. A volume that quelled even White Bear. Kicking Bird removed himself a pace, the two glowering chiefs standing apart.

The ancient wise man was fuming. He tried to keep his face blank, publicly admitting none of the rage that I, being so close, felt radiating from him. White Bear quickly looked down, suddenly very interested in his toes. He glanced up several times, filching peeks from under his brows. Kicking Bird was a bit more dignified than that. Folding his arms across his chest, he turned his head to the side and looked up at the robin's-egg-blue sky. Throughout Owl Man's berating lecture Kicking Bird's angular profile remained dominant, the major muscle of his jaw ticking violently.

It must have been painful for him, yet Owl Man managed to straighten yet another millimeter.

"This issue before us is dreadful," he said. "On the one hand we have the loss of a son whom we have yet to bury and mourn. On the other," he pointed the feather fan in the direction of the shackled and heavily guarded Cheyenne Robber, "we have this son, a most beloved son, who, if he is truly guilty of this terrible crime, faces death himself."

Owl Man tapped the fan against a chin pleated by old age. His glittering eyes, surrounded by folds of sagging flesh dragged down at the corners, stayed with and studied The Cheyenne Robber. I didn't know it then but that trail was a torment for Owl Man. It had been he who had given The Cheyenne Robber the adult name He Will Take From The Cheyenne And Make Them Cry. When speaking *about* him, his name was shortened to The Cheyenne Robber. When speaking *to* him, he was simply addressed as Cheyenne Robber. For all intents and purposes, having named him, Owl Man was The Cheyenne Robber's second father. Had I known the depth of love and pride that old man had for his spiritual son, or the emotional agony that old man suffered but refused to give in to, I would have admired him then as deeply as I admire his memory today.

Again he pointed the fan in the direction of The Cheyenne Robber. "If he is guilty of this vile act, more than his life is demanded as forfeit."

Owl Man turned, concentrating hard on White Bear. He spoke again, his tone rigid and accusing. "He is the son of your sister. He is of your clan. All of his acts of bravery and generosity have been credited to you, as principal chief of that clan. When people have said the name, The Cheyenne Robber, they have said, too, the name White Bear. That is proper, that is how it should be. And how quick you have always been to accept the praise and the credit brought to you by this young man."

Bodies moved to create a path as Owl Man, his eyes boring into White Bear, walked forward with all of the dignity his decrepit body possessed. As impossible as it seemed, the solidity of White Bear appeared to diminish in the presence of this shriveled patriarch. I had to lean forward even more, straining to hear over the unaccountably noisy act of swallowing roaring in my ears.

"If he has truly done this thing," Owl Man shouted, "I blame you. You set the example for your young men to follow. And you are known for your temper. I say to your face that if The Cheyenne Robber killed the nephew of Kicking Bird, he will be banished, his name spoken no more, just as we are no longer allowed to say the name of Kicking Bird's nephew. Also I say that every member of White Bear's family clan will serve for the rest of their days the family clan of Kicking Bird. White Bear will no longer be a chief. He will be a servant, the leader of servants."

White Bear reeled. The men of his family standing in the line facing off the men of Kicking Bird's family became

agitated, muttered loudly, their faces shining with fresh
sweat. They nervously looked to White Bear, hoping hard
that he would take charge of the situation. He did. His
previous reverence and humility toward Owl Man vanished,
his voice booming like thunder over the prairie.

"I am no man's slave! The son of my sister did not kill
the son of Kicking Bird's sister, and I will prove it."

"Will you?" Owl Man said in his croaking voice. "Will
you indeed. Well then, I vote we give you time to prove
your claim. I give you ten days."

"I don't need ten days!"

A movement to my right caught my eye. The Owl Doctor
known as Skywalker lowered his head, closed his eyes, and
grimaced as if in terrible pain.

"Fine," Owl Man shouted. "I give you half that. Five
days. Five days to save the life of your nephew and secure
the freedom of every man, woman, and child of your
band."

As Owl Man turned his back on White Bear, the youngest Owl Doctor of our nation, Skywalker, placed a trembling hand to his brow. Sitting Bear, an aging chief and
leader of the most powerful war society, the Ten Bravest,
sat directly in front of Skywalker. Turning at the waist,
Sitting Bear placed a hand on Skywalker's arm. Sitting
Bear's grip was so strong, I could clearly see the bones of
his knuckles bleached white beneath his dark skin. Skywalker was not comforted by the words Sitting Bear uttered
for Skywalker's ear alone. I clearly heard Skywalker, with
tears in his voice, murmur, "Oh, you fool. You wonderful,
imperious fool."

TWO

The Cheyenne Robber struggled like a bull fending off a pack of wolves. Finally defeated, he was led away. The council had ended.

Men stood stretching their limbs, talking among themselves. Now that The Cheyenne Robber had been given a reprieve of five days, no one seemed especially interested in where he was being taken. The opposing families, hot to talk strategies, formed separate clumps, conferring loudly. The movement all around me was like water heating to a boil, men outside the two families rushing to take sides. There were also those who, voicing neutrality, disproved this claim as they sped toward Lone Wolf. The three factions quickly gobbled up every man present. That is, of course, with exception of the old, the near infirm, and me.

Civil war was coming. Its nearing stride pounded and shook the earth like a gigantic ravenous beast seeking those it could destroy. I looked about, droplets of sweat flying from my hair as my head twisted from side to side. I was the only one still seated. Everyone else had chosen sides, and the ancients, in their sorrow, were going off to lament and throw ashes in the air. I tried to stand but I couldn't. I was numbed by the future I knew was coming.

What I could not understand, what I found truly astonishing was that the men were so excited, so eager to proclaim themselves enemies to their own brothers. Until that day I had lived quite content to walk a solitary path. Technically without brothers, until that day I had not missed what I did not have. It was for purposes strictly my own that I was alone, that I had shunned both doctorly and warrior societies. But sitting there I was filled with sorrow that these men could so easily throw away their priceless gift of belonging.

Their utter selfishness boggled the mind. They were rushing to be on what they believed was the *winning side*. There was no concern for anything else. Power was what they sought. They meant either to have it or be closely allied to those who did have it. The future of the Nation seemed not to matter. I have to believe they simply did not comprehend that this side-taking business would eventually lead to brother killing brother. That must have been totally inconceivable to them, and perhaps it was because I was on the outside looking in that I was able to see all of that coming. Then I felt a hand on my shoulder. I turned my head and looked into the sad but piercing eyes of the Owl Doctor known as Skywalker as he knelt beside me.

"You're to come with me."

"Someone is ill?"

He looked away, smiled wanly.

Hope that this was a legitimate request for my healing specialties began to drain out of me. He looked back at me. Our eyes met and held. He was goading me with silence and I was trapped inside the restrictive confines of courtesy, unable to ask anything more until he answered the first question I had so rudely blurted out. All I could do was wait and squirm. Gradually, his tired smile devolved to a weak smirk.

"I am a representative." He stood and lightly tapped my

back. "As I said, you are to come with me."

A cold chill went through me. Those carefully measured words, words I had dodged all my adult life, words which, had my father lived to hear them, would have made him so proud, were words of conscription. Because they had been spoken to me and I was not such an idiot that I didn't understand their meaning, I had no choice. Civil war was imminent and even though I was regarded as a poor team member, I had been drafted nonetheless.

A noncommunicative Skywalker and I rode to White Bear's camp located five miles from the central camp. White Bear's home base comprised forty lodges, nearly seventy men, two hundred women, ninety children, four herds of horses, and an ever-fluctuating population of dogs. A galloping and whooping throng of men from other camps had passed us by while we were en route. They were already in the camp; even more men were riding in just behind us. All of them were making their way to the shade of arbors. In these cool resting places they would content themselves playing dice games. To the casual observer these men appeared to have not a care in the world, but that wasn't true. They were waiting. Nervous tension was rife. The entire camp was on edge and working diligently at appearing normal. A small pack of dogs trotted to greet us, woofing short protective warnings. Women bustled around with their household chores. Older children yelled and chased one another while small children fussed after harried mothers. It was a butter-yellow, sunny day but the atmosphere was strained. People glanced nervously at us, at each other. When a nation, which is essentially a large family, begins to divide, it is hard to recognize friend from foe. Skywalker and I dismounted, tying the reins of our mounts to a scrub tree. A pretty young woman with a sizable baby straddling her hip walked close to our left. I was astonished by the overly familiar way Skywalker called to her.

"Divine One!"

Far from insulted, she tilted back her head and chortled throatily. "Rogue!"

"How is the child?"

She approached, stood before him, pointedly ignoring me. The sun was so bright that where its light touched her hair it turned black into a gleaming blue. Looking up at Skywalker, concentrating solely on him, she squinted against the sun, her eyes becoming crescents, her face crinkling prettily. She kept her side turned to me. I, in theory, was a complete stranger. But she knew me just as I knew that she was Calf Woman, White Bear's youngest wife. This striking woman had consulted me during the early weeks of her pregnancy. One could say that I was responsible for the toddler on her hip being alive. The baby grinned at me, and clutching the sleeve of his mother's dress in a chubby little fisted hand he brought the sleeve to his opening, drooling mouth. Calf Woman didn't notice as she joked with Skywalker, and the baby quickly forgot me as it began slobbering on and mauling her sleeve. Teething.

Her little boy, her first and only child, was growing more milk teeth. Judging by the sounds he produced, it was obvious he found gumming the sleeve of his mother's pretty dress to be sheer bliss. I smiled at the baby and his bright eyes met mine. Showing off his strength he leaned back against his mother's arm and cooed, a long silver string of drool rushing from his mouth. The string hung suspended from his lower lip, sparkling in the sunlight. When Calf Woman adjusted the baby's cumbersome weight on her hip, the saliva string snapped, becoming a large droplet that plopped to the ground, just missing her bare foot. Were I the kind of man interested only in personal gain, how very different this scene would have been.

She had come to me in secret and in the darkness of night because she was terrified.

"He's so big," she sobbed, meaning her husband. "I'm small. His other wives are of good size but they, they worry for me. They tell me stories of bringing forth his children, how much it hurt, how a few of them almost died. I don't want to go through that.''

"What would you have me do?''

"I want,'' she said, tears spilling, chin trembling, "a potion. Something to kill it in my womb before it grows too big and it kills me instead.''

The fire snapped and popped, illuminating the interior of my bachelor's lodge. The door was closed. No one walking by would be able to look in and see her. It was a warm night, the crickets outside making a merry racket. Inside, the air was growing close, her provocative female scent beginning to disturb me. I had a wife once. She died. She was a good woman. I thought a lot of her. Time has not clouded my memory, making more of her than she actually was. She wasn't beautiful or generously proportioned. What she was, was warm, caring, a joy to know. I wasn't a happy person for many years after she died. I tried to be, but I missed her so much, and with her going something inside me went to sleep.

But I was still a man. I still had . . . needs. They were met by the paid services of a Ute slave woman. Thanks to that slave woman's diligence I was not sexually starved but, confronted with Calf Woman's seductive presence in the private confines of my lodge, the emotional needs inside me just . . . woke up. It was an uncomfortable moment for that to happen and I'm afraid I reacted rather badly. I yelled at her.

"Take a Kiowa life! You would damn yourself, damn me, on the basis of malicious stories?''

Her curled fingers pressed against her lips as she sniffled. "Malicious?''

"Stand up.''

Self-conscious, her eyes darting nervously, she slowly obeyed. "W-What are you going to do?''

Because of stories told by jealous, spiteful women, she, like an idiot, had rushed headlong into certain disgrace. If

White Bear even suspected she had gone unescorted to another man's lodge, he would most certainly divorce her.
Too late she realized her mistake and was afraid. Not only
could I smell her fear, I could see it in her eyes. Because
she had come to my home alone and of her own free will,
legally both she and her child were mine. All I had to do
was throw open the door of my lodge, point to her presence,
claim her before a witness, and her fate was sealed. I was
tempted. Tempted all the way to my soul.

"Turn around."

Her eyes, like those of a whipped puppy, stayed with me
as she turned. She stole furtive peeks over her shoulder as
I concentrated on her backside. (Oh and it was lovely.) The
width and curve of her hips were perfect. She was a natural
breeder. Jealousy of White Bear rose and I tasted bile in
the back of my throat. I swallowed it and the gnawing need
for everything she represented; a beautiful woman to make
love to, someone to bear my children, a companion with
whom I could share my life. Again, I was tempted.

I looked up and our eyes met. Even though she was
White Bear's seventh wife, he was a powerful man. Married to him, her lowly station was far higher than it would
ever be were she the first wife to someone like me. Her
increasing fear of such a fate was evident. She twittered
nervously, wringing her hands. She began to remind me of
a small wounded bird I found once when I was a boy. No
matter how much I loved it, no matter how much I wanted
it to stay with me, once it was cured, it only wanted to
leave. So, as I had with that bird, I opened my hands, letting
Calf Woman, and the moment, go.

"There is nothing wrong with you."

Happiness, excitement came alive on her face. She did a
little jump as she turned, her eyes bright and shining. "You
can tell that just by looking at my—"

"Yes. From now on, do not listen to those women. Believe what I'm telling you. You will have a good baby and
you will not die. Should you ever need to consult me again,

kindly do so in the company of your sisters and with your husband's knowledge and permission. For both our sakes kindly take yourself home just as secretly as you came.''

In her haste to do exactly that, she tossed a silver ring in my direction and ducked out. I didn't see her again but I heard that when her baby was born she amazed everyone by passing him out of her in less than two hours. As for me, barely an hour after Calf Woman left my lodge the Ute slave woman wore a shiny silver ring—in payment for a service rendered.

''Where is your husband?''

Skywalker's question brought me back with a start to the present. Calf Woman tossed her head in the direction of an enormous red-stained lodge.

''In his private home,'' she said. ''A lot of men have come. A lot have gone in there to council with him.'' Her eyes touched mine, guiltily darted away. She tried to rescue her sleeve from her son's mouth as she said, ''There's more trouble coming, isn't there? Not about Cheyenne Robber but about—''

Skywalker pressed a long thin finger against her full lips. He smiled and she seemed to melt under his gaze.

''Divine One, how many times must I tell you? Worry is a backward wish. If you don't speak an evil, it won't hear you and find you.''

When he removed his hand she graced him with an adoring smile, hero worship evident. Realizing she was revealing too much, she turned her face away. ''So many men,'' she said in a sigh. ''It's a good thing my husband has a lot of wives. It will take all of us to cook tonight's meal.''

Calf Woman ambled off in the opposite direction as Skywalker and I made for the huge red lodge. ''I've always wanted to thank you for what you did for her and the child. I love Calf Woman like a blood sister.''

That stopped me. A few paces ahead, he stopped as well. He looked at me, the ghost of a smile relieving the angular

planes of his face. Skywalker was always thin. He was one
of those people who could eat for hours and never gain a
pound. But he was also one of those people who didn't
appreciate this gift. In order to eat properly, one must sit
and take the time to chew leisurely, enjoying all the flavors
of the food. Yet Skywalker's sensory faculties were stunted,
and he could barely taste anything at all. I first believed
this malady was caused by his mind being too often in a
different world. Above The Clouds was his second name.
Anyway, unable to taste foods that weren't liberally sea-
soned with Mexican fire peppers, he easily became bored
of chewing and sitting. After eating just enough to stay
alive, he walked away from a wonderful feast, leaving it to
be squabbled over by diehard gluttons better able to appreciate mildly flavored dishes.

"What are you talking about?" I demanded.

He walked back to me, standing close, his shadow a third
person between us. "You and I are not stupid men."

I swallowed against the enormous lump hastily forming
in my throat. "She—she told you?"

"No."

"Then how—?"

"I saw."

"You saw her come to my house?"

"Not physically."

I cocked my head, studying him. I saw something dis-
turbing flicker across his face like a cloud. His features
tightened, the eyes dulled. The right eye cleared almost instantly. The left took a few seconds longer. Just when I was
beginning to think it had to be a trick of light, it happened
again. This time the left eye did not clear. It remained dull,
the pupil dilating to a dot. I hadn't realized that I had been
studying him with an opened-mouth intensity until he
turned and I, coming back to myself, closed my mouth.

"I see a lot of things," he said, his voice sounding
strained, hollow. "You'll get used to it." I fell into step
beside him, which wasn't easy; he had extremely long legs.

"Just as you'll get used to solving problems for White Bear. But I promise, none of his future problems will be as morally challenging as the one you faced with Calf Woman." He glanced at me and chuckled. "Not many men would have shown your restraint. Calf Woman is quite lovely. By rights, she should be yours. I'm impressed that you never spoke of her foolishness to anyone."

In a ridiculing tone I jeered, "If you were that impressed you could have told me a long time ago."

Holding back the door flap for me to enter the lodge ahead of him, he looked at me without a trace of guile and said, "No, I couldn't. Today was the time I was meant to tell you."

When I've had all I can stand, I am known to be a man of temper. And I was angry in that moment because Skywalker's remark had just trod hard on my last nerve. I ripped the edge of the door flap from his hand and slammed it closed. The action startled the occupants. I knew my time was down to seconds before someone inside reopened the door and confronted us. Speaking quickly, just above a whisper, I sneered, "I think maybe if you actually *saw* all of that then surely you must have *seen* this big trouble coming." I wanted to strike him when he nodded in agreement. "Then tell me why didn't you stop it?"

He answered in an irritatingly calm whisper. "I didn't know what I was seeing until it was too late. I see in dreams. And sometimes they're only that. Dreams."

"Isn't that confusing?"

"Very."

The door flap flew open and the space was filled with White Bear's scowling, beefy face. "Why are you slamming my door and standing out here hissing like a snake?" He looked at me, startled by my presence. "And why is *he* here?"

Skywalker tilted his head toward me. "This is the expert help I told you I was bringing."

"Him?"

"He has a name."

Frowning hard, piggy eyes boring through me, White Bear snapped, "I don't care about his name. He doesn't belong to my family or my brotherhood, so I don't know him. He's not coming in here."

In a patient and near-fatherly tone, Skywalker said, "You've made enough blunders for today. If you keep piling them on, no one will be able to save you."

"I'm not the one needing to be saved."

"Yes, you are. Please don't make me beat you half to death to prove it. Kindly move aside and welcome into your home our new brother, Tay-bodal."

Only my eyes moved, glancing from White Bear to Skywalker. With practiced effort I kept my face perfectly neutral. Never had I heard of anyone daring to speak to White Bear in such a manner. To be blunt, I was not at all impressed that Skywalker had done it. He was so thin that with one swipe of his arm White Bear could snap him in half. I stood there fully anticipating that fatal blow when instead, White Bear's laughter treated me to my very first middle-ear-crushing assault. Grabbing me by the bone choker tied loosely around my neck, he yanked me inside his lodge. I was barely steady on my feet when he whacked me on my back, sending me flying into the sea of his lieutenants.

"Brothers!" he boomed. "This little morsel is called Tay-bodal."

Stepping inside the lodge, closing the door for privacy behind him, Skywalker said in a pained tone, "He's a very useful person. Please try not to hurt him."

The request was ignored. I was manhandled, passed from warrior to warrior. Skywalker, still standing by the door, watched and laughed. Then suddenly he placed a hand to the left side of his head, his face screwing up tightly. He gasped sharply and bent completely double. I saw these things in a space of seconds as I was knocked aside in the almighty rush to Skywalker's aid. White Bear reached him first, a burly arm enfolding him, holding him steady.

In a tender voice White Bear asked, "Are you having one of your headaches?"

With great effort Skywalker wheezed, "Yes."

Panic alive on his face, White Bear looked at me. "You're a doctor, or so I've heard it claimed. Help him."

Skywalker was in agony, pain twisting his features as I questioned him, learning that his vision was blurred by flashing stars. He complained in a tight voice that the light inside the lodge was becoming too bright, that the softest voice reverberated inside his head, adding to an already unbearable suffering. Quickly I had him carried to his own lodge. The men made a carry hammock out of blankets, Skywalker tucked inside like a caterpillar in a cocoon. Carrying him this way protected him from the full light of the sun, but it made for a great disturbance in the village. Seeing the unlikely parade and the bundle in the middle, everyone believed there had been a sudden death and came running, wailing their sorrow for whoever it was that had died. White Bear had to do a lot of shouting to calm them all down, and that didn't do Skywalker a shred of good.

As he was being installed I put the distressed inhabitants to useful employment, had them collect spare blankets and place these blankets on the exterior walls of Skywalker's lodge. This would block out excess light. When their job was finished, bellowing like a bull elk, White Bear shouted at the concerned crowd to go away, and for everyone in the camp to stay away and keep all noise in the camp to a minimum. White Bear's well-intentioned bellowing had Skywalker in such misery that he was on the verge of passing out as he was placed on his bed. Even though the other men were easily dismissed, White Bear bluntly refused to leave. To be honest, I thought his presence would be an extra burden to me as well as Skywalker. Especially if White Bear gave in to hysteria and started yelling again. But he kept his head. I was stunned by that huge man's gentleness as he helped me undress Skywalker. I couldn't help but be touched by the loving concern he displayed as he applied cold compresses to Skywalker's brow and whispered prayers on Skywalker's behalf. And I envied their friendship.

Just when we were beginning to believe he was resting comfortably, Skywalker suffered a seizure. I was instantly more than grateful for White Bear's help because the seizure was so violent that it took the two of us to handle him. Finally he slipped into an agony-riddled sleep. Positioned on either side of his bed, we sat back on our legs and shared a muttering conversation.

"How long has he suffered these headaches?"

White Bear chewed the corner of his mouth as he thought. "I have known him half my life. As far as I can remember, he's always had them. But lately when his head hurts he vomits."

"Can you tell me how many vomiting headaches he's had?"

White Bear's chin snapped back against his neck as he thought. After lengthy deliberation he said, "Ten."

I ran a hand over my face, grumbling, "I wish someone had the good sense to call me."

White Bear yelled in a whisper, "You can help him?" Looking into that big earnest face I saw the love he had for this man he called brother. He loved him so much that I knew without a doubt he would give me anything within his power to give if I even so much as hinted at my ability to provide a cure. Calf Woman's image rose in my mind. All I had to do was offer a glimmer of hope and she might be mine. But something inside me has always been irritatingly honest.

I blame my father, really. All that hard, odorous work he endured catching eagles and I never knew him once to overcharge his customers. After my brief foray into his career, I knew that they would have gladly paid whatever he asked without a single word of complaint. No price he named would have seemed too great in order to save them-

selves the onerous task of digging a pit and sitting under a
flea-inhabited moldering coyote. But he was honest. He was
fair. And I was doomed to his perception of fairness. I
could have done with inheriting from him his more worthy
virtues of patience and the ability to keep opinions to himself. Instead I have always been a man in a great hurry,
and I've never been shy with my opinions. These two
things have always gotten me into trouble, and on occasions
were made worse because I was lumbered with my father's
warped sense of integrity.

"I can't cure him. What I can do is take away the worst
of the pain and help him learn how to live with his afflic-
tion."

White Bear considered me for a long moment, and a slow
smile began to tug the corner of his mouth.

"I've heard about you. They've said that you are an unusual doctor. They've also said you are an honest man."

I cringed, gritting my teeth and cursing my long dead
father as White Bear nodded his head, his glittering eyes
mooning in a smile.

"I didn't believe the stories. Now, I know they're true."

It was then that I realized just how canny White Bear
could be. He had sensed my weakness and had probed it.
Having passed his test he pronounced me to be a doctor he
could trust. To prove it he began to regale me with tales of
troublesome wounds he survived but still suffered. I only
half listened as I leaned across Skywalker, lifting each eye-
lid as gently as I could. Skywalker groaned, his eyes re-
acting badly. There was so much pain in there.

"Stay with him," I said brusquely. "Don't allow him to
get out of bed for any reason."

White Bear had been busily digging at his side, talking
about some scar and a Cheyenne with a lance. I had cut
him off mid-sentence. First he looked irritated, then
alarmed, finally anxiety flashed across his broad face.

"You're leaving?"

"Just for the time it takes to fetch my bags and come

right back. I'm afraid I'll be imposing on your hospitality
for a while.''

"Are you talking about days?''

"Well—''

"I think you should be,'' White Bear said sharply. "You
could make him well today and then he might fall sick
again tomorrow. That would mean a lot of to-ing and fro-
ing when you could be here and handy.''

It took a moment, for I was totally flabbergasted, to realize that in his own roundabout way White Bear was inviting me to join his band, the prestigious Rattle Band. He
rose and grabbed my limp arm, yanking me up to my feet,
positioning me so that I stood in front of him. Brushing the
sides of my arms as if he were dusting me off, he continued
rattling on cheerfully.

"You'll be needing your lodge. I'll send along four of
my wives with you. They're like ants. They'll strip down
your lodge and pack up your goods in a matter of minutes.''

"I—I don't want to be an inconvenience, I—''

He waved a huge hand, cleaving the air between us.
"Oh, it's no trouble. They enjoy it.''

I don't believe, judging solely from their pouting faces and
the waspish manner in which they spoke to me, that White
Bear's grasp of what his wives actually enjoyed was all
that sound. But they were astonishingly efficient, laying
bare the bones of my humble lodge more rapidly than I
could gather up my medical supplies. After packing these
essentials I quite naturally offered my help with what I
considered the nonessentials. My offer was met by a stone
wall of disapproval. The women said nothing. As a unit
they glared at me. I could only conclude that my presence
was nothing more than a vexing hindrance to their remarkable industry. My medical supplies were all I had of special
value and I already had those. I did not have a shield, or
special power bundles that might become tainted if they
were not treated just right. Only warriors endured those

worries. And only wives of warriors had to put up with these inconveniences when it came time to pack up a husband's home. My paltry little everyday things they could handle with no difficulty at all. So I left them to it, escaping as quickly as my horse could run.

Less than a mile outside White Bear's encampment several men on racing horses met me. A young man I knew to be called Big Tree caught the reins of my animal, holding it with impressive strength as it shied and danced, he yelled to me in a hurried tone.

"White Bear sent us. He says come right now. Skywalker's worse."

Kicking the sides of our mounts brutally, we raced for my patient.

He was on his hands and knees, White Bear holding him steady at the waist as he vomited prodigiously into a large bowl. The lodge was filled with men, all of them anxious, all of them helpless in the face of this type of enemy. As I entered, White Bear looked at me with profound relief. As if to explain the presence of so many men, he said, "He was screaming. I couldn't keep him down all by myself. He's stronger than he appears."

Standing on my knees beside Skywalker, his forehead heavily resting against my palm, I asked anxiously, "When did the vomiting start?"

"Just before you came in."

The air was terrible. The sun was beating down on that lodge, the extra blankets on the outside walls holding in the body heat, acrid sweat and the heavy reek of vomitus. Not a healthy environment for my patient. Looking over my shoulder I yelled at the milling warriors, "Open the door wide, leave it open as you take yourselves out!"

I looked back to Skywalker when I heard his rasping voice.

"You came back."

"I said I would."

"Yes, you did. You are a person of exceptional honor."

Then he fainted.

As White Bear and I laid him on the bed, I asked, "Do your wives also enjoy cooking?"

"Well of course they do," he snorted. "They're wives, aren't they?"

I couldn't help the smile. "Please tell them to make a strong broth using only livers and bone marrow. And onions. Lots of onions."

White Bear sent me a look approaching disgust. "My brother lies in agony and you think about your stomach?"

"The broth isn't for me. It's for him."

Shortly after White Bear left, Skywalker woke up. He didn't say anything; he just lay there watching me. Practicing my form of medicine, which involved the laborious use of mortar and pestle, under the watchful eye of an Owl Doctor was a bit unnerving. When I had the mix of herbs pulverized just right, I blended them in a bowl of hot water and set the bowl aside for the herbs to brew. Skywalker offered a weak smile as my fingers pressed against the base of his palm. He didn't know what I was doing, and I didn't bother to explain that at the left wrist human beings have what I call the heart's echo. By placing my fingers just so on the wrist, I can actually feel the heart beating in the chest.

His heartbeat was good, in fact considering his deteriorated condition it was surprisingly strong. In a respectful but soft voice I said, "Would you prefer to be treated by doctors of your own society?"

His eyelids fluttered closed, his voice a hoarse whisper. "They've already done all they can do. Now, I entrust myself to you."

As I treated him, I sang a prayer song I made up as I went along. I thought that if I at least made an effort to seem a bit spiritual while I dealt with the physical, the attempt would please him. My feelings were a bit damaged when he prized open one eye and looked at me in disdain.

"Do shut up. You have a terrible voice and I have a headache."

THREE

The medicine I made for him was vile-tasting, but effective. Taken in moderate amounts it relieves pain; however, a large dose puts patients into a near-catatonic sleep. I've found the latter most useful when having to set broken bones or perform surgery. Normally I never gave out this medicine. It could prove too dangerous for patients using it on their own. The case of Skywalker was the exception. Because his condition was chronic, he would always have to keep a small sack of this medicine with him. During the first days of our acquaintance I taught him how to use it properly, and I always made certain to replenish his supply. When the telltale flashing began behind his eyes, he mixed the proper amount with hot water and drank it, or, in the case of emergencies, he simply placed a pinch of it directly under his tongue. The lights inside his head always warned him well in advance that one of his terrible headaches was coming. Armed with his medicine, he was thereafter able to ward off crippling pain.

After medicating him with his first dose, I ground up more of the medicine for his future use and watched him carefully. Herbs are mysterious and humans have what I call levels of sensitivity. I have known patients to react in the strangest ways. A herb able to severely sicken a huge man may have little or no effect on a slender woman. A doctor must be very careful with herbs. Until I know a patient's level of sensitivity, I never leave them when dosing them. If there was going to be an untoward reaction, typically the unlucky indications, a rash or breathing difficulties, manifested themselves within the first few minutes. I was always there and ready with the antidote. Happily this time, Skywalker reacted in a positive way. His tense expression eased, his eyes became droopy, an idiotic smile stretched his lips. A few minutes more and he was oblivious to his former pain and singing at the top of his voice.

Entering the lodge, White Bear was visibly shocked. "Is he drunk?"

Smiling, I kept on reducing the herbs in the mortar to a fine powder. "No. He's . . . happy."

White Bear sat down next to me. Craning his head, he watched my labors for a few moments. "What you're making there, is that what caused him to be so happy?"

"Yes."

"Can I have some?"

"NO!"

I was not accustomed to being pampered by women. Sitting in the arbor with White Bear and his lieutenants, I was amazed that White Bear's wives saw to it that I was given the largest portions of food, my bowl of refreshing mint water always kept full. White Bear nodded and smiled as he wolfed down his food. Nudging me as my drinking bowl was topped up yet again, he whispered, "You've won them over."

Just then Calf Woman stopped. Her sleeping baby tied to her back, she squatted down beside me, ladling out a generous portion of plums cooked with spices and honey into my newly emptied eating bowl. When our eyes met she sent me a smile that was warm and friendly. I also noticed that she gave me more plums than she had given anyone else. Astonished—and just a little bit concerned that White Bear might prove jealous—I looked warily in his direction. He was grinning broadly.

"Of all my brothers," he said, "Skywalker is their favorite. He's always on their side, you see. When my wives complain that I'm a brute, he agrees and does his best to console." He set his food bowl down, wiped his greasy hands clean against his leggings. "My women tell me Skywalker has managed to keep down two bowls of broth and that he's now sleeping peacefully. Because you knew just how to help him, you're their hero." He bird-eyed my bowl of plums. "Are you going to eat all of those?"

"I was going to try."

"Well, don't. You're pretty small. That many plums might do a mischief to your guts. The last thing we need is for our family doctor to fall sick. I'd better take half."

His first wife, passing behind the circle of feasting men, leaned in between her husband and me, slapping White Bear's hand mid-reach with a long wooden spoon. He snatched his hand away instantly.

Rubbing his injured knuckles briskly, he said, "You really should eat your plums, Tay-bodal. It isn't as if my wives prepare them often. They're a special treat made especially in your honor, to welcome you into our band."

Still nursing his hand, he smiled meekly up at his scowling wife. Knowing she wouldn't leave until every last plum in my bowl was safe from White Bear inside my stomach, I ate quickly.

A common custom after a large meal was known as Resting the Food, which means: Take a Nap. Both stuffed and exhausted, I learned to my chagrin that White Bear didn't actually believe in napping. After we made a quick check on Skywalker, we rode out, leaving a camp of souls quite content to rest *their* food. My envy, as well as my fatigue, vanished when less than a half hour later I met The Cheyenne Robber face to face.

His prison lodge was set on the verge of the central camp, a legion of guards lolling all around it. The guards came to life when White Bear and I rode in. We were questioned to the point of harassment, then finally allowed admittance into a lodge twice the height and width of the average home. Except for his lodge being set up in this isolated place and surrounded by many guards, all of them intently watching his every movement, The Cheyenne Robber was allowed to live as normally as he'd been accustomed to living. As I hadn't had personal dealings with a national idol before, I hadn't the slightest inkling that a royal icon's view of *normal* might be just a bit more skewed than mine.

The lodge was filled with women, young women and their older chaperons. The Cheyenne Robber lay on his stomach in the middle of them, the young women rubbing sweet-smelling oils into his skin.

"Where have you been?" he fumed, staring hotly at his uncle. "I've been in misery."

(As I said, The Cheyenne Robber's perceptions of normal, and torment, were just that little bit out of kilter.)

"There was an emergency," White Bear answered. "Skywalker's been ill. He had another one of those headaches of his and he had to be tended."

Mulling this information, The Cheyenne Robber rested his forehead against his arms. The young women seeking his approval and his attention were even more diligent about rubbing his back. He lost himself to their exertions, grunting like a contented bear. After a moment, without raising his head, he asked, "How is he?"

White Bear waved a hand in my direction. "Thanks to this one, he's very well."

The Cheyenne Robber raised his head, his eyes finding and holding mine. "I saw you today," he said flatly. "You acted very odd."

Before my thoughts became clear, I blurted, "It's been an odd day."

His eyes crinkled, a lazy grin slowly relieving the initially tightly set, too-perfect features. Abruptly he flipped over onto his back and roared, "Leave me!"

I was about to do just that when the women rose and I realized he'd meant them. As they filed out, The Cheyenne Robber brought himself up quickly into a sitting position and White Bear sat down near him. Feeling I should do something besides look the fool, I found a place nearby and sat down. Listening to their conversation I was treated to another mild amazement. The women so devotedly tending him weren't his wives. The Cheyenne Robber didn't have even one wife, never mind a bevy. But he spoke to his uncle worriedly about one woman, a woman he called Otter. Apparently she hadn't been among the women who'd just left.

All doctors are perspicacious. I am no exception. Observing, listening, are vital elements of the healing craft. It is often what a patient doesn't say but responds to that leads to a correct diagnosis. Listening to their conversation, I concluded that The Cheyenne Robber loved this unknown woman passionately and that he was more concerned for her well being than he was his own. White Bear answered his question grudgingly, clearly uncomfortable with the subject. Before I could stop myself, I impertinently put voice to a thing that had been troubling me from the start of the council.

"Why would Kicking Bird believe you wanted his nephew dead?"

They instantly fell silent, eyes slewing toward one another, holding for a second, then turning toward me.

"Have you been living on the moon?" White Bear asked incredulously. "Everyone knows why The Cheyenne Robber wanted that dog's penis dead. How is it you don't know?"

I have a practiced impassive appearance. Even so, the

severity of White Bear's query caused me alarm. Both men were actively regarding me with suspicion and their suspicion was making them angry. I answered slowly, keeping my tone, my expression, perfectly at ease. I had been at Bent's Trading Post in the north of Texas, I explained, studying the fever-reducing properties of alkali water with Navaho healers. Hearing the news of our principal chief's death, I then hastened for the Rainy Mountain, but even so, I'd only arrived in time for the funeral. Anything prior to my arrival was foreign knowledge to me. Satisfied with my answer, with my manner, they relaxed. A trustful atmosphere resumed.

"Well, you missed a treat," White Bear scoffed.

The pair of them talked more to each other than to me. I was desperately trying to make sense of what was being said when White Bear and The Cheyenne Robber began to argue violently.

"Don't talk about her that way!" The Cheyenne Robber yelled.

White Bear jumped to his feet, towering over me and his enraged nephew. Both of them were dangerously angry and there was I, a pig in the middle. I tried scooting back on my haunches but each small inch I gained, White Bear stole, stepping nearer.

"We have all talked!" White Bear shouted. "We have talked to you until our tongues have withered and our minds have gone numb. Still you will not listen. *Everything* is her fault. One is dead and now you face death and it's all because of her. Stop being so stupid. If you would just admit that she is a destructive wanton who has played you false, you might just save yourself before it's too late."

The Cheyenne Robber leaped to his feet and, doing so, I was knocked back. Uncle and nephew bumped chests, both of them livid enough to kill the other. "I will never admit such a thing. She's a good woman. She's *my* woman. She would never be unfaithful."

"You are so blind and so stupid you deserve to die."

"Then I will die!"

"Yes, you will, and the rest of us will die with you!"

Each raised an arm, the power of their need to strike evident in the way their arms shook. In the end, White Bear let go a cry of mournful frustration and stormed out. I scrambled to my feet. The Cheyenne Robber followed after White Bear and I followed him. Outside, The Cheyenne Robber said nothing, he glared at White Bear as White Bear retrieved his horse from one of the worried guards. The Cheyenne Robber was too proud to call his uncle back and White Bear was just too mad to listen even if The Cheyenne Robber had tried. He and I stood just outside the lodge as White Bear swung up onto his horse and rode away. With a saddened expression, The Cheyenne Robber watched his departing uncle while I watched The Cheyenne Robber. He wore only a breechcloth, no shoes. His waist-length hair was untied and draped behind him. His arms lay across his chest, hands resting inside his armpits. He stood with one leg bent at the knee as he stared after his uncle. His well-muscled body was shiny from the oil the women had rubbed into his skin. The sunlight bathed him with a soft adoration. Once again I was impressed. The Cheyenne Robber remains in my mind the most splendid animal I have ever seen.

When White Bear was almost lost from view, The Cheyenne Robber spoke to me in a soft, dispirited tone. "He's angry because he doesn't understand how I can still love her." He turned his head, our eyes met and held. "He blames her for everything. That's his way. Whenever there's trouble and a woman is involved, my uncle blames the woman. I find that peculiar in a man who collects them, can't seem to live without them." He sighed deeply. "But maybe he's right. I think maybe if I were able to view Otter as an evil person then perhaps I wouldn't be in this mess. But I'm afraid I can't do that. I'm stuck. I love her all the way to my soul. And loving her that way, I'd do everything that brought me to this place all over again."

"But do you blame her?"

His answer was a saddened smile and a slow shake of his head.

"Would you like to talk about it?"

He looked up at the sky, that handsome face contorted with grief. In a somber voice, he asked, "Can you give your word you will never repeat anything I say?" He looked back at me, searched my face.

I have always prided myself on being an unflappable person. A doctor knows all sorts of things about his patients, but in that moment, I was disturbed more than I care to admit. In my gut I knew that whatever he wanted to confide in me was bad. Possibly dangerous. But he needed help. And, too, I was unspeakably flattered that a man like The Cheyenne Robber would turn to someone like me for help. So what else could I do but give it?

"You have my word."

He nodded, then moved off toward the shade of a nearby arbor. I followed. When we were seated, he looked off into the hazy distance. I made myself comfortable, tried very hard to relax in his extraordinary presence as I sat and waited.

"That other one," he began slowly, meaning Coyote Walking, "and I were never friends. Never. I know it's dangerous to speak badly of the dead but I wasn't afraid of him when he was alive and I'm certainly not afraid of his idiot ghost. Alive he was an envious, scheming little no-good. I can't imagine that being a spirit will ever improve him."

I heard myself chuckle. The Cheyenne Robber looked at me, laughed soundlessly, then became still. Steeling himself, he said, "That one knew White Otter and I were in love, that we were all but married. I know that's why he interfered." He turned an angry, earnest face toward me. "He didn't care about her. He only wanted to win a victory over me. The day before her father, Run The Bulls, was to announce our marriage, he sent his relatives to plead his—'' his voice faded and The Cheyenne Robber's features began to contort with disgust—"love."

Fury further distorted his marvelous features. "I'm being kind when I say that Runs The Bulls is not a decisive man. Kicking Bird's visit flustered him. He didn't know what to do now that he had two offers for his daughter and from both of the Nation's leading families. Runs The Bulls started dithering. I'm afraid it wasn't a very good time to dither. Believing ourselves as good as married we, uh, we—'' He looked away, wiped a hand across his face. "We had—''

"You'd consummated the marriage."

He looked startled that I had guessed so easily. Then he lowered his head, sounding a sad, empty laugh.

"That's right. For nearly two months we'd been consummating ourselves blind.'' His head jerked up, his eyes finding mine, our mutual stare steady. Again, even before he said it, I knew the worst.

"She carries my child."

For a long moment I couldn't think of what to say. My inability caused an uncomfortable silence between us.

He looked away from me, his face in profile. His mouth began to twitch at the corner, and there was a long, tense silence between us. Finally in a whispery soft voice, he spoke.

"I was happy when she told me about the baby. Happier than I've ever been in my life."

His head whirled so quickly I felt myself jerk. His voice rose, his features hardened.

"Everything would have been all right if *he* hadn't butted in. It was as if he knew everything about us, knew our secret about the baby and was intent on ruining me, disgracing her. I panicked. I went to Runs The Bulls myself. I did everything but tell him he was about to be a grandfather. I thought surely he'd understand subtlety. Obviously the man's hopelessly thick. Can you believe it?" he shouted. "He *raised* her bride price! I didn't know who

I wanted to kill more, Kicking Bird's vicious nephew, or
Runs The Bulls.''

Stunned I said, "Did you say this to anyone?"

The Cheyenne Robber waved his arms wildly. "I said it
to anyone with ears to hear me! I yelled it from mountain-
tops. My beloved was red-eyed, constantly counting on her
fingers, worrying about how long we had before everyone
knew her condition, and the two men I could barely abide,
neither of them owning so much as a cup of common sense
between them, were the cause of all her fears. Of course I
wanted to kill them.''

"You threatened them *both*?"

"Yes."

I lowered my head, resting my forehead against a trembling hand. In an even less steady voice, I asked, "What
happened next."

The Cheyenne Robber snorted derisively. "We were
only in this place two days when Shield Woman, Runs The
Bull's second wife—and I must tell you I find her even
more stupid than her husband—made a great fuss, screaming and carrying on at the top of her voice. *And* she was
waving an article of clothing over her head."

I sat straight up. "Why?"

"You might well ask." Again he snorted down his long,
aquiline nose. "It became the cause of my current situation.
She had a pair of man's leggings. She was screaming that
she'd found them under White Otter's bed. They belonged
to—" He almost said the dead man's name out loud, something quite forbidden. He held his breath for a second, let
it go. "Kicking Bird's fool of a relative."

I must have exhibited distress, or in some small way
exhibited the same biased attitude White Bear had against
White Otter, for The Cheyenne Robber immediately rose
to his knees. Standing on them, he grabbed hold of my
upper arms and held me fast. His face inches from mine,
his words came at me loud and rapid.

"It's a lie. White Otter never knew him. She did not take

him to her bed. She yelled this over and over the whole time Shield Woman was screaming her accusations. White Otter's own mother, Sits Beside Him, shouted her daughter's innocence. She and White Otter share the same lodge. If White Otter had ever allowed a man in her bed, her mother would have known it. But the crowd wasn't listening to White Otter or Sits Beside Him. It was because of those leggings. Those leggings were hard proof and—''

Suddenly overwhelmed with grief, he let go of my arms, his hands dropping heavily away. He bowed forward, his hands braced against his thighs. He wept unashamedly.

Only because he was in great distress and because he needed comfort did I dare touch him. My hands resting nervously on his slumped shoulders, I said softly, ''You're telling me that Runs The Bulls turned his back on his own daughter?''

''Yes.'' He wiped away an angry tear, his voice sounding choked. I took my hands away and he looked at me, his eyes glowing with smouldering fury behind brimming tears. ''I'm telling you that only for my sake and the well-being of our child, she crawled on her belly to her father, begging him to believe her. Do you have any idea what that did to me, having to stand there and watch it? That woman is my heart and my soul and I had to stand and do nothing while she poured dirt onto her head, pleaded for forgiveness for something that wasn't even her fault. But still that sorry excuse for a father of hers refused to look at her.''

The memory became too much for him. Except for me, there wasn't a handy outlet on which to vent his formidable wrath. Becoming a trifle concerned that in a pinch I might suffice, I rushed to assuage him.

''Cheyenne Robber, there was nothing you could do.''

''That's what Skywalker said,'' he snapped. He looked up, not ashamed of the fresh tears sparkling along his lower lids. ''Skywalker held me by my arms. In my ear, he said, 'There is nothing you can do. You will only make everything worse.' I didn't agree with him. I—''

"You didn't confess?" I cried. "Not to the whole nation that you and she—"

His former tension left him and he jeered, "Of course not. I'm not a complete fool. But what I did do was prevent her father placing her hand in the hand of that reptile that, when he was alive, used to be Kicking Bird's nephew. And Runs The Bulls was just about to do it, too. He'd grabbed her up by the arm, was dragging her to her feet. Kicking Bird's nephew was stepping forward to accept her. The words of marriage were on Runs The Bulls's lips. I couldn't let that happen. Not only would that piece of filth have the woman I loved, he would have my son! Could you really expect me to stay silent and lose him as well? If I did I would be condemning myself to watching him grow from baby to man and all of his life thinking himself the son of that—that pile of dung! I couldn't do it. I'd kill myself first. And would you blame me?" he shouted. "Could you really expect me to live with that kind of awful secret? So there was nothing else I could do but break free of Sky-walker and run to stand between White Otter and—"

He shrugged deeply, calming down a fraction. He took a deep breath, expelled it. "I pushed *him* away. And then I accused him of being a sneak and a liar. I said to his very startled face that he had faked everything. That he was the one who had put those leggings under White Otter's bed. And that he'd done it for the sole purpose of winning over me. Of course he denied it. In fact, he was so vocal that for once in his miserable life I almost believed him." The Cheyenne Robber became agitated again, waving his strong arms wildly. "But he was more than ready to take her, wasn't he? He even had the nerve to suggest that White Otter had taken his leggings and placed them under her own bed so that I would leave her alone and let her marry him the way she obviously wanted to do. That's when I hit him."

I felt my blood drain. My head went back onto my shoulders and when my sight cleared I was looking up at the loose weave of the arbor roof. Snatches of the azure sky looked back at me. And through the holes of the loosely woven branches and careless thatching, the sun sent down shafts of velvety light.

"He was a sneak and a liar!" The Cheyenne Robber yelled. "He was all of that and more. The only thing that ever made him seem important was the accident of his birth. If it hadn't been for Kicking Bird, he would have been a nothing, and everyone knew it." I could hear his hand drumming rapidly against his chest as he shouted, "Only I had nerve enough to say to his face what everyone said behind his back! Only I dared to challenge him man to man. And how did he respond? He tried to hide behind a woman. *My* woman."

Thoroughly dismayed, I said weakly, "And everyone in the entire nation heard you and witnessed you hitting him?"

The defensive bluster instantly left him. We consciously avoided looking at each other as he resettled himself, long legs crossed, arms folded and resting against his broad chest. After a lengthy pause, I heard him chuckle. Canting my head, I bird-eyed him. He grinned at me, and his chuckle became a laugh.

"I didn't exactly accuse him and knock him down in front of the *whole* nation. If you'll remember, you managed to miss it."

Absurd laughter erupted from me. It blended with his. A group of guards positioned some distance away, squatting around a lively game of dice, looked questioningly back at us. Our laughter increased. We leaned heavily against each other, laughing uncontrollably. When we were too weak to lean, we fell onto our backs and rolled with laughter.

In a crazy way, the moment felt wonderful.

FOUR

This was the second day of my return to my own people. The first day was spent setting up my lodge in a host camp. Or I should say, setting up my lodge on the fringe of a host camp, for that is the more accurate. I have never done well with grieving. When people I considered worthy passed, my grief for their loss has been both private and profound. In any case, I had kept myself to myself before Little Bluff's funeral, which was this very morning. The events that The Cheyenne Robber described had occurred just yesterday. I too could have been a witness had I not been holed up on my own. Ordinarily, after such a startling occurrence camp gossips would have swarmed like excited hornets, but there are strict rules regarding mourning, and unbridled scandal mongering is definitely against the rules. As impatient as the gossips might be, their tongues were forced to be held until about now, the afternoon following Little Bluff's funeral.

While The Cheyenne Robber talked, my mind went to another place. Although I seemed attentive to him, I was thinking about two things. The first was that gossips are very useful, necessary people. At least they always have been for me. Try to remember that mine is a culture that frowns on direct questions. The logic behind this is unfailingly simple. If there is a thing the speaker wishes the listener to know, the speaker will say it without any need of discourteous prompting. Also, our culture was a classed society. A person such as myself, a member of the lowest class, did not dare question, nor ask questions pertaining to, a member of a higher class. Any male ranking above the Herders society outranked me, so there you have it, my predicament on top of a predicament. If I were to prove myself useful to The Cheyenne Robber, I would have to depend heavily on camp gossips otherwise I'd never learn anything.

The second thing I was thinking was about the motive for Coyote Walking's death. At the council, Kicking Bird had repeatedly said that The Cheyenne Robber had been jealous. I hadn't understood then why The Cheyenne Robber would have been considered jealous of Coyote Walking. Listening as The Cheyenne Robber spoke of his love for Otter, at least the jealousy portion of the puzzle had become clear to me. However, to understand it fully it was necessary to first examine the emotion called jealousy. On its own, jealousy is a flattering emotion, letting another person know that he or she is very special. But jealousy has three dark shadows: possessiveness, envy, anger.

My eyes narrowing, I studied The Cheyenne Robber for a long time. I decided he could be a jealous man. Had he been jealous of White Otter? From the way he talked about her, expressed over and over his deep concern and worry, I would say that, yes, he could be jealous. But jealous only of her time. He wanted all of it. But when she was away from him? I tilted my head, studying him harder, the words he spoke drifting into my thoughts. I was attentive for a moment, really listening to what he said. As he spoke of White Otter, of their unborn child, I realized just how deeply he loved her. And I heard enough to know that when they were apart, he trusted her completely. As her lover it was only natural that he might be a little jealous of her, but neither he nor I could imagine her ever being unfaithful to him. And because he certainly could not conceive of it, it was next to impossible for me to view him as being lethally jealous. Therefore, the only motive he would have for killing Coyote Walking would be to protect White Otter and his unborn child. His next statement foiled that motive.

"I was going to kidnap her. Even though my uncle wasn't convinced that she hadn't soiled herself with another man, for my sake, he agreed to help me. The kidnap was scheduled for today. White Bear was going to council with Runs The Bulls, preventing his announcement that White Otter was now the wife of . . . Anyway, while Runs The Bulls was distracted, White Otter and I, with an escort of twenty, would be riding hard for the Red River. When Runs The Bulls realized his daughter had gone away with me, he'd have no alternative but to accept the bride price my uncle offered. Once she was declared my lawful wife, I had planned to beat the truth about those leggings out of Kicking Bird's nephew."

I thought hard about everything he said. I looked for flaws. There weren't any. His plan of direct action was effective and far more productive than any sudden burst of deadly emotion. He had shown his temper when White Otter was accused by her second mother, but afterward he had calmed down. Apparently enough so to devise a counter-move against Coyote Walking's sneak attack. Such thinking proved to me that The Cheyenne Robber, despite his admission of a public outburst, had actually kept his head. His vocal challenge against Coyote Walking's honor bought The Cheyenne Robber the time he would need to steal White Otter. His ability to think clearly even in the heat of the moment erased in me all trace of doubt that he might be a true subject of violent passion. The Cheyenne Robber was not the type of man who would kill in anything other than a fair fight.

Then a jarring thought occurred. Coyote Walking's body had been found that very morning. His body was still fresh. Hurriedly, I made my excuses and left behind me an aggrieved Cheyenne Robber. He could be so like his uncle. When either he or White Bear had someone's full attention, they didn't let go of it without a struggle. When I suddenly leaped to my feet making a flurry of excuses in my haste to rush off, I irked him.

"If you really want to help *me*," he said, his tone sullen, "then what I have to say is important."

"Granted," I replied. "And I promise I will return. But for now, I must be away. My reason is in your best interest, please believe that."

His expression sour, he looked me over from head to toe. I had been a good listener, but then again, trees are good listeners. Standing away from me and looking again at his uncle's choice for clan champion, I knew The Cheyenne Robber was having second thoughts about me. I couldn't blame him. Were it my life hanging in the balance, I'd look askance at any rescuer who looked like me, too. What I could not tell him was that at dusk Coyote Walking's family would begin the final preparations of the body for burial, washing him completely, dressing him in his best clothing. If I wanted to examine the remains while Coyote Walking was in almost freshly murdered prime condition, I would have to do so immediately otherwise valuable evidence would be lost.

As I rode away from The Cheyenne Robber's prison camp I heard him yelling at his guards. The Cheyenne Robber was a very haughty, autocratic individual. Being a prisoner did not lessen this attitude. Glancing back over my shoulder I saw the guards jumping to obey his every command. It was that sight that impressed on me the importance of saving him. The Cheyenne Robber's nature would not make for a successful outcast. Without lackeys to do his every bidding, he would not survive even a day on his own.

Kicking Bird's camp was a good ten miles away. I rode

as quickly as I could, and during the ride my mind tumbled over everything I remembered hearing at the council. During Kicking Bird's very wordy address I had gleaned that prior to dawn, no more than a hour or two before Little Bluff's funeral, Coyote Walking's body had been discovered by a group of women making their way to the creek to collect water. Coyote Walking had been found lying close to the creek, across the narrow pathway. At first the women believed him asleep and, mocking him, kicked the body. When he did not respond they knew he was dead and ran away screaming, alerting the camp.

Kicking Bird claimed that the cause of Coyote Walking's death was a broken neck. He described at some length the path leading to the creek, that it was only gradually inclined and that a fall and subsequent tumble could not have resulted in the fatal injury. It was on this evidence alone that he singled out The Cheyenne Robber as the assailant and the motive, as stated, jealousy. What Kicking Bird had failed to describe was any further evidence of violence. If there had been a fight, why had Kicking Bird not mentioned evidence of a fight. The ground would most certainly have left traces. Then again, no, it would not, not after the footprints of the women obliterated the area round the body. However, the evidence on the body would remain. Bruising cannot be rubbed out. Why hadn't Kicking Bird mentioned the bruises?

Kicking Bird was a powerful chief and his camp reflected this power. Hundreds of warriors bore him their allegiance, and each warrior could have many wives, thus many households to bring into this single encampment. I counted five large horse herds, and the smoke-blackened tops of tepees stretched out for miles. Because there had been a death here, the inhabitants went about their lives quietly. The children were not allowed to play games, men were not allowed to gamble. As the women went silently about the necessary business of living, children and men sat in small

clumps speaking in low tones and with grave expressions.
My appearance came as a welcome diversion, curious faces
turning in my direction as I walked my horse into the outskirts of this impressive camp. People walked forward to
greet me and in the solemn way of a death camp received
me graciously. Had they known of my recent friendship
with The Cheyenne Robber and White Bear, their faces
would have lost any trace of friendliness. They would not
have invited me to step down from my horse or offered me
a refreshing drink. They would have dragged me down and
beaten me for a spy. I don't believe I would have fought
back. I was a spy. But no matter how low-down I felt about
it, lives were at risk, the most precious being The Cheyenne
Robber's unborn child. So I accepted the beverage, extended my sincerest sympathies for their loss, and lied my
head off.

"He was my friend," I said, rousing compassion along
with one or two blatantly startled looks. "No one knew of
our friendship. I felt it best not to brag of a close relationship between someone such as myself and a noted warrior.
As befitting a person of his high class, he proved towards
me again and again that he was a good and caring person.
And he was so generous, wasn't he?"

Relatives nodded dutifully, puzzled glints in several pairs
of eyes rapidly trying to recall when (or if) this generosity
had ever been extended to themselves.

"I learned only this very morning of his death. I would
have come sooner but I was too overcome with shock and
grief. I come now," I continued, "to offer my respects and
ask, if it wouldn't be too great an inconvenience, for just
a few moments to say good-bye to my good friend."

As I was escorted through the grief-stricken camp, the
small group of relatives walking all around me said to their
cousins whom we passed (with a mixture of incredulity and
wonder in their voices), "This was his friend."

I couldn't make out if their bafflement was because *I*
was the friend, or because it was such a surprise to learn

that he'd actually had one. Whatever was true, I was marched like a prince through the village toward the death lodge and once there politely left alone to vent my grief. It is our custom that after a person dies, his or her best possessions are given away, the rest burned up with their lodge following the funeral. Before a person is buried, mourners stand outside the lodge and wail their misery long and loud. No one ever goes inside the death lodge. That is forbidden. The only people who actually come near a dead person are the people laying out the corpse. So I stood outside Coyote Walking's lodge wailing away until everyone in the camp became oblivious to my presence. Then I quickly stooped and went inside.

The lodge was empty except for the covered body lying on a pallet. Gourd bowls of smoking herbs were dotted around the head. The purpose of this pungent smoke was to help guide the spirit up and through the lofty smoke hole and mask the odor of death. To the living, this smoke is a considerable deterrent, hard to breathe, but the dead aren't bothered. I had to fan my hand before my face in order to breathe small breaths of air and reduce the effects of smoke-sting to my eyes. As there was no time to worry about my physical comfort, I proceeded quickly to the body, knelt close and lifted away the covering blanket.

Happily, as I had hoped, the ritual of bathing and oiling the body for burial had not been done. Judging by the odor, never mind our stern code of hygiene, bathing wasn't a thing Coyote Walking practiced on a daily basis. The clothing he had died in had been removed and replaced by a long shirt as the corpse lay waiting for its much needed bath. For my needs, however, the present condition of Coyote Walking was perfect.

The neck is unimaginably fragile and the skin covering the neck is highly sensitive, bruising very easily. Strangling was a personal violence unheard-of by my people. Even when confronted with the irrefutable evidence that their relative had been strangled, those viewing the corpse had no idea what they were seeing. But I knew. I had seen these marks once before.

When I was about twenty-six I spent the autumn lounging in my favorite place, Bent's Trading Post. Bent's was the gathering place for all the nations and that curious breed of white man who was more Indian than white. One afternoon an Arapaho doctor showed me the body of a dead Navaho woman. In particular the bruises marking her neck. It was thought that she had died of a sudden illness, but the Arapaho shaman examining her said no. He said her life had been squeezed out. At the time I couldn't believe it, couldn't even envision such a thing. To prove it to me he placed his hands over the marks and demonstrated exactly how the killer's tightening hands had blocked off air to the lungs and brain. Without air, the brain, then the body, dies. He said something else that impressed me.

"Only bullies kill people by the neck."

I was appalled by this knowledge, but I knew he was right. I stayed with that old man, never letting him out of my sight, and by watching him I learned something else. That to find a killer one must first learn everything there is to know about the victim. And what we learned of the habits of that Navaho woman led us straight to her murderer.

That young woman had been something of a flirt. She had been given many offers of marriage but coyly took her time considering each one. At Bent's she received yet another proposal, this time from an especially ardent suitor. As she was about to leave him, to go off and "consider" his offer, he grabbed her and she struggled. His hands increased their grip on her throat as he kissed her mouth. When she went limp he thought she was responding, being agreeably compliant. It astounded him that instead she had died. When that old Arapaho announced all of his findings, the young man, another Navaho, did the honorable thing. He confessed.

That memory filled my mind as I sat on the backs of my

legs before Coyote Walking's earthly remains. I knew that whoever had done this to him was not honorable, would not confess. This was not accidental death caused by a kiss. With my fingertips I probed the center front of the throat. The delicate bones inside felt loose, broken. I brushed back his hair and examined the flesh around the eyes and the hairline. I had to look very hard, for Coyote Walking was of an exceptionally dark complexion, but even still, tiny pinpoints of blood were visible around the eyes, along the scalp line. My worst fear confirmed, I re-examined his throat. Judging by the exceptional bruising, Coyote Walking had struggled against his attacker. I picked up his hands, studying them closely. His fingernails were a trifle long for a man and looked as if they hadn't been properly cleaned in quite a while. Amid the encrusted grime under the nails, I found a large bit of desiccated flesh. The cuticles of the two middle fingers were caked with dried blood. This evidence was missed because the blood and the scraped flesh blended perfectly with Coyote Walking's less than perfect form of hygiene. There were no marks on his trunk, but there were minor abrasions on the knees. From this I could only conclude that the killer had been taller, more powerful. During the struggle the killer had forced Coyote Walking to his knees. In this position, fighting for his life, Coyote Walking had managed to wound his attacker. But where? Closing my eyes, I tried to visualize where my hands would go were I on my knees, my air being shut off, my hands clawing.

I heard a noise. My eyes flew open, and with a hasty glance over my shoulder, I looked out the opened door of the death lodge. People walked around in the sunlight but no one approached. I convinced myself that I had imagined the noise, for the victim's family didn't seem especially concerned about where, in my inconsolable grief, I had gotten off to. Whether I'd imagined the noise or not, though, I didn't dare risk remaining too long. Quickly, I turned the body over. Easy to do—he was not a large or heavy person.

My nation was struck by two plagues that very nearly saw the end of the Kiowa people. First was smallpox, then a few years later, cholera. It was that illness that took away my wife. During these epidemics I dealt with more than my share of dead people, and I learned something which has been invaluable to me. I learned that there are stages of death the body passes through and these stages, no matter the cause of death, are inevitably the same.

At the moment the soul departs the body, blood no longer flows evenly. Like stagnant water, it seeks the lowest level, forms a sluggish puddle, and then coagulates, becomes thick and gummy. I have never known this fact to vary. This negative circulation, as I call it, begins during the first hour of death. It takes approximately five hours for the blood to leave the vital organs and sink. During this process, the body stiffens, relaxing again after the blood has permanently settled. Incredible as it seems, knowing these simple stages of death makes it possible to guess the time death occurred. I've never told anyone I could do this. I was afraid I would be accused of being crazy. And morbid.

Raising the overlarge white shirt adorning Coyote Walking's body, I examined his back and the length of his right side. Where the blood had collected and was fixed, his skin was darkly colored. In the areas that had made hard contact with the earth, blood was absent, the skin flat and unnaturally white. These signs were evident on his right side. These signs told me exactly how the body had rested. What I could not find, evidence that would have made the claim against The Cheyenne Robber hard to disprove, was a solid vibrant bruising on the *back* of the neck. According to Kicking Bird's account, The Cheyenne Robber had struck Coyote Walking from behind, the blow breaking the neck. Coyote Walking's neck was most certainly broken, I can attest to that, but the few bruises evident were small rounded spots, where the tips of the fingers had been. A single blow hard enough to break the neck from behind would have produced a bruise that would have covered the area from the base of the skull to the middle of his back. There was no such bruise, but the spinal bones that allow the head to nod were splintered. I could only conclude that his neck had been broken *after* he was dead. Had he been alive, the blood would have been flowing. The blow breaking his neck would have left a considerable bruise. But dead, the blood in his body seeping away from the area, his body was no longer capable of raising a bruise. As abhorrent as it was for me to consider, I was forced to admit what I knew without a doubt. The neck had been broken *after* the victim had been strangled, my best guess, a few minutes into the first hour of the death process. I further mulled what Kicking Bird also claimed during the council, that his nephew had been attacked from behind, had been given no chance to defend himself. That was not true. Coyote Walking had struggled with a frontal assailant while said assailant had him by the throat. Next, I wondered why after killing him in this manner, the murderer had not just run away. Why had he felt the need to break a dead man's neck. A chill, colder than the north wind rushed through me as my mind pictured the scene. Quite clearly I saw this faceless attacker as he suddenly realized that he had killed Coyote Walking. I could almost feel with him his horror and his panic. Then, as he calmed himself, he brutally re-arranged the death and in doing so exploited the known feud between Coyote Walking and The Cheyenne Robber, deflecting any blame away from himself.

Hurriedly I replaced the body and arranged it exactly as I had found it. I timed my exit just right. Outside the lodge I stood with one hand covering my eyes, trying to steady my rapidly beating heart. Someone touched me, a man murmuring comfort, his voice silken and soothing. I allowed his voice, his words, to wash over me. I desperately needed comforting just as I desperately needed the sun to warm my freezing skin. But neither the kind words nor the sun proved effective against what I knew. That among us there existed a soul utterly diabolical, viciously malevolent. Someone so inhuman he could throw away the lives of two men in the interest of protecting his own. Shaken to the core, I was ushered by the kind-voiced man off in the direction of Kicking Bird's lodge.

Kicking Bird was a small man, but he had an aura. All men of great power have it and wear it like an invisible cloak. When with his friends, White Bear removed his, for he craved familiarity. Kicking Bird didn't, not ever. He required everyone, even his wives, to address him with an attitude both reverent and humble. Oddly enough, being in his stilted company just moments after making that hellish discovery actually helped to focus my mind. Had Kicking Bird been halfway friendly, I might have broken down and babbled what I knew like a frightened fool. But Kicking Bird was about as comforting, about as malleable, as dried tree sap, and his lodge was filled with his relatives and subordinates. Certainly this was not the time or the place to lose my head, nor was this a crowd who would appreciate what I had to say on the subject of strangulation and The Cheyenne Robber's innocence. Keeping what I knew close to my chest, I forced myself to look at each face and remember all of them. Someone had intentionally murdered Coyote Walking and was intent on pushing the blame onto The Cheyenne Robber. And that man could be as close to me as the man seated either on my left or on my right. As Coyote Walking had gone to meet his killer in a relatively private place, this killer was likely someone he had known quite well, a description fitting everyone present in the lodge with myself being the one exception.

Even though I sat directly across from him, Kicking Bird rarely looked at me. He wasn't really listening to the men seated around him extolling the merits of Coyote Walking. I had the distinct impression that he was trying to figure a way out of the present mess his nephew's demise inadvertently created, saving not only face but perhaps even The

Cheyenne Robber's life. He finally looked at me and spoke in a measured tone.

"We are grateful for your courtesy. I have heard of you, Tay-bodal. I am given to understand that you are a man of great wisdom. Wisdom is needed in this dire time. Wisdom in great abundance." He sighed heavily. "White Bear and I are not friends but I have long admired his nephew. The Cheyenne Robber has always been a good man to cross the river with."

Heads began to nod, grunts of agreement sounded around the circle of seated men. The river was of course the Red River. Crossing the river meant belonging to a raiding party against the *Tehans*—Texans. Tehans were our natural enemies. Kiowa raiding parties crossed the river regularly, especially during this time when there were too few soldiers protecting too large a country.

"The Cheyenne Robber," Kicking Bird continued in a droning voice, "is a man everyone present here has trusted with their lives, many times. The loss of such a man is measureless and the result of that loss too dreadful to contemplate."

I was right. Not only was Kicking Bird alarmed by the specter of civil war, he actually *liked* The Cheyenne Robber. Bringing charges against him had grieved Kicking Bird just as much, if not more, than the death of his nephew.

A quarter of an hour later I left the lodge with three men following me out and escorting me to my horse. These men, Hears The Wolf, Stands On A Hill, and Chasing Horse, were all maternal relatives of the dead man. Hears The Wolf was the oldest, and, I learned, the younger brother of he dead man's mother. He was a very good looking man who did not show his proper age of almost forty years. There was no gray in his hair, his stomach was flat and hard. He was also comically self-absorbed. On a day so hot that everyone went about in just enough to satisfy modesty, Hears The Wolf was resplendent. Wide copper bands encircled his biceps, a plethora of smaller copper and silver bracelets jangled from his wrists to his elbows. An eagle-bone-and-glass-bead breastplate covered his chest, and a matching and equally wide choker encircled his throat. The tag ends of his breechcloth fell below his knees, and he wore Apache-style knee-high moccasins. His long hair, dressed and oiled, was littered with decorative beaten-flat discs of silver. When rays of the sun caught in the silver ornaments, the effect was blinding. He wore a gold nose ring in his left nostril like a Nez Percé, and each ear was heavily earringed from lobe to the top of the ear. This burdensome attire was presented as a uniform, a costume expected, perhaps even demanded, of him. The man was living proof that there is nothing more punishing, or more rigid, than the required conventions of someone deemed unconventional.

Content to be ordinary, Stands On A Hill, Chasing Horse, and I wore only the essentials. And all of us, to keep the backs of our necks cool but our backs shaded, wore our hair tied up into horsetails. Even so, we were miserable from the heat. Hears The Wolf, burdened with clothing and metal jewelery, sweated profusely as he pretended to be unperturbed by the sweltering temperature. Small children, and of course an inestimable pack of dogs, tagged after us, all of the children intent on the highly conspicuous Hears The Wolf. He preened and reveled in the attention but instead of being insufferably haughty toward them, there was gentleness in his voice as he laughed and tried to shoo off the children. It was the same voice that had comforted me outside the death lodge. While I untied my horse, Hears The Wolf formally addressed me, presumably on behalf of his sister's family.

"We thank you for coming. We thank you for your many kind words. We honor your"—his lips twisted in a half smile—"grief for our departed one."

I knew from the smile that I hadn't fooled him. Still, he seemed unconcerned by my ruse. If anything, he was helpful.

"As his friend," he continued, "I know he would have wanted you to console his beloved. She meant a great deal to him, and now she's suffering. Her father can be such a hothead. Someone needs to talk to that man, convince him to go easier with her. She is only a child and children have such tender feelings. Unfortunately, no one from our camp can do it. Any one of us would only serve to remind him of his daughter's impetuousness, how by rights she should have been an honorably married woman now."

He smiled again, said good-bye, and walked away. Everything he'd said made perfect sense, but the subtle mocking undertone to his words filled me with embarrassment. I knew he considered me to be a miserable liar and I was. Blood hot on my face, I turned towards Stands On A Hill and Chasing Horse. Stands On A Hill had an open, honest expression but Chasing Horse looked very unfriendly, even shifty. After Hears The Wolf departed, Chasing Horse grunted something that was supposed to pass as a polite farewell, turned on his heel, and stalked off. Only Stands On A Hill remained, walked along with me as I led my horse through the maze of lodges to the edge of the village.

"I heard about a man once," Stands On A Hill ventured slowly, "who went up to the land of the dead. He stayed only a little while and then came back. He told about a big village in the sky where everyone lived together. Enemies were no longer enemies. They were good neighbors. And all of the horses were mixed up into one big herd. No one person owned them. Everyone shared."

"I heard that story, too," I said.

Stands On A Hill stopped. We stood looking at each other for a moment as Stands On A Hill struggled with whatever bothered him. Then he blurted it.

"Do you think it's true?"

Taking a deep breath, I gazed up into a perfect cloudless sky. "I have been present," I said, "on the occasions when the breath has departed. I remember most especially a little

boy so young that he hadn't learned to speak. He was very
sick but it was within my power to help him.''

I looked back at Stands On A Hill. He looked back at
me with one eye squinting against the white blaze of the
afternoon sun. His attention to what I said was total.

''That baby boy didn't want my help,'' I said softly. ''He
saw something. I tried to keep his face turned in my direction, tried to force him to focus on me, but whatever it was
he saw off to the side drew him. He wouldn't look at
me, he didn't seem to hear his mother weeping. I know
what he saw was the land of the dead, and I believe what
he saw was beautiful. I believe that far country sparkles
and shines. I believe this because that baby couldn't take
his eyes away from it, and in the end he chose that place
over a life here.''

We regarded one another for a curiously comfortable
moment. ''Anyway,'' I said, turning, preparing to mount
my horse, ''that's just what I believe.''

Stands On A Hill caught my arm, thwarting my move-
ments. I stood against the side of my horse, both hands
gripping the mane tightly as I looked questioningly at him.

''So,'' he stammered, ''you're telling me you don't believe *he* will come back?''

My head rolled slightly to the side, eyes narrowed.
''Your relative?''

He nodded briskly.

I filled with sympathy for him. ''No. I'm sorry. I'm
afraid he's forever dead.''

Stands On A Hill's hand fell away from my arm, his
eyes closed, and he expelled a held breath. ''Good,'' he
muttered. Then he turned and walked away.

I rode a good distance from Kicking Bird's camp, got down
off my horse and, in the shade of cottonwoods and willows
standing along Medicine Creek, I made a small fire. From
a small pouch stored inside my carry bag, a bag always
ready with various essentials and therefore always with me,
I threw some cedar chips onto the fire. Sitting on my

haunches, I purified myself of Coyote Walking's ghost with the cedar smoke, pulling it over my head, arms, and body with my hands. That done, I enjoyed a small meal of dried meat and cool water. Then I filled my little stone pipe with kinnikinnick, a blend of tobacco and sumac leaves, and smoked and thought. As this seemed a day for offering condolences, I decided to go the full route. I knew he had only said the things he was expected to say to a friend of his relative, and that he knew I was not that friend, but nevertheless, I decided to take Hears The Wolf's advice. Still wearing the guise of Coyote Walking's earnest friend, I would pay my respects to Runs The Bulls.

At variance with the affluence and the somber goodwill of Kicking Bird's camp, Runs The Bulls's encampment was small, mean, and the atmosphere thoroughly miserable. I counted six circular places where the grasses were beaten down, black holes in the centers. These had once been the sites of family lodges. These bare places meant the owners of the lodges had pulled up stakes and moved on. Not away from the Rainy Mountain. They wouldn't do that for another five or six days, after the excitement of The Cheyenne Robber's trial. They had merely moved to another camp, distancing themselves from Runs The Bulls.

Success has many claimants, failure only one. Despite his long history as a warrior and a chief, due to his daughter's disgrace, Runs The Bulls was seen as a failure because he was a man not in control of his own family. As an outsider riding into the middle of this dispirited group, my presence caused the entire camp to come to a stop. People stared at me with forlorn eyes. That was the men. The women, a breed given to demonstrative despair, placed hands against their mouths and wept piteously. Hearing them, Runs The Bulls barreled out of his lodge, the sleeves of his open shirt flapping, his ham-sized fists clenched as he stormed toward me. He stopped just inches from my face, spraying me with spittle as he seethed behind clenched teeth.

"If you've come to tell me what you think of my family, I would advise you to leave quickly. Just this morning I beat nearly to death a man offering his opinion."

I hadn't noticed until that moment, but Runs The Bulls was a big man and every inch of his body was made up of hardened muscle.

Hastily I said, "I have come to ask your permission to speak to your wife."

His face pushed further into mine. The veins in his neck stood out in cords, his face churned with fury. "Which one?"

I felt the pull on my spine as I arched away from him. "Sits Beside Him."

His growl deepened. Bending still closer he tested the flexibility of my spine another fraction. He straightened suddenly, stomping away from me. His long hair brushed against his broad back, swinging counterpoint to his gait, powerful legs carrying him away. He did not look like a man wallowing in disgrace. He looked exactly like what he was, a powerful, frustrated warrior badly in need of something to kill. He paused at the entrance of his lodge. He yelled at me but his words were for the benefit of everyone within hearing.

"Her name has been changed. She is no longer Sits Beside Him. She is now known as Brought Him Low."

That public pronouncement made, he knocked back the door flap and disappeared inside his lodge. A rather smug young woman simpered behind him, pausing just long enough to send all of us a highly unattractive smirk. Of course I could have been wrong, a man like Runs The Bulls could have a dozen wives, but I knew I wasn't wrong. The young woman following him had to be Shield Woman, the wife purported to have found Coyote Walking's leggings under White Otter's bed. Even without the smirk she would not be considered an attractive woman. She was fat, her

broad face made to seem even more broad by a wide nose
spreading across the middle. To my eye, the only virtue she
owned was that she was in the bloom of her childbearing
years, and now that she had her husband's undivided attention, she seemed pleased by the prospect that she would
begin to fulfill her only promise. White Otter's mother, because of her daughter's supposed wanton activity, had been
deposed as first wife, which made Shield Woman's discovery very fortuitous indeed. Call me a skeptic, but I've always tended to look askance at random chance. Most
especially when chance honors ambitions which have not
been earned through worthy endeavor.

Curiosity about my presence deteriorated, and the relatives of Runs The Bulls went back to their normal business.
I asked those I could get to pause for a moment where I
might find Brought Him Low, but again and again I was
mildly rebuffed. Finally an old woman who had been
watching me came forward and instructed me to follow her.
She was carrying a heavy basket, balancing it against her
hip as I walked beside her. She seemed affable enough until
I repeated the new name Runs The Bulls had given his
wife. Then she stopped, frowning up at me.

"Don't call her that."

"But he said her new name was—"

"He's an idiot!" she screeched. "He's always been an
idiot. I should know. I'm his mother. When he was born,
the cord was around his neck and his face was blue. You're
a doctor. You know that's the sign of an idiot." She started
walking again.

I was both amazed and appalled. Even if what she said
was true, that her blood son was a long walk away from
the edge of intellectuality, screeching this for all the world
to hear was a grievous offense. I threw off my amazement
and sprang after her.

"You shouldn't talk that way about your protector," I
said. "Suppose someone should hear and—"

She stopped abruptly. "So what!" she yelled. "I'm an

old woman. I'm tired of life and I'm ashamed of that idiot. I look forward to dying, and in death I will do what I was too afraid to do in life."

I glanced worriedly about. People were looking directly at us, intently listening. Even so, she continued on rather vocally.

"What I'm going to do when I'm dead is find a stick and hit that idiot's father on the top of his head for making me the mother of such a stupid son."

She was tottering off once more, and I followed.

"If I had better control of my water," she grumbled, "I'd really enjoy being old. I like making everyone yell because they think I'm deaf." She stopped, looked up at me. "I'm not." She set off again. So did I. "Another thing I like is that I don't have to sew anymore. I've convinced my family that I'm nearly blind." She stopped, I stopped. "I'm not." We both walked again. "I see as well as any of my daughters. I just don't like to sew. Never have."

We came to a lodge set on the verge of the small village. Grass was high all around it, a clear indication that this was a very recent lodge site. A lonely place that was perfect for a wife newly consigned to live outside her husband's favor.

"There are a lot of things I like about being old," she said. Head tilted back, eyes mooned to slits, her expressive face puckered into a network of deep wrinkles. "But the best thing, the really best thing, is that men no longer pester me with their penises. I'm left in peace while they make the lives of younger women a misery. As I said, if I didn't pee myself so much, I'd really love being old."

Even in the dim light of the lodge I saw clearly that both pairs of eyes looking back at me were red and swollen from hours of crying. The women seemed more like sisters than mother and daughter. And, too, they were exceptionally lovely. Runs The Bulls and The Cheyenne Robber shared the torment of having these exceptional women forcibly taken from them. Seeing both of them for myself it was easy to imagine the agony both men felt. It was also easy to understand what might have prompted Coyote Walking. I now doubted that Coyote Walking's motive had been wholly as The Cheyenne Robber assumed, a ploy to disgrace a warrior superior to himself, although that was perhaps a pleasant consequence. White Otter herself had been inducement enough. I have known honorable men to lie, cheat, and steal to have a woman as lovely as she. From the precious little I knew of Coyote Walking, it didn't seem likely that Coyote Walking was an honorable man.

FIVE

Entering the lodge and sitting down with the women, I tried to keep an open mind. The Cheyenne Robber was thoroughly convinced that White Otter would never betray him, that the child she carried was his. What if he were wrong? I have known young women far less lovely who have been more than capable of being fickle. I only had his word for it that she was loyal solely to him. How could he be so certain? If she had yielded to him when they were alone, what would prevent her yielding to yet another suitor? From what I had seen of him, Coyote Walking wasn't an ugly person, and he was a member of a powerful family. On both counts he was The Cheyenne Robber's equal. Perhaps White Bear's opinion of the girl was truer than his stubborn nephew cared to admit. Yet was The Cheyenne Robber so stubborn that he would willingly die before admitting that he had been wrong? Probably.

The old woman, finally introduced to me by her daughter-in-law as Duck, had a lot of venom in her, all of it directed at her son and her second daughter-in-law.

"He only married that slut because her father is his oldest friend. Both of them were embarrassed because none of the other men offered for her. To save his friend's pride, my son married her. Her place in our household was supposed to be as an extra pair of hands so that Sits Beside Him wouldn't have to work so hard and could be near my son more. That intention was not shared by Shield Woman. She's lazy and she's hateful. She didn't help with the work, she only made more.''

I'd heard enough on that particular subject. The old woman's scathing remarks left me feeling sorry for Shield Woman. I turned away from Duck, concentrating my attention on her granddaughter, White Otter.

"Tell me about Kicking Bird's nephew. I suppose he loved you very much.''

White Otter lowered her head. Sits Beside Him placed a weary hand to her brow as once again it was Duck who did all the talking.

"The only person that one ever loved was himself. He pranced around like a strutting prairie chicken, his chest puffed out, his attitude all full of himself. He acted as if he expected my beautiful granddaughter to swoon at his feet whenever he came near her. He behaved disgracefully and my idiot son let him get away with it. But if the father of the girl being courted didn't complain about this appalling conduct, Kicking Bird was powerless to censure his nephew's behavior.''

"Perhaps your son was afraid to reprimand Kicking Bird's nephew.''

"Oh, he was afraid all right. Afraid of the *Ondes*. He's always been afraid of them. He lets them walk all over him.''

Our culture has always been remarkably democratic, but we do have a fixed class system. An aristocracy (the Ondes), a middle class (men of Runs The Bulls calibre), and a lower class (men such as myself). Our class system was not based on personal wealth. For a man to be considered noble to wear the hat made of beaver pelts that distinguished them as Ondes, he was judged solely on his deeds of valor, his generosity toward the less fortunate. Ondes lived by very rigid rules that governed their entire lives. Becoming a member of their unique number often required a lifetime of effort. Only the truly exceptional ever became a member at an early age. It was from the Ondes that the very highest class, the Ten Bravest, were selected.

Coyote Walking wasn't an Onde. However, The Cheyenne Robber was. Surely if Runs The Bulls feared the Ondes as much as his mother claimed, he would have immediately chosen The Cheyenne Robber as his son-in-law. Then again, if it was as The Cheyenne Robber believed, that Runs The Bulls feared being forced to choose between White Bear and Kicking Bird, he would hesitate. White Bear and Kicking Bird were both powerful men in this very powerful class. I certainly wouldn't care to publicly choose between them. Technically, I hadn't even chosen between them in private. I'd been inducted. Therein lay the subtle, forgivable difference, and I clung to it tenaciously. This speculation brought me back to an unpleasant subject.

"Forgive my rudeness," I began lamely. "I am not one to ask impertinent questions, but there remains the question of the leggings. Can any of you imagine how they came to be under White Otter's bed?"

Sits Beside Him, Duck, and White Otter said the same thing in near hysterical voices and all at once. White Otter was innocent of the charge brought against her. None of them could understand how the leggings had found their way under her bed. Kicking Bird's nephew had never been inside the lodge; neither Sits Beside Him nor White Otter would have allowed it. While they yelled, I thought. Thought about how a sneaky person might manage such a thing. Not being a sneaky person, it took a lot of thinking, but when I came up with workable possibilities, I raised a silencing hand.

"Again I beg your forgiveness, but I need to be very

clear in my mind. Exactly where were each of you when the leggings were discovered?''

Sits Beside Him answered first. "I was with my husband. He had important guests and I attended him.''

I looked at Duck. "And you, Mother?"

She curled her upper lip. "I was doing the cooking.''

I glanced at White Otter. She bit the corner of her lip and blushed deeply. "I—I was coming back from a walk.''

"You walked alone?"

She lowered her head, her hair hiding her face. "No.''

"I need a name," I coaxed.

"The Cheyenne Robber," she said in a tiny voice.

I raised my face to the ceiling and took a deep breath. Luck was with me that the women were answering my questions. I pushed that luck further as I mused out loud.

"I am trying to see all of this in my mind but I'm having difficulty. Why wasn't Shield Woman helping with the cooking or there to serve your husband's guests? As his second wife her place was with him.''

"We didn't want her there," Duck snapped. "She can't cook and she's clumsy.''

That struck me as a trifle hard. Wives have their place of honor and to shut her out was cruel. Perhaps being cruel to her had been a playful pastime for them. If so, I could well understand Shield Woman's bitterness and her happy attitude that Sits Beside Him had fallen from her husband's considerable esteem.

"When she was sent away," I asked, my tone thoughtful, "was she sent to your lodge?"

"No," Sits Beside Him answered softly. "And she wasn't sent away. Not by me, nor by my husband. She is his wife." Her voice became even softer and tinged with sadness. "Just as I was his wife. I have never sent my sister-wife away. I would never shame her.''

"You've always been too good to her," Duck screeched. She turned her wrath on me. "If you must know, I sent her away. And it wasn't the first time. I sent her away every chance I got. I hate her and I admit it."

"But did you send her to Sits Beside Him's lodge?"

"No! Why would I do that?"

"I've no idea. I'm just trying to work out why she would go there."

"She shouldn't have gone there," Duck said, her wrinkled face puckered in anger. "She had no business going there. She has her own lodge and besides, I'd sent her to pick berries. She should have been doing that, but instead she was poking her nose where it didn't belong."

"And she found the leggings."

"Yes!" Duck cried. "And now that we have answered all of your questions, perhaps you can tell us how she would find a pair of leggings under the bed of a virtuous girl."

"Two ways," I said when Duck's excited voice calmed. I held up my index finger. "First way. The one who died put them there himself and then pointed Shield Woman in the right direction."

All three women looked at each other, mouths slightly parted. Eagerly they looked back at me.

I held up another finger. "Second way. Kicking Bird's nephew *gave* her the leggings and she simply said she found them under White Otter's bed."

This produced anguished cries from the two younger women and shrieking calls for vengeance from the old woman, Duck. Standing on her knees, shaking a fist at me, she demanded, "Which way do you think?"

I tried to estimate a spurned wife's need for revenge, then I remembered the satisfied look on Shield Woman's face. "Second way."

Wailing, Sits Beside Him pulled at her hair. Sobbing heart-brokenly, White Otter bowed forward, forehead lightly beating the carpeted flooring. Duck produced a knife, and brandishing it made threats against Shield Woman's tongue and her own son's penis.

As it went against her best interests to speak to me, there was no way I could force a confrontation with Shield Woman. If she refused to talk to me, her status as an honorable wife put her beyond my reach. But where other women were concerned, she was a pitifully slow-moving target. Her husband would never lower himself to protect her from women; she would be virtually alone inside a mob of angry females. I suddenly became quite concerned. If there was even the tiniest question concerning Shield Woman's innocence in this matter, it seemed it had fallen to me to protect her.

"If Shield Woman is physically harmed, she'll claim coercion and she will be believed. In order to gain the truth you must be clever. You've lived a long time. Use your wisdom and experience. Save your need for vengeance until you are certain of the truth."

Duck folded her arms beneath pendulous breasts. She raised a heavily wrinkled brow and looked at me out of the corner of her eye. She was sulking, but it was apparent she knew I was right. What was galling, what she didn't care for very much, was having to yield to a male's opinion. It's a common trait among older women. When the physical need for men deteriorates, irascibility sets in. This final stage of life for women is either very freeing or unbearably exasperating. Personally, despite her claims for the former, where Duck was concerned, I believed the latter.

"Please," I said. "I need your help. There isn't much time and too many lives hang in the balance. I must have information if I am to help The Cheyenne Robber. If there are others with information, any at all, even the silliest bit of information, all of it will help."

"We could talk to other women," Sits Beside Him breathed. "And they would spread the word to the other camps."

"Good!" I cried. "Women are the eyes and ears of their families. Whatever they have to share, tell them I will fully appreciate hearing it."

As I was leaving, Duck's last remark, meant to be scathing, warmed my heart.

"My daughter and my grandchild need help. The only men they've had to count on is my son the idiot and White Bear the blowhard."

Sitting atop my horse, I smiled down at her. "Skywalker is their friend."

She clucked her tongue and shook her head. "When that one isn't seeing visions, he generally keeps his head tucked up his backside. What we've been needing is someone with common sense. You seem to have a little bit. Maybe you'll do. I hope so. I think you're all we've got."

It was getting late in the day, nearing dusk. Mentally, I was a thousand miles away as I rode leisurely into White Bear's village. Women of the camp were gathering the evening's rations of water. Some stood in the creek with water up to their knees or sat on the shoreline, chatting happily and paddling their feet in the shoals. As I passed this familiar sight, I saw the women without actually seeing them. Not until *she* stood and waded from the shore to the center of the creek. Her movement caught my vision peripherally, my head automatically turning in that direction.

The serrated clouds at sunset were turning shades of orange and pink. Even though she was in the company of many women, to me she stood alone against this exquisite backdrop. The water gently whorling around her mirrored the sky's colors, the fading sunlight spangling the surface. Overawed by the vision, I stopped my horse and sat for I do not know how long. As I stared, I began to have trouble breathing. What breath I managed to draw was ragged, shallow, my lungs failing to find any benefit.

She stood almost in the center of the creek, the skirt of her dress pulled between her legs, the base tucked into a belt around her trim waist. The sparkling water rippled just below the knees of her exposed legs. Her hair, worked into two plaits, draped her shoulders. The water bladder she was

in the process of filling, its mouth yawned open, gradually
sank beneath the surface. She didn't notice. She had become aware of my admiring stare, and her eyes locked with
mine.

She looked young, but not so young as to be a maiden.
Then it came to me that she was someone's wife, and there
was I, staring at her, showing myself to be insufferably
rude. Inwardly I cursed myself for a fool, yet I couldn't
turn away. Everything about her was exactly right. She was
a good height, slim but not skinny, with good muscle on
her arms and what I could see of her legs. She had a heart-
shaped face, generous mouth, straight nose. If she had a
flaw, it would be that her eyes were very large, surprisingly
round. During my seconds of study, everything else was
blotted out. When a shy smile began to curve her lips and
I knew the smile was for me, my heartbeat was rampant.
Nearly two years ago Calf Woman had woken a need
within me. I had managed to suppress it. But this new
woman triggered it again, and I felt lost. Just that one sight
of her caused a rampage of yearning coupled with an ex-
cruciating ache.

The sound of giggling brought me to my senses. Tearing
my gaze away from her, I realized with horror that all of
the women were looking at me, were laughing at me. Feeling a surge of humiliation, I quickly looked back to the
woman in the creek. She turned her face away. She was
embarrassed and most probably very concerned about what
she would say to her irate husband once he learned of my
unseemly attentions to his wife. I kneed my horse and
bolted away. By the time I found where my lodge had been
set up, I was raging inside. I had been with White Bear's
band less than a day and it had taken me less than a few
minutes to prove myself something of a fool. My anger
boiled over. Shutting myself inside my lodge, I began to
forcefully arrange my house just the way I like it. A barely
habitable mess. Skywalker entered, dodging just in time as
I threw a basket toward the kitchen area of the lodge.

"I'm a friend!" he cried.

Breathing hard, pausing mid-lob of another item, I glared at my former patient. Skywalker walked into my home lightly kicking strewn items out of his way.

"Settling in, I see. Have you never considered the merits of a woman's touch?"

"If you've come to laugh at me I—"

"Oh, do be quiet," he chided. "I'm only a messenger. White Bear has sent me to fetch you. He wants to talk to you."

"I don't feel like talking right now."

A firm hand seized my arm. We studied one another at length. Skywalker's eyes were clear, the whites surrounding the black orbs, snowy. There were no tight lines on his face. And from the pincher-like grip on my arm, I deduced he was feeling remarkably fit.

Stressing each word, he said, "White Bear says you are to come right now."

In a fuming mood, I followed him. Just outside, he turned to me and said, "Do you like children?"

"What?"

"Children," Skywalker repeated. "More specifically, boy children."

Perplexed, I trailed after him.

There wasn't the usual throng lolling inside White Bear's tremendous lodge. In fact, until we arrived, there was only White Bear himself. He was pacing when we entered. Seeing us, he stopped, indicated impatiently that we were to sit. The three of us formed a tight circle and spoke in low, conspiratorial tones.

"Where have you been?" White Bear demanded. "I went back to my nephew, to apologize for adding to his worries, and he told me you had gone to Kicking Bird's camp. His saying that added to *my* worries."

"He's been very hard to live with," Skywalker said with a wry smile.

White Bear gave Skywalker an impatient and reproachful look. Skywalker appeared unfazed. White Bear opened his mouth to speak but before he could deliver what I knew would be harsh words, I cut him off.

"I inspected the dead man's body." That instantly piqued their interest. The tops of our heads met together inside the small circle our bodies formed. I told them my observations and suspicions, ending with my visit to Runs The Bulls's camp and my visit with the women. Talking about the women made White Bear squirm. I knew why. He was convinced the daughter of Runs The Bulls had led both Coyote Walking and The Cheyenne Robber to their destruction. "I believe that she is a victim too."

White Bear's eyes riveted on mine.

"I have spoken with her," I said firmly. "I do not believe that I heard lies in her voice, but I am certain that I heard love. Love for your nephew. The competition between The Cheyenne Robber and Kicking Bird's nephew to have her as a wife is important in this mystery, but it seems unlikely that any fault lies with her." I looked intensely at Skywalker. "As a seer, can you offer any enlightenment?"

He chewed the side of his mouth as he shook his head. "I've had images in the past two days, but they've made no sense to me."

"I'm a bit desperate," I said. "I'm willing to listen."

He was quiet for a long moment, then he said somberly, "I see the dead one's face as he turns. At first he seems smug, then he looks angry. His face tightens in a strange way. A crow flies against the sky and everything turns black."

White Bear looked anxiously to me. "Does that help?"

"No."

Shouting, White Bear threw his hands in the air. "I hate it when he's cryptic."

Skywalker was not insulted. He turned to me and spoke with an air of detachment. "You, Tay-bodal, are in the best

position to solve this puzzle. You've already proven that
you're able to go in and out of the different camps without
being challenged.'' He waved a hand, indicating himself
and White Bear. ''For obvious reasons, we can't. I realize
that what I'm asking is a big favor, especially when asked
of someone so new to our family, but would you be willing
to continue gathering the information we need to save The
Cheyenne Robber?''

I didn't hesitate. ''Of course.''

The two sat back, pleased smiles relieving some of the
tension on their faces. Skywalker reached out a hand and
took mine, shaking it firmly, the handshake affirming my
word to him. White Bear rose and walked to the door,
opened it, and shouted for food. A few moments later, four
women arrived carrying in bowls and platters. One of them,
her.

Mortified, I closed my eyes and wished I could disap-
pear. When my eyes opened again, her profile was all I
could see as she knelt beside me, preparing the oblong
wooden plate set in front of my crossed legs. She was so
close that had I been calm enough to try, I could have
counted all the hairs on her head. My heart was thumping
so loudly I knew she heard it. I forced myself to be perfectly still, but my blood was heating and I felt each droplet
of sweat as it formed then bloomed. My worried mind
spared no thought about her husband. My only concern in
that moment was how I looked to her. Did I look ridicu-
lously sweaty, as I so keenly felt? Did she see me as sad
and ugly? I was so fixed on these questions that when
White Bear spoke I almost jumped out of my skin.

His mouth was full but not so full that he wasn't under-
standable. ''Tay-bodal, I would like you to meet my cousin,
Crying Wind.''

She turned her head, her eyes properly downcast as she
smiled shyly. My throat was so constricted I could only
manage a slight acknowledging nod before she rose and
moved off to serve Skywalker. When she knelt next to him,

he playfully touched the tip of her nose. She looked him familiarly in the face as she giggled, and I felt a burning rip of jealousy. Then Skywalker looked at me.

"This one is a widow."

My heart stopped, everything except her face and the distant sound of Skywalker's voice vanished.

"Texans got her husband last spring. He went bravely, but he is greatly missed. Because he was such a good man, this one has been overly fussy about his replacement."

Everything and everyone in the lodge abruptly reappeared. Images were too clear, too sharp, as my heart jumped, resumed beating at a gallop. That such an incredible woman was still available, that I might just possibly have a chance, was so exciting I was almost delirious. Then Skywalker frightened the life out of me. His elbow nudged Crying Wind's side as he cried, "Woman! I offer myself to you one last time."

I wanted to kill him. But a second later her answer had me turning all giddy again.

"I don't want you." She laughed softly. "You're a big flirt and you're too bony."

Skywalker chuckled. Then he began to eye me speculatively. "Tay-bodal's not bony."

I wanted to kill him again, but then I went all nervous as she seemed to study me in a considering way. I kept my less-than-perfect face in profile, hoping, praying, that she didn't find me terribly unattractive. I couldn't breathe. I sat helpless under her scrutiny. I waited for the same type of playful rejection Skywalker had received. My body was so rigid as the silence stretched that the seconds felt like hours. I willed my eyes to move. From out of the corners I saw that she was smiling. In a rush I realized she wasn't going to reject me and I suddenly went peculiar all over, almost succumbing to a faint. Conversation flowed all around me while I battled mind-warping dizziness.

"Tay-bodal's a good size," Skywalker said to Crying

Wind. "But would he consider a skinny woman like you? Now that's the question."

"I'm not skinny," she cried. "You just see me with bony eyes."

"And your cousin White Bear only sees you with fat eyes?"

"Yes," she said haughtily. "Because he only likes fat women."

White Bear howled with laughter, asking, "I wonder then what kind of eyes Tay-bodal sees you with."

Again the lodge became unnaturally quiet. Everyone looked to me, awaiting a response. I heard my voice break as I managed, "I—I see her with perfect eyes."

Skywalker clapped his hands. "Well said, well said."

White Bear nudged Crying Wind and cackled, "Perfect? You? Do you hear that man? What have you done to fool him so completely?"

She ignored her cousin, her glow of approval rushing at me, hitting me squarely in the chest, knocking the last remaining breath out of me.

I know I ate, but I didn't taste anything, nor do I remember chewing. After the meal, we men smoked cigars and White Bear dominated the conversation. The night was black when I finally left his lodge. The camp was illuminated by a half dozen fires. Because of the muggy night air, doors were open, lodge walls rolled up. Ordinary life inside the lodges was on display in the faint light of gourd lamps. I paid no attention to any of it as I walked along, my head filled with the puzzle concerning Kicking Bird's nephew, and my heart centered on the woman Crying Wind. I was jerked from my reverie when I felt a light flutter touch my shoulder. I turned so abruptly that I startled her. She stepped back, eyes wide, hand going to her mouth.

"Forgive me. I—"

"There's nothing to forgive," I said a little too anxiously.

She visibly relaxed, her hand coming away from that

perfect face. My heartbeat trebled when she rewarded me with a smile. I forced myself to remain calm as she stepped nearer, then took my hand.

"My cousin has given me permission to walk with you." She canted her head to the side, her eyes searching mine. "But only if you wish it."

I experienced another one of those funny turns. After having had so many, presumably I was used to them. But funny turns are like strokes. They come up suddenly and your mind becomes liquidy. My brains by this time, as she took my hand and held it and looked at me, had been reduced to the consistency of watery soup. My mouth opened and closed, opened and closed. It was several seconds before I could produce a coherent sound. And even then, it was badly stammered.

"I—I w-wish it! A lot."

She laughed softly, obviously enjoying her paralytic effect on me. Embarrassed, I turned my head away. When her hand squeezed mine, I stole a sidelong look at her. That she hadn't become disgusted with my pitiful presence and walked off meant that she liked me. Emboldened by that thought, I gripped her hand tightly and led her away from the village. I found a secluded place in the darkness, on the bank of the creek. Above us the stars against the black sky shone bright and huge. Had it been within my power, I would have plucked one down and handed it to her. The glow of the full moon cleaved the inky creek water with a swathe of gently undulating silver, outlined the dark lacy foliage of the giant cottonwoods standing like guarding sentinels on both banks. Crickets chirped, cicadas thrummed. Still holding hands, Crying Wind and I sat down side by side. Fireflies flitted and danced all around us. We were contentedly quiet for a long time. Then she put up her free hand and fireflies flitted and blinked around her fingers.

"When I was a child," she murmured softly, "we girls used to catch fireflies. We pulled the glowing tails out and put them on our cheeks, thinking that the sparkling light made us beautiful maidens.'' She glanced coyly at me. ''If I did that now, what would you say?''

I was finally feeling so comfortable with her that I surprised even myself when I made a joke. ''I'd probably say, 'Crying Wind, what is that nasty goo on your beautiful face?' Then I'd wipe it off.''

My answer delighted her. She laughed, and I laughed with her. But in this moment of supreme happiness, an ugly thought niggled. I tried to control it, but it grew. Before it became so big that my happiness crushed me, I spoke, haltingly, hating that our easy mood was being threatened by a terrible dread rippling through me. She moved, bending her legs at the knees, drawing them to her chest. She rested her arm on top and propped her chin on her arm. She watched me intently as I insisted on making an enormous fool of myself.

''I appreciate your company. My concern is that you are here with me only because your cousin wishes it. If that's true, please reassure White Bear that I—I'm fully on The Cheyenne Robber's side. I will do everything I can possibly do to help him. To help White Bear. He doesn't have to bribe me.''

A heavy silence lay between us. That short span of time will always remain a horrible blur in my mind. My blood pumped dangerously, my limbs felt cold and numb. Clear thought was as elusive as a slippery fish. My heart was in my throat. I fully expected, even waited for her to quietly stand and walk away, leaving me alone and desolate. You must realize that had she done so, I would never be able to look on her again. My pride as a man, our customs as a people, would never allow it. Her act of rejection would forever be final. In the seconds that flittered by, I began to mourn my second crippling loss. I was thoroughly enjoying this great trove of pity that I had stored up for myself over the years when her softly laughing voice reached me.

''If you're talking about me, I'm very flattered. I've never been a bribe before. I think I like it.''

My head swirled on my neck. I looked at her with wide, love-hungry eyes. She continued to regard me calmly and to speak with that soft, near musical voice.

"If you want to know the truth, my cousin objected when *I* asked *him* for permission to walk with you. He didn't want to give it. He thinks our being together is a bad idea. He believes you are more devoted to your healing craft than you would ever be to a woman, and he knows what a selfish person I am. He said that I would always want all of your attention. That I would bring disharmony to your life. He did not believe you would even walk out with me. He warned me that my even asking you would get my feelings hurt. He said when he found me tomorrow crying about your rejection, he would change my name to She Never Listens To Good Advice."

Ambushed by a surge of happiness and supreme surprise, I gasped sharply. "I would never hurt your feelings. They're too precious to me."

Everything stood still, the singing insects and the night birds became mute as she leaned against me, her soft lips touching mine. The last vestiges of my reserve teetered on the brink, then fell. My years of loneliness fell away with it. I took her in my arms and kissed her with all the love that was mine to give.

I don't know how long we stayed there. The moments seemed captured in eternity. We kissed a great deal. We lay on our backs and stared up at the stars and talked about so many things. We got to know each other so well that I felt as if I had always known her. Couldn't possibly imagine that until this very night, I hadn't even known she existed. That thought, when it came to me, seemed so odd that I felt I must surely be thinking of a stranger. I couldn't possibly mean myself.

Crying Wind, Crying Wind. Her name was as sensuous as a warm sigh being breathed down my back. As she spoke I raised her hand to my lips and kissed it. Laughing softly, she rolled her head toward mine and looked at me.

"Careful," she smiled. "I've been a long time without a man, and I find you very attractive. If you keep kissing me, I just might lose control."

She erupted into a storm of giggles as I frantically kissed her hand and then her arm to the elbow. An instant later and we were rolling around like a pair of snickering children, kissing so much and with such fervor that eventually we couldn't kiss anymore because our mouths had become all puffy and sore.

Hand in hand we walked through the heart of the village. This was the silent, outward sign that our official courtship had begun. Sitting in the cooler air outside their lodges, men nodded to me their approval. Women threw away their sewing, running off like giggling little girls, talked behind their hands as they glanced meaningfully in our strolling direction. Feeling so proud I could barely stand it, I gripped her hand tightly, raised it to my mouth and kissed her knuckles for all of them to see. She looked up at me, sent me a prideful smile that glowed from her sloe eyes. I felt myself balloon with even more pride. I was complete now. I belonged, to her, to this band of people. But my joy was a fragile thing and, with a jolt, I knew it.

The ghost of the man waiting to be buried at dawn rose up between myself and this incredible woman. The ghost demanded revenge. But the ghost of a man I would have found unappealing had I known him in life was a secondary consideration. What was important to me was The Cheyenne Robber, his wife and unborn child. And no less important was keeping safe the families of my newly adopted band. Most especially this one woman. Crying Wind had a child, a little son; he was important to me too. Suddenly, the monster responsible for the death of Kicking Bird's nephew was my greatest enemy. Finding out who he was, setting right everything he seemed determined should go wrong, was personal.

We stopped outside the lodge Crying Wind shared with other women. From inside I heard rustling, women whispering. Being a widow, she owned nothing. She and her son were totally dependent on the goodwill of her relatives. But not anymore. Now, they were my responsibility. It was a burden I was eager to accept. Immediately. The thing staying my eagerness was Crying Wind herself. Placing her hand against my chest, just above my boisterously pounding heart, she lay down a series of tiresome rules.

"I know this is not the first marriage for either of us and that second marriages usually have all the romance of a man tapping a woman on the head and grunting, 'Follow me.' But I like romance and I will not follow after anyone too lazy to be bothered to court me properly. Men think that's peculiar. Do you?"

When a laugh escaped me, the hand that had rested on my chest slapped my arm. I couldn't stop laughing and so she slapped me again.

"Stop that!" she cried, trying to sound angry. "I'll have you know women think you're a little peculiar. Very attractive, but peculiar."

Mirth died. Startled, I replied, "They do?"

Tugging at her ear, she turned away grumpily, muttering, "You know they do." Turning back to me, she took my hand, placed something inside my upturned palm. In a very bossy tone she said, "All through our very passionate courtship I want you to wear this. Everyone knows it's mine and your wearing it will signify that you are mine. I suppose I should tell you, I'm a very jealous person."

All of that flew past me. I was too taken by the richness of the gift. It was Navaho. Where she got it, she never said. It was a tiny sand-cast silver fetish of the animal so sacred to the Kiowa that its name could never be said unless it was a name given to a human. As in the case of White Bear and Sitting Bear. And from this small icon on two strands of thin silver hung tiny blue stones sacred to the Navaho. This earring was of immeasurable worth for both nations.

"I—I have nothing to equal a gift like this."

"Yes, you do. Give me your earring."

With fumbling fingers, I unhooked the simple bone-and-bead earring hanging from my right ear. I handed it nervously over, half expecting her to look at it with utter disdain and fling it to the ground. But my love was a worthy woman. Joy was on her face as she admired my very common earring, then slipped it through the small puncture in her earlobe. When I made no move to follow suit, she snatched the priceless silver piece from my hand and stuck the hook through my lobe herself. I was still standing there staring at her like a wide-eyed dimwit when she grabbed me by my hair, yanked me forward, her mouth colliding with mine. Our noses touched when she finished kissing me while still holding me by the hair.

"Remember," she warned in a husky whisper, "I expect flute music, presents for all my family, full courtship, and—"

"Groveling?"

"Yes," she agreed quickly. "Groveling. A lot of groveling. And don't forget to brag about how lucky you are to be engaged to me whenever my name is mentioned."

In a flash she was gone, disappearing inside the lodge where she was greeted by a chorus of delighted squeals. There was nothing left for me to do but make my dazed way home. Which took an inordinate amount of time for I was truly dazed and, too, I'd forgotten by this time just where my home had been placed. When I eventually found it, Skywalker was sitting in front of the open door, smoking a cigar.

"Congratulations," he chortled softly.

Remembering to brag, I promptly replied, "I am the most fortunate man alive."

His shoulders bounced as the chortle turned to full-fledged laughter. "No married man is fortunate," he hooted. "What he is, is married. No other characterization is needed."

My people are known for their black humor. This was merely a first volley, one expected when following the bragging-man-hopelessly-in-love road my darling decreed I must walk. Ignoring the jibe, I settled down beside him, crossed my legs, and stared off into a love-fogged middle distance. The long silence Skywalker and I shared was comfortable, and I rested in it.

"But I am fortunate," I said fervently. "I cannot believe that she would choose me, or that White Bear would so easily give me his precious cousin."

Skywalker rolled the cigar in his mouth, inhaled deeply, expelled the smoke that marginally repeled a small swarm of flying insects. "White Bear has a lot of cousins. Besides, he's jealous of you."

"He is?"

Skywalker canted his head, his amused eyes locking with mine. He chuckled deeply in his throat. "Yes, he is. All that lovely freedom you've enjoyed. No one tying you down, no one nagging you. It got on his nerves. If this cousin hadn't suited you, he would have kept on trotting them out until you gave up and finally picked one."

"How do you know?"

Again the deep chuckle. "Personal experience. I've married two of his cousins and one niece. I am so related to him, it brings on one of my headaches trying to work out just how related."

"I hadn't realized that you were married at all."

He sat back, made a humphing sound as he inhaled again. "When the rapture of the honeymoon dissipates, women are content to go their own way. My wives show up now and then whenever they want a new baby." He sighed dramatically. "I do my best to comply."

I was chuckling now. "Irksome task, is it?"

Using his middle finger, he tapped away ash from the cigar. "Well, when all that work became too tiring, I could beg off because of my headaches. That was handy. Now they know about the medicine you've given me. Now that the headaches are under control, I'm bracing myself for renewed assaults against my person."

Suddenly the warmth of Crying Wind's body, the lingering sweet taste of her mouth, became too fresh in my mind. It left me in no mood for casual jokes about sex.

"I'm going to bed," I said a bit tersely.

"Mind if I hide out with you?"

"Yes!" I shouted as I stood. "It's dark inside my lodge. And in the dark, you would do."

Skywalker was laughing hilariously as I entered my lodge and slammed the door behind me.

SIX

My body was exhausted but my mind wouldn't rest—recalling, reexamining the events of the long hot day. Insects were a further torment. The little beasts inside the lodge flew close to my ears, their whine working me into a near frenzy while outside, the cicadas were singing their mating song a steady, obnoxious throb that could only attract another cicada and is so grating as to set one's teeth on edge. Something landed on my cheekbone and proceeded to bite. I slapped myself hard. Frustration and the gummy heat of the night both worked to boil up my blood. My hand, lingering on my face, drifted slowly toward the ear holding Crying Wind's gift. My fingers touched the silver fetish, felt its outline, drifted to the tiny blue stones hanging from it. It soothed me and I relaxed, my thoughts focusing on Crying Wind. Eventually I drifted away, only to be troubled by dreams.

I was in a strange place. There was a creek nearby, the shade from many tall trees further cooled by a breeze wafting across the surface of the murmuring water. I breathed

*in the coolness, my scorched lungs expanding gratefully.
My moment of complete peace was disturbed as Coyote
Walking came toward me and then passed me by. I called
to him, but he didn't hear, he just kept on walking away.
A moment later a second man approached. He didn't see
or hear me either. I knew then that I was an invisible witness to the last moments of Coyote Walking's life.*

*Coyote Walking waited, his expression tense and his
body language impatient, until the second man caught up
with him. Then he began to speak and his tone was upset,
angry. His image was very clear, but the second man was
nothing more than a looming shadow. A shadow as black
as a crow's wing. The size of the shadow filled me with a
fearful dread, but Coyote Walking didn't appear to be the
least bit apprehensive. If anything he was foolishly arrogant, as if he had a power over this frightful specter. Muffled words were exchanged. I strained to understand their
conversation but could only register gibberish, as if they
were speaking some unknown language. I felt enormous
anger begin to pulsate from the dark shadow. Again, Coyote Walking didn't understand his jeopardy. He continued
to rail at the shadow, talk to it as if it was of no consequence. Complete surprise was apparent on his face when
powerful hands seized his throat, gripped so tightly that the
slightly built Coyote Walking was forced to his knees. He
struggled, his claw-shaped hands pulling at the wrists of
his attacker. His face purpled. He couldn't breathe. He became more frantic. He—*

I started awake, bolting upright in my bed. My eyes were
wide open but blind in the darkness of my lodge. Even
though I felt as if I'd only managed a few moments of
sleep, when I looked up through the smoke hole I was
forced to accept the fact that the night sky had changed
from black to a murky gun-metal gray. Dawn was approaching and whether or not I felt any of its value, I had
slept for a few hours. In fact, I'd overslept! Wrestling

around in my bed, I fought to untangle my legs from the light blanket twisted around them and sprang from my bed. Groping in the darkness, I dressed.

A second after erupting from my lodge in the same fashion a lead ball explodes from a musket, I stood in the drab light. The morning stars were gone, hidden behind an impenetrable blanket of cloud. Humidity pressed against me like a heavy hand. Around my feet and legs a mist swirled gracefully, stretching up the length of my tensed body, caressing my face as it coiled away from me. My people have long described this eerie phenomenon as Mother's Spirit Stirring. A poetic phrase for steam rising from the earth to meet a steadily building thunderhead. My good sense told me that it was going to rain sometime soon, but my immediate concerns were fixed on other issues more important than the weather. So, in my hurry, I was wearing only a light summer shirt, my breechcloth, and moccasins. My mind filled with the images of my dream, I untied the leg hobbles of my horse, saddled and bridled it.

I stirred up the camp dogs as I galloped out of White Bear's camp. They barked and chased along after me until my horse put them to shame. They gave up, slinking back into camp, tails between their hind legs, to be confronted by cursing women brandishing sticks. I knew the women were cursing me too for being the cause of the early morning commotion. Because of me and the dogs, the women had been denied the little luxury of another hour or two of sleep. In a foul temper White Bear's camp would shuffle to life, outside cook fires rekindled, nursing infants bawling to be fed, men still in their beds, yelling for the women to keep their activities quiet, and the women yelling for the men to get up and go get them some fresh meat for the day's meals.

This was simply ordinary life, nothing to get worked up over. But knowing that I now had a place in these lives, that I was an accepted member of this band and all these people were my relatives, filled me with elation. I stood in the rawhide stirrups of the light birch-wood saddle, my horse running full flat, the hooves beating the earth sounding louder than the yelling voices or the ominous thunder rumbling behind me.

Even though I was late, I still managed to be on time for the funeral. This was due to the dead man's not being especially popular. It would be unseemly to bury a person while his entire clan stood about dry-eyed. When I arrived, the dead man's relatives were still working hard at getting themselves into the proper mournful attitude. The storm that had threatened White Bear's camp had advanced, and, sometime during all the required singing, reached Kicking Bird's camp, where it seemed quite content to linger. The burial of Coyote Walking was carried out in the slamming rain.

The body, tied into the sitting position, head bowed, knees drawn to the chest, was placed inside a prepared hole. It was covered over by muddy earth and the mound was slowly encased with rocks. As a mourner, when my turn came, I lifted a good-sized rock from the stockpile that had been collected for the event, positioned it just right on the built-up mound. I was the only one attending the ceremony without protective clothing or a sheltering blanket. And I was freezing, my fingernails blue from cold as I placed the rock just right, the palms of my hands white and wrinkled from prolonged exposure to the rain. If the dead man was half as inconvenient in life as he was proving to be in death, small wonder he was not a well-liked person.

After placing the rocks, a good horse was slaughtered next to the grave. The only thing left to do was the customary burning of the dead man's lodge. Because of the storm, that part of the ceremony had to wait. A fire would never have caught during that downpour. So people scurried for the protection of their homes instead. As I was passed, no one extended an invitation for me to shelter with them and, as I had no place to go except my patiently waiting horse, I heaved a dejected sigh, headed in that direction, and tried to think out what I should do now. Nearing my horse a strong had captured my shoulder. I turned and was surprised to see Hears The Wolf, overdressed as was his tendency, in all his vain but drooping splendor. He found only a modicum of shelter beneath the blanket his arms tented over his head. I could barely hear him as he shouted at me through the lashing rain.

"I have coffee."

"What?"

"Coffee!" He jerked an impatient head to the side. "Come with me."

He opened an arm, and with the sodden blanket attempted at least to save me from the worst of it as we huddled close together hurrying out of the rain.

Because I hadn't formed any expectations concerning his lifestyle, the opulence of his lodge momentarily stymied me. I just stood in the doorway afraid to move as he pegged the corners of the soaked blanket between two lodge poles where it would eventually dry. Without a word he gathered kindling from the stack of wood kept inside and on the right of the door hole. He carried the kindling to the fire pit, feeding the glowing coals a stick at a time. The fire sprang to life, its light chasing away dark shadows. I was able to see the evidence of his wealth more clearly. Almost to the top of the smoke hole, Hears The Wolf's lodge was filled with the things a man demanding great comfort requires. They were very expensive things. Navaho rugs carpeted the earthen floor, brightly colored woolen blankets draped the inner walls, providing him both insulation and privacy. And he had a lot of white man's cooking pots, metal plates, and cups.

"Please close the door and come all the way in," he said.

Startled, I hurriedly did as I was told, walking to the right of the lodge as was the polite thing to do. A guest must never walk straight in or walk to the left. The correct way to enter a lodge is to go along the right then stand and wait

until the host decides the place you are to sit. Hears The
Wolf directed me to a spot on the other side of the fire and
I went there. There was a good blanket draped over a heap
of pine needles. It would make comfortable sitting, but I
was worried about soiling the blanket, so I just sat over it,
behind my knees and on my haunches. Because I was cold,
my legs immediately cramped, but I refused to give in to
the soreness. I did not wish to ruin such a fine blanket and
cause my host to regret his generosity to me.

Hears The Wolf did not notice my discomfort. He sat on
his legs very close to the fire. He held a flat rock about the
size of his hand, and he smashed the rock against a larger
fire pit stone. On the flat surface of that stone he had already gingerly arranged a pile of nut-black coffee beans.

"There's a secret to this," he said. He raised the rock
in his hand and again smashed the coffee beans on the fire
stone. "You just want to crack them. Broken just a little
bit they release their flavor when they're boiled. Anyway,
that's the way I like to do it. Some people think it's better
to crush the beans into small pieces. I don't like to do that
because of the danger of the pieces being swallowed during
drinking. I accidentally swallowed a piece once and my
body was nervous for several days. If you get a piece in
your mouth, Tay-bodal, take my advice and don't swallow
it. Always make certain you spit it out."

My eyes danced from corner to corner. *Where?* I wondered. Spitting anywhere in this luxurious lodge seemed to
me an unforgivable offense. I made up my mind not to get
any of the pieces in my mouth, but if I did, to spit it back
into the cup. That pesky problem solved, my mind flitted
off in another direction. The only interest I've ever had in
coffee is that it's the one herb I've never quite understood.
Taking one of the whole beans from the bag containing a
hearty supply, I held the bean between two fingers and studied it as he scraped the crushed beans from the stone into
the coffeepot, filled the pot with water, and then placed it
on the cook stone closer to the flames of the fire pit.

Coffee beans came to us a long time ago, when I was a little boy. White traders brought them up from the southeast where the bean bushes grow. It's a food product of the eastern people and at that time unknown to us. Being good traders, these venturing white men knew that it was good manners to give away presents before any actual trading. They gave to the children hard, crystallized lumps of sugar and to each woman they gave a small handful of coffee beans. The children enjoyed their treat, the women put the beans into storage. These were good gifts and everyone approved of the traders. The band chiefs then allowed these white men to make serious trade with their bands. I remember that time clearly because it caused me great distress that my sweet was melting too quickly in my mouth. The sweet taste was so nice I wanted it to last and last. When it finally dissolved, I refused to speak for hours. I kept my mouth shut tight, swallowed only when I absolutely had to, hanging on to that sweet flavor just as hard as I could.

The beans didn't quite have that same success with the women. My mother got her first iron cook pot on that trade day, and the first thing she cooked in her new pot were the coffee beans. She softened them up with hot water the way dried beans are supposed to be prepared, then she added chunks of meat, onions, and dried laurel leaves and crushed sage. Needless to say, our supper that night was rather awful. Mother thought it was all the new pot's fault, that maybe it was unnatural to cook food in a metal pot. She wanted to throw the new pot away.

Father said no, don't do it. He'd heard other people complaining about the beans, which they had cooked in the usual way inside a buffalo-stomach pouch with water and heated up by hot stones placed in the water. Feeling vindicated, my mother scrubbed clean the iron pot and cooked up something different. The pot made a very good meal on the second try, and my mother never cooked with anything other than that pot for the rest of her life. But she wouldn't have any more of those beans no matter how urgently new traders offered them out as inducements for trading. Those beans had mortally shamed her to her husband and son. She called coffee "bad luck beans."

Years later, of course, my people adapted to the concept that the beans were for brewing, not for eating. Being an herbalist, what fascinated me was the hidden properties of coffee. A little bit of coffee was soothing. Too much made the heart excitable. And I realized that coffee was addictive. That opinion was formed by the steady increase of a lot of hardened coffee drinkers in the Nation. None of them would ever admit their addiction but, let me tell you, they would do anything to get their hands on bags of coffee beans. To my mind, anything that powerful is scary, which is why I only drink coffee on rare occasions and always simply to be polite.

I felt Hears The Wolf's eyes on me. Timidly, I replaced the borrowed bean, hunkered closer to the fire, extending my hands toward it. It was unmannerly to shiver, but I couldn't help myself. I was very wet, very cold, and sincerely mortified that I was dripping all over Hears The Wolf's expensive blanket and floor rugs. Fortunately, he didn't appear offended. He stood, went to the storage area of his lodge, his back to me for a brief moment. This gave me another opportunity to survey the surroundings. Each furtive glance revealed another costly treasure. Hears The Wolf's dress sense might be comical, but his furnishings were solid proof of his extraordinary bravery. Only an exceptionally brave man going out on countless raids could ever hope to amass such a fortune. His trove was a testament to his daring. It caused me to look again at Hears The Wolf, see past the narcissistic adornments and see the man. What I saw was that he was not only extremely brave but a kind and considerate host, for when he walked back to me, he draped a red and yellow heavy wool blanket over my trembling shoulders. As I dried myself and wrapped up tightly inside the blanket, I added this to my certain knowledge that he knew I was not Coyote Walking's friend, that

I had never been. That meant that no matter how superficial he might seem, he was most certainly no one's fool. I have always liked canny individuals and I realized that I certainly liked him. Even so. I also knew to tread carefully because this man whispered directly into Kicking Bird's ear.

His voice startled me back into the moment. "You're cold on a mild day because you have no blood."

Holding the blanket close to me, I watched him as he made his way back to the cushion he'd been sitting on.

"You wear no clothing when it's hot, almost no clothing when it's cold. Stupid." He sat down, crossed his legs, picked up pieces of wood and added them to the blaze of fire. "When you do that, you confuse your blood. I, on the other hand, wear clothing all the time. My blood temperature stays the same. I'm never too hot or too cold."

I precisely recalled yesterday how, because of all his clothing and jewelry he had sweated enough water to fill to overflowing his white man's coffeepot. Wisely I kept this to myself. If this accounting was meant as justification for his peculiar dress sense, who was I to argue? A warrior of the Onde class hardly need explain himself to me. When it was ready, we drank coffee and talked. He spoke, answering my unasked questions without the slightest hesitation.

"You said yesterday my relative was generous. Perhaps he was, but only with you. No one else knew this side of him. To those of us who knew him best he was insufferably selfish. What's more, he was a blatant opportunist. He used his status as Kicking Bird's nephew to his every advantage, and he could be cruel to those he felt were beneath him as well as aggressively cunning against those who were above him. He made many enemies and both the low- and the highborn watched their backs for his knife whenever he was present. It is unfortunate for everyone concerned that his final enemy was The Cheyenne Robber. Had that young man not acted out in public, there would have been many suspicious persons to choose from. Kicking Bird would not have so readily singled out The Cheyenne Robber, but because The Cheyenne Robber had publicly denounced Kicking Bird's nephew only hours before the body was discovered, I'm afraid my cousin was left with no other choice but to accuse him.''

''The Cheyenne Robber hadn't any choice either,'' I said inside a deep sigh. ''White Otter's father was about to—''

So much for my treading carefully. When I realized what I'd said, I glanced up quickly. Hears The Wolf's sly smile told me that I had just caught myself out. One lie only buys a person five more. Knowing that I had already tripped myself up in one lie, I decided that it would be more prudent to walk a more truthful path. Not only did that ease my torn-up integrity, it saved my pathetic memory trying to keep up with the lies.

I confessed that I was not a friend to his newly departed relative. That prior to his death I couldn't even recall of ever hearing of him. To my intense relief Hears The Wolf did not pretend to be astonished nor was he incensed. What he was, was curious as to why I would even make the effort. Why would I grieve for someone I didn't even know? Still trying to mend the tear in my sleuthing disguise, I did what all married men do. Or in my case, an almost married man. I blamed my wife.

I had done it, I told him, for the sake of Crying Wind, my beloved. I was back on the lying road again, but some things cannot be helped. Even then I tried to stay within the realm of truth no matter how viciously I mauled that truth. Extolling Crying Wind's beauty, her virtue, and my passion for her, I painted a picture of a man so in love that he had been driven into deceit. Because of Owl Man's edict, my all-consuming love for Crying Wind was threatened. As she was certain to be subjugated to Kicking Bird, I knew that it would be within Kicking Bird's power to permit or forbid our marriage. So, I had tried to ingratiate myself to him. I had pretended friendship with his nephew as a way to make myself seem favorable to him. My actions were unforgivable but I had seen no other way. I was a wretched man on the brink of despair. I understood that my behavior was disgraceful, but I asked Hears The Wolf's compassion. Then I bowed my head, appeared to wait for the ax of castigation to fall. I waited and I waited, becoming more nervous by the second. His soft voice froze me to the marrow.

"You have done a miserable thing. You deserve the highest punishment. But I understand your reasons, Little Brother. I once loved someone just that way. And like you, I would have done anything for her. Anything."

I lifted my eyes. He had turned his head. I saw pain etched on his profile. My lie had affected him more deeply than I had imagined. Keeping my voice low, I encouraged him to speak.

"What happened?"

He stared into the fire without seeing it. His reply was a wistful utterance that was just above a whisper. "I was young, I was poor. I was not related to Kicking Bird then. I was simply one of his many good friends. It was my sister's marriage to him that eventually changed my fortune. I should have waited for that, but I didn't. I was a young fool wildly in love. I went to the camp of the girl I had to have. I offered her father everything I owned, which amounted to one old horse, two blankets. Her father's answer to me was the wrath I have decided to spare you. For what happened to me is the fate awaiting all young men daring to mock or intentionally lie to their betters. And you intentionally lied to Kicking Bird. Look closely now, Little Brother. See the punishment for that crime."

He stood, removed his shirt, showed me a broad back that was crisscrossed with ugly white scars. My breath left me and I was too stunned to draw another. And all the time that I stared as if caught in a trance, Hears The Wolf continued to speak in a soft, dead voice.

"He said my offer mocked his daughter, mocked him.

He claimed that I had played a cruel joke against everyone in his family. That I had been put up to it by other pranksters. He then wondered how long they would laugh after they found me. Like you, I hadn't thought beyond my great love, I hadn't thought of the consequences. So I didn't understand what he meant until his sons tied me between two trees and he used a whip against my back. He beat me until I could no longer stand. I hung between those two trees hearing my darling girl crying for me as they broke camp and left me there.''

He put on his shirt, resumed his seat, stared at me but through me. His gaze traveled far into the past, where the hurt against his body, his pride, was born, still lived.

"Kicking Bird found me the next day. He said that all though the night during his ride to the camp of my beloved's father, he heard the howling of wolves. There were many wolves. They had caught the scent of my blood and followed it down from the hills. I was surrounded that night as I hung between the two trees. I was weak and defenseless, and there were so many wolves. But there was one especially. The dominant wolf. He came forward and sat down before me. I talked to him and after a while, he talked to me.

"We made a pact, that wolf and I. His promise was that he would not allow his brothers to eat me until I was dead. I promised that if I survived, I would never kill another wolf or own a wolf pelt. Thanks to Kicking Bird, I did survive. Barely. I was sick and weak for a long time. When I was eventually well again, I changed my name. I have kept my promise to the dominant wolf, who, while I suffered my greatest torment, spared me additional pain.''

Only when he became silent did I remember to breathe. With a shaking hand I held out my cup for more of the coffee he offered. As he poured I asked, my voice shaking as badly as my hand. "And the girl?''

Hears The Wolf smiled languorously as he replaced the pot on the heating stone. ''Her name, when I loved her, was Fortunate Girl. Her father gave her that name because she was so beautiful he knew she would make a good marriage. His hope for her didn't work out so well. She was in love with me, you see, and after what he'd done to me, she hated her father. She became so unpleasant that he finally married her off, but to a mediocre man from an unimpressive family.''

"Who?''

His tongue lightly touched his upper teeth. He made a sucking sound, then said, ''Runs The Bulls.''

Our eyes met. He smiled. There was only sadness in his smile. A knot formed in my throat as Sits Beside Him's face became as defined in my mind's eye as any image captured in a photograph.

''She was worth the beating, wouldn't you agree?''

I didn't know what to say to that. I felt humbled. I simply lowered my head and remained quiet. Eventually, warmed by both the blanket and the coffee, I slowly spoke the thing worrying me.

''I was wondering if the relative we buried this morning loved White Otter.''

My head shot up when I heard him laugh contemptuously. ''I think maybe the person that one loved the best was himself. White Otter's costly mistake was being timid.''

''You mean she should have told him to his face that she didn't like him?''

He chuckled again. ''No. That would have only made her a greater challenge. What she should have done was throw herself at him. Then he would have done to White Otter what he did to that poor little girl who really had loved him.''

''What?''

''Abandon her.''

''He did that?''

''Oh, yes. And that sweet little girl's only shortcoming had been to believe him when he swore he cared for her.''

Hears The Wolf settled comfortably, leaning against the backrest, sticking his long legs out, crossing them at the ankles. I was still hunkering, wondering if I was finally dry enough to risk sitting down. As my legs were almost totally damaged from the uncomfortable weight they supported, I gambled on the full measure of his hospitality. It felt so good to sit on the soft bundle of blanket-covered pine needles, I almost groaned. But he wasn't watching me. He was looking into the fire, brooding.

"Her name was Grass Stem. Do you remember her?"

"Yes," I yelped. "That was the girl who shamed her family when she ran off and married a Cheyenne two summers ago."

"That's right," Hears The wolf grunted. "The summer season we camped with the Cheyenne up on the Arkansas. It was on account of the dead one that she did that." He raised a hand, silencing the question I was about to ask.

"It went this way. The dead one was not an unattractive person. He had many faults but being ugly in the face or body wasn't one of them. When he pressed his attentions on Grass Stem, she quite naturally believed he was a serious suitor. And she was flattered that a handsome young man of good family wanted to marry her.

"Grass Stem became very proud and responded favorably to his suit. That was Grass Stem's mistake. Not only did she make herself obtainable to him, she went about bragging what a wonderful fellow he was and how lucky she was to be his chosen bride. He decided that she was right. He was much too good for her. Besides, she wasn't fun anymore. Chasing after a girl who was eager to be caught became boring. So he stopped coming to see her; there was nothing she could do. Their courtship had not been formalized, he could throw her away without any hesitation. When he had been chasing her he'd led her along with the lie that he was preparing to speak to her father, but he hadn't. And once he tired of her, he had every right to pass her by as if she didn't exist.

"That poor child suffered terribly. She could no longer go out in public for all the teasing directed at her. A lot of people thought she had the teasing coming for all the bragging she had done. Hiding from the teasing only made everything worse. I went to her myself, tried to coax her out, make her face the ordeal with her head high. If she had had that kind of courage, people would have respected her for it and would have eventually left her alone, placed the blame where it belonged, on him. Until she did that, no other man would look at her as a likely wife.

"Then we camped with the Cheyenne, and evidently one of their men spotted her. She always kept to herself and because of this she was easily accessible to that Cheyenne warrior. Before even her parents suspected, she was in the Cheyenne camp and married. There was nothing anyone could do without starting a major war, so she went with her Cheyenne husband and her parents sang her death song. This is why I'm telling you White Otter made a crucial mistake. Her heart is with The Cheyenne Robber and always will be. Her greatest error was allowing Kicking Bird's nephew to realize this. For him she was an irresistible challenge. A challenge he would delight in conquering every time he bedded her."

The rains had decreased to a light drizzle when I left Hears The Wolf's lodge thinking about what an utterly loathsome human being Coyote Walking had been. As I walked through the village, people were coming out of their homes. Because of the fresher air, activity was more brisk than it had been on the previous muggy day. I saw a nearby group of young men greet other young men; then all of them squatted down, chatting and laughing, readying themselves for a friendly gambling game. Two of these were of my acquaintance, Chasing Horse and Stands On A Hill, but only the latter seemed pleased by my approach.

Stands On A Hill stood up, smiled broadly, waved an arm toward his body, signaling me to join them. When I came to stand beside him, he took my arm with both of his hands and gave me the shake of welcome.

"I saw you earlier," he said, good humor apparent in his tone. "I thought you left."

"Hears The Wolf offered me shelter from the storm," I replied.

Stands On A Hill nodded. "He's a good man, my cousin. I think a lot of him."

A surly Chasing Horse turned his head, looked askance at Stands On A Hill, snorted, and muttered something to those around him. They snickered. I looked questioningly at Stands On A Hill. He was blushing. He fidgeted, balancing himself first on one foot then the other. When he spoke again, his initial happy mood had turned anxious. Resting an arm across my shoulders, he forcibly led me away from the group of young men. We walked through the center of the camp, his heavy arm still around my shoulders, our strides matching.

"They meant no disrespect," he said close against my ear. "Hears The Wolf is a valuable person, a good relative. My cousin-brothers . . ." He went quiet.

Both of us reflective, we continued our promenade, I still in the throws of wishing Coyote Walking dead all over again, Stands On A Hill pondering the thing he wished to confide. Whatever it was, was a struggle for him. Finally he took a deep breath, let it go, sent me a timorous half smile, hugged my shoulders in an affable manner.

"We're all very protective of Hears The Wolf. But I know you to be a good person. A caring person. I've told my cousin-brothers this. I've told them too that you will be good for Hears The Wolf."

I stopped as revelation bolted through my brain. Stands On A Hill placed his hands on his slender hips, tiny beads of the drizzling rain sitting like jewels in his hair, on his mildly curious expressioned face.

Finally I found my voice and blurted, "You're telling me Hears The Wolf is *Hwame*?"

His chin snapped back against his neck. "Of course he is. Aren't you?"

"NO!"

A startled look flashed across Stands On A Hill's young face. Then he looked seriously confused. His hands fell as he took a step back, half turned away from me, shook his head as if trying to clear it. He canted his head, looked back at me over a partially turned shoulder. "You're certain you're not a Hwame?"

"Very certain."

He lightly tossed his hands in unison with puffing his cheeks and blowing air through his mouth. "Then I don't understand," he said flatly.

"Understand what?"

"What you're doing here. I know very well that you were not friends with—" he lifted his shoulders in a shrug. "You know. Him."

"And how would you know that? Did you know all of his friends?"

"Yes. He only had one."

"And who was that?"

"Chasing Horse."

We began to walk again, this time in the direction of my horse, which was hobbled very near Hears The Wolf's lodge.

Stands On A Hill proved to be a bounty of information. I listened eagerly.

"That's why Chasing Horse was rude to you. He knew you were lying. And, he didn't like it that you were being cagey. If you were here for Hears The Wolf, he said you should just come out and do the honorable thing and declare yourself. He said until you did that he would not believe you cared for our cousin the way you should. That you were going to hurt his feelings. I took you off to warn you that if you did, Chasing Horse and the others would get you for that. As I said, we all think a lot of Hears The

Wolf. He's special. We would allow only a very special outsider to love him.''

As I unhobbled my horse I told Stands On A Hill that I understood. Another lie. I didn't understand at all. Hears The Wolf had shared with me his secret love for a woman, a woman he endured a brutal beating for, and now his relative was telling me the exact opposite. If Hears The Wolf was Hwame, why hadn't he simply told me that? In our culture Hwames did not hide. So why had he hidden from me? I meant to go home. I had not eaten and was very hungry, but despite my growling belly, the puzzle of Hears The Wolf eventually pulled me in another direction. There was only one person I felt I could trust to tell me the truth and that person was the only woman Hears The Wolf had been known to love.

Sits Beside Him.

I rode through Runs The Bulls's little camp without pausing, not even for the young woman who tried to stop me by waving her arms over her head and calling after me. I continued undaunted until I was on the outskirts of the camp. Just as I neared Sits Beside Him's isolated lodge I spotted her pacing back and forth, and when she turned her head, saw that it was me, she ran to greet me, worry vainly attempting to despoil her remarkable good looks. The instant I reined up my horse, her hands reached up and grabbed on to my arm and my leg.

''I couldn't stop them!''

''Couldn't stop who?''

''My mother-in-law and my daughter.''

All thoughts of Hears The Wolf promptly faded as I quickly slid off my horse, stood before her. ''Where have they gone?''

''Separate directions,'' she said hurriedly. ''Duck, to confront my sister-wife, Shield Woman; my daughter, to The Cheyenne Robber.''

"She went to him!" I shouted. "What made her suddenly decide to do that?"

Sits Beside Him threw up her hands in mental surrender. "She crawled out the back of the lodge while I was gathering dry firewood. I didn't see her go. When I came back she was gone. Love makes people stupid. She had to be with him and she wouldn't listen to good sense so she ran off."

I wasn't actually that concerned about White Otter. It wasn't as if she could heap more disgrace on her father. At least with The Cheyenne Robber she would know a little happiness before his trial. And afterward, well, because of that baby inside her, she was already doomed to whatever sentence was passed on The Cheyenne Robber. No, it was the old woman and what she might be getting up to that caused me grief.

"Tell me about your mother-in-law."

Sits Beside Him placed a hand against a worried brow, shook her head, spoke as if she were speaking out loud to herself. We walked as she talked. My horse, led by the reins, plodded obediently behind.

"My mother-in-law is what she is. No one has ever been able to control her. Not even her husband, but he used to laugh, call her spirited." She took her hand away, looked me squarely in the eyes. "What she is, what she has always been, is a woman behaving badly. My secret name for her has always been Tantrum. Her husband named her Duck, because that's what he did most of his married life."

I chuckled, and as worried as she was, Sits Beside Him managed a chortle or two herself.

"Life with her has always been interesting," Sits Beside Him said. "But I've come to love that old woman more than I ever believed I could."

Close by her sad little lodge I hobbled my horse and then followed her inside. We sat by the dying fire, each of us silent, lost in our own thoughts. Staring into the low flames, I broke the silence.

"I went to the funeral this morning," I said. The real reason for my visit had returned to me. The need to know the truth outweighed any urgency of whatever Duck might have gotten up to. "Afterward"—I turned my head, looked at her, anxious to see her reaction—"I sat out the worst of the rain with Hears The Wolf."

She flinched, hard, recovered quickly. So quickly I began to wonder if I'd seen the flinch, or imagined that I had. Now her expression revealed absolutely nothing. Her lovely features could have been cut from stone. I watched her profile as she pondered the information I'd given.

"Hears The Wolf told me that he knew you. I must confess that I was surprised by just how well."

"That was a very long time ago," she said crisply. "I haven't seen him or thought of him since. Anyway," she said as she tossed her head and ran a hand through her soaked hair, "his name was different then. When I knew him his name was White Clay." She became still. For a second, her mouth and throat muscles tensed. Closing her eyes briefly, I could feel her willing herself to remain calm. This inner will produced a second brilliant recovery. I hadn't imagined the flinch.

"He's aged well. Admittedly he's no longer an impetuous young man," I said gently, "but he's still tall, still strong, still beautiful. And he's something else."

Her laugh sounded forced and hollow. "Oh, yes? And what would that be? Married eight times over? The father of twenty children?"

"No. I'm told he has become Hwame."

She looked away quickly, stared into the near-extinguished flames. "I don't believe it," she whispered so softly that I barely heard.

To me, and in a very composed tone she said, "I suppose people change."

SEVEN

Sits Beside Him found it hard to remain stoic. She tilted her head back and looked up toward the smoke hole. Outside, sunlight and blue sky were managing to break through the thinning dark clouds. Golden light filtered down past the lofty ears of the soot-blackened smoke hole, highlighting her rigid mien.

I gently said, "Anything you might want to confide in me would go no further."

Her chin bobbled. Tears welled in her eyes, slid free of the corners, glided across her upturned face, became lost in the hair surrounding the temples. She couldn't bring herself to look at me.

"We loved each other very much. Too much. For a long time I thought he was dead and I felt dead inside too. Finally, when I heard that he was alive, I wanted to run away, be where he was. But I couldn't. I could only trust that he would understand and forgive me." She lowered her head, wept quietly into her hands for a moment. When she finally raised her head and looked directly at me, her mouth open, about to speak, it confirmed what I had just surmised, the lodge door flew open and Duck shouted at both of us, me especially.

"They told me you were here. You'd better come quick. She's telling the truth for once in her miserable life and you don't want to miss it."

Whatever Sits Beside Him was about to say was immediately forgotten. Jumping to her feet she dashed past me. I wasted no time following her out of the lodge. Running, we caught up with the old woman toddling rapidly away. When I was at the old woman's side she looked up at me. She was excited, looking extraordinarily pleased with herself. She chuckled, satisfaction glowing from her eyes.

"Where is she?" I said breathlessly.

"In the lodge of my son the idiot."

"Maybe she's escaped."

"Can't. My daughters and my nieces won't let her."

I caught the old woman by her shoulders, forcing her to a halt. "You didn't use your knife, did you?"

Duck looked guilty.

I gave her a shake. "I told you not to do that."

Her hands flew between my arms, knocking my hands from her shoulders. "Well, I tried it your way, tried being nice, but that didn't work. It was only when I hit her with a stick that she agreed to talk. Then I was told that you were here. I told her to wait to do her talking because you would be extremely interested in what she has to say, too. That you're being a smart man, as soon as she confessed to you, you'd not only clear my grand-daughter's reputation, you'd figure out who really killed Kicking Bird's nephew." Duck cackled an ugly laugh. "You should have seen her face. She turned a sick green."

The lodge of Runs The Bulls was crowded with women. Just women. Perplexed, I looked at Duck. She snorted the answer to my unspoken question.

"He's hunting. He's never around when he's needed. You're going to have to be our male witness."

Women had equal voting rights and an equal voice at

council. However, in matters of a woman or as in this case, a group of women accusing another woman before the council, a male voice blending with theirs carried tremendous weight. I, it would seem, had been elected by these women to be that voice.

Taking my hand, Duck led me through the throng to the center of the lodge and there my doctorly eyes were treated to a terrible sight. Horrified, my heart instantly went out to their victim.

Shield Woman's clothing was in tatters, her hair in wads as if it had been almost yanked from her skull by many pairs of hands. The left side of her face was swollen, one eye just a slit, and her mouth, split in several places, was bleeding profusely. More than a simple stick was the cause of that much damage. I fought down the urge to throttle Duck. Hurriedly kneeling down before Shield Woman, I pushed back the sleeves of her ruined dress and saw that her arms were covered with welts and bruises. Before I could examine the rest of her body for further evidence of maltreatment, Duck was beside me. Her old hand covered my face, and she roughly pushed me back, causing me to fall clumsily on my rear end.

"Doctoring comes later. After the slut's talked."

"I have nothing to say," Shield Woman said sulkily.

Duck menaced her by advancing a step, raising a fist. "Oh, yes you do! You're going to talk and talk and talk. Go back on your word now and I will beat you to death."

I recovered quickly, righting myself. I pulled at Duck's raised arm, forcing her to look back at me. "How can you do this!" I shouted. "Not only are you dishonoring your son, you're dishonoring his first wife and child whom you claim to love."

Duck twisted me off, and in a snarling voice said, "Him I don't care about. The other two I love because they are separate from him." Then she was towering over Shield Woman again, the fisted hand poised to strike.

Shield Woman looked hastily toward me, licking blood

from her lower lip. "Can you get me out of here? Away from this crazy old woman?"

"Only if you tell me the full truth," I answered rapidly. "Promise me that and I will take you to Sitting Bear's camp. If the chief of the Ten Bravest can't keep you safe, no one can."

Shield Woman licked at her bleeding lip again, her eyes, most especially the left, were swollen almost closed. What little I could see of them sparkled with genuine fear.

"Agreed."

Her eyes cut toward her mother-in-law, Duck. The old woman snarled for effect and Shield Woman further recoiled from the old woman hovering too near.

"But not here!" Shield Woman cried. "I'm not saying anything until you get me away from that crazy old woman."

Duck began screaming as I lifted Shield Woman, carrying her battered and ponderous body awkwardly in my arms.

"Make her talk! Make her talk right now."

"No!" I shouted. Shield Woman's portly arms went around my neck, held on too tightly. Her weight very nearly breaking my back, she was now suffocating me in the bargain while I elbowed my way through the feminine crowd. "I'm taking her to Sitting Bear before you all do something even more incredibly stupid." I tried to sound commanding and masculine, hoping these personas would intimidate the women surrounding me. Not an easy task when you're wheezing.

The old woman pushed along beside me. She resembled a nightmare, eyes wild, flecks of foam caught at the corners of her snarling mouth. She was caught in a seizure of fury and would only back away from a greater strength. I stopped my ungainly escape and did my best to give her that impression.

"Old woman! If you try to prevent my going, if you so much as touch this woman again, I will personally haul you before the council and charge you with assault.''

"You would do that to me?'' Duck screeched.

"Yes.''

She became confused. I could see in her crumbling face that she was trying to work out which was more important, avoiding condemnation or revenge against Shield Woman. Meanwhile, I was sweating buckets. If she chose the latter and I was forced into a fight, I knew I was in big trouble. Admittedly Duck was old, but she was spry. Not only that, but she had a horde of women eager to take her side in a fight. I might have won against only Duck, but never against all of them. Then too, I was severely handicapped by the load in my arms. While the laborious thought process temporarily subdued the old woman, I used those precious seconds to escape. Duck's indecision seemed to melt the wall of women. They stepped away, allowing room for my departure.

Shield Woman had been so brutalized that riding a horse on her own was unthinkable. Besides, taking a horse from Runs The Bulls's herd without his permission would only create more unnecessary strife. Shield Woman would have to ride behind me to Sitting Bear's camp. My horse was hobbled near Sits Beside Him's isolated lodge, not a very long walk but more than the battered Shield Woman could manage.

The day had just passed noon and as the protective cloud cover had dissipated, it was now very hot. I carried Shield Woman on my back, praying with each step that Crying Wind would not suddenly appear, see me piggybacking a fat woman, and get the wrong idea. Logic told me that my beloved was miles away but newly found love often makes one a trifle paranoid. My paranoia soared and my pace quickened, becoming an awkward jog.

I was forced to tie her to me. A belt around her waist secured to mine. Even so, she wobbled badly behind me, passing out, coming to again. She'd suffered so many blows to the head, I worried she might be concussed. I couldn't let her go to sleep. I tried to keep her talking.

"Did Kicking Bird's nephew give you the leggings to place under White Otter's bed?"

Nothing.

"Did you find the piece of clothing and then falsely claim the place you'd found it?"

No reply.

"Woman! You promised me the truth. Now speak!"

She passed out, almost fell from the horse, and I struggled to keep her in place. As we slid toward its belly, my frightened horse broke into a faster trot. Bumped along, the unconscious woman and I almost fell off. Finally I managed to hoist Shield Woman upright, her cheek resting against my spine. Anger bolted through me. Thanks to Duck's beating the blood out of her, the answer to the question about the leggings was stalled. If I ever hoped to get the answer from her, I'd have to make certain she stayed out of Duck's way. Kicking my horse to greater speed, I took Shield Woman to the safety of Sitting Bear's camp.

I'd never before had any direct dealings with Sitting Bear. I admired him in the extreme, but was always careful to keep a good space of ground between us. I worried now that I would be forced to speak directly to him. Sitting Bear was of an age to remember that part of our history all but forgotten by everyone else. Staunchly traditional, he followed the old ways. Whereas we more modern men plucked our faces of all stray facial hairs, some men including their eyebrows, Sitting Bear allowed every hair on his face to grow at will. Thus he had wild eyebrows, a scraggly mustache and a long goatee, all of it gray, none of it flattering. He was the chief of the Ten Bravest, men who not only faced death, they ran to embrace it.

The Onde wore hats but the Ten Bravest wore sashes draped over the right shoulder and training behind their feet. The sashes, unlike the hats of the Onde, were not merely the outward manifestation of high office. The sashes were the outward sign that the wearer was completely ready to die in battle, for during a battle, an arrow shaft was stabbed through the train into the ground. The man wearing the sash was literally staked out, he could not run away, he had to fight until he was either killed or freed. Because when he was staked out this man was also a Contrary, the one freeing him was forced to speak backward.

"Stand firm against the attack" meant in the language of the Contrary, "Run away! The battle is lost."

What frightened me most about facing Sitting Bear was that he had been known to fight off his rescuers just as valiantly as he had faced down the enemy. That he was still alive was a testament to the courage and stubbornness of his own men hauling him away from a fight. I'd heard too many grisly stories of his struggles to remain on the field, and I believed them because I had doctored more than a few of Sitting Bear's rescuers.

We caused something of a stir as we rode through Sitting Bear's sprawling camp of seventy lodges. Bewildered people stopped what they were doing and trailed after us. Being the kind of chief he was, it wasn't so unusual that those in trouble arrived at Sitting Bear's door seeking sanctuary. But a man riding in with a beat-up, unconscious woman behind him was unusual. Even the great man himself ventured from his lodge and joined the clamor being raised. While I struggled to dismount, pull Shield Woman with me then hold her limp body steady in my arms, Sitting Bear peered incredulously at me. With Shield Woman's dead weight growing heavier by the second, Sitting Bear continued to regard me from beneath feral brows.

"My son," he said in a strong but age-graveled voice, only just managing to be heard over the din of the crowd, "why have you abused this woman?"

"I didn't do it, Father. The women of her band took clubs to her."

"Why would they do that?"

"She was deceitful against her sisters."

Sitting Bear opened his mouth and nodded his head in a silent *ahhhh*. Then, squinting his eyes, he studied me harder. "Why have you brought her to me?"

"To save her life."

"And where is her husband?"

"They say he is hunting, Father."

"And do you think this is true?"

"No."

Sitting Bear shook his head in disgust. A man in hiding from his womenfolk was the lowest form of coward. "The woman is safe with me until her husband takes hold of himself and finds his own balls. After that, her welfare is his responsibility."

At an over-the-head wave of his arm, several of his wives took charge of Shield Woman, lifting her away from me, taking her off to be tended. My numbed arms, now empty, fell limply against my sides.

Sitting Bear clamped a hand on my shoulder. "I believe you have a lot of things to tell me. Isn't that right?"

I nodded mutely.

"First you will eat and we will smoke. Then, you will tell me everything."

I've only known three genuine heroes in my life; my father, Little Bluff, and Sitting Bear. I've always held them in exactly that order. The first two were lost to me. I thanked our Creator most profoundly that the third, never mind that personally I found him scary, was still here.

The meal he provided was wonderful. I ate until I was on the verge of being sick. Then I reclined against a backrest and smoked from a small clay pipe Sitting Bear handed me. He had his own pipe, his own recliner. The two of us were alone in the cooling shade of the arbor. After the women had removed the remains of the meal, no one ventured near. As naturally nosy as the members of his considered band were, and as badly as they wanted to hear what I had to say to Sitting Bear, none were so nosy or so foolish as to disturb his privacy. The atmosphere between us was comfortable and oddly familiar, as if we had enjoyed one another's company many times before. Sitting Bear was intentionally making me feel that way. At the time I was too relieved not to be afraid of him anymore to see through his tactics. I simply basked in the comfort and the safety of his presence.

Shield Woman certainly knew she would be safe in his protection, which is what likely prompted her willingness to talk to me. I pondered the things I believed she would eventually tell me as I smoked and allowed time to drift away in the comfortable silence Sitting Bear and I shared. I felt like a child finding protection under his father's arm. It was not only Sitting Bear's reputation, but his wisdom that made me feel that way. I knew that I was simply one of many of his spiritual children, but in those moments I felt as if I were his favorite son. It had been too long since I had been anyone's son, favorite or otherwise. Whatever the age of a child or a man, an orphan is an orphan. Loving parents are missed. Missing my blood father acutely, I told my spiritual father everything, left nothing out. And like my blood father had done so often in the past, Sitting Bear remained silent and listened.

When I was finished, I felt completely drained. He waited for a few moments, then spoke to me in a low tone. He approved of most of my actions but was a bit appalled by two—the pretense of being Coyote Walking's friend, and then examining the body. He forgave me those things, as he himself was unable to think of any other course of action.

"But all that lying," Sitting Bear scolded, "and then rolling around with the dead." He shuddered, then looked hard at me. "I know as a doctor you can't help being around dead people. But you shouldn't be around them when you don't have to be. You're pushing your healing power beyond its purpose. One day your nails and all your hair will fall out on account of your gruesome curiosity. That's what happens to people unnecessarily fooling around with the dead. I can only hope you had the good sense to cleanse yourself with cedar smoke after you'd done this thing."

"Yes, Father. I did. I have been very careful."

"Well, that's something at least."

I lowered a contrite head, fighting the smile that threatened. Further discussion was abruptly interrupted by a new furor in the camp. A lone horseman rode in, scattering the camp population like squawking chickens. White Bear executed a running dismount and with a blustery attitude stormed our way. He raised an arm like a lance, pointed it directly at my heart.

"I want to talk to you!"

I stood, experiencing a jolt of fear that he had heard about Shield Woman sharing a horse with me and misunderstood the reason. I was afraid that he was furious because of the embarrassment my doing this might have caused Crying Wind.

As it happened, White Bear hadn't heard about Shield Woman. Therefore, I was able to tell him that Shield Woman had been attacked, and using Sitting Bear as my witness, I hastily explained that I had only brought her to safety. The three of us stood in the arbor, White Bear with his hands on his hips listening irritably to all I had to say. During my last placating sentence, he interrupted me, throwing a hand away from himself.

"I don't care about that! I have more on my mind than my cousin's tender feelings. Besides, Crying Wind will sort you out herself when she hears about it. And don't try running to me. I have enough problems with my own wives. You're a reasonably good-sized man, I have every confidence you'll be able to hold your own against one skinny woman."

He brought his huge fist back to his hip, leaned toward me, and yelled into my relieved face. "Are we all finished with the trivial? Can we now discuss a *real* problem?"

Sitting Bear and I nodded in unison.

"Good! I'm here because of The Cheyenne Robber. He's lost his mind. He's declared himself married to White Otter and she's with him. When I tried to pull her out of his lodge and annul the marriage, my own nephew defied me and threw *me* out. When that girl's father hears about this foolishness, he'll shoot my lunatic nephew before his trial ever begins."

"No, he won't," I answered mildly.

White Bear slapped his thighs. "Another one that's lost his mind!"

I was pleased that he was unarmed, for when he turned back toward me, murder was in his eyes. I kept my voice steady, my tone clear.

"Runs The Bulls will not oppose his daughter's marriage."

White Bear was completely still for a long moment. In an open-mouthed daze he looked to Sitting Bear for confirmation.

"Tay-bodal's right," Sitting Bear said in his gravelly voice. "So now, you great lump, stop blowing off your mouth and listen to me. You'll leave that girl with The Cheyenne Robber and you'll leave them both alone. Whatever the council decides, those two have chosen to face it together." He turned to leave, stopped, peered at us over his shoulder. "One more thing. You're to stop yelling at this young man. I admit he's a bit unconventional, but I like him anyway. I like him a lot." His eyes sought mine. "Go home, Tay-bodal. Enjoy being with your woman. The problem you've left at my door can wait. Come back tomorrow. I'm an old man, and I like to sleep late in the morning, so early afternoon would be a good time."

"Thank you, Father. I will come directly after the noon meal."

"Good. Then I won't have to feed you again."

White Bear twisted his lips to the side as we watched the stately chief depart. "Well," he huffed, "it would seem you've made yourself a powerful friend." He snorted a laugh as he glanced my way. "But you'll notice he offered you no protection from Crying Wind."

As my face registered alarm, White Bear chuckled evilly. "You're not going to tell her!"

"Oh, yes, I am."

We ran a foot race through Sitting Bear's camp, each of us attempting to reach our horse first. Spectators whooped, jumping up and down and cheering the contest. Because his legs were about four miles longer than mine, White Bear won.

His horse was faster, too. His large frame was a moving dot on the horizon that I followed, punishing my horse brutally. I didn't see White Bear anywhere in the camp when I finally galloped home a soundly defeated second. I might not see him, but I knew White Bear was somewhere happily spilling his guts to Crying Wind. That left me with no alternative. I would have to do something terribly romantic to soothe her temper.

Never a great musician, I didn't even own a flute. So while White Bear contented himself with enraging my beloved, I tore up the camp trying to beg, borrow, or steal a flute. One was finally given to me by a woman who couldn't stop laughing. Her ill-contained mirth was all the evidence I needed that word had spread like a blaze. My misadventure with Shield Woman was now common knowledge and most probably distorted forty miles wide from the actual truth. If people were laughing at me, then they were teasing Crying Wind unmercifully. And as I knew my little sweetheart wouldn't care for that very much, it was pitifully easy to reckon that I was in deep, deep trouble.

Romance was in the twilight air. The creek purled, newly bloomed flowers were fragrant with sweet perfume, the sky a breathtaking display of red and purple, the First Star shining brightly, the full moon beginning its ascent, and there was I clumsily producing shrill notes from a flute. What woman could resist?

Crying Wind.

She slipped up quietly behind me as I squatted less than a yard away from her lodge, grabbed that flute out of my hands, and cracked me over the head with it.

My eyes crossed and watered, my injured brain dizzy, my ears registering her words as if she were speaking— angrily—under water.

"I understand you spent your day carrying off a woman in your arms. That she then rode behind you. That everyone saw this."

I tried to stand on wobbly legs. "I—I can explain—"

She shoved me back down. I sat at her feet, my legs inelegantly splayed.

"Oh, you're going to explain all right. And you'd better be convincing, otherwise our engagement is finished."

"But, dar—"

She grabbed the ear from which her earring dangled and pulled. Hard. My head and my complete attention followed.

"Don't you *darling* me! I'll decide if I'm your darling. So start talking."

I did, and faster than a ripping breeze on a blustery day. At some point during the discourse, her interest in the secret things I confided soothed her ire. She let go of my throbbing ear and crouched in front of me absorbing all of it. When I went quiet she whistled softly through her teeth. Then she regarded me with her oddly rounded eyes, the rims of which brimmed with tears.

"My poor little soul," she said, sniffing back a sob. "Please forgive me for doubting you. You've been working hard to help all of us, and that rascal cousin of mine has been playing games again. But then he would. He thinks making trouble is funny. I should have known better. I should have listened to Skywalker."

"Why? What did Skywalker say?"

She hesitated, then said quickly, "Nothing worth repeating."

Her nervous attitude negated her words. Suddenly I felt it was very important that I should know what Skywalker had had to say about me. "Tell me. Tell me exactly what he said."

"You might not like it."

"Try me."

She let go a loud sigh. "Well, all right, as you're so insistent. He just said you weren't very attractive. That you were so happy that a woman such as myself actually loved you and consented to marry you, that you would never risk my love foolishly. He also said he was certain that that woman had only ridden with you because she was desperate."

"Oh, he did, did he!"

Her eyes narrowed into dangerous slits. "Are you implying that wasn't the case? That you didn't think about my feelings? That Runs The Bulls's slut of a wife was eager to be with you?"

"I—"

Divine wisdom stopped me. Crying Wind was eyeing me like a starving turkey buzzard impatient to tear into a still-breathing feast. Any defense of my trampled pride would only be used against me. So I humbled myself the way only a very worried man can.

"I thought about you the whole time. I only saved that woman because she will be needed as a witness at The Cheyenne Robber's trial. If it weren't for that, I swear on all my love for you, I would not have raised a hand to help her. But she is needed for the trial. Everything she's done is the direct cause of all of our troubles."

Crying Wind made me squirm, taking an inordinate amount of time to reflect. When she spoke again her words held an intentionally badly disguised threat.

"I had a dream about you last night, Tay-bodal. In my dream you were talking to a group of admiring women.

Then suddenly, your hands went to your throat and you went all white in the face. Blood poured out from your hands as if your throat had been cut. Isn't that awful?"

She smiled indolently, showing no teeth. I managed a sand-dry swallow.

Realizing that I was sufficiently cowed, she stood, offered me her hand. We walked toward the creek, following it until we were well away from the encampment. Near the bank, concealed by trees and scrubs, we sat down.

"Do you really love me, Tay-bodal?"

Her voice was soft, tinged with a baffling nervousness and need for spoken reassurance. That such a beautiful, coolly confident woman would be quietly worrying about my feelings for her blasted me senseless.

"I'm an unattractive man," I answered, "staggered by my great good luck. You know I love you."

She chuckled, her uncertainties gone. "That really got to you, didn't it?"

"Yes, it did."

She turned her head, looked at me, her expression amazingly shy. I was learning quickly that she was a woman of many moods. I found I liked this shy mood best. Shyness is only another term for fearful. I was still a stranger to her. She needed to feel safe loving me. And I wanted her to know she would always be safe. I raised her hand to my lips and kissed it.

"Even if I were as handsome as The Cheyenne Robber," I said earnestly, "I would still count myself very lucky that someone like you chose to love me. You will always be the best, the most vital, part of me. I will love and honor you with all my heart, with all my soul, for the rest of our lives and then throughout eternity."

"Oh, Tay-bodal!" she cried, flinging herself at me.

Sitting Bear would have been pleased to know that I was no longer rolling around with the dead, that I was rolling around instead with a very live, incredibly passionate, woman. He would have declared that to be the proper thing to do. But as the woman in question was White Bear's cousin, I knew White Bear would declare it something else altogether. *That* sobering thought had me clawing myself loose from Crying Wind. Frantically, I pushed my hand between our foreheads, breaking off the deep kiss.

"We can't do this," I gasped.

"Oh, yes, we can."

Her mouth was on mine again, and she pinned my arms next to my head, her strength frightening the liver out of me.

"Tay-bodal," she growled huskily, "I have been without a man for two years. If you're not going to help, the least you can do is hold still."

When I returned from the edge of oblivion, she lightly kissed my mouth.

"Now you are forever mine," she breathed.

As my eyes rolled to the back of my head and the lids slid closed, I nodded.

I am hers. And because I'm hers I have, since that night, strenuously avoided groups of women. I've only one throat and I've never been anxious to find it cut.

We stood outside her door, Crying Wind snuggled against me inside my arms as I begged disgracefully.

"Please come home with me."

"I can't."

"Please! I want to fall asleep holding you."

She placed her hands on my chest and pushed away, looking up at me, her face made white by the light of the moon, her unusual round eyes resembling two large black holes.

"You know I can't. White Bear would have a fit. He likes everything done just right. A marriage between us will only receive his blessing when he takes my hand and places it in yours in front of witnesses. Then there must be a great feast and a giveaway. Don't forget about that. I am his blood relative and it would shame him if he didn't provide presents for everyone witnessing our marriage. That's the way it has to be, Tay-bodal. If we simply elope, he will be mad at us forever.''

She was speaking good sense. White Bear's pride was already chaffing because of The Cheyenne Robber's elopement, and a second hurried marriage would send him into a fury. But good sense and lust have nothing in common and now that I had recovered from my—surprise, I was a man consumed by deep-heated lust. I pulled her back against me, groaned slightly from the torturous pleasure of her breasts crushed against me.

''Then let's go back to the woods.''

I felt the sting of her slap against my upper arm. ''Be quiet,'' she whispered through clenched teeth. ''Sharp ears are near and listening.''

My eyes slithered to the corners toward the lodge looming like a black specter positioned against a starry sky. In that lodge Crying Wind lived with three maidens, two widows, and the children of the widows. All of these women, White Bear would hold on to for as long as he could. A supply of strong, marriageable women was another mark of his wealth. With so many hands required for the smooth order of his extensive camp, that meant he would also let go of them reluctantly. His elusive promise of my marrying Crying Wind was an unabashed bribe, one he would dangle in front of me for as long as he believed he could get away with it.

He knew that I would labor as a doctor or as a useful spy—anything he chose for me to do—to have Crying Wind. But once I was contentedly married, my continuing to carry on as his menial would be a matter of my own choice. I would be bound to his band by marriage, but I would no longer be his dogsbody. Therein lay the inconvenient difference.

No matter how softly lined a trap, it still has teeth. Teeth that bite deep. I felt those teeth tearing me apart as she left me, disappearing inside that conic silhouette. I stood there for an indeterminate time, giving Crying Wind plenty of

opportunity to change her mind, come out of there, and run
with me either back to our trysting place or home to my
lodge. I stood there until my feet and legs fell asleep. She
had more sense than I. She did not change her mind.

I heard her whisper, "Is he still out there?"

The flap pulled aside a fraction, a single eye appeared.
The flap closed quickly and then a feminine titter, "Yes!"
Sniggering promptly followed.

I was defeated, I was being a fool. Dejected, I slunk off.

EIGHT

The next morning I awoke feeling better than I had in years, clearheaded and full of energy. Making love does that. It's the sharp contrast between making love and paying for sex. I, more than anyone, am well aware of the difference. The thought that I might have impregnated Crying Wind only served to make me more pleased with myself. I was grinning like an opossum as I lay in my bed imagining her fat but incredibly beautiful as my child grew inside her.

All of this dreamy imagining gave me an inkling of how it must feel to be The Cheyenne Robber. I was instantly sobered. The woman he loved was pregnant with his baby, and White Otter's pregnancy was not a wishful daydream. And that baby's life was in danger. This was day three of the five allocated by Owl Man. Even though White Otter was now with him, I knew The Cheyenne Robber was still frantic about her safety. Neither she nor the child would truly be safe until he was free to bring her to his home in White Bear's camp.

I shared another thing in common with The Cheyenne

Robber. The woman I loved wasn't entirely safe either. And she had a child. A boy. Little *What's His Name*. I ran a hand over gritty eyes. I knew she'd said his name, but for the life of me I couldn't remember it. I'd have to meet him, make friends. Finding out first exactly which child he was among the horde of children tormenting the camp dogs would be enormously helpful. As it was still very early, I might manage to make his acquaintance before he became lost in the crowd.

My first sight of him made me laugh. He was standing just outside the women's lodge. He was buck naked, rounded belly protruding, back arched, hands behind his hips, yawning hugely as he urinated. He could have been one of several children belonging to that lodge, but I knew he was Crying Wind's. He had her distinctive eyes. And with his child's stubby body, the strangely round eyes made him look like a baby brown owl.

Not bothering with formal niceties, I startled him by grabbing his hand. "Not here," I growled. "Women don't appreciate men peeing in the doorway."

His little legs hurried as he tried to keep up with me. When we reached an appropriate place, lots of protective scrub trees, I let go of his hand and proceeded to relieve my bladder. The child looked from my stream, to me, back to my stream.

"Pee!" I shouted.

He comically mimicked my stance, dribbling out the last bit of water left in him. When we were finished I took his hand again, leading him home.

"What is your name, little man?"

"Hungry." He was barely five. His answer sounded more like *Hunggwy*.

I stopped and looked down at him. He peeked up at me, the sun causing him to squint. His upper lip was curled up toward his button nose. The tiny milk teeth revealed by the squinting grimace were more like little white stones.

"That's a baby name," I said solemnly. "A boy old

enough to know the proper place to pee is too old to have a baby's name.''

Still holding my hand, still looking up at me, his free hand scratched the back of his head becoming instantly lost inside the wealth of hair.

"I think I'm going to call you Tay-bodal's Favorite Son."

"Who is Tay-biddal?"

"Me."

"Tay-biddal me daddy?"

"Yes. From now into forever, I am your daddy. And never let me catch you peeing by the doorway again."

I picked up my son and carried him back to his mother.

She was standing outside, wringing her hands, looking worried. Relief shuddered across her face when she spotted us. Being Crying Wind, aggravation promptly followed relief.

"Where did you take him?" she demanded. "And why didn't you tell me you were taking him? I was worried."

I knew that the lodge was filled to the top with listening ears. I also knew that if I was ever going to assume the tone of a full and proper husband, be a genuine role model for Favorite Son, now was the time to make my stand. If she hit me over the head again and hit me so hard that this time I died, at least I would have a score of witnesses to attest my final act of bravery.

"Woman, I don't need your permission to go off for a pee with my son."

Crying Wind's head snapped back, her round eyes flaring and rounding even more. But she didn't say anything, and I took that as a good sign. I handed the boy over to her.

"Another thing, he's too old to run around naked. He needs shoes and a breechcloth. I've also changed his name. From now on you will call him Tay-bodal's Favorite Son."

"B-But we're not married."

"We're almost married. That gives me the right to regard him as my son."

"No, it does not," she sharply countered. "Not until White Bear says so. And just what's so wrong with the name I gave him? It fits him and he's used to it."

She went on and on in this arguing fashion. I coughed, clearing my throat once, twice, just as my father used to subtly do when he wanted my mother to shut up. Crying Wind wasn't attuned to anything that subtle. I could have coughed up my lungs and she would have continued on unfazed with what she had to say on the subject of my brash perspective toward her son. I glanced at the little boy in her arms. His small face was pinched with worry. It isn't good for adults to argue in front of a child. Raised voices affect them deeply. But in this instance it couldn't be helped. I raised mine.

"Woman! Stop your carping. Your point has been made. Many times over. Now understand *my* point. I have walked out with you in the moonlight, twice. I have played the flute for you. True, you hit me with it, but nevertheless, I was playing it before I was assaulted. After all that, if you fail to concede to the fact that we're almost married and that as your husband I have certain rights, then you have just publicly proclaimed yourself to be a woman of shameless virtue."

Crying Wind sucked in nearly all of the morning's freshened air. A snickering female face appeared in the doorway, then jerked away. Crying Wind, rendered speechless from shock, jostled the child in her arms as she bristled, her face glowing a hot red. I had gotten the better of her and all of those women still inside the lodge had heard me do it. Crying Wind's nostrils flared as she sent me an evil look.

"All right," she said through gritted teeth. "I acknowledge the fact that we're as good as married, that you have certain rights. But I have rights, too, and one of those rights is to inspect the home you intend for me to share with you. If it's a shamble I'm telling you right now that the marriage day will be postponed until you provide something that's fit to live in."

It was my turn to gasp sharply. I was quickly learning that my beloved could be exceptionally crafty when angry. She already knew my lodge was a wreck. White Bear's wives had made fun of it, mocked the many patches littering the walls. They'd also said that they had been worried that it would shred to pieces as they took it down. Remembering all of this made me mad. Mad at those women, mad at Crying Wind. And it struck me as grimly funny that last night the condition of my lodge hadn't concerned her one little bit, but in the strong light of morning she was ready to forget all about that.

Carrying Favorite Son, she simpered past me. "I have to see this hovel you call home," she said airily.

Walking away with her, both of us as mad as hornets, I heard that damnable giggling again. Which further incensed me and caused me to wonder if those women ever had anything other to do than hide inside that lodge listening to my life.

When we reached my admittedly sad lodge, her anger abated, turning to wide-eyed shock. She set Favorite Son down and then just stood there, silent, mouth agape.

"It could do with a little improvement here and there," I stammered defensively. "But it's roomy enough."

Slowly she turned her head toward me, her face pale, her eyes black orbs against a sea of white. When her husband had been declared dead, Crying Wind, his widow, had been allowed to remove things precious to her. Then her female relatives were allowed to take what they thought would be useful. Then her home, along with the remaining contents, was burned. She had come to her cousin White Bear literally destitute, a son on one hip, a bundle of belongings on the other. I knew in her memory she was comparing her lost home to one I now offered. And I was humiliated by the comparison.

"How many hides would be needed to make a new home?" I asked worriedly.

"At least forty," she answered, her tone thoroughly dismayed. "And all of them tanned just right, which means forty brains for the tanning."

I staggered slightly, then recovered. "All right. I'm not a poor man, I can afford that."

She suddenly became excited, happy that I was showing myself to be a generous husband. "I know my sisters would help me with the work. We could have the hides finished in no time at all. But I'm not very good at cutting the hides properly. My first husband paid a professional to do it."

I felt myself becoming irritated with a dead man. In a grudging tone I said, "Then I'll pay for a professional."

"You will? Really!" Animated, she cheerfully called her son away from the lodge door. "Don't go in there, my little soul. You'll get fleas."

"Woman!" I yelped, "I don't sleep with fleas."

"Don't be absurd," she chortled. "Fleas are all that's holding it up. And while we're on the subject, those poles have been worn down to sticks. There's no head room. Walking around in a crouch will give me a bad back. The poles will have to be replaced as well." She chewed the corner of her mouth as she did a quick calculation. "For a lodge cover of forty hides, we'll need at least sixty poles. All of them twice the size of these." She stooped to enter my humble abode. "Now I have to see the things you expect me to cook with."

"What about the fleas?" I shouted after her.

"I intend to bathe immediately."

Favorite Son and I loitered about as she did her inspection. When she came back out, she was peeved again.

"Gourds," she spat. "Old-fashioned gourds and one old black kettle missing its handle. You cook like a wild man in a raiding camp. A civilized human being does not live that way. It all has to go. Fortunately, I still have my cooking kettles and eating bowls. By the way, what are you keeping in those little Taos jars? Whatever it is, it stinks."

"Those are medical herbs. You cannot throw away my medical supplies."

"Well, I'm not going to live with them. We'll keep this little joke of a lodge for a storage shelter. You can keep all of your smelly things exactly the way you have them now. Does that suit you?"

"Perfectly."

"Fine."

"Fine!"

She kissed me brusquely. "It's lucky for you I find you so irresistible. Otherwise I'd leave you to your fleas and noxious Taos jars and never look back."

The morning held a trace of a cooling breeze with the sun steadily climbing against a clear sky. The earth had greedily absorbed the moisture of yesterday's deluge of rain and was losing its muddy softness, turning hard, more compact, under the soles of my feet. All around me vegetation was rejoicing, fairly bursting with renewed life. The freshly washed trees and pines flashed splendid hues of brilliant greens and stood proudly, thoroughly rejuvenated. Prairie grasses greeted me in shades of greens and yellows as they twisted and bowed with the freshening breezes. And the air was sweet, tinged with a delicate piney fragrance.

On this perfect morning, evidence was in abundance that Grandmother Earth's misery had been alleviated, and her joy was infectious. So infectious that I had to fight off being in a good mood to stay angry with White Bear for the little prank he'd played on me. As I walked toward his private domain, I wound myself up, making myself really good and mad.

The escapade had very nearly annihilated my delicate relationship with Crying Wind. It didn't matter to me that this hadn't been intended or wasn't meant to be spiteful. It was just another one of his infamous jokes. In his mind, stirring up Crying Wind, sending her after me with blood in her eye and the need to mete out physical abuse, as she proved when she whacked me on my head with that flute, was funny. The prospect of watching me for days tagging after her, begging her forgiveness, would be even funnier. I knew he looked forward to that part with childlike glee. But I had outmaneuvered him. And there was a certain amount of danger to that. I had, after all, declared myself to be her husband without his consent. It was well within White Bear's emotional range to change from sublime good humor to instant rage. All I had going for me was justifiable anger. So I nursed that, winding myself up tighter than a braided rawhide lariat, and was idiotically eager for the confrontation.

What I failed to notice was the rather estimable company he was keeping at that time, all seated in the sheltering arbor enjoying the day's first meal. My sights were trained only on White Bear. Gripped by righteous anger, I failed to notice Lone Wolf, Big Bow, Stumbling Bear, Long Horn, Big Tree, Skywalker, Quitan, or White Horse. All of them chiefs of the Onde class, and three of them, Big Tree, White Horse, and Big Bow, were *To-yop-kes* (war chiefs).

"I have a few things to say to you."

Startled, White Bear looked up from the bowl in his hand. He had food in the fingers of the other hand, which was poised halfway to his mouth. His surprised eyes locked with mine. The men around him tensed. Skywalker emitted a low chuckle.

"I have come here specifically to tell you that I am going to marry your cousin known as Crying Wind. That I've adopted her son. Even as I speak to you now, she is beginning the preparations for our new home. So, whatever the bride price you demand, I will pay it and be done with you. I didn't think it was necessary to ask your permission because of yesterday's trouble you mixed up between us."

White Bear sat there looking at me, his mood brooding, taciturn.

"I see," he said somberly.

He set the bowl down, put his fingers in his mouth, scraped them clean of food, chewed. During the entire process, his glittering black eyes never broke their hold with mine. When his mouth was empty of food, he spoke in a chesty rumble.

"And my cousin, Crying Wind, she simply scampered off to begin the work for your lodge without any word of argument?"

I hesitated, the first ray of common sense dawning in me. It was then that I noticed the other men, their chiefly status and their tense silence.

"Well," I said, feeling myself beginning to shrivel, "as a matter of fact, yes, she did."

White Bear stood. With measured strides, he approached me. My anger vanished. Now I was afraid. So petrified my feet felt bolted to the ground. Then he was standing before me. There was barely enough breathing room separating us. I fully expected to be struck down. What he did was grab me up into a laughing bear hug, lifting me off my feet.

"Welcome to the family!"

Setting me down, he turned me toward the arbor, forcing me to face our audience of chortling men.

"Let it be known that the recklessly brave man known as Tay-bodal will soon be my full cousin. A member of the Rattle Band. That he has conquered the unconquerable, my less than good-natured cousin known as Crying Wind." He slapped me hard on the back. "Wish him good luck with her. He'll need it."

The men began to chortle, White Bear looked down at me with a very self-satisfied expression. "She's a fine woman," White Bear said loudly. "She just needs a firm hand. Never let her forget who's the boss, and try to ignore any stories you might hear about her first husband running in front of that Texan's bullet on purpose."

Sitting in the shade of the arbor, surrounded by august persons, I thought hard as I ate with a voracious appetite. So, Crying Wind had a temper and because of that she had been considered hard to marry off. So what? As far as I was concerned, her temper had saved her from being married to

someone other than me. I counted her temper a blessing,
put it out of my mind, and ate everything placed before me.

"You are a glutton," White Bear sourly complained.

"No, he isn't." Skywalker glanced at me, winked. "He's
gathering his strength for the honeymoon."

White Bear pounded my back and I swallowed a large
lump of food that wasn't quite ready for swallowing. .

"That's right! Everybody give Tay-bodal anything left
in your bowls. He intends to wrestle a demon, he'll need a
lot of muscle. Especially the muscle hanging between his
legs."

White Bear nudged me with his shoulder. In a stage
whisper, he teased, "By the way, should you need a witness
while you fight to consummate the marriage, you might ask
Big Tree. He's a virgin. He'd appreciate—"

Big Tree slammed his bowl to the ground. "I am *not* a
virgin!"

White Bear leaned toward the offended young war chief.
He grabbed a chunk of Big Tree's cheek, pulled, and cooed.
"Yes, you are, baby-man."

Big Tree slapped White Bear's hand away and sat sulking, rubbing the offended cheek as the other men laughed.
I didn't laugh. I was studying Big Bow, trying to work out
what he was doing in White Bear's home. That he was
sitting close to Lone Wolf outwardly meant that he was in
White Bear's camp as a neutral. But Big Bow was a man
of strong opinions. It went against his nature to be neutral
about anything. During the course of the meal Lone Wolf
spoke of his concerns for the Nation, and in a roundabout
way tried to convince White Bear that in the interest of the
better good, for the sake of unity, White Bear should try to
appease Kicking Bird.

Big Bow nodded as if in full agreement. An attitude that
did not fit at all with what I knew about Big Bow. In fact,
the only thing that did fit was that Big Bow was seated as
far away from Skywalker as he could possibly manage.

I've told you that for years I had been viewed as a loner.

I was. But even my former hermitic habits fade in comparison to Big Bow. He was renowned for being antisocial and a-religious, and a stunt he pulled against Skywalker was the cause of his being driven into temporary exile. He wasn't banished, mind you, only sentenced to two years of life among the Comanches out on the Stake Plains. All of that happened just after he had earned the rank of To-yop-ke—war chief.

Owl Doctors, more than Buffalo Doctors, go out on raids. Not only are Owl Doctors useful as formidable warriors, they are also needed to make powerful medicine prayers before any fight. During the night prior to a dawn battle, nervous warriors generally consult with the Owl Doctor regarding any visions the doctor might have had concerning them. If a young man is fated to die the next morning, it's a good thing to know. Knowing a death-day enables a warrior to use his last hours properly, preparing his heart and cleansing his spirit. He will also be a better fighter, willing to sacrifice himself to save the others. It was during such an activity, Skywalker consulting with a young man concerned about his destiny, that the newly appointed To-yop-ke, Big Bow, made a swaggering fool of himself. A night camp just happens to be the worst possible time and place to air one's religious views, or in Big Bow's case, his lack of religious views. His boastful narration, his slurs against Skywalker's power and integrity, stole the heart out of everyone hearing him. The raid failed and the only one to distinguish himself in the face of this terrible defeat was Big Bow.

His victory won him no prizes. He was rightfully sent by Sitting Bear into exile.

"Go to the Comanches, you big-mouthed bragger. They don't have any religion either. Maybe after spending time with heathens, you'll come home a human being."

Big Bow spent the allotted time with the Comanches and, to everyone's deep chagrin, while he was with the Comanches he distinguished himself in a big fight against the Navaho. He came home dripping with war honors, completely unrepentant. Still, he didn't want to be with the Comanches anymore, so he had at least learned to keep his mouth shut. He continued to treat Skywalker and all of the Owl Doctors with utter disdain, but he refrained from accusing them of being fakers. But he still *thought* of them as fakers. Which was why he wouldn't sit close to Skywalker, wouldn't even look at him, and curled his lips back like a snarling wolf whenever Skywalker spoke.

It was difficult for me to equate such a self-centered person with someone likely to be worried about the unity of our nation. Anger burned within me over his presence here in White Bear's camp, Skywalker's home, and his arrogant treatment of Skywalker as if Skywalker was the interloper. But the thing that really made me angry was that he was allowed to get away with it. How could White Bear be so fickle? Didn't his brotherhood with Skywalker mean anything to him? Was his faith in me so slight that he was beginning to feel desperate for support? So desperate he could be grateful to a man as unpleasant and as condescending as Big Bow?

That rankled. So much so that my former hearty appetite died. I stood up and abruptly left. Walking out of the arbor, I didn't see Skywalker's head signal to Big Tree, or that Big Tree followed me until he caught up with me a few minutes later.

Although Big Tree came from a poor family, he was a nominee for the Onde class. Which said a lot about the young man I was surprised to find walking quietly by my side. He was incredibly young for such an honor. A nomination for a place among the Onde was an honor his father couldn't possibly afford to help buy for him, and like his title of To-yop-ke, Big Tree had earned the nomination and the means to pay for the required giveaways and feasts on his own. He was White Bear's chief lieutenant, and that meant White Bear trusted him with his life. It is the job of the chief lieutenant to guard the back of his chosen chief.

Not only in battle, but also during times such as these, when political strife caused a chief to look again at the men surrounding him.

Big Tree was short, somewhat slender. His face was as pretty as a girl's. And like a girl, he had a tendency to blush, even giggle. All of this was deceptive, hid the fact that he was deadly. Those who knew him knew that he was quite capable of blushing and giggling as he cut a man's throat.

When it became apparent to me that he would not speak until I spoke, I asked, "Is there something I can do for you?"

He tilted his head and answered flatly, "No."

We continued walking. When I could stand the silence no longer I stopped, and placing my hands on my hips I turned on him. "Would you mind very much telling me why you are following me like a shadow?"

"Skywalker ordered it."

"Why?" I shouted.

Big Tree shrugged lamely. "I don't know. I didn't ask."

We simply stared at one another for a space of minutes, and in that time I drew my own conclusions. Skywalker had most probably sensed my anger and, concerned, felt it was best that I not be on my own. My anger began to settle as I realized that perhaps this young man might possibly have the answers to the questions I had regarding two other young men of his age group.

"Big Tree," I began carefully, "have you ever ridden with the ones known as Stands On A Hill and Chasing Horse."

"Many times," Big Tree replied. "What of it?"

"I would like your opinion of them."

Big Tree placed his hands on his hips, twisted his full lips to the side as he looked off. Then he made a clicking noise with his tongue, shook his head. He glanced back at me, his tone terse. "You know about the trouble between White Bear and Kicking Bird?"

"I know they don't like each other."

Big Tree grunted, sucked at his upper teeth. "They liked each other pretty much until a few seasons ago. A season when it was White Bear's turn to hold the buffalo."

Big Tree's reference was to a method of hunting reserved for a time when one or more bands came together. Holding the buffalo is a misnomer. It's virtually impossible to contain a herd of buffalo that stretches for over a dozen miles in width. What a chief and his band of warriors actually hold are impatient hunters. It was the chosen chief's responsibility to prevent any and all random hunters from scattering the herd. Only when the chief had assembled enough men for a combined assault would he then lead the charge against the herd. All of his hunters would ride in a straight line, shooting arrows because the use of guns would stampede the herd. A great many buffalo could be taken this way. Enough to feed everyone and supply the Sun Dance camp its needed supply of tongues—both a delicacy and a part of the religious ceremony.

Big Tree started walking again. I fell into step alongside him.

"Kicking Bird's two relatives ruined that hunt," he said angrily. "They rode out before White Bear was ready. They fired guns and the herd went crazy, running everywhere. White Bear went crazy, too. As you know, holding the herd is a great honor and a great responsibility. By scattering the herd, those two not only ruined the hunt, they shamed White Bear. So he rode them down. When he caught them he whipped them with his quirt, killed their horses, and tore up everything they had with them—saddles, weapons, even their clothing. While he was doing this, they were shouting that they had only done what Kicking Bird told them to do. White Bear went even crazier, sent them back to Kicking Bird's camp on foot, beat up and naked. He had turned the shame back onto Kicking Bird.

"Much later, he found out that those two had been less than truthful. Kicking Bird hadn't even been aware of their mischief. He certainly hadn't told them to do it. White Bear tried to apologize, even gave Kicking Bird a lot of presents. But Kicking Bird, as I'm sure you're aware, can be a little"—he paused midsentence, searched for an appropriate word. When at last he found one he glanced at me and spat, "Rigid. Kicking Bird is rigid. Oh, he shook White Bear's hand, said there were no hard feelings, but there were. And still are. What Kicking Bird has never been able to understand is that White Bear is the kind of man who lets go his temper, gets it all out, and then it's over. He can't understand it because Kicking Bird is the kind of man who holds everything in. He never lets anything go. Therefore his anger is never over. Since that incident Kicking Bird has made it his business to provoke White Bear every chance he gets. White Bear always retaliates and it's gone back and forth like that between them for years now."

"So the two I've asked about are more than capable of lying."

"Oh, yes," he laughed. "The truth, as they see it, is relative to their needs."

"What about their cousin, Hears The Wolf."

"He's a good man," Big Tree said. "As a matter of fact, he's the only man I know of who has any kind of control over Stands On A Hill and Chasing Horse. He keeps them out of trouble most of the time and makes amends for them when they do get into trouble. I don't know why he bothers. I don't think he likes them very much either, but they seem to love him."

He stopped, looked at me curiously. "Why are you asking me these questions? Why does Hears The Wolf concern you?"

"I was told something. I'm having a little trouble believing it."

"Then take my advice," Big Tree snorted. "If what you heard came from either one of those two, continue to question what you were told."

"I wonder if you know the truth."

"It's more than possible that I do. But I won't tell you."

"Why not?"

Big Tree came to an abrupt halt and leaned toward me. I felt a twinge of distress. His too-pretty face was taut, his words clipped and angry.

"No To-yop-ke, no one of the Onde society, would *ever* speak to anyone about one of their own behind his back. You could get into a lot of trouble just asking me these questions. What I've told you about White Bear I've told because White Bear has given all of us his permission to answer should you ask. He said that you are our brother now and that it is your right to know everything pertaining to his history." Big Tree's voice became raised as he jabbed his chest with his index finger. "But now that you've dared to ask about another, *I* have the power to decide what I will share. If you have personal questions about Hears The Wolf, I would advise, and strongly, that you brace up your courage and ask him yourself."

Sound advice. He was right of course, not only wouldn't an Onde speak about another Onde, their lessers would be too terrified to do it. Stands On A Hill had just managed to slide in what little I had learned because he had supposedly believed he was giving fair warning to his cousin's lover. After he realized I wasn't that lover, Stands On A Hill refused to speak any further.

Big Tree left me alone to flounder, trying to work out just how I would tactfully inquire of a distinguished upperclass man his sexual preference. I couldn't think of a preference, but badly put or not, I knew I would have to ask. The question, I had to admit, was simply a curious aside, having nothing to do with the more important issue closer at hand. Nonetheless, it continued to drive me to distraction. Watching Big Tree's back as he walked away from me, I also wondered if he had been sent to me by Skywalker to divulge something that our subsequent conversation had missed entirely. The trouble with being given permission to ask questions, I found to my deep chagrin, is that typically the wrong ones are invariably asked. Still, I was more the wiser than I had been and I suppose I simply settled for that.

I was going for my horse, walking through the center of the village. It was time for me to journey back to Sitting Bear's camp and question Shield Woman and I was deep in my thoughts, centering on just what questions to put to her. As I mentally formed, then rejected, a flurry of questions, the bustle of daily life in the camp I was presently in failed to register in my consciousness. Only when I heard shouting was I jerked back to the present. People were streaming past me in a noisy hurry. I managed to grasp a running woman by the arm.

"What's the matter? What's happening?"

She answered in rapid-fire speech. "Black Shield! His son has been injured."

"How?"

"A horse knocked him down. Stepped on his leg."

"Where is the child now?"

"Black Shield's got him. The boy is screaming with pain."

I released the woman. She loped off. I marked her direction, knowing she was going to join the excitement encircling Black Shield's lodge. Once I knew which route would lead me to the place where I was needed, I hurried for my own lodge.

Crying Wind was standing just outside, holding Favorite Son on her hip. Her anxious face appeared and disappeared as the flow of running people past her. An adult being gravely injured would have brought out only the stoic in the population. Especially if the adult in question had reached a good middle age. But a child with the promise of a long life falling victim to a grievous injury was considered a major calamity to the parents, the family band, indeed the entire nation. Favorite Son felt his mother's anxiety and reacted to it in the manner of a five-year-old unable to understand. He was crying at the top of his lungs, and bouncing him around on her hip as Crying Wind was absently doing, only made the child cry harder. Trying to reach her through the rushing mob was like trying to swim against a torrent. When I managed it, she screamed at me over our son's wails.

"That little boy! That poor little boy. If he doesn't die he's going to be lame!"

I felt myself beginning to bristle, becoming irritated that she could so easily dismiss my singular talent. "Have some faith in your chosen husband, Woman."

She gaped at me, recovered from her moment of stunned silence, and then followed me inside my lodge and scolded me like a magpie.

"You can't do it, Tay-bodal! You must leave it to the Buffalo Doctors. If you treat him and fail, Black Shield will blame you. He's my blood cousin. I've known him all my life. He's the kind of person who holds a grudge. If you fail to heal his son, he will ruin our lives."

Crying Wind had been very busy during our brief time apart. She had the lodge so tidy, so organized that I couldn't find anything. Not without digging through packed cases and flinging contents around.

"Look what you're doing! I had everything just right. If I had known you were such an inconsiderate person, I would never have consented to marry you."

"Too late," I grunted. "White Bear has blessed the event of our future marriage in front of witnesses."

Ignoring her censure, our son's wails, I stuffed the necessary medical items into a carry bag. When I was ready to make my hasty departure, I faced her.

"I truly appreciate that you are a tidy person, my beloved. But I must insist that you do not extend this virtue toward my medical supplies."

Kissing her mouth just as she opened it, I effectively silenced her before she could berate me further. Then I dashed out, running swiftly for the distant lodge.

• • •

Long before I reached the lodge, even over the loud voices chanting prayers on his behalf, I heard him. Whatever was happening to him in that lodge, those attempting to make right what the weight of horse had made wrong were making his torment worse. The child's screams sent a shiver of cold dread through me which helped to block out the fact that if I accepted his case, I was wagering not only my tenuous reputation as a healer, but my entire life. If I failed, in recompense I would owe the parents of that child everything I owned. White Bear, as a matter of pride, would not allow his cousin to marry an impoverished, downfallen man. He would have no choice but to disavow the betrothal, drive me out of his camp. This was why Crying Wind tried to stop me. She knew the risks and the ramifications. But I knew as I hastened for Black Shield's lodge that if I did nothing to help that little boy I would never be able to live with myself, let alone make a life with a woman as worthy as Crying Wind.

Skywalker, Big Tree, and Quitan stood on the fringe of the crowd. When he saw me, Skywalker's tormented expression instantly changed, became glad. The three ran to meet me. Big Tree relieved me of the heavy bag I carried, and the four of us made a combined assault on the crowd, shouldering our way through, my three body guards shoving and pushing grief-stricken immobile people out of our way.

The Buffalo Doctors were already at work, waving feather fans and buffalo tails over the writhing boy. His father holding the damaged leg, lifted it toward the blessings and prayers the Buffalo Doctors intoned. Jagged white bone stabbed through the skin just below the knee. Lifting a leg in that condition was the worst thing the child's father could do. When my temper exploded, Black Shield did the second worst thing. He dropped the leg. The boy let go a long soul-wrenching scream that was raspy from the many screams preceding it. In my fury I did a most unseemly and

foolish thing for a man of my nebulous status. I began
laying hands on unnerved men, relatives and attending Buffalo Doctors alike, bodily hurling them from the lodge.
There were a lot of them. I was aided by Skywalker, Quitan, and Big Tree, who characteristically giggled with
delight with each body he tossed.

Black Shield was harder to get rid of. As Skywalker and
Quitan used their combined strength to stuff him out the
door hole he shrieked at me.

"Cripple my son and I'll have you, Tay-bodal. I swear
on my eyes, I'll have you!"

My shouted reply froze even the frenzied Black Shield.
"At least with me he has a chance at staying alive. Your
tender mercies were killing him."

His highly colored angry face instantly drained, became
chalky. Being told he had added to his son's torment caused
him to stumble in his strength and all of his anger against
me deserted him. Skywalker and Quitan were able to see
him out without further protest.

Huffing for breath, Skywalker turned toward me. "Tell
us what to do. We're prepared to help."

I was in no position to refuse. The fact that Skywalker
was a recognized Owl Doctor saved me from the fate of
the jealous Buffalo Doctors whipping the crowd into riot,
and from the rioting mob dragging me out and doing me a
terrible violence. They would be entitled to do that because
the father of my patient was not happy that I had taken on
the case and bodily evicted him from his own home. As a
healer belonging to neither healing society I was only allowed to attend the sick and the injured when the patient
or the relatives of the patient asked for me specifically. I
was walking on dangerous ground.

"You," I said to Quitan, "go to the creek. Cut thick
portions of cottonwood bark about this length." I indicated
the length with my hands. "I'll need three pieces."

Quitan nodded that he understood.

"Big Tree!" He jumped forward as if obeying a command from a superior chief. "Get a kettle. Fill it with water. Tell women to gather firewood. I'll need that water to be boiling hot. And give them this." I handed over one of my Taos jars, the one filled with solidified buffalo tallow. "I'll need that melted into a hot liquid."

Without a word, Big Tree followed Quitan out.

"What do you want me to do?" Skywalker asked.

"Pray. Use your best prayers to convince that crowd out there that conventional healing methods are being used. While you're doing that, stay out of my way."

The first thing to do was to stop the pain. The boy looked to be nearly eleven and was of a good weight. I gave him a strong dose of the herbs I kept already ground into a fine powder for Skywalker's needs. Because the child's need was immediate, I placed the powder under his tongue. I held his mouth shut in case he tried spitting the bitter powder out. But the child was shivering with pain, suffering so badly, his tearful eyes so anguish-riddled, he offered no resistance. His beseeching look, the silent plea for mercy in those dark, tear-brimming eyes nailed me through the heart more surely than any groan or whimpering sound he might have uttered. I crouched next to him and spoke softly against his ear. Gradually my voice, along with Skywalker's droning chant and the dissolved herbs, took effect. His face gradually lost its grimace, his eyelids became heavy, and finally were completely shut. His tear-dampened face turned toward me, nestled trustfully against my palm. Mercifully, he drifted off into a deep sleep.

I was halfway finished when Black Shield was allowed back inside. During the hour I tended his son, the calm, clear baritone of Skywalker's singing voice had rankled the man's nerve ends more than his son's piteous screams. With the boiled water, I had cleansed the break in the skin, washed away the blood. The melted tallow was poured into the abrasion, purifying the nasty wound. With the boy sedated, it was easy to maneuver and reset the bone, stitch closed the ruptured skin. The splints of stick supplied by Quitan neatly surrounded the leg. I was tying the cast tightly into place when the extremely ashen-faced father crept inside, answering Big Tree's summons.

"Is—is he going to be all right?"

I looked up from my task. "Given time," I answered. "And patience." I finished the last knot, sat wearily back on my legs, wiped the trickle of sweat from my brow. Taking a deep cleansing breath, I gave the thoroughly contrite man a series of instructions.

"For two days, he isn't to move from this bed. I will leave medicine against further pain with your wife. On the third day, I want him up but moving only inside the aid of your strong arms. He is not to try walking on his own. Not until I've examined him again. He will complain about the splint. He will tell you his leg itches. He might even beg you to untie it and remove it for just a little bit. Don't do that. No matter how much you're tempted, you're to let his leg itch. A small discomfort now will prevent a lame leg dragging behind him for the rest of his life. Do you understand?"

"Yes, Tay-bodal," he replied, eagerly nodding and quickly adding my position in his family, "soon to be the husband of my cousin."

His repentant attitude, his acknowledgment that I was practically his relative, served to lessen my open hostility. But I still remembered his threats against me. I have always been good with grudges when I could afford to be. Because I had gotten to the child before he had been damaged beyond repair, was able to treat him early on and countervail infection, in this instance I could afford to be. I raised my voice so that those crowding around outside the lodge could hear as well.

"You are to ask me before doing anything other than the instructions I have just given you. If you have any questions, any worries, do not hesitate to summon me. I tell you now that I am always available. Do not wait for a more courteous hour if this child needs me. To do so places your son at risk. I will blame you if he becomes sick with fever. Is that understood?''

''Yes, Tay-bodal.''

''You are a real hero.''

I pushed White Bear's weighty arm from my shoulder. ''No, I'm not.'' Embarrassed, I looked away from the group of men clustered around me, concentrated on the patch of ground between my feet.

''Yes, you are,'' White Bear insisted. ''Only a fool or a hero would have rushed in to tend that child the way you did. You are not a fool. You are a brave and competent man. A good doctor. From now on when I go out on raids, you're coming with me.''

I gasped in horror. I was a doctor, not a warrior. I had so devoted my life to the study of the complex mechanism that was man, I had never been on a raid in my life. I hadn't had the time, the inclination, or the necessary skills. (Or the courage.) It was a little late to expect me to muster together those gifts at this juncture of my life.

I lifted a defiant chin. ''No, I'm not.''

''Yes, you are.''

''No, I'm not.''

''Then you force me to tell Crying Wind that you're stingy. That you don't care about earning for her the many fine gifts the other women have come to expect. She won't like that.''

My only response was to stand there looking thoroughly appalled.

Quitan and Big Tree's arms covered my stooped shoulders. ''Don't worry. We'll protect you,'' the two laughed.

I looked eagerly to Big Tree, a young man who might be as pretty as any girl I'd ever seen, but was also mean enough to terrorize an army of howling enemies. ''Do you promise?''

"Absolutely. We're afraid of Crying Wind, too. We have been ever since she became a widow that first time. If we let it happen again, she'll be really mad. I think maybe I wouldn't want to be anywhere around her if you got wiped out too."

This from a man who had beaten almost to death a Cheyenne virtually twice his size.

Day three was getting away from me. I hurried home to stash my medical bag. Crying Wind was furiously employing a broom to the hard earth floor of my lodge, sweeping out rocks and other debris before she replaced my thin carpeting. When I tried to enter, she used the business end of the broom, stabbing me in my chest with the bundle of slender twigs.

"I was there for most of the time. When I couldn't stand it anymore, I left. But I heard what you did. Everyone was in a great hurry to tell me. How could you?" she cried. "If you hadn't been able to help that child, that mob would have torn you apart. And here was I, just getting used to the idea of being your wife. I'm warning you, I don't like being a widow. If you only knew how many men I fought off waiting for just the right one to come along, you wouldn't be so reckless with your life!"

Her words struck a nerve. But not the one she would have considered flattering. "You've had a lot of other offers?"

"Well, of course I have."

I worried my lower lip with my teeth as I considered, mused aloud. "Attractive women always get a lot of offers. Not simply two."

"I've had dozens, you idiot. Not just two. And I'll have you know—"

I flung the medical bag at her feet. "Good-bye."

"Now, where are you going?"

NINE

As I galloped toward Sitting Bear's camp, my mind was crowded with questions. First and foremost was the question Shield Woman had promised to answer, the riddle of the leggings. I felt I knew the answer already and was a bit too confident that I would be able to present this truth, lay it at White Bear's feet in less than a few hours. After I finished with Shield Woman I would go next to The Cheyenne Robber's prison lodge. Not only would I help White Otter pack up her few things, I would let her know that her honor had been completely vindicated. Proof of her innocence would be a prize to delight The Cheyenne Robber's heart and being happy, possibly he wouldn't mind the few tricky questions I needed to put to White Otter. Yet no matter how many various ways I mentally asked the number and the names of her other suitors, the image of The Cheyenne Robber's livid face rose up before me.

Then there was a second angry face, this one belonging to White Bear. I could clearly imagine the veins popping in his neck as I came into his camp with White Otter, but with her name cleared, he would have no choice but to welcome her into his safekeeping. Like it or not he would be publicly forced to announce himself as her protector should The Cheyenne Robber be sentenced to banishment. Knowing the kind of man The Cheyenne Robber to be, he would face certain death valiantly and without regret, but only so long as he knew that his beloved White Otter was safe and her child was recognized as his. If I could do nothing else for him, I felt confident that I could at least prevent a death sentence being passed on his wife and their unborn child.

The wonderful hope for my first round of questions was dashed moments after I entered Sitting Bear's camp and he greeted me with a sour expression.

"Get down, Son," he said formally.

To which I responded with equal formality, "Here I am, Father."

The atmosphere of his camp, the people pretending to go about their own business, was strained. Furtive glances were sent our way as I dismounted and Sitting Bear stood waiting with a posture that was ramrod straight. When both my feet were planted firmly on the ground, he turned and walked toward his chiefly lodge. My throat constricted. Something was terribly wrong and whatever that something was, Sitting Bear would only tell me privately and ceremoniously.

I sat inside his lodge, waiting with impatience as the subchiefs entered, took their seats. Sitting Bear proceeded to light the pipe of his high office, offering the smoke to the Four Sacred Corners, then to the earth and sky. Seated immediately on Sitting Bear's left, I was the last to smoke as the pipe was passed from man to man. I gave it back to Sitting Bear, who extinguished the smoldering tobacco in the pipe's bowl, and lay the pipe across his knees.

"What I have to say to your face is very serious. The woman you have come to speak to is gone. Her husband came for her last night and he made a big racket."

I felt my blood sink.

"This man accused you of many things," Sitting Bear continued gravely. "Vicious things. I won't bother to repeat what he said. I'm afraid that man hates you. He said to my face that if you go to his camp again you would regret it."

"But the woman?" I said a bit recklessly. "She promised me she would talk to me. Did she have anything to say?"

"No. She just sat on her horse looking pleased. Which wasn't an easy thing to do seeing as how her face was all swollen up," he snapped. "The thing is, you can't go near her again without his permission, and he has made it plain that you don't have his permission. If you try talking to her again, he will have every right to kill you. I'm sorry, I know this makes your task harder, and your days are running out, but that's the way of it."

Outside Sitting Bear's lodge a trio of women stood waiting for me. Two of them looked frightened, the one in the middle determined. She stepped forward.

"We were told," she said in a secretive tone, "that if we had information to share, that you would listen."

"That's right," I agreed. She motioned for me to follow and I did, following them at a discreet distance until we reached the relative safety of a stand of trees. Again, the more forthright woman spoke.

"We know of two things you might find of interest," she said, still careful to keep her voice low. "First, the second wife of Runs the Bulls wasn't as bad off as she appeared. While we tended her, she was awake and very agitated."

"She bossed us around," one of the more timid women interjected. The first woman quelled her with a look.

"That's right," the first speaker said firmly. "Then she ordered us to leave her alone." The woman then grabbed the hand of the third woman, pulling her forward. "Tell him," she said in a near growl.

This third woman looked hesitant, her eyes sending the other two begging glances. Finally she steeled her nerve and spoke in a small whispery voice, her words choppy.

"I saw her. Later. She spoke to boys. Gave them something. The boys ran away."

"I see," I said, for I did, quite clearly.

"Second thing," the first woman said, moving closer to me. "You said you would be interested even if it was silly."

I nodded that this was true. All three of the women looked hesitant: finally the first woman finished what she was about to say. "This has been a woman's secret for many years. Perhaps it will not help and my telling you does Sits Beside Him a great disservice, but her child, the young woman known as White Otter, was born too early."

I rode fast for The Cheyenne Robber's prison lodge. The guards weren't in any better a mood than Sitting Bear's had been. I braced myself for more bad news and I wasn't disappointed. They must have viewed me as a sympathetic listener, for they listed a score of complaints. The Cheyenne Robber was churlish—not an easy person for them to deal with. But their primary complaint was that he had too many visitors, mostly women, and White Otter's taking up residence had evidently set off a major altercation.

"I heard White Bear caused a scene," I said as I was escorted by two of the harried guards.

"White Bear wasn't a problem," one said flatly. "It's those women. Four of them got into a hair-pulling fight and we had to break it up. Have you ever stepped between warring women?"

"No."

"Well, don't. They're tricky. Worse than Mexicans."

"What were they fighting about?"

"You wouldn't believe it."

"I'm willing to try."

We stopped, the guard waving his arms as he spoke, or

more accurately, yelled. "They were fighting about who was the better natured."

"You are joking."

"You weren't here. Otherwise, you'd believe me. But I'm telling you that's what started the fight. One said that The Cheyenne Robber's chosen wife was spoiled and selfish and that he deserved better. Meaning, I guess, herself. The others agreed but cited themselves as the more logical choices for this living image of virtue. That's when they started to fight. It stopped being funny to us when blood and hair began to fly. We were forced to intervene and Kills With A Gun got the worst of it. They knocked two of his teeth loose and a well-placed kick bent him double. If The Cheyenne Robber hadn't stopped it, those women would have gotten us all."

"He jumped into the middle of that?"

"No," the guard said, his expression peeved. "He just stuck his head out the door and told them to stop before they made him *really* furious." The guard sounded a mirthless laugh. "Try to imagine it. His guards, men assigned to protect him, were being stomped into the dirt and his only concern was that we were being too loud with our noisy cries for help. He said the riot was upsetting his wife.

"Kills With A Gun's mouth was bloody and he was hobbling around with a groin swelling up the size of a Wichita watermelon, and The Cheyenne Robber was getting mad on account of his wife's sensitive nature. I'll be glad when this is all finished. I'm sick of The Cheyenne Robber, sick of being a member of his guard. I wish I were anywhere but here."

"I'm quite sure he feels the same way."

The guard sent me a sour look that clearly said he didn't believe me for a second. His words confirmed the impression.

"Why is everyone so worried about him? He's living a pampered existence and he's treating us as if we're nothing more than his servants. If I were sentenced to days of indulgence and had women fighting over me, I wouldn't be afraid of banishment either. But no, I was born under a black sign; no one ever accuses me of being anything other than stupid.''

He and his equally peevish men stormed off. I had to admit that from the guards' point of view, The Cheyenne Robber did seem unusually lucky. But no matter how it is dressed up, banishment is still a death sentence. Anyone so condemned was sent out naked, without a horse, without any type of weapon. I have never known of anyone who survived that terrible fate. The most horrific aspect is that with no one to see a banished person properly buried, there was no guarantee of life in the afterworld. Anyone other than the very young, or the very dense, knew that there weren't enough days of luxury to cover the cost of a human soul.

Life is a temporary adventure and must be lived wisely. The forever belongs to the Creator. He shares his home only with the worthy.

Those are the two things we Kiowa have always fervently believed. And that is why banishment was the ultimate punishment.

The Cheyenne Robber and White Otter were napping in the cooler air of the arbor. I stood for a moment viewing them in this vulnerable state. But even in sleep, White Otter curled against him, his weighty arm draped over her, he appeared ready to spring to her defense. It would be an attitude he would know constantly if they were banished and he was her only protection from the many enemies eager to kill them. As I moved closer, he heard me, coming fully awake, pushing her behind him with a fluid movement. Only when he recognized me did he exhale a relieved breath. White Otter, mewled awake, sat up knuckling her eyes.

''Forgive my intrusion.''

The Cheyenne Robber greeted me with a scathing expression. "If you're here on my uncle's behalf, spare yourself further trouble. I've told him and now I'll tell you, I will not send my wife away."

Considering my recent failure at Sitting Bear's camp, it was no longer in my power to take her away and place her in White Bear's protective custody. For a day that had opened with such delightful promise it was rapidly becoming too abysmal for words.

"I haven't come about that. May I come forward?"

He studied me for a moment. With an indifferent wave, he invited me into the shade of the arbor.

Sitting down, crossing my legs, I stared at White Otter's taut face. Even with her face screwed up with worry she was inexpressibly lovely. I knew I was right. It was inconceivable that such an attractive young woman had known only two suitors. The odds were high that men had begun offering for her following the first day of her first menses. It was paramount I know the names of these men.

"This is difficult for me," I said weakly. "I beg your patience."

I glanced at her, relieved that her expression was open and concerned. The Cheyenne Robber, however, was glowering. His attitude would certainly make anyone diffident, but there were things more important than his pride. As tactfully as I could I began to put my first question to her.

"I have knowlege of only two suitors, one of them dead, the other"—I nodded to The Cheyenne Robber—"present. As hurtful as this question may be for you, I need to know if there were others."

Lowering her head, shielding her face behind a flowing curtain of hair, she answered softly.

"There have been many. I've forgotten most of their names. Mostly they were old. Thankfully, my father listened to my mother when she told him they were too old. She said that he should choose for his only child a young man from a good family. A family that would bring him honor and a virile son-in-law to provide him many healthy grandchildren.''

''Tell me about the young men.''

She squirmed, looked hesitantly at The Cheyenne Robber. In a faint, tremulous voice, she said, ''There was Big Tree.''

I sat up smartly. The initial dismay I'd felt began to leave me when I heard The Cheyenne Robber chuckling.

''I knew about him.''

''You did?'' she gasped.

''Yes. He started talking about you during the first days I began to notice you, too. We settled the matter peaceably.''

''How?'' I blurted.

His expression became abashed. He squirmed. White Otter stared at him intently. So did I.

''We, uh . . . threw dice. Best two out of three.''

''What!'' she cried.

His speech accelerated. ''We're brothers. We couldn't just fight it out. Brawling would have made bad feelings inside the family. Besides, I won didn't I?''

Her face puckered with fury. ''Did you throw dice with Chasing Horse as well?''

The Cheyenne Robber sucked in a lung-load of air. I was a bit knocked back myself. The Cheyenne Robber recovered from the surprise first and he readied himself for a heated argument. White Otter, looking satisfied, was more than prepared to take him on. But as I didn't have time to politely wait out a lengthy lovers' quarrel, I cut them off.

''Please! White Otter, tell me about Chasing Horse.''

Their tempers deflating, they reluctantly turned their attentions back to me. The Cheyenne Robber held his tongue and his temper as White Otter took me into her confidence.

''Father thought he was all right, but he was a little confused by the relative who spoke for Chasing Horse. The speaker wasn't as flattering as a suitor's speaker should be. But even so, the speaker was a powerful man, well thought of. My father was excited about being related to him. Then White Bear showed up, speaking for The Cheyenne Robber. My father became even more excited. Suddenly Chasing Horse was no longer a subject my father wished to discuss with me. The Cheyenne Robber was all he talked about. He encouraged our courtship, allowed us great freedom in being together.''

The Cheyenne Robber took her hand, gave it a gentle squeeze. She glanced at him and smiled shyly, a blush growing in her cheeks. She was apparently remembering just how heated their courtship had become. Much like my own courtship with Crying Wind. Too much freedom and hot-blooded couples behave badly. Especially if they're in a secluded wood in the moonlight. Feeling my temperature beginning to rise and my pulse quicken, I shook my head, clearing my addled brain of the erotic memory.

''We were married,'' she said, her tone defensive. ''The only thing keeping us apart was the settlement of the bride price and then the announcement of our marriage at the Sun Dance. But Kicking Bird appeared, speaking for his other relative. My father became . . . confused and worried.''

We were all silent for a lengthy space of time, The Cheyenne Robber and White Otter remembering the subsequent events and I thinking long and hard about Runs The Bulls's dilemma. He'd suffered no confusion in the matter of choosing The Cheyenne Robber over Chasing Horse. True, Chasing Horse was Kicking Bird's relative as much as Coyote Walking had been. But Chasing Horse, aided by Stands On A Hill, had caused major trouble for Kicking Bird. Because of that, Kicking Bird refused to speak to Runs The Bulls on Chasing Horse's behalf. His failure to do so was all the evidence Runs The Bulls had needed to know that a marriage between his daughter and Chasing Horse would not necessarily align him with Kicking Bird or Kicking Bird's substantial prestige.

But White Bear had spoken for The Cheyenne Robber,

hence Runs The Bulls's initial excitement. With White
Bear's nephew courting White Otter, Runs The Bulls had
felt himself growing more important with each passing day.
Everything was perfect. Until Kicking Bird, ever eager to
prod White Bear, appeared and spoke for his own nephew.
Suddenly a very dull-witted man felt himself trapped inside
an ongoing feud and the power play between two illustrious
families. Whichever family he chose, the other would feel
slighted, might even become his enemy. No matter who his
daughter married, Runs The Bulls would continue on as a
man of the middle-class. He could not afford an enemy of
the Onde class.

I looked again at White Otter, one last question needing
an answer. "The person who spoke for Chasing Horse. Do
you remember his name?"

"Yes. I've known him all my life. When I was a child
he used to give me presents. But when I changed from child
to maiden, I didn't see him so much. Come to think of it,
I don't remember really seeing him again until he spoke
with my father about Chasing Horse."

"What is his name?" I barked.

"He is the man known as Hears The Wolf."

"And he used to give you presents?"

White Otter shrugged deeply. "He gives all children
presents. It's his way. I was just a child in the crowd of
children."

I remembered our walk through Kicking Bird's camp and
the numerous children swarming after Hears The Wolf. He
had been gentle with them and they appeared to adore him.
Children are notoriously hard to impress and presents from
a person they think very little of only serve to make them
greedy for more. No, the children I had seen tagging after
him had wanted only his attention, for they had genuinely
loved Hears the Wolf and he them. For someone who presented a face to the world that was vain, self-absorbed, he
seemed to have the hidden nature of a man owning remarkable depth. Just then my conversation with Big Tree

came back to me, in particular his bold advice that I question Hears The Wolf myself.

I jumped to my feet and with hasty words of assurance that they shouldn't worry—that everything would be all right—I left. Riding quickly I made for Kicking Bird's camp, certain with every fiber of my being that the mystery began and ended, there.

There was a new mood in Kicking Bird's camp, a threatening atmosphere. It overpowered me as I walked past lodges leading my horse by the reins. Incensed expressions immediately formed on the faces of people I passed. They then stopped whatever they were doing and fell in behind me, anger pulsating through the growing mob dogging my footsteps. A warrior standing just outside Kicking Bird's central lodge saw me and my surly followers. He quickly ducked inside the lodge. Just as I neared, Kicking Bird and a group of men came out, Kicking Bird not all pleased to see me as he walked toward me.

"You are no longer welcome here," he said, his mouth tight, his eyes hard on mine. "I know who you are and I now know exactly why you came here the first time. You came among us as a spy for White Bear."

The crowd surged tightly around me. In the group of men backing Kicking Bird, I was stricken by the sight of the conceited smile on Big Bow's face. I became livid. It was because of Big Bow that Kicking Bird had learned the truth about me. Now Kicking Bird knew too of my impending marriage to Crying Wind, knew that I was considered to be a relative as well as a member of White Bear's band. I could not deny that I was a spy.

"I can only ask your forgiveness," I said in as clear a voice as I could manage. "My only intention was to learn the truth. I know your heart, Kicking Bird, and I know your sorrow. I beg you to allow me to help in any way I can."

"Enough!" Kicking Bird cried, waving both arms. "I will not listen to more words from White Bear's pet snake.

You leave my camp. Now! And I warn you, if I ever see your face here again, I will kill you.''

As if on cue a team of six mounted warriors whooped in and grabbed me, dragging me up and placing me on my horse. Then holding my mount's reins they led me around and through the heart of the village while I hung on to the animal's mane and children hit my legs with sticks. Women shrieked, shouting obscenities concerning my parentage, mortally defaming my mother. Finally I was escorted in this manner to the edge of the village where a man grabbed a stick from one of the children. Lifting my horse's tail he used the stick to poke the animal, sending my horse into a startled gallop. Mocking laughter followed after me as I hung on as best I could. It didn't need to be said that if I had the audacity to return to his village, Kicking Bird would let his women have me, an appalling fate reserved for an enemy warrior felt too beneath them to kill with any degree of dignity.

Thanks to the wagging tongue of the egocentric Big Bow, my usefulness as White Bear's private agent was finished. Runs The Bulls had cut me off from Shield Woman, now Big Bow had made certain that I would learn nothing from Kicking Bird's relatives. There was nothing more I could do until the day of The Cheyenne Robber's trial but mend the pieces of my shattered pride and think. But I wouldn't get any thinking done amid the bustle of my home band. White Bear would rant at me for being a failure, and Crying Wind would be after me about the hides she needed to make our new home. Then there would be the anxious father of my newest patient, who, at my invitation, wouldn't hesitate to bother me day and night with his worries about his son's leg. I needed peace from all of that. I needed to be alone.

I rode leisurely in the opposite direction, away from all the camps, staying along the crescent edge of Rainy Mountain Creek as I gnawed the imponderables, moving my thoughts toward one view, then away again. I was so deep in concentration that I spared no thought to the horrific fact that I was a man alone, without a weapon and much too far from the safety of my home camp.

I was jarred from my musings, made aware of my predicament when I heard two horses, both of them running directly behind me and coming up fast. I reined in and sat looking over my shoulder. Fear began to seep through me that the riders were from Kicking Bird's camp, that his warriors weren't finished with teaching me a lesson, that they intended to send me back to White Bear beaten up and on foot. Just as I kicked at the sides of my horse, shots were fired. It finally occurred to me that perhaps they had a little more than a beating in mind as a bullet smashed into the trunk of a tree very close to me, showering me with woody fragments. Thoroughly panicked, I slapped the neck of my horse harder, and the poor tired brute galloped as fast as it could but only managed enough speed to keep me clear of the firing range. Again, I was riding in the wrong direction.

I had been in minor skirmishes before, but, never one for reckless daring, I knew the value of retreat. I retreated just as fast as I could. Shots zinged past me as I rode flat out. I dodged around trees trying to foil a clear aim. The nerves and flesh of my back were sensitive to its vulnerability. I fully expected that any second one of those bullets would strike me there. The expectation was more awful than you can possibly imagine.

They were gaining on me, the hoofbeats sounding louder and louder. There was no way I could make a stand even if I were inclined to fight and die the way a proper Kiowa ought to do. I had nothing, not even a knife. I had gone totally unarmed into Kicking Bird's camp. A friend visiting the camp of another friend had no need of a weapon. Besides, even if I did have a gun, chances are high I would not have attempted to make a stand. I didn't want to die like a proper Kiowa, I wanted to live. Live to be Crying Wind's husband and Favorite Son's father. Throwing that away for the dubious honor of dying like a proper Kiowa was not an attractive prospect. To my horror, the Washita River came into view and I was quickly running out of maneuvering room. I did not have time to panic further.

The head is a hard target to hit even in the best of times. Mine was bobbing all over the place because I was in a fast gallop and I have never been an elegant rider. My deplorable horsemanship may have saved me from having my brains blown out when a bullet scraped along the top of my ear. My back wasn't so lucky. A second bullet hit and stayed in my left shoulder, hurt like nothing I'd ever known, and bled prodigiously. The pain of being shot yielded to blind fear. Then there was a sinking weakness. As is my perverse wont, I was transfixed by analyzing the effects of being gun-shot as I fell sideways off my galloping horse.

I was still conscious when they reached me. I didn't see anything more than feet, and those through silted eyes as I lay belly down and very still, holding my breath, pretending I was dead. But I was listening. Unfortunately, they did not speak. When my lungs had had enough of being starved of air, my brain protected itself.

I passed out.

Waking up again was gradual, grudging. My head hurt, my shoulder was on fire, and I felt captured under a great weight that threatened all the bones in my spine. When my eyes opened, they were greeted by darkness and tiny fragments of light. I lay there concentrating on the weak light. That's when it occurred to me that I was under a pile of rocks. My assassins, believing my ruse, thought me dead. To cover up their crime, they had buried me.

I was as weak as a newly born pup and stank with that oddly coppery, acrid smell of dried blood. I lay gathering my strength for a good long time, gauging my heartbeat, clearing my mind. Then I began to push myself out of the grave. Deprived of the anesthetizing rush of fear, I felt every ache and pain while laboring to the point of exhaustion to free myself. I crawled away from the grave and lay gasping and spent. I touched the side of my head the bullet had grazed. That wound felt hard, caked with dried blood. I couldn't reach the wound on my shoulder, but carefully rotating it, it felt tight. That wound, too, during however long I had lain perfectly still and confined, had scabbed over.

Good. If I were very careful about not breaking open the scab, at least I would not bleed to death. The fact that the bullet lodged inside me would cause internal tissue to fester was a factor I drove from my mind. To survive the murder attempt, I needed help. Painstakingly, I stood to my feet. Then I walked.

Every step was an effort. Because of searing pain in my head, I could not hold a clear thought for longer than a second. Acting solely on instinct I staggered toward the river. The water was below me. My thirst felt like a hideous torture, and only the incline lay between me and my need. I stood on the edge of the bluff, trying to puzzle out how to climb down. My reeling stance took the decision away from me. I fell. The fall did little good for my already too dizzy head and no good at all for the wound in my back. The tumble down the bluff seemed endless, and then I rolled to the river's edge. Stupidly, I tried standing again only to fall once more, this time face-first into the water.

Like a flailing otter I turned over, coughing up the river water I swallowed. Breathing deeply, luxuriating in the gentle coolness of the water, I floated comfortably, too woozy to be concerned that I was floating away from the shoreline. It simply felt too delicious not to struggle. Through heavy-lidded eyes I watched the puffy white clouds drift and change shapes against the cobalt sky as the river took me in its lethargic current.

Tears filled my heart as I said good-bye to Crying Wind, mentally begging her forgiveness for making her a widow even before we were officially married. Her image filled my mind. At first she was angry, telling me off for having the nerve to die when I should have known how upset my dying would make her. Then she wept, calling my name. My heart filled with such sorrow, I felt it break. I was giving myself up to die and felt enormously sorry for myself. The sky darkened with a brief but spectacular sunset. Then the garish colors gave way to dark gray and one by one, stars began to appear. It's a wondrous thing to drift in suspension and watch stars come to life. I can describe it only as watching flowers come to bud and then bloom gracefully before your very eyes. It's a good thing to watch while giving up your life. It prepares you for the eternity you're about to enter. With my ears under water I could hear only the movement of the current and my own death-wishing thoughts.

Until a voice disturbed them. A male voice. One I knew quite well, yet it sounded . . . different. Finally I recognized it. It was Little Bluff's voice. But not his old man's voice. This was his voice when he had been young and vital.

"Brace up! This is not your die day. Prepare your heart. Be strong. You are still needed."

"But I am dying," I whimpered to the voice shouting at me from inside my own head.

"Others have lived through worse than this, and they did not have your purpose. Are you less than they? I tell you again. Brace up!"

"How, Father? How do I fight this?"

"Stay awake, you idiot."

This was the hardest order his spirit could have given me. I ached for oblivion. I had readied myself for death, had begun to think of death as a wonderful lover able to comfort me with a single tender kiss. Little Bluff took that from me. Tore it up and spoiled my final moments. I began to hate Little Bluff. In my fury, The Cheyenne Robber's troubles seemed insignificant. The threat to the Nation? So what. Great nations come, great nations go. What difference did one nation more or less make in the scheme of eternity? Why struggle so hard to keep a nation together when it made more sense simply to let go?

And Crying Wind. My darling Crying Wind. Another man would soon come along. A man more worthy of her. I felt lucky to have known as little of her as I had. But Little Bluff's command nourished that tiny spark inside me that didn't want to let go of my life, my love, or my nation. That spark flamed, and the fire kept me awake against my will as I floated past the trees on both shores. Reaffirming life, cottonwoods rained their seasonal down of seeds, the downy tufts of cotton floating on the water's surface all around me, glowing soft white, like millions of flower petals. Together we floated toward some unknown shore to take root, to live.

I thought of so many things. Thought about two years ago when many bands of the Nation wintered together in the Palo Duro Canyon. Kit Carson, with an army trudging through deep snow, invaded the canyon. Little Bluff, with the old men in the furthest encampment, was the first camp to come under fire. Those old men, most of them blind, put up a good fight holding Carson back, buying time for Little Bluff as he swung up onto a horse and rode it so hard in the freezing cold that its lungs bled. The animal was covered in its own foamy blood when Little Bluff finally reached the primary camp and told of the attack. Then, on a fresh horse, that valiant old man led the assault on Kit Carson, driving the invader out of the canyon, cutting Carson's fleeing army to pieces. I fought in that battle, too. I hadn't been afraid. Just crazy mad that our winter resting place had been violated. Remembering all of that, I felt myself getting crazy mad again. For a long time this anger kept me fully awake as the miles of shore passed as if it were moving, not I.

When I had exhausted that memory, my mind switched to the events of just last year when a man named Leavenworth came to us. He said the warring between the Blue

Jackets and the Gray Jackets was almost over and that the
Blue Jackets were winning. He said we had better make
peace with the Blue Jackets, let them come back into our
country if we didn't want trouble. White Bear thought what
Leavenworth said was funny. He told that man to his face
that the fort belonging to the Gray Jackets (Fort Cobb) had
been burned down and the Gray Jackets had run off back
to Texas. He boasted that he had helped to free all the
Comanches and other Indians the Gray Jackets had living
around that fort. Except for the Cherokees and the Chick-
asaws and the Wichitas. Those Indians didn't want to be
free. They wanted to be farmers. What kind of Indian didn't
want to be free? White Bear couldn't understand their attitude. He blamed it on the white man. He said all white
men were corrupt. They had ruined perfectly good Indians
and that if the Blue Jackets tried to build forts in our country, White Bear would burn down their forts and scatter
them the same way he'd scattered the Gray Jackets.

But Little Bluff considered Leavenworth's words of
warning carefully. So carefully that his thoughtful quiet
stunned into silence his bellicose subchief. At the end of
the day, no one was more surprised than White Bear when
Little Bluff signed Leavenworth's paper. And ever since
the signing of it, Blue Jackets have been moving steadily
into our country.

So far they weren't bothering us. They were too busy
remanning an old abandoned fort to the south (Fort Ar-
buckle), using it as a base while they built a new fort near
the Wichita Mountains (Fort Sill). I wondered mildly what
would happen to that new fort now that Little Bluff was
dead and unable to control White Bear, who was still determined to burn the forts down and scatter the soldiers.
White Bear would fully expect me as a member of his band
to be with him for all the burning and scattering. I was
groaning with the prospect when the crown of my head
bumped against the trunk of a fallen tree that lay extended
across the water. I knew that this collision was a sign that

there was to be no more floating. I had arrived at wherever it was I was supposed to be.

It took a long time, using the tree trunk to keep me upright, my head above water, I struggled to avoid getting myself trapped inside the clawing branches as I maneuvered toward the shore. Reaching the shallows, I dragged myself onto muddy, rocky land and lay on my stomach feeling unnaturally heavy after so many hours of being wonderfully buoyant. Falling into a deep sleep my last thoughts were to wonder how I would manage the strength necessary to walk the too many miles separating me from home.

Voices brought me sluggishly awake and the first sights greeting me were a twilight sky and a face. A face as black as a shadow. Then there was the hair. Thick and short and . . . fuzzy. I had never seen a black human being before. I went from being transfixed to mortally afraid. The black man held me in his arms, studying me as hard as I studied him. When he realized he was holding on to a live Kiowa and I realized he was no illusion, we both began yelling loudly and in unison. The black face whirled away and over my high-pitched screams of utter terror, shouted something in the *Ame-a-can* (American) language. A language I did not speak.

The white men I had encountered previously at various trading forts and had ventured to speak to were not considered by us to be true white men. We thought of them as Indian men because they dressed as we dressed, married into our nations, and spoke to us in our languages. This was proper because these men were in *our* country. It was only later that new white men came to us speaking their garbled language, demanding that we understand them, but there was no music in the sound of their language and it was still *our* country. Why should we bother to learn it? This second group of white men were forced to speak to us through interpreters and now, in the crucial moments when an interpreter was not available, I felt aggrieved by my own arrogance for I couldn't even hazard a guess at what was being said all around me. It was only later that the events of my rescue became known to me.

"He's alive, Captain!"

Captain Mac sat on his horse, irritably chewing the nub of a cigar. Captain Mac was the white officer in charge of the platoon of the Tenth Cavalry, a division made up mostly of ex-slaves. "Damn," he swore. "Just my blasted luck."

Finding a wounded Kiowa and failing to give aid would have been a serious breech to the terms of the Leavenworth Paper. The Blue Jackets could not afford a big war with the Kiowas. Captain Mac knew that whether he liked it or not, he'd better save me. He didn't like it but he had his men build a travois anyway and they placed me on it. I drifted in and out of consciousness as they transported me to Fort Sill.

I have no memory of entering the fort. There is only the memory of waking up and seeing a young man leaning over me. He seemed very earnest in his concern for my welfare and he was remarkably handsome for a white man. Except for a pair of heavy dark eyebrows that met at the bridge of his nose, he had no facial hair. On his head he had very dark hair that was almost as curly as that black man's hair. He studied me with brown eyes as round as Crying Wind's. His nose was perfectly straight and he had a generous mouth. When he smiled his teeth were very white and even. Happily, he spoke a little Kiowa. He sounded like a child, but I was too relieved that we could converse, even on such an infantile level, to judge him too harshly.

His hand touching his chest in the center of his exceptionally white shirt, he said, "Me, Harrison O'Kelly."

He said this many times, encouraging me to repeat it. But we don't have that peculiar tongue-rolling sound in Kiowa. I've never been able to manage it even though I came to understand it. The best I've ever been able to say is *Haw-wee-sun*. Or just Hawwy. During all the years I knew him he answered to it, so that was all right. But he never did tell me what thing or purpose a Haw-wee-sun was. It would have been very bad manners for me to ask. I had to wait for him to tell me. He didn't. I can only assume that a Haw-wee-sun must be something either truly exceptional or highly embarrassing, for I never knew another white man who was called that.

In Kiowa he said, "Doctor." But he failed to say which society, and even though my mind was in a muddled state, it was functioning well enough to register concern. I needed more than bleeding and prayers. I needed that bullet out of my back. I couldn't get to it myself, so as patiently as I could I told him he would need to take it out for me.

"Did," he said.

My eyes closed in relief. He was a practical doctor. I went back to sleep.

I woke up so weak that I was disoriented about time. I hoped this was still day four, since if this were day five or day six, everything would be all over. The Cheyenne Robber and White Otter would have been banished, the Nation would be dividing as White Bear declared war on Kicking Bird, and my lovely Crying Wind and our little son would be in the middle of the conflict. Overwhelmed by panic, I bolted upright in the bed.

The sudden action startled Hawwy. It must have truly alarmed him to be in a closed room with a fully awake wild-eyed Kiowa.

"How many days have I been asleep!" I shouted.

Hawwy canted his head and looked at me incomprehensively. Alarm melted from his expression, slowly replaced by concern and bafflement. Stilling the frustration welling inside me, I spoke again more slowly and in the baby talk I hoped he would understand.

"Days. How many me sleeping?"

He squinted his eyes, twisted his lips to the side as he puzzled out the question. Then it dawned. Looking enormously pleased with himself he answered, "One days."

A full breath I hadn't realized I had been holding left me in a rush. There was still time. If I could only manage to take out this one white man, then steal a horse, I might just make it home before The Cheyenne Robber's life, my life, were irrevocably ruined.

"I going now," I said, twisted my legs free of the light blanket, swung them over the side of the bed. Standing, I wobbled and began to fall. Hawwy caught me, holding me in his arms. The room was spinning and my stomach lurched with each rotation. Despair wafted through me. There was no way I would be able to fight even this one white man and my big plan of stealing a horse was laughable. My only hope was Hawwy. But the idea of trying to talk to him with his limited vocabulary was more tiring than the prospect of crawling through the fort looking for a horse.

"Need talking man."

He raised one of his massive eyebrows. He didn't understand. Panting, I tried again.

"Need talking man. Man talking for me and you."

"Interpreter?" he shouted.

His voice went through my throbbing head like a spike.

"All right," he said hurriedly and in Ame-a-can. But I understood him because he was nodding his curly head rapidly. Then he reverted to mauled Kiowa. "Restings you. Me came back."

I tried not to chuckle as he eased me back down onto the bed. When he had made me as comfortable as I could be, he ran out. I heard him speaking to someone standing outside the door.

Gathering my strength again, I tried sitting up in the bed in stages. The room was spinning badly but I sat there taking deep breaths until the spin lessened and became manageable. Then I began standing up in the same stages. With my arms stretched out before me, I staggered toward the solidity of the log and mortar wall. Reaching it, I collapsed against it, letting it bear my weight while I collected myself. The window was reached in painful, inching degrees. And when I reached it, I discovered the most wondrous thing.

There was a barrier. A barrier so transparent, so clear, that it seemed invisible. The window was divided into equal squares and the invisible barrier was framed inside the squares. I could see the outside world through those little squares. My hands touched one. It felt smooth and cool. The sky beyond the barrier was all clouded up, patches of blue showing. A breeze soughed through the trees that were standing only a few yards from Hawwy's little house. I could see the evidence of the breeze, marvel that I was witnessing this act of nature through a very un-natural device, but the breeze couldn't penetrate the clear barrier. Locked out, that lovely breeze couldn't toss my hair or refresh my clammy skin. I needed that outside air. Needed it badly. I felt sick and on the verge of blacking out again. The only thing that would help me, keep me awake, was that breeze. Balling my fist, I plunged it through the nearest squared barrier.

It didn't yield softly. Not the way an invisible barrier ought to do. This one made a big noise as it cracked, be-came jagged, cut open my hand and my arm. As I pulled my hand and arm back through the broken barrier, the breeze rushed in washing over me. I was enjoying my hard-earned treat, just standing there, leaning against the wall, watching my hand and arm bleed all over the wood-planked floor when Hawwy rushed in.

"Oh, my dear God!" he cried.

A vague smile curved my mouth as he caught me. Look-ing up into his emotionally fraught face, I chuckled and said.

"I understood you. You said a prayer."

"What?"

Another man, one I couldn't focus on, mumbled unin-telligibly. Hawwy answered him. Then this second man spoke to me, reaching my fogging brain in a near-perfect Kiowa.

"He says, yes. He was praying. He prays for you."

"Oh, no," I heard myself whine. "He's an Owl Doctor."

The man mumbled again and Hawwy laughed.

TEN

I was steady enough in my head to be stubborn about lying down on the bed. Lying down only made me weak and I couldn't afford the time to go through all that again. So Hawwy had me sit on a type of worktable while he stitched up my arm and the back of my hand, which the barrier had sliced open. There were a lot of things marvelous about Hawwy. But stitching up wounds wasn't one of them.

The bandages he used were the best. I had one around my head and another that crossed my chest and wrapped around my ribs. The bandages were of a white material I had never seen before. They were very light, extremely comfortable. The second thing were all the shiny instruments he had placed just right on a smaller table near him. His instruments looked very clean and were all different shapes, each tool useful for probing and cutting. While he worked I wondered how I could steal some of them without his noticing, or if I couldn't steal them, how much he would ask for them in trade. The only thing I had of value with me was my knowledge and judging from the way Hawwy stitched me up, he was badly in need of what I could teach.

For one thing, Hawwy used a black thread on a curved needle to do the stitching. Both things were bad. The funny shaped needle offered no control, so the stitches were sloppy. They would leave scars. But the cloth thread was the worst. Stitching made of thread would have to be removed, causing a patient—me—additional discomfort. Fine thread made of gut dissolves. There is never any need to remove it. When a wound sealed with gut threads heals, the threads just fall out. Hawwy didn't use soothing tallow to disinfect and lubricate the wound. He used a clear liquid that had a sharp odor and an even sharper bite when applied. When he bathed my cuts with that stuff, I yelled. The stinging, which felt as if I was being attacked by wasps, seemed to go on indefinitely.

Hawwy had a lot to learn if he ever wanted to be a proper doctor.

But what was really stupid, what snapped my patience and caused me to shout at him, was when a black man brought in a tray of *solid* foods and Hawwy offered me the tray expecting me to eat! Even the worst doctor knows that solid foods are no good for a person who has lost a great deal of blood. I spoke so rapidly to the interpreter that even he had trouble following me. But eventually he understood and translated for Hawwy.

"He says he wants broth made of livers and marrow. And if we have ever heard of onions, those should be cooked in the broth, too. He says he's a doctor and he knows what he's talking about. He also said that you're very young. Therefore he has decided to forgive you your many mistakes. But you're not to touch him with the alcohol anymore. He wants to know which jar contains buffalo tallow. He'll cleanse his wounds himself."

"Buffalo tallow?"

"Buffalo tallow, sir. He wants some."

"I—I don't have . . . tallow—"

"I wouldn't let him know that, Lieutenant. I get the impression he thinks you're a pretty stupid doctor."

With a muddled expression, Hawwy turned to regard me. The interpreter yelled at him.

"Lieutenant! You just keep looking straight at me and nod your head like you're gonna get him that tallow."

The interpreter spoke for a long time. Hawwy didn't look at me again. He stared at the interpreter and nodded his head so much, I worried for his brains swashing around inside his skull. Then he turned to the black soldier holding the tray of food and spoke to him through gritted teeth and a grimace of a smile.

"Corporal? Please go to the kitchens and fetch our guest a large bowl of beef broth. With onions."

The broth was weak and the large chunks of onions floating in it were fresh, not cooked into the broth as they ought to have been. In order to gain all the goodness from the onions, I had to chew them. It became clear when he bandaged up my arm and hand that Hawwy didn't have any tallow to lubricate and keep clean my wounds. White men. They're so backward, with a limited knowledge of doctoring and cooking. I tried not to dwell on their shortcomings as I spoke to the interpreter.

His name was Jenkins. He was a grizzled man, lots of wild brown hair and a short beard that covered up his face. He also stank of old body odors. But he spoke pretty good Kiowa and I was in no position to be snobbish. I talked to Jenkins, impressed him with the fact that if word was not immediately sent to White Bear of where I was, that I was safe, there would be a big war. But I meant a big war among the Kiowa. I couldn't seem to make Jenkins understand that part. He wrongly assumed I meant a war between the Blue Jackets and the Kiowa because I was such an important man. I tried twice to correct him. He still wasn't following me. Shaken, Jenkins turned and spoke to Hawwy.

• • •

"I have to get to that village, Lieutenant. He says I best get going now. That ole Satanta'll hit the war trail come dawn if he don't have word about our boy here."

"What will happen if Satanta goes on the war path?"

"We'll all get kilt! There'll be a mass-a-cree bigger'n Dallas. An' all cause of this here fella Captain Mac dragged in. Ole Satanta ain't nobody to mess with, Sir. An' what you been a doctorin' up so good is the number one boy in Satanta's tribal band."

"You're sure?"

"He said so hisself. An' if he said it, you can take it to the bank. Ain't no Kiowa gonna lie about somethin' that big."

Lieutenant O'Kelly ran a hand across his worried brow. "Mr. Jenkins, I think you'd better speak to Captain MacDougal immediately."

"You got that right. An' you best put away all your pretty little doctoring knives. That broth seems to have bucked him up. You don't want him gettin' his hands on nothin' sharp."

Lieutenant O'Kelly's face went unnaturally white. With a tremor in his voice he said, "On your way out, Mr. Jenkins, kindly double the guard on the infirmary."

Jenkins stood. "Gotcha. An' a pair of guards inside the infirmary wouldn't do no harm neither."

"Whatever you think best, Mr. Jenkins. You're our natives expert."

Jenkins's leaving panicked me. I shouted after him, "Are you going to White Bear?"

"Yes. Just as fast as I can ride."

"Make certain you tell him everything I said. It's very important."

"I will. I promise."

The wait was interminable. It was made worse because Hawwy was suddenly proving to be less than the gracious

host. He put away all of the instruments I wanted to talk
to him about, locking them up in a cabinet, pocketing the
key. Then two black soldiers came in. They each carried
the new rifles White Bear was all the time talking about.
Guns that didn't require the laborious task of being re-
loaded. White Bear had a lot of guns. He'd stolen them off
a Gray Jackets' wagon convoy. The Gray Jackets had intended those guns for the Caddoes, who would have used
those guns against us. That was what the Gray Jackets
wanted. Fighting the Blue Jackets, the Grays didn't have
the strength to protect Texas from raiding Kiowa and had
enlisted the Caddoes to protect Texas for them.

But White Bear got to the guns first, then had a big fight
with the Caddoes, punishing them for their betrayal. Next
he made it his business to tear up Texas using the Texans'
guns, punishing the Gray Jackets. White Bear was happy
with those guns for a long time. Until he saw the new ones.
The Blue Jacket guards accompanying Leavenworth had
the new guns. Leavenworth's guards put on a big show for
Little Bluff to demonstrate Father Washington's new
power. It was very impressive.

Leavenworth called these new guns *e-pee-tas* (repeaters).
He said they had been invented as the ultimate weapon to
end the war between the Blues and the Grays. The Grays
didn't have *e-pee-tas* and now the Grays were giving up
because these new guns were too fast, too accurate. The
new guns were the reason Little Bluff signed Leavenworth's paper.

I walked right up to one of the guards and stood very
close. I was as curious about the black man as I was about
the gun he held in both hands close against his chest. He
tensed, held the gun tighter. He tried not to look at me, his
eyes darting like startled minnows, beads of sweat breaking
out and shining against his dark skin. A nervous twitch
tugged the corner of his full mouth. He had a different smell
from Hawwy's. And Hawwy's smell was different from
mine. Amazing. Three different types of human beings,

three different odors. The black man's eyelashes were fascinating, too. They were short and curled up. My interest in his hair was uncontrollable. It was very black. So black that the sunlight from the window gave it no other color. Not like my hair, which would shine silvery blue, or Hawwy's, which showed bits of red. And the curls peeking around his soldier cap simply begged to be touched. When I reached out my hand, the nervous soldier jerked back and before I knew it, the muzzle of his repeating rifle was hard against my chest.

"Private Washington!" Lieutenant O'Kelly bawled. "Put that gun down."

"But he gonna take my hair, Sir!"

"He doesn't have a knife, Private."

"Please, Lieutenant," the black man whined in a curiously high voice. "Make him leave me be."

I was startled by both his name and his reaction. *Washington.* Was this the man the Blue Jackets always used as a threat against us? The same Great Father Washington who would be mad at us for raiding wagon trains on the Santa Fe? For pestering Texans? Was Father Washington only a sweating black man pointing a gun at me? And because of the gun jabbed hard against my chest I was very compliant, standing rock still, my hands raised level with my head. Hawwy lightly touched my shoulder and I moved only my eyes in his direction.

"You scaring he," Hawwy said in a quiet tone.

"Father Washington?" I laughed. "He has the gun and I'm scaring him?" My comment was too fast and too fluent for Hawwy to follow.

"You scaring he," Hawwy said again. "Tay-bodal sit."

His request made me feel like an errant camp dog but I had no choice but to obediently follow at his heel. Sitting down glumly, Hawwy and I stared at each other. My frustration was getting the better of me. There were so many things I wanted to say to Hawwy. So many things I wanted to ask. But the barrier between us was just like the barrier in the window; clear, yet tangible, and any attempt to reach through, dangerous. Then there was the worry of White Bear's reaction to Jenkins riding into his camp. I could only pray that White Bear would at least have the courtesy to hear the man out before shooting him.

The close air and too many people breathing it was getting to me. My head was swimming again and I was very thirsty. I managed to convey both of these things to Hawwy, who relieved one of them with a cool drink of water. The second he seemed to worry about for a long time. Finally, feeling the need for fresh air himself, he helped me to stand and with a command to Father Washington, who sprang to open the door for us, Hawwy led me outside to the covered porch.

A rocking chair is a frightening thing for someone who has never sat on one. At first I thought it was my head behaving badly, moving back and forth. When I realized it was the chair, I cried out and tried frantically, arms and legs flailing, to extract myself. Before I could do damage to all of Hawwy's stitching, he jumped from his chair and held me down in mine, speaking calmly and slowly in Ame-a-can. Having no idea what he was saying, I depended heavily on the calm meter of his tone. When he could trust me not to pitch another panic-filled fit, he eased himself back to the other chair and sat down. With a pleased grin on his face, he rocked back and forth, back and forth. It made my stomach roll just to watch him. In the meantime I kept my arms on the wide armrests, hands holding on to the ends with a white-knuckled grip and my feet pressing hard the flooring of the covered porch. The only things I enjoyed during our stay on the porch were the shade, the wafting breezes, and my view of the infant Fort Sill.

There wasn't much to see during those early days. There was a sawmill churning out planks of wood for the construction of planned buildings. The only solid buildings

thus far were the infirmary, the big cook house, the barn
for the blacksmith, and the commander's office. All the
men lived in white canvas tents. The officers had nice big
tents, the common soldiers little two-man tents, all of those
tents set in perfectly straight lines. The fort was laid out on
an open plain, meaning there were no protecting walls.
White Bear could burn this place down easy. Small wonder
the mere mention of his name had sent the interpreter into
a flap. This place was indefensible. I could not see the
oppressive danger Little Bluff had seen compelling him, for
the survival of our nation, to seek a peaceful coexistence
with the whites. From what I saw, we hadn't actually made
a peace treaty with white men. We'd mistakenly made
peace with black men, who outnumbered the white officers
by at least twenty to one. Knowing White Bear, this fact
would occur to him just as quickly. And any treaty made
in error wasn't viable. White Bear's reaction, when his current troubles were all cleared up and he was elected as our
new principal chief, would be to kill off the few whites and
then tell the blacks to give him all of their guns and horses
and go away. Honoring Little Bluff's word given to Leavenworth's fallacious treaty, White Bear would cordially
grant the black men their lives. But only once.

I peeked at Hawwy. It made me sad in my heart knowing
White Bear would kill Hawwy. He was such a young man.
And he meant well. But White Bear's killing him would
not be White Bear's fault. That blame lay with Leavenworth's misrepresenting himself and his paper to Little
Bluff. Leavenworth had not mentioned that the land Little
Bluff conceded was for the use of black men. He'd only
talked about whites. Leavenworth was a liar. His paper was
a lie. Even Lone Wolf and Kicking Bird would agree with
White Bear on that. Poor innocent Hawwy. I could feel
only sorrow for him. And as he was a young man not long
for life, I determined I would not cause him too much trouble. No matter how ignorant he proved himself to be as a
doctor, I resolved not to embarrass him by pointing out his

errors. A man needs to die feeling proud of his life. Besides, I was growing stronger by the hour. Whatever he did to me, I knew I was gaining the strength to survive it.

After a few more moments of sitting frozen in that terrible chair, I grew weary. Hawwy helped me back inside and I gratefully lay down on the bed. He dismissed Father Washington and the other black man. Then I watched with drowsy amazement as Hawwy raised the barrier in the window and fresh air rushed in, cleansing the small room. Hawwy placed a light blanket on me, and as I drifted off into much needed sleep, I made another resolution. To repay Hawwy for all of his kindness to me, I made a promise to myself that I would not be there when White Bear killed him.

When I woke much later the room glowed with a soft light. The light came from a strange source. A tiny fire behind the same kind of barrier in the window, but this barrier was shaped like a buxom woman with a big butt. There was a murky liquid inside this container that seemed to feed the small flame. I lay there watching the small flame, completely fascinated and thinking what a wonderful present this would be should I manage to steal it and give it to Crying Wind. I easily imagined the pleasure on her face as I presented it to her and then the pleasure of the reward she would give to me.

Hawwy was sleeping, curled in the fetal position on a small bed near mine. When I stirred, his eyes popped open and we lay there looking at one another.

"Thirsty," I croaked.

Dutifully, Hawwy unwound himself and fetched me a drink, holding me up by the shoulders as I drank every drop of water in the metal cup. Then we both settled down again. Hawwy back to sleep, me lying wide awake with all my many worries.

I had been right to worry. Jenkins had gone to White Bear with an escort of a dozen black troopers. Disconcertion was rife in that camp twenty-five miles from where I lay convalescing. The black men got the worst of it. Surrounded by inquisitive Kiowa, those poor souls were touched, their strange hair pulled and their flesh rubbed hard to see if their color would stay on if scrubbed. Their curiosity had Jenkins's troopers begging either for mercy or the right to shoot in self defense. But Jenkins wouldn't let them shoot nor could he save them from the mob. He was too busy defending his uninvited presence in the camp to an insulted and livid White Bear. If Skywalker hadn't intervened, White Bear would have killed Jenkins immediately. It was only because of Skywalker that White Bear heard Jenkins out. Then the interpreter and his terrified and slightly pummeled troopers were held under close guard as White Bear summoned the outlying chiefs, Kicking Bird included, and those chiefs discussed Jenkins's message and argued about it all through the night.

"This changes nothing," Kicking Bird said adamantly. "The Cheyenne Robber's trial is tomorrow."

"You fool!" White Bear shouted. "Tay-bodal has proof of my nephew's innocence, that's why your agents tried to kill him."

"His being shot has nothing to do with me," Kicking Bird retaliated. "I have no knowledge of any proof he might have for or against The Cheyenne Robber. And I certainly did not send anyone after him."

"Then why was he attacked outside your camp?"

"It did not happen outside my camp. I heard no shots."

"You liar!"

"Don't you accuse me of lying."

"PLEASE!" Lone Wolf shouted. "This is getting us nowhere."

"Lone Wolf is right," Sitting Bear said. "This fighting among ourselves is disgraceful. What we must do is review the facts calmly. Fact one." He raised an index finger. "We have a useful person all shot up and in the hands of the whites. If only for that reason, we can't leave him there. Fact two.'' A second finger joined the first. ''If it is true what White Bear says, that Tay-bodal has information pertinent to The Cheyenne Robber's trial, we must hear what he has to say. For these two very sound reasons, we have to think about Tay-bodal's welfare. The trial must be postponed. Now, we'll vote on those two things.''

He lowered his hand and went quiet while everyone settled down and mentally mulled over the facts presented to them. When Sitting Bear believed everyone was of a cooler temperament, able to make an unbiased decision, he called for the vote.

''Everyone in favor of Tay-bodal's immediate rescue, raise your hand.''

Had I been there to see it, I would have been enormously proud of the voting. All hands went up.

''Those in favor of delaying the trial until Tay-bodal is able to speak for The Cheyenne Robber, raise your hand.''

That vote count wasn't as flattering. As a matter of record, it barely passed. But it did pass and the trial was duly postponed. The Cheyenne Robber was given a few extra days of idyllic comfort in the arms of his beloved.

But my own beloved was in a snit that I had allowed myself to be shot and taken prisoner by the whites. When White Bear eventually emerged from the council, Crying Wind was all over him like a worrisome rash. She insisted on being included in my rescue. White Bear refused. That was a bad chiefly decision, and she let him know it at the top of her voice. To protect himself from total humiliation, he pointed out to her that it would be unseemly for a lone woman to ride off with so many men. Being a lone woman with an army of men would give her a bad reputation. Crying Wind countered that other women would go with her.

''This is not a camp move!'' White Bear thundered. ''This is a rescue party.''

''Fine. Then give me and the other women coming with me, guns.''

"Riding with a pack of armed women is more dangerous than riding into the whites' stronghold!"

"Then we'll arm ourselves and ride behind you."

That stopped him. He stood there with his mouth hanging open, as a clear picture formed in his mind. A picture of himself riding to my aid with armed troopers in front of him, dangerously armed women to the back of him. If one of the guns in the hands of a woman accidentally went off, the nervous soldiers would believe themselves under attack and start shooting. The women would fire back. With himself and his men directly in the middle of all this mindless firing, it would be like being caught in the middle of a free-for-all turkey shoot. White Bear hastily relented. The women could go. But none of them would be allowed a gun. Or luggage.

That last part was treated with a silent contempt. How like a man to expect women to travel that far without the necessary changes of clothing, hair brushes and hand mirrors, soap for bathing, pots of sweet floral scents, and a bit of jewelry to dress up in before reaching the fort. Did he really expect them to present themselves to the whites as a swarm of unkempt wild women? And what about food? Men might be content with slabs of dried meat and a small pouch of drinking water but women had more refined tastes. When White Bear clambered out of his lodge a few hours later, having had only that scant amount of sleep, he was bolted awake by a quick hard slap of reality across his aghast face.

"You cannot take those mules!" he thundered.

"Yes, we can," Crying Wind said with a dismissive tone. "There are five of us and all of our things. With great sacrifice to ourselves we've kept our luggage limited only to the necessities. These three mules will be all we require."

"You can't have any mules!"

"Why not?"

"I stole them from the army. They'll demand them back.

I think a lot of Tay-bodal, but he isn't worth three good mules.''

Crying Wind and her cohorts ignored him, kept on packing their bundles onto the heavily burdened mules in question.

"If you're so worried about your precious mules, we'll hobble them away from the fort. The soldiers will never even see them. Now stop yelling and go get the men awake. We women are ready to leave.''

Skywalker related all of this, word for word, to me weeks later. Fortunately for my own well-being, I had plenty of time for rest and peaceful thought. White Bear in the meantime was being sorely tried. There is only a one-day fast ride between Fort Sill and the Rainy Mountain. But hampered as he was with women and a mule-train in tow, White Bear endured a hard day and a half's slog.

The next morning I felt strong enough to eat real food. Besides, that broth I had been drinking for my meals was terrible, I was glad I didn't need more of it, and I was curious about what white men ate. The breakfast was odd, but good. Flapjacks, Hawwy taught me to say. And coffee. As much coffee as I wanted. But as I told you, I've always been leery of coffee, so to be polite, I had only one cup. Lunch and dinner was the same food. Meat and beans, with more beans than meat, and cooked together in a type of peppery gravy. All of this was served on rice. It was strange that white men ate rice the same way as the Caddoes. But the corn bread, almost like the corn bread the Wichitas ate, was the best. I ate a lot of that. And I drank cow milk. It was good. Very smooth.

The fort had three interpreters, Jenkins being the primary interpreter-cum-scout. Jenkins spoke Kiowa, Cheyenne, and Arapaho—and all of those reasonably well. The second interpreter only spoke Cheyenne, and the third was a young Texan named William Dilly who spoke fluent Comanche. I speak very good Comanche myself along with passable Navaho and enough Cheyenne to get by. I've never tried to learn Arapaho. I've always held the opinion that Arapaho was purposely complicated. Besides, it sounded too much like the Arapaho just made it up as they went along. Anytime I ever needed to talk to an Arapaho, I used my hands. Even *they* couldn't complicate a traditional hand sign.

Of the three interpreters, I liked Billy the best. He was easy to be with and he seemed to genuinely like me. The other two were pleasant enough but they remained guarded when in my presence, almost as if they expected me to attack them. Billy told me stories, made me laugh. We ate together out on the porch and when I refused to sit in the moving chairs, he sat on the floor of the porch with me. This showed me that he was a very considerate person and in my culture we have always made room for anyone who proved himself to be considerate.

Billy was a tall, slender young man with a long, curved nose and thin lips. He constantly wore a shapeless black hat pulled down on his head. His nose and his lips, when his head wasn't turned away, were all I could see of his face. It was obvious by the way he kept his face hidden in the shadow of his hat that he wasn't comfortable with anyone looking at him. Because he was considerate to me, I returned the favor by never looking directly at him, but I studied him closely whenever he was turned away from me.

His hair was long, dark brown, and left untied. He wore white man's trousers, the cuffs stuffed into the boot tops allowing him to show off the ornately decorated hand-tooled designs worked into his expensive boots. He wore every day the same faded plaid shirt, but the article of clothing he was really proud of was a gray canvas material coat that hung all the way down to his feet and was always unbuttoned, flapping to the sides, the gun in his side holster in full view as he strode through the fort. He looked dangerous and I couldn't help but notice the way soldiers avoided him and walked away quickly as he approached. Odd that they would treat one of their own in such a manner. It made me wonder if Billy was an outcast.

Whatever he was, I liked him. He was funny, especially when he spoke. Being a white man, his mouth, tongue, and throat were all wrong to speak clearly. He annoyed me slightly when he threw Ame-a-can words into our conversations. His hand signing was completely accurate and he used his hands in the required way as he spoke to me. So I intently watched his hands while he spoke. Because I had come to like him, I told him in confidence that trouble might be coming and that maybe he should go back to Texas.

"Naw. I'm an orphan. I've sucked the tit of Mother Texas bone dry. Besides, the army needs me to talk to the Co-manch up on the Anadarko. They me pay cash money for that. I'll take my chances an' just hang out here with you Ki-o-ways. Ya'll ain't as mean as the Co-manch. Plus you got real polite manners. If Injuns is gonna get me, might as well be Injuns a man respects."

"Thank you, Billy."

"Welcome, Meat."

Meat, that's what Billy called me after I explained to him in Comanche the Kiowa meaning of my name, Tay-bodal (Meat Carrier). I didn't take the abbreviation of my name as an insult. It was just another instance of Billy being Billy.

That night, following supper, all that strange food started playing games in my guts. Hawwy's too. After a while the air inside the doctor house became so rank that Hawwy opened the window. It no longer mattered if I escaped or not. We had to breathe. In our beds, we chortled about our buttocks' explosive condition until finally we went off to sleep. The next morning was flapjacks and coffee again. I ate quickly because Hawwy had promised that I would be allowed to bathe before he applied my new bandages. I also complained about my teeth.

Kiowas have always been fastidious about hygiene, bathing twice, sometimes three times, a day and enjoying sweat

baths to purge the system. But we have always been inor-
dinately fastidious about our teeth. We used salt, rubbing
it over teeth and gums. Hawwy was getting pretty good at
sign and I made the teeth cleaning sign. Understanding,
Hawwy gave me a wonderful present. My first toothbrush.
It was made of wood with tiny bristles in it. But the teeth-
cleaning powder wasn't so good. It tasted nice but it didn't
clean my teeth properly.

Stripped down to skin, standing behind the doctor house
dousing myself with buckets of warm water to rinse off the
sudsy lather, I attracted a crowd of gawking black men.
Had I known what their brothers endured in White Bear's
camp, I would not have been as peevish about their staring.
At least none of them tried to touch me or steal chunks of
my hair. But their watching and discussing me while I stood
naked and wet did make me mad, and when Billy realized
this, he sent them off rather quickly. Hawwy tended me
after I dressed, and with a full stomach, clean body, and
fresh bandages to protect my wounds, I felt almost as good
as new.

The three of us decided it was much too nice a day to
huddle inside so we took to the shady porch. Billy sat down
beside me, both of us sitting cross-legged on the floor.
Hawwy went straight for the nearest chair. The three of us
enjoyed the day, talked for hours. Billy was an invaluable
help with my talking to Hawwy.

"It was lucky that your wound healed over before you
went into the water," Hawwy explained through Billy. "If
you had gone into the water with a fresh wound, you would
have bled to death. Water causes blood to flow faster.
That's why menstruating women should never bathe until
their menstrual time has finished."

I looked at him for a long time. What he said was fascinating, but hard to believe. Menstruating Kiowa women
bathed all the time. Nothing untoward had ever happened
to them. The only restrictions I knew of were that they were
never allowed around men during their time of the month,

nor were they able to eat undercooked meat. Blood in the meat was dangerous for them. Water purified, made a stay in the women's lodge with other women bearable. It gave me the shivers trying to imagine a lodge full of women not bathing for days. How utterly savage.

"The second lucky thing," Hawwy continued on through Billy, "was that by being in the water, your wounds stayed clean and free of maggots."

"No, no!" I shouted, unable to contain myself through more of his nonsense. "Maggots are good things. They eat away putrid flesh, prevent blood fever. I use them all the time."

After Billy translated, Hawwy went quiet as he stared at me, rocking in that chair that I refused to have anything more to do with. Rocking chairs were bad for my stomach and my head. Sitting on the solid floor of the porch was infinitely preferable. But watching Hawwy as he rocked made me feel equally queasy so I looked away feeling a little sad that he didn't believe me about maggots any more than I believed him about water drawing blood. To ease an embarrassing moment for us both, he changed the subject. He talked about something I could believe.

"The bullet was lodged in your muscle, touching but not imbedded in the bone. I could feel it just under the closed-over skin. I cut it out without any trouble at all. You are a very lucky man."

"The tools you use," I said hesitantly. "Where do you get those?"

"Medical school."

"Is this a place I can go to trade for some of those tools?"

"No." Hawwy laughed. "That school is in Boston. A long way away. But I could give you two tools."

"Really?"

"Yes," he said, smiling. "A fellow doctor should be well equipped."

Hawwy rose and I sprang to my feet. The three of us

went inside the little doctor house, and I took my time as Hawwy, through Billy, explained the uses for all the tools. It was hard deciding just which two I would choose out of the many Hawwy showed me. Finally I chose a sharp-edged cutter and a tiny spoon-shaped probe. Hawwy was so pleased by my wise choice that he even gave me three rolled-up balls of the bandaging material and a lot of the square-shaped pads that went under the bandaging. He gave me a small leather bag and I carefully placed all of my treasures inside it. Hawwy was a good person. I decided as I tied up the leather bag that I would not allow White Bear to kill him after all. Hawwy had given me valuable gifts. I would give Hawwy his life. We would be even.

Billy stood looking out the window in a trancelike state. Then he started yelling to Hawwy in Ame-a-can.

"Holy Jumpin' Judas! Satanta's here! An' he's got an army an' a whole load a' women with him."

Hawwy started for the window, and I ran with him. Our three heads wriggled around as we competed for position, tried to look out that single small window, the barrier in our way. When I saw her, I couldn't believe it. But my heart raced with love and pride. She was so beautiful. And she had come all that way for only one reason.

Me.

"My wife!" I shouted, excitement ripping me apart. "That's my wife, Crying Wind."

"Which one?" Billy asked.

I tried to point, almost putting my hand through the dangerous barrier again. "I want to go outside. I want her to see that I'm all right."

Billy hurriedly related all of this to Hawwy. Hawwy was only half listening. He was staring hard at the impressive procession.

"My God, they are splendid," Hawwy breathed.

"Yep!" Billy crowed. "Ki-o-ways are the best of the best. Wild as an ingrown hair, an' with the manner of kings.

You can go to Glory feelin' real privileged if a Ki-o-way
has lifted your hair from yer noggin'."

I badly wanted to go outside. Rudely, I pulled Billy's
arm and restated my fervent request. The second he finished
translating, the three of us were all heels and elbows going
for the door and then comically trying to squeeze through
it all at the same time.

Had I not been so impatient for her to know that I was
all right, I would have done the civilized thing: stood quietly while the fort commander and his officers received
their important guests with speeches of welcome. But
where Crying Wind is concerned, I'm a bit of a barbarian.
I couldn't wait for all of those speeches. I waved my arms
overhead and shouted at the top of my voice. White Bear
and the others ignored my unseemly display, grimly dis-
mounting, stepping forward to greet the commander with
the customary handshake. Crying Wind kicked her horse
and, with the other women following her, rode in a gallop
toward the little doctor house. I ran down the three steps
and met her just as she jumped free of the horse.

She came into my arms so hard she almost knocked me
down. My arms went around her and I hugged her tightly,
lifting her off her feet, rotating both of us as we embraced
and she wept, her tears bathing my neck.

"I thought you were dead," she sobbed against my ear.
"I was so afraid. And—and then the soldiers came—"

"I almost did die," I crooned. "But I fought off death
because I couldn't leave you."

She wriggled, forced me to put her down. Then she stood
glowering at me, angrily flinging tears from her face with
the back of her hand. "Don't you ever! Ever! Do that to
me again. I deliberately chose to marry a peaceful man, a
doctor, not a warrior. And what does this peaceful man do?
This doctor I'm so proud of? He goes off and gets himself
shot."

"Beloved—"

"Don't you dare interrupt me when I'm yelling at you!"

Her eyes cleared and in that second she saw the bandages,
the one around my head, the big one covering my chest
and ribs. Both hands flew to her face, covering her gasping
mouth and most of her nose. Inside her hands, she cried,
"How many times did you get shot?"

"Twice."

Her knees buckled. I managed to catch her mid-swoon.
Oddly enough I couldn't manage her weight as I had so
easily done a brief moment ago. Hawwy and Billy helped
me get her up onto the porch and then into the doctoring
house, jabbering women following behind. We laid her on
my neatly made bed and Hawwy fetched a small vial from
his medicine cabinet. He held this little vial under Crying
Wind's nose and one whiff brought her instantly awake. In
my great concern for her, which lasted a great deal of time,
all of it spent hugging and kissing and reassuring each other
that we were both alive, well, and together, I didn't notice
that Hawwy was staring at a young woman in an open-
mouthed way. Hawwy's stare was directed at Cherish,
White Bear's sixteen-year-old niece and the blood sister of
The Cheyenne Robber.

We call that stare the Thunderbolt, because it's exactly
like that. Like lightning striking and flashing throughout the
body, leaving it feeling tingling and numb and the mind
dead to anything except a smiling female face. When I finally looked away from Crying Wind toward Hawwy and
saw his expression, saw Cherish batting her eyes, turning
her lovely head as she smiled shyly, I knew my new friend
was in mortal danger. If White Bear knew a white man was
looking at his niece like that, he would most certainly kill
him. And if just somehow I managed to restrain White
Bear, there wouldn't be enough of me left over to stop The
Cheyenne Robber. In the seconds that flew by I cursed myself for not having escaped in the night through the un-
locked window. I had been strong enough to meet White
Bear halfway. And had I done that, he wouldn't have come
to the fort. Nor would Cherish. Hawwy would never have

seen her. I cursed again as I watched them, knew all the way to my feet what was happening. I should have known, for the very same thing had happened to me when I saw Crying Wind standing in the creek. Hawwy's being struck by the Thunderbolt was a complication I could have done without. I needed the burden of Hawwy and Cherish the way I needed another bullet hole.

The name Cherish hadn't been given to her by accident. From birth she has been the most cherished female ever born to our people. She had been a beautiful baby, an adorable child. Now, she was all grown up and the female counterpart of her older brother. In a word, Cherish was breathtaking. And Hawwy's breath was most certainly taken. And, because while staring at her he had forgotten to breathe, he was turning a little blue around the lips. I left Crying Wind abruptly, running up behind Hawwy, whacking him hard on the back.

All of the women, including Crying Wind, giggled and tittered as Hawwy sucked in a lung-load of air and then coughed because he was choking on it. I failed to see the humor. Hawwy was making a dangerous spectacle of himself. I continued pounding his back and yelling over my shoulder to Crying Wind.

"Get Cherish out of here."

Laughing hilariously, Crying Wind had the audacity to yell, "Why?"

My seething stare put an abrupt end to her laughter. And as Crying Wind looked uncertainly at me (she'd never seen me angry before, only love-struck and defensive), laughter from the other women evaporated.

"You know why," I said huskily. "Take her and keep her away from this Blue Jacket."

Crying Wind quickly left the bed, grabbed Cherish's arm and tried hauling her toward the door. Cherish dragged her feet, whining, "But I like him, too. He's pretty."

As other women strove to help Crying Wind with Cherish, I dealt with Hawwy. He was a very strong person and he didn't want Cherish taken out of his house. Billy came out of his temporary stupor and helped me pull Hawwy back.

"Why does she have to leave?" Hawwy yelled as the women ushered Cherish out. "Couldn't she stay a little while? A drink!" he cried. "She must be thirsty. I could get her a drink."

Hawwy proved to be as stubborn as he was strong. Billy and I had him sitting on the cot, Billy explaining over and over again that Cherish was White Bear's favorite niece. That he would not like Hawwy's noticing her. He wouldn't like that at all.

To this Hawwy said, "Bud-da-mik" (buttermilk).

Evidently the stone-lined water well had bud-da-mik cooling inside it in buckets, and was considered a precious delicacy. Hawwy was positive Cherish would like bud-da-mik and he was determined to give her some. Through Billy I explained that giving her anything was a very bad idea. That it was not something he would be allowed to do. That the only man allowed to give presents to a maiden was the man intent on marrying the maiden.

And Hawwy said, "That's right. That's just what I'm going to do. I'm going to marry Cherish."

"If you even try to court Cherish, White Bear will kill you."

"Then I'll die happy. But I am marrying her." With a radiant boyish grin, he looked up at me and said happily, "Isn't she the most beautiful woman in the whole world?"

While Billy duly translated, I closed tired eyes and groaned.

Why hadn't I escaped?

ELEVEN

"Hawwy," I said sternly. He looked up at me and then expectantly to Billy. Billy was like a foreign echo, repeating my words in Ame-a-can, his voice almost on top of mine. Hawwy looked back to me as he listened to Billy intently.

"Hawwy, Kiowa women are no good for white men. You must get Cherish out of your mind. You wouldn't know how to handle a Kiowa woman. They're too independent and stubborn, used to getting their own way. White men need docile women. Women who are timid and obedient."

What I told Hawwy was the truth. I had seen enough captive white women to know. The ones I had seen were not strong creatures. They cried all the time, were hysterical, and always begging for mercy. Obviously they were a breed of women used to being bullied. A Kiowa woman under no circumstance would ever act that way. Cringing white women proved to be of no value to us for anything except trading back to their relatives. White Bear made a good living doing this as white women were easy to catch and worth more than the stolen horses and mules he routinely sold back to the army. The only white females the Kiowa ever kept were females taken as young children or babies and raised up properly in adoptive families. When those little girls became women, they had too much dignity and spirit to ever go back to their own people. They married Kiowa men instead and were accorded full rights as members of the Nation. Rights they would not have in the white culture.

I shall never forget the appalled look on Leavenworth's face when his paper came up for the vote. He had been appalled because our women were allowed to vote too. He had said his paper was *Man's Business*. Little Bluff gently corrected him. He had said, no, this was Nation business. Kiowa women are, have always been, full and honored members of our nation. Leavenworth was used to the idea that women were only the dutiful possessions of men. Therein lay the marked difference between our two cultures and the real impossibility of Hawwy ever marrying Cherish, even if White Bear were to suddenly suffer a stroke and approve their marriage. Hawwy would never be able to control Cherish the way he would naturally expect to control his wife.

As for Cherish, she was a spoiled and willful young woman. She would want Hawwy only while he was excitingly forbidden. When he was accepted, considered a member of her family, the excitement of his being different would fade. She would become bored with Hawwy and run off. That type of thing had happened before, and I'm ashamed of the memory. The first case I knew of happened when I was a member of the Herders and about fifteen. One of our young women was captured in a raid by the Cheyenne in an attack on her family band. Everyone thought she was gone forever because she was an attractive maiden, and a Cheyenne would most certainly marry her. But two seasons later she came home, not married to a Cheyenne but married to a white man. A white trader. We couldn't pronounce his American name (Charlie) properly because of that funny rolling sound, so we called him *Taslie*.

Taslie had traded the Cheyenne for that girl and then he married her. He thought a lot of her, and when she said she wanted to go home, Taslie took her. At considerable risk to himself, I might add. Kiowa policy during those years was to simply wipe out any white man who had the bad luck to pop up. But the girl was in love with Taslie during that time, and because he had saved her from the Cheyenne and thought enough of her, at the risk of his life, to bring her home, killing Taslie would have seemed . . . rude. So Taslie stayed with us for years and became one of the family. He had three children by his Kiowa wife, and everything was peaceful. And then she ran off with a Kiowa warrior, abandoning Taslie, her own children. She went to that warrior's band and then sent word that she wasn't coming home again until "that white man is gone." She said she was finished being a white man's wife because poor old Taslie was boring. She instructed her mother to take her children and care for them until her eventual return.

Without a Kiowa wife, Taslie was no longer a Kiowa, he was an interloper. He realized this, and with a broken heart he did the right thing. He left. I don't know whatever happened to him. We never heard from him after that. His children grew up with no memory of him. But my memory of that well-meaning white man, Taslie, made me desperate to save Hawwy from the same fate. I talked and talked, tried to make Hawwy understand that even if everything went smoothly and his marriage to Cherish was accepted, his greatest hurt would come from Cherish herself.

Hawwy wouldn't listen.

"No, Tay-bodal," Hawwy said, his expression determined. "I acknowledge your superior intelligence of the ways of your people, but you didn't see the way she looked at me. I know she cares for me the way I care for her. Cherish would never hurt me. I would never hurt her."

Spoken like a true victim of the Thunderbolt. As a victim

myself, I knew further talk was pointless. And if I wouldn't
listen to anything anyone said about Crying Wind, how
could I possibly expect Hawwy to listen to me about Cherish? I looked at Billy, my only true ally in this separate
fight which I now found myself embroiled in.

"You understand how bad this is, don't you."

"Yes," Billy answered gravely.

"You'll have to help me keep him away from her. I have
other concerns to face, and young lovers are tricky. They
have to be watched all the time. I won't be able to watch
them without drawing White Bear's attention. I'm making
Hawwy your responsibility, Billy. My wife will watch over
Cherish. Maybe if we're all lucky, they will get over their
mutual infatuation."

"But you don't think so."

"No," I said with a sad shake of my head. "Trying to
fight the Thunderbolt is like trying to stamp out a prairie
fire with your bare feet. All anyone can expect from that
effort is to be badly burned and scarred for life."

Hawwy and Billy escorted me to the council. I leaned
against Hawwy, shuffling along on dragging feet for dra-
matic effect. That performance, plus my many bandages
provoked the sympathy in my brothers that I hoped for.
Had I just sprinted along on my two good legs, they would
have all been fuming mad at me for not having escaped, as
I now realized, too late, that I should have done.

White Bear and his company of thirty men sat cross-
legged in the shade of the trees. The fort commander, Colonel Edmund Wilkins, stood at the forefront of his officers,
talking to the listening Kiowa through an interpreter we
have all known from way back. A man named Haw-ace
(Horace) Jones. Jones was a little banty rooster of a man
in his midfifties. He may have been a Territory interpreter,
but he would have none of the buckskins the other scouts
and interpreters wore. Not Haw-ace Jones. He only wore
good white man's suits, white shirts, and vests. He had a

beard that went all the way to his chest, and he habitually stroked it as if it were a pampered pet. He thought a great deal of himself despite the fact that he was inclined to be a drunkard.

Jones was in charge of all the army interpreters; therefore, he was always moving between one fort or another. Whenever there was anything important going on between the army and the tribes, Jones made certain that he was there, strutting around like a big important man and talking in a hard voice to warriors as if he was their father and they his errant children. Jones could get away with that attitude because he made certain that armed soldiers always surrounded him. He made extra certain after his humiliation at the trading store belonging to the Shirley brothers. Jones had been caught alone that day. He didn't have a single soldier with him because he was buying illegal whisky from the Shirleys.

Jones came off lucky that day because it had been Stumbling Bear, a cousin to Kicking Bird, and Stumbling Bear's men who had walked into the Shirley store. Stumbling Bear and his warriors offered no threat to Jones, but Jones didn't see that. He only saw a lot of Kiowa, only saw that he was without his usual guards. Jones peed himself. Stumbling Bear, of course, told everyone, and after that, whenever Jones talked in his hard voice, those listening to him smiled. Some even went so far as to make the hand signs for peeing or of a knife passing across the throat. Jones carried on talking loudly, pretending that he didn't see any of it. But he did. Coming to terms with the idea that it was better to be a thirsty live man than a dead drunk, Jones was never caught alone after that. Which sorely affected his drinking habits and caused him to talk even harder to the Kiowa whenever the chance came his way. When I arrived, Jones was publicly berating White Bear. I felt myself seething because Jones's new chance to be a big man, talk hard to our chiefs, was all my fault.

Jones's presence at the council equally undermined Jen-

kins. That Jenkins had jeopardized his life to make this
council possible mattered not a whit to Jones. Jenkins had
to stand to the side and say nothing as Jones strutted
around. The colonel would say a few words and then Jones
spoke for a long time, adding lengthy worthless opinions
as well as veiled threats to whatever the colonel needed to
be translated. That little man was completely insufferable.
He needed killing. And if the stormy expression on so many
Kiowa faces was any indication of their mood, there were
many within the sound of Jones's voice who were ready
and anxious to grant that ill-mannered man's latent death
wish.

White Bear was shifting on his haunches, visibly chaffing
for a fight. His attitude was partly due to the hideous adventure of traveling with carping women for two days, but
mostly it was due to being made to suffer Jones's lashing
tongue. When White Bear glanced my way, his expression
was tight, his eyes narrowed to slits, his mouth a mean line
cutting across his face. I made a point of wilting against
Hawwy, my legs buckling at the knees; Hawwy struggled
to help me sit down at the back of the council amid the
company of ordinary warriors.

Hawwy knew I was faking but he was more than happy
to go along with the ruse. If I appeared too weak to travel,
that meant the Kiowa would stay. Because of Cherish,
Hawwy wanted the Kiowa to stay. Through Billy he spoke
happily and rapidly, talking about needing to see to a proper
camp for the fort's Kiowa guests. Gesticulating with one
arm, he talked about going over to the long log building
he called *Supply*. He was more than glad to see to the comforts of the women himself, and *Supply* supposedly had
everything their tender feminine hearts required.

Hawwy was gloating as he said this to me. He was much
too clear in his intention to give Cherish presents. A lot of
presents. He was even more clear that there was nothing I
could do to stop him. Hawwy was like an ignorant, blind,
deaf and dumb man joyously dancing toward his own pri-

vate hell. But he was absolutely right about one thing. As he was stubbornly determined to go there, I couldn't stop him. But what I could do was trip him up, make his mindless journey harder.

"Billy," I said anxiously, but in a guarded tone, "anything he gives to Cherish, make certain he gives the same thing to all the women. Don't allow him to single her out. Tell my wife, Crying Wind, everything I've said. She'll understand."

Billy ran after Hawwy, the coattails of his long canvas coat flying. Billy might profess that it was an inestimable honor to be killed by the Kiowa, but he was a long way from being ready to be so honored. He would be Hawwy's shadow. I believed I could trust him not to let a love-struck young officer start up a major war that the army was not yet prepared to fight. Besides, I had no choice but to trust him. Now that I had put in an appearance at the council, I was trapped. And White Bear was looking back over his shoulder at me. But his gaze skimmed past me. He glanced at someone further to my left, nodded, then looked away. Curious, I leaned forward, looked in the direction of White Bear's brief and silent exchange, and received the shock of my life.

Skywalker wasn't dressed right. All the chiefs were dressed in their best clothes and wore the regalia befitting their rank and separate societies. Skywalker wasn't wearing anything more than a ragged-looking breechcloth and moccasins that were almost worn through on the soles. Even more astonishing than his clothing, he was sitting among the ordinary warriors. He was an Owl Doctor, an Onde, a To-yop-ke. He did not belong among menials. Feeling my stare, he glanced my way, looked into my astonished eyes, hurriedly glanced away as if he hadn't recognized me. I sat back, felt my blood pooling in my backside as my benumbed brain floundered, tried to fathom Skywalker's shoddy appearance, his presence among inferiors.

Finally Jones shut up and it was White Bear's turn to

speak. He stood, crooking an index finger to Jenkins, beck-oning the secondary interpreter, a man he knew to be of few words and courage, to stand beside him and speak for him. Jones, close to the colonel, turned bright red in the face, but there was little else he could do. Jones's scolding tirade had pushed White Bear to his less than interminable limits, and for once Jones had the wit to realize that one more word would find him in more trouble than even his armed guards could handle.

Our *Orator of the Plains* was in fine form that day, but I heard little of what White Bear said after he introduced the chiefs and subchiefs. As soon as I heard the name Big Bow, my mind, which had just begun to recover from the shock caused by Skywalker's shameful dress and humble attitude, went numb again. And then I slowly became a mass of fuming rage.

How dare Big Bow be here! He had betrayed White Bear to Kicking Bird. He was the reason behind the attack on me. I had very nearly been killed! The more I thought about that, the madder I got, losing all sense of reason. Sky-walker, I promptly decided, had been demoted because of Big Bow. That was why Skywalker sat in the back during the council. And that was why Skywalker had looked away from me with a shamed face. Because of Big Bow, Sky-walker was a nobody even among men who were his less-ers.

My mind pulled hard in another direction, thought about Hawwy being struck down with love for Cherish and the awful consequences of that love. That, I decided, wasn't my fault after all. In a blaze of hatred I blamed that on Big Bow too. My mind then began pulling from all directions at once, and then *everything* that had gone wrong since the dawn of the first day in history was somehow all Big Bow's fault. I was so maddened during White Bear's discourse that if I'd had a gun I would have stood to my feet and shot Big Bow right in the back. But all I had was slobbering rage. Worked up in this rabid state, I vowed that if White

Bear could be so stupid as to trust a snake like Big Bow, then he was too stupid to be a chief. Especially *my* chief. I'd make peace with Kicking Bird, or even better, I would side with Lone Wolf. Lone Wolf was handier anyway. He was already there. Kicking Bird wasn't. So I made elaborate plans to offer myself to Lone Wolf and at the same time extract from him the promise that he would take in Crying Wind, too. With her safely with me, I would happily abandon White Bear to his duplicity and gross stupidity. Any man who could forsake a valuable brother like Skywalker deserved to be Kicking Bird's lifelong slave. It was too bad about The Cheyenne Robber and White Otter, but I was too maddened to be concerned. I easily tossed them out of my thoughts with an indifferent, *They're young, somehow they will survive.*

I was still in this state when Kicking Bird and his men rode in and the council was thrown into an inflamed turmoil. I sat there chuckling evilly as White Bear, Lone Wolf, and Kicking Bird shocked the colonel with their three-way, very heated war of words. The more they shouted at each other the more sourly happy I became. I actually hoped it would all come down to civil war right then and there. I wanted to kill something. No, I wanted to kill someone. First Big Bow, then White Bear.

It simply wasn't my day. There I was with my bowels in an uproar, for once in my peace-loving life anxious and ready to go to war, and those three hotheads had the nerve to calm down, call a truce. I sat there simmering and grinding my back teeth as they all shook hands. And then Lone Wolf and Kicking Bird sat down, magnanimously yielding the confused and stricken colonel's attention back to White Bear.

That was enough for me. With either one of those three in charge as principal chief, maybe I didn't even want to be Kiowa. Maybe the thing to do was take Crying Wind and go off with The Cheyenne Robber and White Otter. Maybe Skywalker and his family would come too, and we

would just start up our own nation. That struck me as such
a fine idea that I stood up and walked off. I didn't reel or
wobble even one little bit the way I had done during my
approach. I wanted White Bear to see that there was nothing really wrong with me.

He did. And my walking away, perfectly normal, cut him
off midsentence, made him forget his thought. He, along
with everyone else, just stared after me. I felt White Bear's
beady eyes on my back. I could feel his temper fix on me
as I walked away. I didn't care. I was going after Crying
Wind. It no longer mattered to me that White Bear hadn't
officially given her over to me to be my wife. I was going
to take her. Take her and leave. Take her and our son and
just get as far away from White Bear and his miseries as
we possibly could. And I knew just where to go. We'd go
to Quanah out on the Staked Plain. Crying Wind might not
like being Comanche, but she'd get used to it. I determined
in my half-crazy brain that I would love her so hard that
to be with me she would eventually accept anything. Even
being Comanche.

My walking away in a maddened huff sent White Bear
into an abnormal stammer. While he floundered, Skywalker
rose and discreetly followed after me. It was on account of
Skywalker that Crying Wind and I never became Comanches.

It took Skywalker a long time to find me. Having been there
for three days I knew what was what concerning the fort.
Skywalker didn't know anything, so he was having to skulk
inconspicuously around. That was hard work for a tall, naturally skinny Kiowa man dressed in a poor breechcloth.
Against the backdrop of well-fed, finely dressed black
troopers, Skywalker looked like a half-starved Indian beg-
gar. While he was doing all this skulking, I was taking my
temper out on Hawwy.

Wouldn't you know that Hawwy had decided that the
best place for the Kiowa to make camp was near his little

doctor house. That's where I eventually found him, Billy and all the women. From this place he kept calling *Supply*, Hawwy had purloined two officers' tents. He and Billy and four troopers were setting these tents up while the women sat in a semicircle on the ground, eating and watching the activity. It was unseemly for men to make a camp, but Hawwy didn't know that. He didn't know he was making a fool of himself. But Billy knew and Billy was caught up in an anger that almost matched my own. When Billy spotted me out of the corner of his eye, he stopped holding the staking peg the black trooper steadily pounded into the ground and ran toward me, waving his arms, hollering loudly.

"I couldn't stop him!" Billy cried. "It's not my fault."

When he reached me, we both stopped, Billy standing in front of me still waving and shouting.

"I told him I would explain to the women how to put the tents, but he wouldn't listen. He wanted to do everything himself. He wants to impress her. He has. She now thinks he's simple. That's good luck for you, but it's bad luck for me. All those women think I'm simple, too."

Billy's plight took some of my own anger away from me. I felt very sorry for him, but I was relieved Hawwy had managed to make himself look silly to Cherish. Not that I cared during that moment about White Bear or Cherish. I only cared about Hawwy. If his being silly put him out of the way of Cherish's fascination and saved him from White Bear's wrath, then I hoped Hawwy would do a million silly things.

"It's all right, Billy," I said, feeling my hot head cooling slightly. With my hands on my hips I lowered my head and stared at the ground between my feet. "What else has he done?"

"Given the women sweets," Billy snorted. "And blankets to sit on. It was just as you said. He tried to give those things only to Cherish, but I made him give sweets and blankets to the other women, too. Then he got out those

tents. And beds and more blankets. When the women tried
to help with the camp he made a big fuss, made them all
sit down. He won't even let them gather firewood. He's got
two troopers out doing that.''

I sighed deeply but with a peaceful relief. Hawwy had
dug a very big hole for himself. Cherish would certainly
see him as a hopeless simpleton and reject him because of
that. The women joined us, Crying Wind close against my
side. I wrapped my good arm around her shoulders and felt
that modicum of relief wither as the women jabbered at me
all at once.

"Do you see what that white soldier is doing for us?"

"Isn't he lovely?"

"Do all white men spoil women so wonderfully?"

"He hasn't allowed us to lift a thing."

"Those tents have *two* rooms inside them."

"He says he's going to give us *ca-ake*. What is *ca-ake*?"

Crying Wind began to bounce excitedly, her face as radiant as a happy girl's.

"He took us to a long building. It's filled with wonderful
things. All we had to do was point at a thing and he gave
it as a present! I have a new metal bucket. He just gave it
to me! I tried to trade my necklace for it but he wouldn't
take the necklace. So now I have the bucket *and* my necklace.

"Weaving Woman got two knives. Makes War got a big
roll of blue cloth. Sits Alone got a big bag of coffee, and
Cherish got a big metal box filled with sweets that she
shared with us. The sweets are all gone but she will have
the box forever. It's beautiful with painted pictures on it."

With a despairing groan, I said, "You've been having a
wonderful time, haven't you?"

"Yes," she beamed. "The best time. We all like your
friend very much. How long do we get to stay here? Did
my cousin White Bear say?"

"He—he's still making talk with the chief of this fort.
I—I didn't get a chance to speak to him."

"I hope we get to stay a long time. I think that soldier will give us presents every day. He's like that," she nodded solemnly. "Generous."

I stole a glance at Cherish. She stood looking over her shoulder, pride radiating from her as she watched Hawwy's approach. She was even more proud when he came to stand next to her. She lowered her face and eyes like a modest woman ought to do, switching her weight from foot to foot, smiling a secret smile as Hawwy spoke to me.

I must say he did cut a dashing picture. Without a hat his curly head glowed. Highlighted by sweat, the bits of red in his hair were shining like tiny fires. To impress Cherish with his manly physique, his shirt was partially unbuttoned. The dark brown fur on his chest peeked out. The long sleeves of the shirt were rolled up past his elbows. His arms were hairy like his chest. Cherish kept stealing glances at his arms. I didn't even care to speculate on what was going on inside her virginal little head. Nevertheless, her desire to be held in those arms was clear enough. She moved to stand more closely beside Hawwy, enjoying the coolness his eclipsing shadow provided.

Hawwy's hands rested lightly on his slender hips. His massive brows became a single wrinkled line as he squinted and spoke to Billy, expecting him to translate to me. The whole time he was speaking, his eyes kept venturing down toward Cherish.

"I chose this place because it was more convenient for your wife."

I snorted down my nose and replied, "And I suppose the fact that Cherish will be near had nothing to do with the selection of this campsite."

Billy translated. Sarcasm was lost on Hawwy, he just kept talking.

"You still need to be in the *Infirmary* under my care. You shouldn't be walking around so much in this heat, Taybodal. You're a sick man."

Billy was using hand talk along with the Comanche language. All of the women easily followed the exchange. Crying Wind became excitable. Because she loved me too much, she started a fuss.

"You get right in that *In-fammy*. You do what he says. White doctors have a lot of power. He wouldn't say a thing that wasn't true and risk losing his power." She grabbed up my arm, began tugging me. "Don't you worry about anything, my darling. We will stay in this place for just as long as it takes to get you completely well again."

The chattering women worked together in their determination to push me toward the confines of the doctoring house.

"Billy!" I cried.

"Right behind you, Meat."

What saved me from all-out depression was Crying Wind's being alone with me in the doctor house. It was the first time we had been alone together in what felt to be a lifetime. She lay down with me on my bed. Laying partially over her, I hungrily sought her mouth, savoring the sweet taste of her, the feel of her body pressed close to mine.

"SSSSSSSH!"

I drew back a bit, looking questioningly down at her. Crying Wind grabbed me by the hair, pulled my mouth back to hers.

"SSSSSSSSSSSSSSSSSSH!"

I drew away, again looking anxiously over my shoulder toward the raised window. Skywalker came slithering through like a sleek otter. Caught in our compromising position, I yelled angrily at him, and Crying Wind shrieked in dismay. Chuckling, he stood with his back to us, very interested in the raised barrier of the window.

"What is this thing?"

"A magic barrier," I said grumpily, worming myself off Crying Wind. I left the bed and went to him. We stood side by side, our backs turned toward my bed. A moment later, the door of the doctor house opened and closed. Crying

Wind was gone. Skywalker's untimely intrusion had me mad all over again.

"What do you want?" I yelled loudly, pointedly ignoring his hand sign to speak quietly.

In a secretive tone, he said, "I have to talk to you."

"I think maybe I don't want to talk to you."

He glanced obliquely at me. His mood, until he heard the anger in my tone, took in my livid expression, had been good-humored. Now he was genuinely perplexed.

"What is the matter with you?"

"What's the matter with me?" I cried. "How can you even face me after you've allowed yourself to be so thoroughly disgraced?"

"Why would you say something like that? And kindly keep your voice down. I don't want that Blue Jacket to find me."

I waved a hand away from me. "The soldier they have put in charge of me is called Hawwy. You have nothing to worry about from him because he won't even notice you. He's too busy making a fool of himself."

"Really? How?"

"That isn't important," I snapped. "What is important, is you."

"Tay-bodal," he said with an irritating calmness, "other than being shot in the head, what is ailing you?"

"You!" I said, nearing hysteria. "Just look at you. Do you have any idea how poor you look?"

"Yes."

My eyes flared in surprise. "You do? And you don't even mind about White Bear humiliating you?"

"White Bear hasn't humiliated me. Why would you think that?"

I flapped my arms like a big bird preparing for flight as I paced away from him. "Then tell me this, if he has not been stripped of his rank by a superior chief, what kind of Onde shames himself by wearing a poor man's clothing to an important council?"

For the first time, Skywalker raised his voice. "An Onde who doesn't want to be recognized by his enemies as being an Onde. An Onde who is better able to serve his brother by being his extra pair of eyes and ears during that council."

I stopped pacing. Mouth agape, I gawked at him. He came to me, his tone no longer raised and angry.

"I've always done that for him, stood back, whispered in his ear. White Bear is a good talker but sometimes his mouth gets away from him. That's when my whispering works. Today while he was talking, my job was to watch the soldiers, read their faces and, if I could, their minds."

"Did you learn anything?"

"Yes," he said, exhaling a deep breath. "From their expressions I read that they're very nervous. From their minds I picked up a word. *Shuman* (Sherman). Have you heard them speaking of a Shuman?"

"No."

"Well, whatever a Shuman, is they're waiting for it. The fort chief is anxious for it to come. That chief doesn't think in images. He thinks in his own language, but still, his impressions were very clear. When Shuman comes, that chief will stop being so nervous."

"A Shuman must be a new and even more dangerous gun."

Skywalker twisted his lips to the side, thoughtful for a long time. "I think maybe it's a dangerous person. There was one image that white chief held as he mentally said Shuman."

"What?"

"Fire. A fire that went all the way to the sky."

Fear crawled through me, gathered and became a single strangling knot.

Skywalker sat down on my bed. With a complete change of subject, he startled me out of my grim thoughts.

"Now tell me why you're so concerned about Cherish and this person you call Hawwy."

I averted my eyes and stared at the far wall while he patiently awaited my answer. Being òne of the unlucky ones who are powerless against an Owl Doctor's uncanny ability is the principal reason I have always hated and avoided seers. Now I had a new best friend and he was one of the better seers.

My joy was unbridled.

TWELVE

"Neither Cherish nor Hawwy is important right now," I cried. "I want to know what Big Bow is doing here. Why he's suddenly so friendly with White Bear."

"They've always been friends," Skywalker said mildly.

The flames of temper as hot as a firestorm devouring a drought-stricken forest roared through me. Skywalker was taken aback by the way I began shouting and pacing the room again as I shouted.

"How can he be friends with a man who despises his brother!"

Skywalker pointed a finger at his chest and mouthed, "Me?"

"Yes, you!" I screamed in his startled face.

Skywalker had the audacity to laugh. I stood rock still as his laughter increased. He held his sides as he laughed. Stripped of my righteous anger, I felt suddenly naked. It took everything I had to stitch it back together again, face him with a bit of dignity when his laughter finally subsided.

"He doesn't hate me as a man," Skywalker hooted. "He only hates me as an Owl Doctor."

"And there's a difference?" I sneered.

"Of course there is." He dried his eyes on the back of his hand. "Oh, Tay-bodal. For a wise man sometimes you can be as thick as a tree stump."

He sniffed deeply through his nose, cleared his throat, spoke to me in that gratingly reasonable tone of his.

"As a man, as a fellow To-yop-ke, Big Bow respects me. It's only on the matter of religion that we . . . differ. I'm a rabid believer in the unseen. He's a skeptic. If he can't taste it, touch it, or kill it, for Big Bow, it simply doesn't exist. He thinks that when a man is dead, he's no better than a dead dog. That there is no other world for a dead man's spirit to go to. There are no such things as guiding spirits.

"You must remember, Tay-bodal, the Creator has given each of us the gift of free will. If a man wants to believe in one thing and not in another, that is his choice. And his right to choose comes from the Man Above. It is not my place to be mad at Big Bow for what he believes any more than it is his place to be mad at me for my beliefs. So we have formed a truce, Big Bow and I. He now holds his tongue whenever I practice my craft, and I never try to convert him to my views. It has taken us years to come to this agreement. Please don't ruin it for us with your blind loyalty to me. I assure you that when it comes to Big Bow, I can take care of myself."

I was not put off so easily. My flagging temper rallied. "Oh, yes!" I shouted indignantly. "Well, good for you. But what about White Bear? How would he feel if he knew that Big Bow betrayed him to Kicking Bird?"

Satisfaction rushed through me as Skywalker lost his smug expression and looked up at me aghast.

"That's a very serious charge."

"It's meant to be," I said arrogantly. "It's the reason I was shot."

Skywalker rose from the bed. His color was ashen, his shoulders rounded from the weight of my accusation. In a low voice, he said, "I think you should say all of this to Big Bow personally, and in White Bear's presence."

"Gladly."

Leaving Hawwy's doctoring house, we did not have to walk far to hunt down either Big Bow or White Bear. The talks with the fort's chief were finished, the white chief now busy with overseeing the preparations for the evening feast he promised. With nothing else to do, all of the Kiowas had wandered in the direction of Hawwy's little campsite. They found the women, who were more than happy to display their accommodations, Crying Wind herself leading White Bear, Big Bow, Lone Wolf, and Kicking Bird through one of the two large tents Hawwy had worked so hard setting up. I heard every word of her excited jabbering voice.

". . . and see, this little back room is where three of us will sleep. That front room is where we are supposed to eat."

The crowd in the tent began to emerge, Crying Wind still talking, still showing off.

"This overhead flap is the best part," she said, meaning the awning supported by two long metal poles everyone was now standing under. The men looked appreciatively up at the thick rainproof canvas material directly over their heads. "It's like having a built-in arbor. Isn't that smart? We can sit in the cool shade without ever having to leave this little home."

"Did he give these tents as gifts?" Lone Wolf asked.

"Yes."

Kicking Bird leaned forward and asked, "To which two women?"

That shut Crying Wind up. She just stood there looking perplexed. There were five women, only two tents. Cherish and her cousin were standing in the shaded awning of the second tent. Cherish began looking evilly at her cousin, silently daring the younger girl to even try to make a claim on that tent. That girl, equally determined, screwed up her face and glared right back at Cherish.

The remaining two women were standing away from the first tent Crying Wind had taken the tour through. A second after Kicking Bird had innocently asked the fatal question, those two women began snapping at each other. Clearly all five women wanted one of those tents. Three were destined to lose, but not without a fight.

Hawwy's good intentions, which were meant to impress Cherish, were now predictably going awry. I was only sorry he wasn't around to witness the havoc. I should have just let it happen, said nothing and allowed Hawwy to come off looking bad. Doing so would have spared him the immeasurable grief he faced throughout the subsequent years, but like him, at the time, my intentions had been good. I wanted to save my new friend from looking bad in the eyes of men who knew how to provide fairly for a lot of women. Hawwy's giving only two tents to be clawed over by five quarreling women had indeed made him seem asinine in the minds of these men. The men stepped away, sadly resigned to the fact that the women would now fight it out. Everyone, even Kicking Bird, seemed pleased when I intervened.

"Those tents are not presents!" I cried. "No more than the doctor house I have been sleeping in has been intended as a present to me. These are only borrowed shelters. When we leave this place the white doctor will have his house back, and the soldiers will pack up those tents and keep them for their own use."

"But he said they were ours!" Crying Wind protested.

"He meant that they are yours while you are here," I said, looking hard at her. "White men talk backwards. When he said those tents were for you, he didn't know how he sounded. But the most important thing you should know is those tents are not as strong as tepees. They wouldn't last through a winter or keep out the cold. They are no good to us. Amuse yourself with them while we're here, but forget about keeping them. Besides, I would never marry you if you insisted we live in that thing.''

Crying Wind's face puckered; she sent me a hateful glare as the men and even the women began to laugh. She flounced back inside the tent, slamming the flap door behind her. I knew she was brewing up a lot of things to say to me later.

Worrying about my allegations against Big Bow, Skywalker didn't join in the revelry. As Crying Wind continued to hide away, nursing her sulk, the women lost their battling attitudes, started working together to make a fire from the kindling the soldiers had piled up between the two tents. They busied themselves making coffee, and the men all sat down to wait for it. Skywalker nudged White Bear and Big Bow, twisting his lips to the side, pointing toward the porch of the doctoring house. He nodded to me the four of us walked in that direction. Seeing us walk off, knowing something important was going to happen, Lone Wolf and Kicking Bird rose and followed.

I didn't want them there but as neither Skywalker nor White Bear objected as Kicking Bird and Lone Wolf climbed the porch steps and sat down, there was nothing I could say. Forming a circle, we were all quiet for a long time, my nerves becoming stretched and thin. Finally, Skywalker spoke.

"This one," meaning me, "has something serious to say."

"I have a few serious things to say to him as well," White Bear huffed. He looked directly at me, pinning me with an angry stare. "What do you mean by hobbling into council looking beat up and pathetic and then getting up in the middle of my talk with that white chief and walking away? Was that sacred ground you briefly sat on? Did you undergo a miraculous cure? And were you so overcome by your instant healing that you forgot yourself and had no idea you were shaming me to a white man?"

"No."

White Bear waved his arms wildly. "Then what did you think you were doing?! You made me mad."

"That was my intention."

"What?" he cried, his tone high, incredulous. Skywalker touched White Bear's meaty arm. White Bear angrily shook him off. Before the storm inside White Bear could rage out of control, I jumped to my feet and went on the attack.

"I had every reason to be mad at you!" I shouted.

White Bear's eyes snapped open, his lower jaw dropped. His surprise at my outburst rendered him speechless. Pointing my arm like a challenging lance at Big Bow's heart, I kept up the assault.

"*TWICE* I have seen you welcome to your heart a man who is nothing but a traitor."

Voices murmured all around me. White Bear continued to stare up at me with glazed-over eyes. Big Bow's face began to mottle with fury, but I was too angry to be afraid of him.

"Ask him where he went after he left your camp, after he ate with you like a brother."

White Bear's eyes shifted toward Big Bow, then crawled slowly back to me. He didn't ask Big Bow anything. He simply waited for me to supply the answer. I happily obliged.

"I'll tell you where he went. He went straight to Kicking Bird. He told Kicking Bird that I was your spy. Then when I went to Kicking Bird's camp to question his two relatives known very well to you as Chasing Horse and Stands On A Hill regarding what part they played in The Cheyenne Robber's troubles, Big Bow stood in the crowd grinning at me as Kicking Bird first denounced me, then threatened me, and then had me run out of his camp. It was while I was journeying back to your camp that I was chased down by two riders, was trapped against the river and shot. My attackers, believing I was dead, buried me."

Disconcerted voices hummed as I breathed hard, my chest ballooning rapidly, and I concentrated a malicious

stare at Big Bow. It pleased me to watch anger drain from
him. What wasn't pleasing was Big Bow's assuming an
expression of genuine absorption. His utter lack of offense
effectively reduced my hard truths to the level of fascinating fables. But the thing that made the others look from me
to him was his near-mesmerized tone.

"And what happened then?"

Even I found the tension of the moment waning. Struggling to hang on to it, I jeered, "Do you even care?"

"Yes," he answered, sounding the soul of innocence.
"As a matter of fact, I do."

He wasn't fooling me with that one. I was seething. But
now part of my rage was for Skywalker, as he just sat there
with his head slightly angled to the side, fighting off a trace
of a smile.

"For your information," I said, my tone loaded with
contempt, "I dug my way out of that grave and managed
to make it to the river. Then I fell in and floated on my
back all night long."

Knowing how strongly Big Bow disbelieved in spirits, I
delighted in adding the part about Little Bluff talking to
me, telling me to brace up, that it wasn't my time to die.
Big Bow grimaced, his eyes dancing from side to side,
thoroughly loath to believe or even pretend any interest in
that part. He only became riveted again when I told the
final half of the story of being found by the soldiers, my
initial reaction to the black men, and then being transported
to the fort where I was held captive.

"And now," I snarled, "you're here and I know why.
You came only because you knew I would tell the truth
about you."

"That's not true."

That he would have the gall to deny a truth so blatantly
obvious made me see red.

"Yes, you did. You have two mouths, Big Bow. With
one mouth you talk to White Bear. With the other you talk
to Kicking Bird."

"Ha!" Big Bow laughed. "There I have you, *Storyteller*. I have had only one mouth, one tongue my whole life. I have never been afraid to speak straight no matter who I might offend, and any man ever knowing me knows that to be true. But as you seem delighted to wallow in ignorance, make up very exciting stories concerning me, I'm afraid I shall have to embarrass you with the truth.

"Yes, I did go to Kicking Bird's camp as you say. But hear me when I say that I went there only because Lone Wolf urged me to accompany him. It was Lone Wolf who counciled with Kicking Bird. I said nothing, not one word as Lone Wolf counciled with Kicking Bird the same way he had counciled with White Bear.

"I sat beside Lone Wolf and never once opened my mouth, so I most certainly did not say anything to Kicking Bird about you. White Bear trusted me with the secret of your investigations on behalf of The Cheyenne Robber. The Cheyenne Robber happens to be a good friend of mine. I would do nothing that places his life at risk. Besides, you, you poor little man, mean absolutely nothing to me. Whatever your puffed-up pride may tell you, the truth is I never concern myself with carrying tales of my inferiors."

Humiliation swept over me like a roaring flood. Big Bow had effectively reduced me to the status of a stepped-on bug, its guts glued to the underside of his shoe. I swallowed hard and managed to rasp, "Then why were you standing there grinning while I was being threatened."

"Because you looked scared. That was funny. It made me laugh."

Oh, how I wanted to hit him. Shouting at the top of my embarrassed voice, I said, "If you didn't tell Kicking Bird, who did?"

Kicking Bird raised a hand. We all swirled our heads in his direction. In a small placid voice he said, "I think maybe I have the answer for that one."

"Who?" White Bear roared. "Who was it?"

"Stands On A Hill. He said he learned that Tay-bodal was a spy from Hears The Wolf."

"Him again!" White Bear cried. "Stands On A Hill is the biggest troublemaker I have ever known. The second biggest is his cousin, Chasing Horse." White Bear looked quickly up at me. I was lost in thought, my mind turning in a swiftness I have never experienced since. "You said two riders," White Bear said angrily, trying to interrupt my thoughts.

On one level I heard him, but my mind was moving faster than a tornado. But unlike a tornado, instead of everything being torn up, things were falling into place with an audible click.

"Those two riders shooting at you had to be Chasing Horse and Stands On A Hill."

I waved a dismissive hand as everything became startlingly clear. Looking to Kicking Bird, I asked, "Did Stands On A Hill accompany you to this fort?"

"He did," Kicking Bird nodded.

I ran a hand over my mouth. My heart was beating rapidly as I said, "I request permission to question him."

Kicking Bird's eyes never left me as he considered. After a lengthy pause he said, "Your request is granted on one condition. I must be allowed to hear what you ask and what he answers."

"Agreed."

White Bear made an impatient move, but Skywalker's hand stayed him. Kicking Bird rose and stood near the edge of the porch and summoned one of his men and told that man to find Stands On A Hill.

Stands On A Hill looked very worried. He was only a few paces from me as we stood in the center of the circle of seated chiefs. He sent me beseeching looks which I promptly ignored.

In a cold voice I asked him, "Is Hears The Wolf Hwame?"

White Bear slapped his thighs hard and cried, ''Have you gone crazy?''

Skywalker's blanching face first turned toward me, then his gaze traveled wonderingly to Stands On A Hill. The young man was sweating profusely.

''Answer!'' I shouted.

''N-No.''

''You lied to me.''

''Y-Yes.''

There are two types of lies. One for gain, the second to protect. Stands On A Hill had nothing to gain.

''Now answer this. When was the last time you saw your dead relative alive?''

He did not want to answer. His body shook as he wept. Finally, my heart went out to him and I stepped toward him, taking him in my arms. ''When?'' I said against his ear.

In a sobbing whisper he said, ''Just before he died. I spoke with him. I brought him a message. But I wasn't the only one. Chasing Horse spoke to him too, he—''

''It's all right,'' I said, cutting his words off. I leaned back, holding his weeping face in my hands. ''Everything is all right now.''

I sent the distraught young man away.

White Bear threw a fit. ''He knows the name of the real killer and you just let him walk off?''

White Bear's tantrum failed to break Skywalker's invisible grip on my mind. While he ranted, Skywalker and I continued to stare at one another. Skywalker's gaze began to bore into me. I felt the front of my skull melting, giving way as he entered the dark recesses of my mind. It was invasive, unspeakably personal, and almost erotic, like a highly experienced man coaxing an apprehensive virgin during the moment of penetration. And there was nothing I could do to stop him. Pressure inside my head began to build. Images of my life skipped by in seconds. I was a boy, a young man, a man. I was with Coyote Walking, examining his lifeless body. Next I was with Hears The Wolf, seeing his scarred back. Lastly, I was riding for my life. Then I was on the ground looking at the feet of my assailants. I was trapped inside my past and yet still vaguely aware of the present. That part of my brain that wasn't being raped knew exactly where I was and I could still hear White Bear's oddly faint voice.

Had the white chief felt all of these things when Sky-walker crept into his mind? He must have. And he must have believed that the heat was playing tricks with his mind, was making him temporarily delusional, for that white man couldn't have known what was actually happening to him. Not the way I knew. But my knowing made the invasion all the more terrible, for there were things in my life I held in private, desperately wanted to hide. But I couldn't hide. I couldn't do anything but stand trapped inside Skywalker's black, bottomless eyes. His face very pale, Skywalker began the process of letting go.

White Bear's voice began to reach me, to sound stronger. He wasn't talking to me, he was yelling at Kicking Bird.

"I've told you repeatedly that those no-goods, Stands On A Hill and Chasing Horse, are responsible for the hard feelings between us. Everything is their fault. Isn't that right, Tay-bodal."

Answer.

Can't.

Yes, you can.

"No," I managed in a strangled voice.

My speaking snapped the final frail threads of the spell and hastened Skywalker's withdrawal. The sensation of his abrupt departure felt as if I had been thrown violently away. And with him gone, I felt utterly alone. I breathed in deeply, coughing and spluttering exactly as I had done when rolling onto my back in the river. I had narrowly escaped death by drowning. Now the private world inside my mind had been invaded, literally looted. Were you to ask me which I considered the absolute worst, I'm afraid I wouldn't have an answer. As a survivor of both ordeals I am left with the conviction that there is precious little difference between the two.

Knowing he had completely drained me mentally and physically, Skywalker was there when my legs began to fold. He caught me just as my knees buckled. Lone Wolf scrambled to his feet, rushing to help hold up my other side.

"He's very weak," Skywalker said. "This council has been too much for him." He called to a thoroughly startled White Bear. "You better get that white doctor back here. If we hope to leave tomorrow, Tay-bodal will need all the medicine that doctor has to offer."

White Bear stood and approached me. He stared down at me as I hung between Skywalker and Lone Wolf. "You know who killed Kicking Bird's nephew, don't you."

My failing sight moved to Kicking Bird's anxious face hovering just behind White Bear's shoulder. I was so drained, all I could manage was an affirming nod.

"Then tell us!" White Bear boomed.

"No," I heard Skywalker answer. "Now is not the time. The Cheyenne Robber was publicly accused. He deserves the right to be publicly acquitted."

White Bear's mouth moved as if to argue. He pulled a face, made a noise of disgust in the back of his throat. Then he left the porch.

Inside the doctor house Lone Wolf helped Skywalker ease me onto the bed. Skywalker pulled up a stool and sat near me. Lone Wolf said something to me I didn't catch, and left. I sucked in air through tightly clenched teeth as I adjusted my head on the pillow. Mind rape leaves in its wake a very nasty headache. Skywalker placed a soothing hand on my forehead and looked down at me with a faint, sad smile. We no longer had any need for spoken words. What do you say to the one human who knows everything about you? The good and the bad? That was why I was so drained, you see. In a matter of seconds he had whipped through every memory I owned. He had been with me in the eagle pit with my father, shared the unbearable pain I'd felt when my parents and then my sweet-natured little first wife died, rejoiced in the depth of my new love for Crying Wind, agreed with my concerns for Hawwy and Cherish . . . and now knew just as certainly as I knew, the face of Coyote Walking's killer.

The evening feast was sumptuous and noisy. Neither Skywalker nor I attended, but we were brought food on trays and we could hear everything that went on just outside the doctoring house. Because of my apparent relapse, Crying Wind forgot about being mad at me. She brought in a second tray and looked equally proud and excited.

"This is ca-ake," she said as she stuffed chocolate cake in my mouth. Crying Wind has always been proud and a little bit pushy with anything new that she's learned. She was certainly pushy with the cake. I was barely rallying and she was choking me to death with it, cramming cake into my mouth before I could manage to chew and swallow properly. I was more concerned with suffocation than appreciative of the cake's sweet taste.

"Don't kill him with it," Skywalker scolded.

"He has to eat quickly before my cousin comes in here demanding what little bit he's left for others."

Have you ever tried to protest with a mouth full of cake? It can't be done. The more I muffled, the more cake she crammed inside my mouth. And I was growing alarmed that as Skywalker enjoyed his piece of cake, he'd forgotten all about my struggle to breathe.

"This kind of food would make White Bear greedy all right," Skywalker said between bites.

"He's acting like a wolf," Crying Wind grumbled. "You'd think that man had never had a decent meal in his life. I had hoped there would be enough ca-ake to take home to share with my sisters, but White Bear's proven that a useless ambition."

"Perhaps Hawwy will provide more of this ca-ake," Skywalker replied mildly.

His evoking that name gave me the impetus to survive Crying Wind's lovingly intentioned mugging. I flung her hand away, sat up swallowing and hacking in unison. When I managed to clear my windpipe, I wheezed at Skywalker in anger.

"We . . . can't."

Crying Wind pursed her lips. Another pout was on its way. In a clipped, impatient tone, she cried, "Hawwy won't mind. He likes giving us presents. It makes him happy."

"Giving presents to Cherish makes Hawwy happy!" I shouted. "What he chooses to ignore is that he must also give presents to everyone else. If Cherish wasn't there to smile at him, Hawwy wouldn't give you anything."

As punishment for my unseemly demand for reason, Crying Wind ate what little of the cake remained in her hand. And she positively glowed with satisfaction when Skywalker outvoted me.

"Hawwy's a good person," Skywalker said evenly. "And some things cannot be prevented."

There it was. His final say in the matter of my fears for Hawwy. I could expect no help from Skywalker in my attempt to thwart the inevitable. With a heartfelt groan, I fell back against the bed. Skywalker looked away from me to the open window. He became transfixed with whatever was going on just outside in the darkness, while I lay flat on my back flogging my brain for avenues of escape from the fate meant for Hawwy. Meanwhile, Crying Wind contented herself with the cake crumbs remaining in the palm of her hand. Had I known that Hawwy and Cherish were alone in that darkness, I would have saved myself the bitter effort. I would have instead fought with my own beloved for my share of the crumbs of cake. That was a fight I might have won.

•   •   •

Hawwy was Jones's pupil in the early years he spent trying
to learn the Kiowa language. His eventual mastery was due
to his patience and fixed determination. I certainly never
helped him. If anything, I tried hard to impede his awkward
progress, making him always talk to me in Ame-a-can so
that I could learn his language. On that night all he had
was his inane baby talk and a heart full of love. The latter
proved to be his greatest weapon. Women respond to slath-
ering adoration more readily than they do to well-spoken
phrases. And, too, Hawwy had two more gifts for Cherish.
Gifts he couldn't possibly provide the other women.

Clasping the gold locket on its chain around her neck,
he said, "Me mother."

Cherish knew he wasn't calling her his mother. She was
being given something valuable that had belonged to his
own mother. Placing her hand over the locket, holding it
close to her heart, Cherish fell madly in love with Hawwy.

Skywalker grunted, shook his head, turned away from the
window. I felt my blood run cold.

"What?" I demanded. "What did you see?"

"Nothing," he answered. "It's very dark out there."

Skywalker benignly resumed his previous captivation
with his piece of cake. As I told you, Owl Doctors can
never lie. But they can be evasive. I knew he'd seen something in his mind.

Hawwy's second gift was a thing Cherish didn't understand
nearly as well as she had the locket. He gave her a gold-
cased pocket watch. He held it against her ear, and she
gasped hearing the soft ticking sound.

"It's alive!" she cried, trying to struggle away from the
thing in his hand.

Hawwy held on to her more tightly, willing her not to
be afraid.

"Father."

Cherish duly calmed down, reluctantly accepting the

watch he closed her fingers around. "Father." Then re-
verting to Ame-a-can, "It was a gift from my father just
before I left for the Territory. One day you will give it to
our son."

"Father?"

"That's right!" he cried. "That's right, my little darling."

He scooped her up, hugged and kissed her hard again.
Perhaps he wouldn't have been so jubilant had he known
that in three days Cherish would present the watch to her
father. Or that his trusting her with his new and modern
eight-day windup watch would frighten him with its soft
ticking. Frightened the man so much that he opened it,
smashed the glass and the watch face, forever stilled the
heart of the mainspring, then stuffed the gold case with
herbs guaranteed to ward off evil spirits.

THIRTEEN

B illy managed to find Hawwy a few minutes after Hawwy and Cherish had scuttled from their hiding place and parted company. When Billy finally spotted him, Hawwy was standing innocently to the back as soldiers watched several young Kiowa men dancing. Presumably their dancing was to thank their hosts for the food, but in reality they were showing off in front of the Blue Jackets. Those youngsters got their comeuppance when the black men began clapping their hands and two of their own began to dance. Crying Wind was outside for the dancing. From the tales she regaled me with throughout the next day, I concluded that those black men had been impressive dancers.

After spotting Hawwy, Billy left the dancing and happily reported to me that everything was all right. Skywalker and I just listened and said nothing to the contrary. Billy was so pleased with himself it would have been criminal to yell at him, make him understand just how badly he'd actually failed. It wasn't Billy's fault any more than it was mine. No one could fight the inevitable; listening to Billy as he made repeated assurances of his ability to keep Hawwy and

Cherish apart, I came to heartsick terms with the inescapable.

A little later, Skywalker and Billy left together. I was alone for only a few minutes. The festivities were ending, Hawwy came in, humming. He hummed while he undressed, hummed as he blew out the light glowing inside the bosom of the lamp I called the Big Butt Woman, hummed as he lay down on his bed, and eventually hummed himself off to sleep. He was a happy man. A thoroughgoing idiot, but happy nevertheless. Snoring replaced humming. I lay there with my eyes open, seeing only the faint silver light of a dwindling crescent moon that was carried in through the opened window on a breeze as soft as a contented lover's sigh. Listening to his snoring, I mentally let go of Hawwy's hand. In my vivid imagination our hands slowly parted, fingertips lingering for one final instant. I could have caught hold of him again. As his friend, I should have done that. But I didn't. Hawwy fell away, became lost in the vortex of a tempestuous future he should never have made for himself.

The black of night was tapering into drab predawn slate. I awoke, lay on my bed tired to my bones, watching the few stars I could see through the window, fading. The darkened mass of completely still trees loomed against the murky sky like inky wraiths. And I listened to what had pulled me from my barely managed sleep. The soft, almost imperceptible sounds of muttering voices and the muted thudding of hooves as horses were led in a slow-walking pace. The camp just outside the doctoring house was breaking up.

There would not be a great show of leaving. When the fort woke up, the Kiowa would simply be gone. This was not rude. It was simply the way things should be done. It's only when a raiding party is going out and the young men belonging to it might never be seen again that Kiowas make a big farewell with lots of war whoops, tears, kisses, and hugs. When a group is simply leaving, merely moving on, there is rarely a wave and never a backward glance. Because he had reasonably learned advisors, the fort's chief knew that and quite rightly kept to his bed.

I wanted Hawwy to stay in his bed, too, so I picked up the bag of medical tools he had given me and slipped out of his house. My escape would have been perfect if Billy had not been sleeping on the porch of the doctoring house. I had no idea of his presence until I stepped on him. He came awake yelling his head off, throwing the light blanket away, sitting up on the porch. Because the sun had yet to climb as high as the trees, Billy was to my straining eyes nothing more than a moving shadow.

"Meat! You just stepped on my hand."

"What are you doing down there?"

"I camped here. Wanted to be certain sure we got to say good-bye."

"Oh."

I stood silent for a moment, feeling immensely uncomfortable. Billy was honoring me like a favorite relative, and I was at a loss as to how to respond. I needed a lot of things in my life. A white brother was not one of those things. The second thing I didn't need was Hawwy waking up. But hearing Billy, Hawwy did wake up. Through the cracks of the closed door I saw the faint glow as the coal lamp came on. Two heartbeats later, Hawwy emerged, hastily buttoning up his pants. Billy scrambled to his booted feet.

"What's going on?" Hawwy growled to Billy.

"The Ki-o-ways is leavin', Sir."

"Now?"

"Yessir."

"But it's dark."

"Ki-o-ways sees real good in the dark, Lieutenant. Don't bother 'em a-tall. Why they could pick up a pissant's trail on a moonless night."

• • •

Hawwy's formidable silhouette was highlighted by the satiny ochre light spilling through the opened door. In its glow his almost ethereally beautiful face changed, the shadows deepening around his mouth, his narrowing eyes resembling half-moon holes drilled into his skull. His palpable mood was one of wide awake, angry, our flimsy friendship forgotten. Hawwy just stood there, silently accusing me of being a false friend. He saw the Kiowas' predawn departure as nothing more than a vicious plot to spirit Cherish away. His flinty look said all of this as, without a word, he rushed off the porch, clambered down the steps. Then I followed Hawwy, and Billy followed me.

Completely oblivious to the flower of forbidden love blossoming, turning fragrant beneath his very nose, White Bear was understandably flustered as Hawwy rushed toward the camp yelling for Cherish. Cherish was never one for discretion, in that so much like her brother The Cheyenne Robber it was frightening. Cherish ran full tilt for Hawwy, throwing herself bodily into the emotion of the moment and Hawwy's arms. Lone Wolf and Skywalker quickly grabbed White Bear, holding on to him. They had him prisoner, but they could not stop his yelling.

"Cherish! You get yourself off that Blue Jacket right now."

Before Cherish could obey her uncle, Hawwy captured the back of her head and pulled her to him, kissing her on the mouth in full view of everyone. Dumbfounded by the boldness of Hawwy, the brazenness of Cherish, White Bear staggered. A second later, never mind that Hawwy and Cherish were still in each other's arms, still kissing, White Bear broke free of Lone Wolf and Skywalker, grabbed up his single-shot rifle and tried to fix Hawwy in the sights. Skywalker and Lone Wolf jumped him again, struggled to prevent his getting a solid fix.

"I'm going to kill him!"

"Not here," Lone Wolf pleaded.

"Listen to me," Skywalker begged.

"Both of you, get off me!"

White Bear struggled for control of the rifle, the barrel first waving dangerously down at their feet, then swinging harmlessly skyward.

"This is a good morning he's chosen to die," White Bear bellowed, "and I'm going to help him."

"Will you stop!" Skywalker pleaded. "You'll kill Cherish, too."

"Perfect! They can continue with their kissing in the Forever."

A pair of arms wrapped around me. Cutting my eyes left, I saw Crying Wind, her lovely face tense, her exceptionally large eyes brimming with tears.

"Do something," she whimpered.

"There's nothing I can do. This is beyond me. Hawwy won't listen, and Cherish is behaving badly. Whatever White Bear does to them, they deserve it."

Gripped by sudden anger, Crying Wind flounced away from me, stood at arm's distance. When she was in a fighting mood I knew better than to try to reach for her. So I merely stood, returning her stare, trying to let her know that I was the boss, that I knew what was best. But in my heart I knew I was defeated. On the issue of courtship, a man's logic is always frustrated. Women only see romance. And the forbidden liaison taking place before all of us was simply too delicious to be swayed by anything as ambivalent as reason.

Through tightly gritted teeth, she warned, "If my cousin shoots Hawwy, I'll shoot you."

I was still all bandaged up from the previous attempt on my life. I was a pathetic sight, really, but Crying Wind was as blind as a fence post to me, to my bandages. All of her former teary-eyed sympathy for my recovery, for my near brush with death, dried up and flew away like a twirling dust devil. Being shot is a terribly painful experience. Even the threat of being shot again made me cringe. It took about a second to search for the hero inside myself and realize he wasn't home. Therefore I did what any craven would do under the circumstances. I immediately relented.

Armed only with the knowledge that I was more afraid of my wife than I was of her powerful cousin, I left Crying Wind, running to join the conflict. As I passed Hawwy, he was taking the defensive posture, shoving Cherish behind him, covering her with his own body. White Bear's aim was no longer skyward. Anger had redoubled his normal strength, and he was more than Skywalker and Lone Wolf could handle. In spite of their efforts, the barrel of the rifle was dancing in a tight circular pattern on Hawwy's chest. And White Bear's finger was on the trigger. I was wondering if Crying Wind would weep for me when I was stone-cold dead as I placed myself between White Bear's wobbly aim and his target.

His eyes were firestorms of hate and rage. "Get out of the way, Tay-bodal!"

"You can't shoot him."

"Yes, I can."

"He hasn't done anything wrong!" I shouted at the top of my voice.

To my near-fainting relief, Skywalker finally managed to yank the gun from White Bear's hands. "Listen to him," Skywalker cried. "And listen to me."

White Bear was breathing hard, but his bluster was draining. His hateful glare shifted from me to Skywalker.

"I am ashamed," he seethed. "Ashamed of this day."

"You have no reason to be," Skywalker said calmly. "That young Blue Jacket is an honorable man. I've seen his heart, I've read his thoughts. In my opinion, he's much too good for your niece."

White Bear jerked back as if Skywalker had just kicked him in the groin. Then he recovered, came back hotly denying Skywalker's statement.

"I'll have you know that Cherish is the most wonderful

girl in our nation. Not only is she the most beautiful, she's sweet.''

"No, she isn't," Skywalker replied, "she's a brat. And there are only two people I know in this world who refuse to acknowledge the truth. You, and now, Hawwy."

"That's a lie!" White Bear roared.

"Is it?" Skywalker chuckled. "Putting aside the fact that I am unable to lie, ask yourself how many offers of marriage you've received for Cherish. And she's well past marriageable age. The truth is, no one among our kind has the courage to marry her because everyone knows that few things ever delight her. What man in his right mind wants a wife impossible to please? The only other woman I know to compare with her is Crying Wind."

Behind me, my beloved sounded a little squeak. Vindicated, I managed a slight smile. Neither White Bear nor Skywalker noticed as Skywalker continued speaking.

"Remember how long it took you to marry off Crying Wind that first time? And it hasn't been any easier a second time. You had a long wait for someone like Tay-bodal to come along. And even now, he could still change his mind."

A second barely passed and Crying Wind was beside me, taking my hand, looking up at me imploringly.

"You wouldn't do that, would you?" she asked, her voice low and strained, words barely audible.

"Don't you ever threaten to shoot me again," I yelled. Hearing male chuckles, I looked abashedly toward a grudgingly smiling White Bear. Skywalker was visibly grateful for the affirmation I had unwittingly supplied his arguments.

"See what I mean?" Skywalker said, tossing his hands in the air. "You've allowed the females of your family to get away with too much. There aren't that many men with the guts to stand up to them. And their leader is Cherish. I'm telling you to your face that the only man fit to be her husband is a man unable to understand a word she says."

Still facing White Bear, Skywalker pointed toward Hawwy. "And there he stands in all his splendid ignorance. Shoot him and Cherish will be your responsibility for the rest of your life. Let him live and you have not only a solution to your problem, you'll have an extra pair of ears in the white camp."

"That makes sense," Lone Wolf said ingenuously.

"Everyone shut up!" White Bear shouted. "I'm thinking."

His time for thinking was long and laborious. I squeezed Crying Wind's hand, letting her know that everything was all right, that *we* were all right, that no matter how scathing Skywalker had been toward her, I loved her. But while I was reassuring her, I stared in amazement at Skywalker. Amazed not because he'd effectively defused a dangerous situation, but because it had occurred with an awful certainty that he did not like Cherish. And that was so amazing because Skywalker was a man who loved women. Women responded and loved him right back, but for some reason there was an invisible wall between himself and Cherish.

As with all things concerning White Bear, Skywalker's persuading argument had its limits. When his thinking was finished, he approached Hawwy. I turned and summoned Billy. Billy tried very hard to ignore me. I called him again; he apprehensively came forward but stopped, standing well away from Hawwy and White Bear. He was not anxious to be caught in the middle if hard words, then blows, were exchanged. To his credit, Hawwy did not back down. With his eyes perfectly steady, raised chin jutting out, mouth a grim line, he stood toe to toe with White Bear. Locking his stare with Hawwy's, White Bear yelled at Billy.

"You tell this Blue Jacket I do not approve of him. He isn't good enough for my niece. I don't want him related to me."

Stuttering badly, Billy translated. Then Hawwy spoke.

"You tell him I don't care what he thinks. No matter

what he says, I'm marrying Cherish. Even if I have to take her at gun-point.''

''Lieutenant,'' Billy trembled. ''Do you know who you're a-talkin' to?''

''Yes.''

''Well, I do, too, an' I ain't about to tell Satanta nothin' like that.''

''Do it!'' Hawwy yelled straight into White Bear's face.

I could tell by the way Billy spoke that he wasn't translating right. That he was lying his head off.

''The Blue Jacket officer wants to know the bride price. He says he will pay anything.''

''Forty horses, twenty mules!'' White Bear shouted into Hawwy's face. ''And twelve of the army's new guns and five boxes of bullets. Each!''

''Done,'' Billy said, without bothering to translate to Hawwy.

A pleased expression came over White Bear. Perplexed, Hawwy turned to Billy.

''What just happened?''

''You got yourself a bride, Lieutenant.''

''I have?''

''Yeah. But the wedding's a long ways off. It's gonna take us a spell to gather up the necessaries. Bride price for a genu-wine Ki-o-way princess is awful high.''

''Whatever it is, I'll pay it.''

''That's what I done tol't the man. Now, shake his hand afore he changes his mind.''

White Bear rumbled a chesty laugh as Hawwy grabbed up his hand and worked it like a water pump, Hawwy babbling in Ame-a-can like a rain-flooded brook.

The crisis passed. The excitement over, the morning growing bright, the Kiowas returned to complete their preparations for departure. No one watched as Hawwy hugged and kissed Cherish. When she skipped happily away from him, I couldn't help but notice the subtle difference in the way

she was treated. No one was overtly rude or unkind. But
then no one was as welcoming or congratulatory as they
normally should have been to a newly engaged woman.
Cherish had crossed an invisible line, and too pleased with
herself she failed to comprehend that she was no longer
one of us. Swinging up onto his horse, White Bear was the
first to ride away, placing physical as well as psychological
distance between himself and his favorite niece. White Bear
now saw Cherish as a race traitor for conniving behind his
back, choosing for herself a Blue Jacket husband. She had
made herself one of them . . . white. Once the bride price
was paid and White Bear handed her over as promised,
everyone except Cherish understood that he would say her
name no more. That she would be dead to him.

Finally realizing the level of severity of everything that
had just transpired, Crying Wind worriedly chewed the corner of her mouth.

"I—I don't think your being involved with this thing
was such a good idea."

Finally! Cold logic occurred. But then, helped along as
it had been by a visual aid, it would. Anger began to build
inside me, gathering a dangerous momentum as she continued to sniffle.

"I—I think you should just keep out of it from now on.
Let Skywalker deal with it. White Bear never holds a
grudge against him. But he would hold a grudge against
you if he knew how much you've helped Hawwy."

"I haven't helped Hawwy!" I cried. "I said everything
I could say to talk him out of his love for Cherish."

"Oh, that's good," she beamed up at me. "Just stay with
that story and you'll be all right. Now all we have to worry
about is him being mad at me for inviting her to be part of
our rescue of you."

"My darling," I seethed. "Sometimes I could just—"

I was silenced by a kiss. I had only just begun to enjoy
it when she pulled away.

"Oh, no!"

"What now?" I cried irritably.

"White Bear's stupid mules. He didn't want the soldiers to see them, so I hid them. Now I can't remember exactly where. If you don't help me find them, he will never forgive us for losing him his niece and his mules."

The other women had noticed the absent mules as well. Their proud horses were balking at being treated like pack animals. Taking their cue from White Bear, the warriors ignored the women's predicament, leaving the camp in droves. In the time it takes to blink twice, the only men left in the camp were me, Hawwy, and Billy. Leaving a wounded man with a group of lagging women could hardly be described as a stirring rescue. I'm not surprised that this one exploit never made the list in the lengthy catalog of White Bear's gripping legend.

Because helping me out one more time bought him another opportunity to be with Cherish, Hawwy behaved like an excited long-legged puppy. Cherish responded and was just as happily engrossed with him. That the rest of us shuffled all around them failed to turn one hair of their interest. This made the three remaining women very angry. Cherish wasn't doing her fair share of the packing up, and they were mad, said they wouldn't do another thing for her. That started off a lot of yelling and complaining. I just left them all to it, silently packing up whatever anyone insisted they wouldn't dirty their hands with. Relief washed through me when I spotted Billy leading four mules toward the demolished campsite. I dropped the bag in my hands, running across the field to meet him.

Handing me the lead ropes, Billy said soberly, "These are part of the bride price. Will you see that White Bear gets them . . . please?"

"Have you enlightened Hawwy to the size of his promise?"

"No."

"Are you going to tell him?"

"No. I'll just get things to White Bear as I lay hands on

them. It's better to keep the lieutenant out of it. The mules
and the horses wouldn't bother him too much, but the guns
would make him crazy."

"How are you going to get the things to White Bear."

Billy looked at me, both surprised and bewildered. "I'll
just get them to you. You'll—"

"No, I won't," I railed. "I'm finished. I'm having nothing more to do with this. Skywalker's your man. You give
the things to him."

"Wait," Billy cried. "Is Skywalker that long skinny
buck that looks at a man like he can see inside him?"

"That's the one."

"Forget it. I'm not going near him, Meat. He gives me
the shivers. I think maybe he talks to the dead."

Taken aback by his last statement, I looked hard at Billy,
burning him into my mind. As was his wont he wore his
hat pulled low onto his head, the long coat, the side pistol,
and the tooled boots he thought so much of. He was standing there looking like a white man, and his Comanche ac-
cent was as deplorable as any white man's would be. But
he had just made a bad mistake with his disguise. The last
part of his speech, and the inflection had been perfect. And
even though at that time I could not speak the Ame-a-can
language, I knew enough about them to know that no white
man would ever begin a sentence with "I think maybe . . ."
That's pure Indian. By unthinkingly using a speech pattern
deeply ingrained in all Indians, Billy had made his one and
only slip.

With a swipe of my hand, I knocked Billy's hat off. He
was too astonished by what I had just done to move. And
I was too astonished by what I was seeing. So we simply
stood there staring at each other for an indeterminate length
of time.

Finally, I asked softly, "What tribe are you with, Billy?"

Billy's jaw tightened and twitched. He turned away from
me, picking up his hat, slamming it back on his head, pull-

ing it low, the shadow of the brim once again hiding the high cheekbones, the dark eyes.

"No tribe," he said sullenly. "My father was just passing through when he raped my mother. Then when I was a little boy and she couldn't hide me the way she had when I was a baby, she took me to the orphan home. She told them she'd found me in the street. Asked if they would keep me until my parents came. I understood every word she said. I just stood there holding her hand, knowing no one would ever claim me. That it was my own mother giving me away. And I knew why. I was beginning to favor my father, and it hurt her to look at me. So when I got old enough to leave that place all by myself, I got this hat. No one would ever have to look at me. Not even me."

I was filled with a terrible sadness. How many more Billys, I wondered solemnly, were out there. The little lost ones, our own precious babies born out of violence, condemned to lurk in the shadows of the chasm dividing two very separate worlds. I now understood why he was such a great admirer of my nation. Why he felt it would be an honor to be killed by one of us.

"Your father was . . . Kiowa."

"No tribe!" he yelled so loudly everyone turned in our direction. He lowered his voice to a husky whisper. "I'm mixed blood. Nobody wants me."

"You're wrong," I said calmly, swinging up onto one of the mules. Looking down at him as he fumed and fidgeted, I said as gently as I knew how, "When you're tired of playing white man, you know the direction home. And your brother, Tay-bodal, will welcome you."

Leading the trailing mules, I rode for the women.

By midday we found the hidden mules. Waiting with them was a single warrior, Chasing Horse. I found his presence irritating and suspicious. He was just as uncomfortable while he helped me readjust some of the packs on one of the mules.

"I—I just wanted to know if you were"—he shrugged deeply—"all right."

"I'll live," I grunted.

"How badly were you hit in the head?"

That finished off any remnant of good humor. I rounded on him and gave him a good telling off.

"My head, thank you very much for your interest, works just fine. My memory is clear, my abilities to think unimpaired. You may tell certain members of your family that I am more than prepared to speak on The Cheyenne Robber's behalf. Now unless you're anxious to tell me more of your fat lies, my good advice to you is that you get away from me and that you stay just as far away from me as you possibly can."

Chasing Horse had the grace to look ashamed. He began to walk away, stopped, and turned. "I had my reasons."

"Reasons for doing a thing you know is wrong is never an excuse. Learn that early and you'll live to be a wise old man. But not if you linger long around me."

His dancing eyes studied my face for a moment; he tried to smile, sounded a fainthearted laugh, swung up onto his horse, rode away.

As for the women and myself, after we ate a quick meal, we all started for home. We made good time, arriving in the camp in the middle of night. No one bothered to greet us, no one seemed interested in the fascinating tales we had to tell about the fort and the soldiers as we turned our horses out, unpacked the mules. Crying Wind worked beside me and we were silent. We both understood that Cherish was the cause of this lackluster welcome. Stunned relatives not knowing what to say, or simply too afraid of White Bear's temper, prudently stayed inside their homes.

Cherish was oblivious to the discomfort she caused us. She prattled away in a loud voice, for the benefit of all those hidden but listening ears, about how her rich Blue Jacket husband would give her this thing or that thing, that all she would ever have to do for the rest of her life was simply point at a rich gift and he would give it to her. I knew this was all terrified bravado. That the enormity of her commitment to Hawwy had finally dawned on her. That Cherish was working hard to convince herself that her life as a Blue Jacket's wife was a thing to envy. But Crying Wind was becoming so irked that her right hand clenched and unclenched. She ached to slap Cherish's bragging mouth.

In a fury she whispered that and more, concluding with, "I can't sleep with her tonight. I might do something violent."

"There's my lodge," I whispered back.

"I can't go there! My cousin will go crazy."

We were standing on the other side of the grazing mule, hidden behind the mule's wide body. I took Crying Wind in my arms, kissed the top of her head.

"He has so much on his mind I don't believe he would notice if we ran hand in hand, stark naked through the middle of the camp."

She laughed softly, her entire body shaking. I held her hard against me, enjoying her quiet laughter. Pressing the moment, I brazenly begged, "Sleep with me. Please. I want you in my bed and in my arms so badly, it's tearing me apart inside."

"Only if you promise to wake me before dawn."

"I swear it on my life."

Years of sleeping alone had dulled my memory to the realities of sleeping with a woman for the first time. A woman you love. A woman you want to impress with your perfection. There are too many things to worry about when you want to seem perfect, and the chief worry I had that night was all those beans I'd ingested at the fort. Beans have a terrible propensity to backfire. Curled up on our sides, Crying Wind snuggled against my chest, I was rigid, my buttocks locked so tightly, beads of sweat bloomed on every inch of my skin.

Only when she went dozed off first did I finally relax and drift slowly away, resigning myself that whatever happened during our sleep was not my fault. It felt like only a few moments later when I awoke with a snort, unable to breathe. Coming fully awake, I realized Crying Wind was holding me hard by the nose. I could see her angry face very clearly in the light pouring down through the smoke hole and with the fragmented rays peeking through the laces of the wall seams.

"You snore!" she screamed in a whisper.

I pulled her hand off my nose and yelled huskily back at her. "No, I do not. I'll have you know I sleep as quietly as the dead."

"I don't know what kind of dead person you're talking about. I personally have never heard of a dead man able to breathe well enough to rattle the walls of a lodge. I thought I was in the middle of a tornado."

My pride mortally wounded, I sat up. "What time is it?"

"It's morning. And you didn't wake me up the way you swore on your life you would do. Now I'm trapped."

Morning! And I was late. Everyone would be waiting for me. Most especially The Cheyenne Robber. "Make yourself useful," I cried.

It was very important to look my very best. No matter how much she scolded as she worked to make certain I looked just right, I could not have managed without her. She helped change the bandage on my shoulder, eased me into a covering buckskin shirt, clean breechcloth, and my best pair of leggings. While I sat putting on my good shoes, she brushed out my hair and oiled it to a gleaming shine. A wife is an invaluable treasure. Because of her, I looked better than I had in ages. And because I looked so well, I left for White Bear's lodge brimming with confidence. I needed to be brimming. In fact, I could have done with an ocean of confidence. For I was marching forward to meet the most difficult day of my life.

● ● ●

White Bear's private lodge was packed with silent men. I slapped the outside wall of the lodge, announced myself, waited for permission to enter. When it was given and I ducked inside, only White Bear glanced at me. Everyone, even Skywalker, kept their eyes down. Everyone was counting on me, and their last-minute doubt was as tangible as the lodge walls.

"You're late," White Bear said in a throaty growl.

"I overslept."

"Typical," he sneered. He stood and everyone stood up with him. I stepped back as they wordlessly filed past and exited.

I had the unnerving feeling that I had lived all of this before. The council was exactly the same as it had been those long days ago. But instead of sitting in the back, behind the boys and in the harsh sunlight, I was now in the row of chiefs, seated in the dark shade between White Bear and Lone Wolf. The Cheyenne Robber was brought out exactly as he had been, lashed to a pole lying across his shoulders. But this time he didn't fight. Today he held himself straight and tall, his eyes never leaving me as he was paraded to the center of the hushed council.

It's an awesome responsibility, being a worthy man's only hope. I began to review everything I'd learned, trying to find fault in my theory as Kicking Bird most certainly would try. So in those final moments, I attacked my theory exactly the way Kicking Bird could be expected to attack it. My trembling was not lessened by the realization that my theory held. That I could actually prove it. For this theory would destroy almost as many lives as it would save. And there was nothing I could do but tell the truth.

Owl Man stood. The moment to speak my truths had arrived. My heart was beating hard in my chest, my brain lost inside a numbing stupor, my ears unable to discern the words Owl Man spoke. Then, from beside me, White Bear answered a question I could only suppose Owl Man had asked.

"Tay-bodal speaks for me, for my nephew."

After saying this, White Bear turned his head in my direction, his narrowing eyes grabbing hold of mine. Days before, this dreadful moment had seemed years away. That it had finally arrived came all over me like a vile surprise. My stomach was fluttering violently. My hands were clammy and shaking. I felt sick. Standing on legs I barely trusted to hold me upright, I walked forward. When I came to stand before Owl Man, my back to the waiting assembly, that gracious ancient placed a steadying hand on my quivering shoulder, and he spoke to me in a low voice that only I could hear.

"Speak the truth as you know it. Brace up. Do not be afraid."

He withdrew his hand and left me. As the tension mounted behind me, I glanced at The Cheyenne Robber. Looking at me, he smiled wanly, his uncertainty evident in the slight tremor of his lips.

I took a deep breath, exhaled it, turned.

FOURTEEN

"The task I faced was hard," I began simply. And as I continued speaking, uncertainties began to fall away, little by little, like the gentle, silent falling of golden leaves, turning slowly, gliding downward, and coming to rest at the base of an autumnal tree.

"Allow me to go back to the beginning." Even to my own ears my voice sounded clear and strong. "Begin with the day the incriminating leggings were displayed by the second wife of Runs The Bulls, the woman known as Shield Woman. As you all know, this woman made a great fuss, yelling about how she found the leggings belonging to Kicking Bird's nephew, under White Otter's bed. What she said was a lie. She hadn't found those leggings at all. They had been given to her."

Kicking Bird began to bristle. Looking directly at him, I cut his temper off at the root. "No, not by your nephew. I really can't say for certain, but I'm under the impression he hadn't any prior knowledge, nor was he in any way a partner in the planned conspiracy against White Otter. I imagine he stood in the crowd just as surprised by Shield

Woman's accusations as everyone else. But, Kicking Bird, you know deep in your heart that your nephew was not the kind of man to let an opportunity go by. His had been a rather strong, self-serving personality and he wasn't known for being devoutly honorable. He hadn't upset you too badly in the past because his indiscretions had mostly been trivial. Nothing that couldn't be settled peacefully with a handshake, a few presents. But this was a big thing. This was a woman he wanted very badly. During the moments she was being accused of taking him as her lover, it was within his power to clear her name, yet doing so would also most certainly cost him her.

"Standing there in the crowd, thinking it through, he was probably feeling pretty good about himself. You know how young men like to brag. The trouble is, bragging about virtuous women from good families can get young men into serious trouble. In this case, Shield Woman was doing all the bragging for him. The other young men most probably were looking at him and thinking him a lucky fellow. Pride in a man not overburdened by conscience is a dangerous thing. It causes him to be more self-centered than he normally would be. That was why your nephew chose not to do the honorable thing. That was why he didn't stand tall, publicly confess that those leggings had been stolen, that he had never in his life seen the inside of White Otter's lodge.

"The saddest thing is that his doing the right thing would have saved his life, spared the Nation all this misery, but your nephew," I nodded to Kicking Bird, "was not a person capable of thinking beyond the moment, and most certainly not a person prone to be sensitive to another's distress. Even if that other person also happened to be the woman he supposedly loved and wanted to marry."

I glanced away from Kicking Bird, seeking and finally finding Runs The Bulls. "But then neither was her father moved by her tears or her cries of innocence. And he, better than Kicking Bird's nephew, knew she was telling the truth,

because it was Runs The Bulls who stole the leggings and
instructed his second wife in exactly what she was supposed to do and say.''

A single gasp sounded from the crowd of men. The
Cheyenne Robber bellowed, made a lunge in the direction
of White Otter's father. The guards sprang to restrain him.
White Bear began bawling at the top of his lungs, protesting
the way his nephew was being manhandled. Runs The Bulls
leaped to his feet and over White Bear's din started screaming that I was a liar. During all of this, Owl Man calmly
waved his feather fan and several young men, on this cue,
rose and made their way toward Runs The Bulls, effectively
surrounding him. Those men had been sent by the ever
prudent Owl Man to prevent any attempt by Runs The Bulls
to leave the council or worse, attack me. When everything
gradually calmed down, I was permitted to speak again.

"Runs The Bulls's motive for planting evidence against
his daughter is easily explained. First, White Otter was
courted by The Cheyenne Robber. Runs The Bulls was
enormously pleased. His daughter's marriage to The Cheyenne Robber would unite him to a powerful family. Being
related to someone like White Bear presented him the pos-
sibility of his bargaining or buying his way into the Onde
class. He wanted that honor very badly. So badly that he
went so far as to allow the courting couple outlandish freedom. With his blessings they went off on numerous occasions without any type of chaperon.

"Then Kicking Bird came to him, speaking for his own
nephew, and that nephew began turning up at his door.
White Bear retaliated as has been his habit during the last
years whenever Kicking Bird moved to get the better of
him. Kicking Bird and White Bear began literally drowning
a thoroughly disconcerted Runs The Bulls with friendship
and gifts, pulling him back and forth between them. He
was a small man caught in the middle of an ongoing feud
between two of the most powerful men in the Nation. Imagine Runs The Bulls's terror. If he willingly chose one over

the other, his doing so was tantamount to making for himself a terrible enemy.

"By his mother's own admission, Runs The Bulls is not the smartest of men. What he did next was not only despicable, it was unbelievably stupid. He couldn't get his hands on anything belonging to The Cheyenne Robber because we all know The Cheyenne Robber to be a fastidious individual. If even so much as a brush belonging to The Cheyenne Robber went missing, he would raise a commotion. Nor would he stand idly by, mentally calculating the benefits to himself while something belonging to him was used to falsely accuse the woman he loved.

"On the other hand, Kicking Bird's nephew was an acknowledged sloven. Stealing from him was incredibly easy. His life was such a jumble, he most likely never even noticed that a pair of his leggings was missing until that fateful day. Also, he was so devious himself that as long as the situation clearly benefited him, Runs The Bulls could count on him to go along with the farce both of them knew very well to be a lie.

"In theory the end result of this sad pretense would see Runs The Bulls handing over his daughter to Kicking Bird's nephew. How could White Bear possibly blame him for the impetuous actions of a pair of young lovers? The answer is, he couldn't. But being a dull-witted fellow, Runs The Bulls failed to remember all of those private walks he'd allowed his daughter to take with The Cheyenne Robber. He failed to see that those two young people were desperately in love and he failed to draw into the equation the kind of man The Cheyenne Robber is. Which is ironic when you consider that he'd been afraid to steal so much as an article of clothing from The Cheyenne Robber. I'm astounded he actually believed that The Cheyenne Robber would do nothing as he gave White Otter to another man. She's the most precious thing in The Cheyenne Robber's life, but Runs The Bulls wasn't thinking about that, nor was he thinking of the other consequences.

"I believe with all my heart that it simply never occurred to him that his little scheme might touch off a civil war. Just as it never occurred to him that by enlisting Shield Woman's aid, he was elevating her over his much-loved first wife.

"Her very name announces how he feels about her. Sits Beside Him. A name that means treasured wife. A wife he always wants close to him. Only after the event did it occur to him that by shaming his daughter, he had also condemned Sits Beside Him. He became almost uncontrollable with rage when he realized that his first wife had lost her right to be considered an honorable wife and a good mother. But Shield Woman had known all along. Her husband's foolish scheme fit wonderfully in her ambition to replace Sits Beside Him, to be Runs The Bulls's first wife. Realizing all of that she wasn't difficult to persuade into going along with her husband's feeble plan. It was only when everything blew up in his face that he finally realized what he had done to his first wife. But he was caught. No matter how the issue of White Otter's disgrace was settled, he'd forever lost Sits Beside Him. So he tried shutting her out of his mind. He sent her into isolation, changed her name, blamed everything on her, but he suffered her loss so acutely that he had to take himself away for a while. The excuse he used was that he was hunting. What he was actually doing was hiding from his demanding second wife and her hold on him, and weeping with misery for having thrown away his first wife.

"But as I've recounted to you, Runs The Bulls's greatest mistake was expecting The Cheyenne Robber to believe his miserable lie and do nothing while White Otter was being shamed. That grievous miscalculation was the actual cause of everything falling apart. The Cheyenne Robber effectively foiled what should have been White Otter's wedding day and prevented her father from handing her over to Kicking Bird's nephew when he stepped forward, challenged Kicking Bird's nephew, struck him and knocked him down. That challenge against his manhood made it impossible for Kicking Bird's nephew to claim his prize until the matter of his honor had been duly settled. The Cheyenne Robber had no intention of wasting his time settling anything of the sort. His challenge bought him the time he needed to arrange White Otter's kidnapping. That was what he was busy doing while his hated rival was being murdered.''

I paused for a deep breath. It was during this brief second that I realized just how tightly I held my audience. They were all leaning forward, arms resting against crossed legs, all eyes following my every movement. As I slowly exhaled, I listened. There was no bird song, no hum of insects. The atmosphere was so unnaturally quiet that an earthworm's yawn would have sounded like a clap of thunder. Clearing my throat, I began to pace as I resumed speaking.

''During my days of discovery, another problem rose to confront me. On the face of it, it was a minor problem, more annoying than anything else, but nevertheless I was baffled by it. This was a problem put to me by the persons known as Stands On A Hill and Chasing Horse. Now, I didn't know these young men. The Nation is such a big place that I had never even heard of them. But I learned later that they are considered to be troublemakers. Of Chasing Horse, I could believe it. He was never friendly. He presented himself to me as a churlish, deeply angry young man. Stands On A Hill was the exact opposite. I learned early on that he hadn't cared all that much for his recently departed relative. To be blunt, our first conversation dealt with his worry that his dead relative might come back to life.

''The next time I saw them both was the day of the funeral. It rained hard that morning and after the burial I spent one or two pleasant hours in the company of Hears The Wolf. Leaving him I again encountered Stands On A Hill and Chasing Horse. Chasing Horse didn't have anything to do with me, but Stands On A Hill took me aside and told me the thing that had me puzzled for days.''

I stopped pacing, looked out over my captivated audience. ''That was where Stands On A Hill made a mistake. He couldn't know that Hears The Wolf had, only moments before, confided in me a secret vital to his life. Not knowing that, Stands On A Hill blatantly lied, told me that Hears The Wolf was Hwame.''

I waited stoically for the gasps of surprise and the turning of heads and buzz of excited conversation to die down. During the wait, I scanned the gathering, found Hears The Wolf. He smiled sadly and nodded. I hand signed, ''I'm sorry.'' He lifted his shoulders in a resigned shrug. Regaining my audience's attention, I ventured on, sorrowing in my spirit that the truth can sometimes be a coldhearted beast.

''There are two types of lies,'' I said. ''One type is for gain, the second, protective. That was the kind of lie Stands On A Hill told. Protective. Next I had to think out why Stands On A Hill would believe Hears The Wolf needed protecting. That answer came from Hears The Wolf and Sits Beside Him.''

Looking fully at the crowd, I observed my listeners. They had settled in like children gathered around the fire anxious to hear a story from an exceptional teller. I knew this part of the drama would not disappoint them.

''It all goes back to a time when Hears The Wolf was known as White Clay. To a time when this young man, White Clay, was in love with a lovely young girl and I know personally that she was in love with him.'' My gaze traveled back to Hears The Wolf. ''She still is.'' His expression tightened and Hears The Wolf lowered his head. ''This girl's father was terribly cruel to White Clay, tried to kill him. That awful old man did not kill White Clay's body but he managed to kill White Clay's heart when he married his daughter to Runs The Bulls. After all that, White Clay changed his name and tried repeatedly to commit suicide by going out on raid after raid, being brave but reckless. To his great disappointment all that ever earned him was not the death for which he longed but great wealth and high honors.

"Now you're asking yourselves, why would such a man want to die? Why didn't he simply choose another woman, make a good life for himself? Those are the very same questions that wouldn't leave me alone even after I'd settled the lunacy of the Hwame business—knew it to be a lie. Although I'll admit, that Hwame thing did have me convinced for a while. On the face of it, it was entirely believable. He was a man without a wife, a rich man almost comical in the way he dressed, the way he pampered . . . children."

I snapped my fingers and the entire council started as if they had suddenly popped out of a trance.

"That was it! Children. That was the real reason why for so long Hears The Wolf had wanted to die. That was the thing he found unbearable. Children. Or more accurately, *a* child. A little girl he saw all the time but did not dare approach without calling undue attention to him, to her. A little girl he could only speak to when she was with other children. So he made a point of attracting children, especially her little playmates. And how did he attract them? Simple. He used gifts and wildly eccentric clothing. The combination of the two was irresistible. Children flocked to Hears The Wolf in this very calculated way, allowing him to be close to that one child. His daughter. White Otter."

I heard a thud. Turning swiftly, I saw The Cheyenne Robber sitting on the ground, his legs splayed. History had come so very close to repeating itself that the force of the truth had knocked him off his feet. In a stupor he looked up at me. Horror radiated from his eyes. I knew he was struggling to come to terms with just how narrowly he had missed suffering the same fate as Hears The Wolf. Unfortunately, I didn't have time to comfort him. Runs The Bulls

had rallied. When I turned back, he was shouting and pointing accusingly toward Hears The Wolf.

"Then he's the one who killed Kicking Bird's nephew.
To save his bastard child, to get his revenge on me, he did
everything."

"No." I looked coldly at Runs The Bulls. "He didn't
kill anyone."

That long-ago Arapaho doctor's voice reverberated
through my mind. *Only bullies kill people by the neck.* He
had been right then, he was right even now.

"Hears The Wolf knew long before the body was ever
discovered by the women that his relative was dead, just
as he also knew the identity of the murderer. But he was
so trapped inside his own dark secret he didn't dare speak
out. However, he knew I could speak, which was why he
shared part of his secret, confessed to me his love for Sits
Beside Him when that kind of confession wasn't really necessary except to send me in the direction of the real killer.
And he did that twice. *Twice* he sent me straight to—You."

Every drop of blood drained from Runs The Bulls's blus-
tering face. "Th-that's not true."

"Yes, it is. Just as it's true that it was you and your wife
Shield Woman who tried to kill me. The motive behind
that attempt is painfully clear. I had saved Shield Woman
from the brutal wrath of your own mother but before I
saved her, before I extracted from her the promise that she
would tell me the whole truth regarding the leggings and
her accusations against White Otter, your mother said an
interesting thing. She said that Sits Beside Him and White
Otter were nothing to do with you. I knew then that White
Otter was not your blood child. What I needed from Shield
Woman was the truth about the leggings and to find out if
she knew the truth about White Otter as well. She tricked
me when she managed to hide behind a faint, forestalling
the inevitable. Once she was in Sitting Bear's camp she
bought favor from a group of boys who in turn got word
to you of where she was. And you came running.

"If there is one thing that can be said about that wife of yours, it's this: she's sly. Being sly, she knew that I had already guessed the identity of the one who had given her the leggings. Which was certainly easy enough. It hardly requires a robust mind to work out the identity of the one person in this world with the power to force her to do anything, the one person it is in her own best interest to guard. So when you got her back from Sitting Bear, she didn't waste any time telling you that I was dangerous. And she rode with you when you set out to attack me because you had bungled everything else so badly she no longer trusted you to kill me on your own."

"You can't prove any of this," Runs The Bulls fumed.

Spoken like a diehard idiot.

With a grandiose wave of my hands I dismissed The Cheyenne Robber's now unnecessary guards and beckoned them to follow me. Then I marched straight for Runs The Bulls. The guards already around him kept him in place. When I reached him, he had the sense not to fight me as I grabbed up his arm, pushed back the sleeve of his summer shirt, and saw exactly what I expected to see. A series of deep and vibrant gouges Coyote Walking's clawing finger-nails had made on Runs The Bulls's upper arm. The dying man had raked his killer from the shoulders to the elbows. And the wounds weren't healing well. They were red and swollen with infection. Runs The Bulls hadn't availed him-self of a doctor's treatment. The chances were in his favor that any doctor he chose would have tended him without a comment, even though any doctor would have found it strange that a man would have scratches on that part of his arms. To a doctor, a patient's confidentiality is paramount. But even a doctor being aware of his wounds wasn't some-thing Runs The Bulls was willing to risk. Not until after The Cheyenne Robber had been pronounced guilty and was safely banished.

"Here is the proof," I said to Runs The Bulls's face. "I imagine it all happened this way, please stop me if I err.

Two men sent word to Kicking Bird's nephew to meet with them. One man was you, the second, White Otter's real father, Hears The Wolf. Both of you knew you were speaking to Kicking Bird's nephew in turns. Hears The Wolf certainly knew who you were, but his identity was never revealed to you. When you felt you were safe from being identified as the murderer, you were planning to find out who he was, even if you had to beat Sits Beside Him, forcing her to speak his name. Then you would have killed him, too.

"Now it comes back again to Stands On A Hill, his need to protect his favorite relative behind a lie. I know that of all the men in his family, indeed the entire nation, Stands On A Hill reveres only Hears The Wolf. When one man idolizes another it stands to reason that that man would know everything there is to know about his hero. *Everything*," I stressed. Not for Runs The Bulls's benefit. He was too busy flogging his simple brain with ways to save himself. No, I was talking to the council. I turned back to Runs The Bulls even though he actively ignored me.

"Stands On A Hill knew the true paternity of White Otter. He also knew that that one truth could be turned and used as a motive against Hears The Wolf. It's more than probable that he even believed Hears The Wolf was the actual murderer. So to me, a man Hears The Wolf had already confided the truth to, Stands On A Hill, came up with the Hwame debacle. It was a desperate lie and told only to me because Stands On A Hill knew that I was a spy. So he believed he was being clever, that he had successfully hidden Hears The Wolf behind the guise of a man who does not care for women. Bear in mind that the whole time he worked to remove suspicion from Hears The Wolf, Stands On A Hill believed him to be the actual murderer. He believed that Hears The Wolf had been driven to murder in order to protect his only daughter from a brutal marriage to a scheming no-good. Stands On A Hill completely believed that was how it had happened because he knew that

Hears The Wolf had arranged to meet their mutual relative, because he had carried the message between the two."

I turned just enough to see Stands On A Hill's blanching face. "You told me this yourself."

Stands On A Hill wiped copious tears from his eyes and face. In a rasping voice, he said, "Yes. Yes, I did."

"And the first day you spoke to me, you weren't afraid of ghosts so much as you'd been terrified that your cousin would come back from the dead and name Hears The Wolf as his attacker."

Stands On A Hill looked away.

I turned back to the still mentally calculating Runs The Bulls.

"When their mutually despised cousin turned up dead, Stands On A Hill couldn't be blamed for believing Hears The Wolf was responsible, because he didn't know anything about the previous meeting the dead man had with you. But Hears The Wolf knew. He simply couldn't prove his suspicions without making everything worse. He needed me to do that for him, and that's why he confided in me. I'm a good listener and a reasonably trustworthy person, but I was a stranger to him. One does not trust a complete stranger with something so painful, so personal as the secret of unrequited love without an ulterior motive. He had one. He knew the truth about me. Knew that I was working secretly for The Cheyenne Robber's cause.

"But Hears The Wolf became a little frustrated that I was going in and out of Kicking Bird's camp more than I was concentrating my attentions on you. As I said, he'd already set me on your trail twice. Doing so a third time would only draw my attentions right back to him. Had Hears The Wolf known just how close I was, that I was coming up behind you with the truth about the leggings, he would have left me alone and you wouldn't have gotten the chance to run me down and shoot me. But he didn't know. All he knew was that I was coming in and out of his own camp unnecessarily. He wanted me solidly onto you, so through the ever-compliant Stands On A Hill, he exposed me as a spy to Kicking Bird. He knew how enraged that would make Kicking Bird and exactly how I would be treated. Then, with Kicking Bird's camp closed to me, I'd have no choice but to go back to your camp, and he was counting hard on your being stupid enough to reveal yourself in fairly short order. The trouble was, he didn't know you were in a blithering panic caused and continually stirred up by your wasp of a second wife. Nor had he realized just how dangerous you were until the news filtered back to him that I had been gunned down. Learning that, Hears The Wolf knew a panicked moment or two himself, which is why he sent Kicking Bird to the fort. Not because he felt that Kicking Bird should be in on any council taking place between chiefs and the fort's chief, but because he was desperate to know if I was all right. He proved to be so desperate that he unknowingly revealed himself to me for the third and final time. He sent to me the one person I knew was a liar when he discreetly inquired about my health. He sent Chasing Horse.''

Shaking my head disapprovingly I looked again at Hears The Wolf. ''That really was sloppy.''

His smile was broad, unembarrassed. ''Sorry.''

I huffed a mirthless laugh. ''No, you're not.''

Turning again to Runs The Bulls, I said, ''Your killing Kicking Bird's nephew was an accident, wasn't it?''

It was sad the way he jumped for that faint gleam of hope. Hearing the question, he saw it, I believe, as his chance for a pardon of the unpardonable. He was like a lion of a catfish sounding for a tidbit of bait wriggling just above the surface from a suspended hook.

''That's right! That little weasel. He'd changed his mind. He said he didn't want White Otter anymore. He said she was a disgrace and he didn't want anything more to do with her. He said she was a slut and a . . .'' His words trailed off.

What Coyote Walking then told him must have come as

a severe blow. To have only one child, a beautiful child
that was the pride of his life, only to learn in the callous
manner I imagine Coyote Walking had used, that that child
wasn't actually his, must have been terrible. But no matter
how despicably Coyote Walking behaved, it still didn't al-
ter the fact that Runs The Bulls had been ready, eager, and
willing to sacrifice that same child, first upon the altar of
prestige, next on the altar of convenience. Her feelings had
never once mattered to him.

"Did you try to force him to name her real father?"

Runs The Bulls, looking down at his feet, nodded his
head, spoke in a contrite voice.

"Yes. But he wouldn't do it. All he would say was that
I wasn't important to him anymore. That only her real father was important. That her *real* father was going to give
him a big herd of horses and all he would have to do was
drop all claims on her. He said he was happy to do it even
if her real father only gave him one horse. He called her
names again. Called The Cheyenne Robber names. When
he started laughing and calling me names as well, when he
said he was going to tell everyone what a fool I had been
for years, I—"

"You grabbed him by the throat to make him shut up."

Runs The Bulls was nodding hard and weeping, tears
streaming his face. Unable to feel anything but disgust, I
turned away from him. I wasn't moved by his tears, or even
convinced that he was sorry for all the wrong he had
caused. But I knew most certainly that he was sorry about
one thing. He was entirely sorry that he had failed to kill
me.

Dismissing Runs The Bulls from my mind, I began to
fix on the puzzle of how Coyote Walking had found out
the truth of White Otter's paternity. He certainly hadn't
known about it prior to the final hours of his life. If he had
known, he would have profited from that knowledge early
on, really put the squeeze on Hears The Wolf. Just as he
planned to begin squeezing Hears The Wolf on the night

he died and why he was so anxious to rid himself of Runs The Bulls's inconsequential presence. Coyote Walking would have kept Hears The Wolf's secret. For a lifelong price.

The answer to this final quandary came to me like a bolt from beyond as I caught sight of Chasing Horse's nervously sweating face. Chasing Horse fidgeted, looked like a man about to jump out of his skin.

"Chasing Horse," I shouted. "You evil, poisonous little toad. I hope that after today I never have to see you again. You're the one who told your dead cousin about White Otter. Because you are close to Stands On A Hill, he mistakenly trusted you with Hears The Wolf's secret. And trusting you with that secret was all right as long as it seemed that your dead cousin was going to marry White Otter.

"But among his other failings, your dead cousin was a coward. He didn't want to face The Cheyenne Robber's challenge. In fact, he was worried about it and was looking for any excuse to throw White Otter away. It wouldn't have bothered him that she would then be in terrible disgrace. He'd disgraced another girl and that girl had run off and become a Cheyenne. The only difference between that first girl and White Otter was that he hadn't actually offered for the first girl so she was not a problem for him when he changed his mind about marrying her. But White Otter he'd publicly claimed. He couldn't just throw her away, pretend none of it had ever happened the way he had before. No, to get rid of White Otter, to avoid The Cheyenne Robber's challenge, he needed a valid reason to offer her aggrieved father. And you gave it to him.

"You've never loved Hears The Wolf like a brother. You only loved that he was brave and wealthy and generous and allowed you to walk in his reflected glory. It wasn't enough for you that he got you out of trouble whenever you fell into it. You wanted what he had. You wanted it all. Through your equally greedy cousin, you saw a way to have all of his wealth because you knew Hears The Wolf would do anything to protect his daughter. The horses he agreed to pay was just the beginning. If Runs The Bulls hadn't killed your partner, the two of you would have stripped Hears The Wolf of all he had.''

Chasing Horse confirmed his guilt. He jumped to his feet and ran away. Men stood shaking their fists, cawing after him as he fled. He wouldn't be banished; Chasing Horse managed to escape that form of punishment, but he would become a non-person. Someone no one talked to. No one loved. Not ever again.

Sitting Bear's expression was stony as he faced the assembly, speaking for all the chiefs.

''I think maybe we've heard enough. Tay-bodal has proved to all of us that The Cheyenne Robber is not guilty. Untie him.''

Skywalker and White Bear rushed to The Cheyenne Robber and cut away the bonds, hauled him to his feet, dusted him off, and hugged him in turns.

''As for Runs The Bulls,'' Sitting Bear said in a flat, toneless voice, ''for killing Kicking Bird's nephew, trying to blame an innocent man, and then attempting to murder Tay-bodal, those crimes demand our harshest retribution. Everyone here knows the penalty for one Kiowa taking another Kiowan life. Banishment. The same punishment Runs The Bulls was happy for The Cheyenne Robber to suffer in his place. So hear me now, Runs The Bulls, for I have just said your name for the last time in my life.

''You and your miserable second wife, known as Shield Woman, are to leave our nation. You will both be stripped of clothing, horses, weapons, everything you own. All of those things will be given away. Your lodges will be burned to the ground. Naked and ashamed, you and your woman are turned away from us. If you live or die, that is not our concern. Your first wife, known to all of us as Sits Beside Him, is divorced from you. I now give her over to her rightful husband, Hears The Wolf.''

A triumphant shout blasted behind me. Turning slightly
I saw out of the corner of my eye, Hears The Wolf rocking,
his head thrown back. He let go another joyous whoop,
thrusting his arms skyward, his hands fisted. Then he
laughed like a drunken fool. Struggling, weeping, begging
for mercy he had not thought to show others, Runs The
Bulls was led away. Hears The Wolf jumped to his feet,
spat in Runs The Bulls's face as he passed near him. Hears
The Wolf then turned. He looked at me, quietly sending all
the gratitude it was within his power to send across the
crowd dividing us as he was clapped on the back and con-
gratulated by a flurry of well-wishers.

The truth had not been so terrible after all. It had
unmasked the unsavory among us and had set two very
noble men free. I was happy that The Cheyenne Robber
was all right, that he and his wife and child were safe. But
I was so happy for Hears The Wolf, I wanted to weep. His
years of torment were over. The woman he had loved for
so long was his at last. The daughter denied him, publicly
acknowledged. How much sweeter all of this would be
when he was told that he was also to be a grandfather. That
the little baby he had missed out holding would, by next
spring, place her own baby in his arms. I silently prayed
that holding that baby would wipe away any remaining
traces of his pain. Hears The Wolf was a good man. You
cannot fool children or dogs, I thought, chuckling silently,
remembering walking beside him and being confused by
the horde of children and dogs eagerly following after
Hears The Wolf.

"This has been quite a day," Skywalker said, ambling
along beside me.

I looked back in the direction of the council. It was different, yet very like the first. Men were again gathering in
clumps, the biggest group surrounding White Bear and The
Cheyenne Robber.

Power was still a seductive magnet. Having power or

being aligned with the most powerful side. How amazing
that men found those two things more valuable than their
own lives, and in the case of Runs The Bulls, more valuable
than the lives of others. Ironic that one of the few men I
knew ever to have both was walking away from it, seem-
ingly content to be lost in the rush toward White Bear to
be with lowly little me. Now that I had served my purpose,
I was a nonentity again. White Bear and The Cheyenne
Robber were the real men of the hour. If he had wanted it,
Skywalker too would have had his full share of the glory.
But Skywalker was amazing. He wore power and influence
like a pair of comfortable old shoes, happily taking them
off whenever he felt more at ease in being barefoot.

"I was worried you wouldn't be able to prove the truth.
You didn't make me aware of the scratches."

I stopped, turned on him and yelled in his face. "Are
you telling me there's a spot in my brain you actually
missed?"

"Yes," he said, laughing. Playfully he touched the side
of my head with two fingers. "This spot where the bullet
went. All that's left in there is a big hole."

I slapped his hand away. "Very funny," I growled,
walking again.

"Stop walking so fast," he complained. "I want to ask
you something."

"Then ask."

"I want to know if you'll allow me to be your disciple."

I stopped short again, looked at him utterly dumbfounded. In a thoroughly disbelieving voice, I breathed,
"You want to be my what?"

"Your disciple," he said flatly. "You're a very intelli-
gent man and an excellent medical doctor. I could learn a
lot from you."

Flustered beyond endurance, I threw my hands away and
yelled at him. "I don't want a disciple. Certainly not an
Owl Doctor disciple. I'm happy just as I am. Alone."

"Ha! But you're not alone. Now you have a wife, a son,

a family band, and countless brothers. You're never going to be alone again. Not ever. We'll make sure of it.''

My anger wilted as this realization settled over me. For a man who, just moments ago, had thrown around truth like a righteous avenger, having it thrown back into my aghast face caused me to undergo a bit of an internal struggle. Alarm became a carnivorous worm eating up my vital organs. Wife, family, brothers, all the things I had wanted so badly during the last days, now were unequivocally mine. As were the varied pitfalls of this new lifestyle, things I had failed to see during my headlong quest. The lengthy list began with now being answerable for my every movement and ended with the complete loss—forever—of bachelor freedom.

From now on if I lolled around with healers of different nations when the bands moved, my new brothers would be sent out to hunt for me, and when I was found, I would be taken home to a wife who would nag and a chief—White Bear—who would yell at me for having sloped off in the wrong direction. (Something I was habitually prone to do.) Suddenly all of the benefits of the married life I had longed for evaporated. What I was left with was the grim reality that from here on out, I was in for a lot of yelling.

Oh, no.

As if I were nothing more than a piece of the glass we had both found so fascinating in the window of Hawwy's little doctoring house, Skywalker saw my fears, felt my knee-knocking panic. Never being the sympathetic sort, he threw back his head and laughed.

I tried to remember her face as I was led forward through the center of the village belonging to my new family, the people of the Rattle Band. Even squinting, the only mental image that came to me was a perfect body standing knee-deep in a sparkling river. But no face. That part of her was obscure. Which meant that I was in the process of marrying a faceless stranger. Terrorized by that thought, my anxieties grew with each step that carried me closer.

What if the emotion I'd been lost to was not love, only lust? How could I expect myself, expect her, to build a life on something so insignificant as that? But, hoping for the absolute best, say we are indeed in love and we managed to make everything work out all right, what about her son? Oh, he's sweet now because he's a baby. But what happens if he turns out to be another Chasing Horse? What would I do then? Certainly I would never have the option employed by Chasing Horse's own father. I could never disown Crying Wind's son. Not because I wouldn't want to but because an adopted child, no matter how that child turns out or what terrible crimes are committed and laid at its father's door, can never be disowned.

My heart was beating treble its normal rhythm. I sweated profusely. And in my very best clothing, buckskins tanned so soft and bleached out so white that I wore them only on very special occasions and was always, always, careful when being inside them. But that day, I couldn't be careful in my clothing. I was too much of a wreck. Behind me walked Big Tree and Skywalker. Before me, in front of his lodge, which looked too red and garish in the late afternoon sun, stood White Bear. People lined both sides of the pathway we trod. They were smiling, waving encouragement to me, the groom, on my wedding day. I smiled, my teeth gritted so tightly I heard them cracking. But still I walked on, toward my fears, my uncertainty when everything inside me was screaming for me to run away.

Then, as White Bear called her out, and she appeared, looking so beautiful my heart stopped mid-beat, all of those things became so negligible that I felt the fool for ever harboring even a twinge of apprehension.

Of course I loved her. Loved her with every fiber of my being, and whatever the future had in store, that future was ours to share. Then I wanted to run again. But this time I wanted to run straight for her, grab her up in my arms and never let go. Evidently I conveyed this, for Skywalker placed a restraining hand on my shoulder.

"Dignity," he muttered.

I swallowed hard, breathed rapidly through my mouth. The walk toward her seemed to last an eternity. Finally it was over. I stood before her, smiling like a pleased idiot; Crying Wind, looking down at her feet, managed to blush like a maiden. White Bear made a big speech. One of his more impressive ones. At least, I was told it was. I didn't hear a word.

Light blasted through me, a light stronger than the sun, as White Bear placed my wife's hand in mine, pronounced us married. Then she looked up at me. She was smiling but her eyes were wet. When I took her in my arms, everyone cheered. They were all so happy for us. Somehow, over that noise, I heard her sweet voice whispering words of love against my ear, words that were pure, unadulterated Crying Wind.

"Don't you ever die on me, Tay-bodal. If you even think about it, I will hurt you."

My head rolled back onto my shoulders as I held her hard against me, and I laughed as I realized then what I know now. Being bound to someone you intensely love, someone you trust to love you back, is a man's only true freedom. And it's the one thing any of us ever really owns. Everything else, most especially power, is fleeting.